12 JUN 2016

AN ANCIENT PEACE

Essex County Council

3013021106675 7

ALSO AVAILABLE FROM TANYA HUFF AND TITAN BOOKS

THE CONFEDERATION SERIES
Valour's Choice
The Better Part of Valour
The Heart of Valour
Valour's Trial
The Truth of Valour

THE ENCHANTMENT EMPORIUM SERIES
The Enchantment Emporium
The Wild Ways
The Future Falls

The Silvered

AN ANCIENT PEACE

PEACEKEEPER BOOK I

TITAN BOOKS

An Ancient Peace
Print edition ISBN: 9781781169766
E-book edition ISBN: 9781781169773

Published by Titan Books
A division of Titan Publishing Group Ltd
144 Southwark Street, London SE1 0UP

First edition: October 2015
1 3 5 7 9 10 8 6 4 2

This is a work of fiction. Names, characters, places, and incidents either are the product of the author's imagination or are used fictitiously, and any resemblance to actual persons, living or dead, business establishments, events, or locales is entirely coincidental. The publisher does not have any control over and does not assume any responsibility for author or third-party websites or their content.

Copyright © 2015 by Tanya Huff. All rights reserved.

No part of this publication may be reproduced, stored in a retrieval system, or transmitted, in any form or by any means without the prior written permission of the publisher, nor be otherwise circulated in any form of binding or cover other than that in which it is published and without a similar condition being imposed on the subsequent purchaser.

A CIP catalogue record for this title is available from the British Library.

Printed and bound in Great Britain by CPI Group (UK) Ltd, Croydon, CR0 4YY.

DID YOU ENJOY THIS BOOK?
We love to hear from our readers. Please email us at:
readerfeedback@titanemail.com or write to us at Reader Feedback
at the above address.

To receive advance information, news, competitions, and exclusive offers online, please sign up for the Titan newsletter on our website.

www.titanbooks.com

For Fiona

Who put up with a lot while this was being written.

ONE

" **A**nd we will create a place for Humans alone!" Eyes
... blazing, nostrils flared, Richard Varga threw both arms
up into the air, directing the roar of the crowd. When the sound
began to die down on its own, he lowered his arms—giving the
impression the sound had fallen on his command. "A place for
Humans," he continued, "where we will not be tempted by the
di'Taykan. Where we will not be forced to live among those who
use their bodies as licentious tools of conquest!"

Most of the di'Taykan Torin knew would laugh themselves
sick at the phrase "licentious tools of conquest." Taykans in
the di phase were undeniably the most sexually indiscriminate
species in known space, but when it came to conquest, a smarter
man than Varga would remember that they'd only barely
managed to broker a planet-wide peace—a peace enforced by
half a dozen heavily armed satellites—when the Elder Races
made first contact. And they'd been as happy as Humans had
when given a chance to apply their knowledge of war to the
Confederation's engagement with the Primacy.

"A place where we will not live under the threat of the Krai's
unnatural appetites!"

As the Krai's appetites weren't unnatural to the Krai, Torin
thought *all-encompassing appetites* would have been a better
description; although Varga wasn't particularly concerned with
either accuracy or overt speciesisms. In fairness, even Torin

found it a bit disturbing that the Krai considered Humans to be the tastiest thing on the menu—or would, had not a number of very explicit laws been put in place.

"We were there when the Elder Races needed us." The fingers of both hands curled into fists, Varga shifted into an exaggerated fighting stance. "We fought in their war!"

Torin gritted her teeth and mirrored the reactions of the men and women around her who were stomping, howling, and forgetting that Varga had never been a part of the military *we*. Had never fought. Had never watched friends blown to pieces by Primacy artillery or seen them bleed out too fast to save. Had she not already been under orders, Torin would've taken him down for that lie alone.

Three years ago, Varga had been a less-than-successful actor who found his natural stage when he'd joined Human's First. When he'd realized that true belief wasn't as important as discontent and a willingness to blindly follow rhetoric, his rise to the top of the organization had turned a whiny fringe group with a misplaced apostrophe into an armed force. He'd gone looking for Humans trained to violence by the Navy or the Corps and unwilling or unable to settle into the peace of civilian life, then he'd layered the new shape of the organization around them.

Human's First had stopped being a distasteful example of the Confederation's belief in free speech and had become a threat when they took over the small station orbiting Denrest and killed the station crew, three of them the Humans they were supposedly putting first as well four di'Taykan, whose small freighter they stole after dumping the bodies out the lock. It wasn't entirely clear if they'd taken a shuttle up from Denrest or if they'd had Susumi capabilities before they'd taken the station, but they definitely had them after, opening up all of known space.

Then they took another small station, another ship.

And another.

Having watched him in action for over two tendays, Torin would bet her pension Varga had referred to the dead as collateral damage.

"We have done their dirty work, and what has it got us?" he demanded.

The old garage, long empty of drills and excavators, rang with variations on *sweet· fuk all.* The communication unit implanted into the bone of her jaw pinged twice short and fast. A heartbeat later, once more. Her people were on the move and not a moment too soon. Torin touched her tongue to the pressure point just long enough to make the ping distinct, snarled at the sallow-faced, young man who'd just stomped on her foot, and let the motion of the crowd carry her away from him toward the wall.

A tall, thin man, hair and beard gone naturally gray, stood in the half circle of upper echelon behind Varga on the dais, his eyes locked on his slate. He might have been checking on his kids— there were, unfortunately, no laws preventing assholes from breeding—but Torin's intell said he was monitoring the crowd's comm traffic, his own implant slaved to the slate. Implants significantly improved the odds of veterans finding civilian employment, so both officers and NCOs kept their military comm units when they left the service even though nonmilitary techs charged an arm and a leg for upkeep. Both legs if they had to crack the bone. Given the size of the crowd, Torin estimated another ten to fifteen implants in the garage creating sufficient background noise to hide her team's coordinating pings.

Or the fraction of her team acceptable to Human's First aggressive recruiting. Ryder. Mashona. Her.

Today, new recruits mixed with old hands in an abandoned mining facility on the dark side of a small moon, in the old heavy machinery garage that smelled of sulfur and sweat, having their stores of meaningless rhetoric topped up.

"No more . . ." The crowd around Torin quieted as Varga dropped his voice to a conversational level. She settled into the same expectant stillness, although her expectations were entirely different. "No more will the Elder Races keep us from what is rightfully ours. Humans first!"

"HUMANS FIRST! HUMANS FIRST! HUMANS FIRST!"

At least they drop the apostrophe when they're chanting. Torin covered the last three meters to the open decompression hatch, stepped over the lower lip, and out into an access tunnel that had clearly been a part of the old mine. She drew in a deep lungful of air and said with complete sincerity, "Stinks like the latrines after burrito night in there. I need to breathe a bit."

She found it interesting that Varga's security stood facing the garage rather than down the tunnel. Had been facing the garage before Torin had moved toward the hatch. Varga was clearly smart enough to realize he hadn't built stability into his organization.

At 1.8 meters, Torin wasn't small, but the woman standing with impressive arms folded and a scowl that told Torin she'd made master corporal, at least, before leaving the Corps topped her by a good 15 centimeters. "Don't wander off," she growled.

Torin tongued her implant, grinned, and said, "Wouldn't think of it."

The guard's scowl shifted to a frown.

First ping back.

"Think you're smart, eh? You can't be hanging around out here."

The double ping back removed the need for Torin to respond.

Eyes locked on the guard's face, Torin lunged forward, driving her fist into the other woman's solar plexus, her weight behind the blow. "Actually, I can be," she muttered, turned, and hauled the hatch closed to the sound of a large body hitting the floor and flopping a bit, the guard's ability to give the alarm reduced to a barely audible wheeze.

Years of neglect had nearly rusted the locking wheel into place. Using the heel of her hand, Torin slammed it left, then right. Metal ground against metal and red-brown flakes drifted toward the floor.

Left. Then right.

Left.

Then all the way right. The battens slid home into the cleats on either side of the hatch.

The problem inherent in turning people into a mob was that, at some point, they had to be gathered together and people crowded into an area with limited access were inherently vulnerable. Control the access; control the space.

First ping.

Torin tongued her implant and dropped to one knee, checking

the guard's diaphragm spasms had stopped when she'd lost consciousness. Labored but regular breathing suggested they had, so Torin hooked a thumbnail over the end of the zip-tie hidden in the outer seam of her military surplus trousers and yanked it free. Woven from Mictok webbing, the zip-ties were undetectable and unbreakable. Torin'd had to call in a few favors to get them, but she didn't use plastic with another option available. The guard's wrists secured, she pulled another zip-tie from the inner seam of the same leg, looping it around and through crossed ankles.

No implant. Torin let the guard's mouth close and scrubbed her thumb against her sleeve. Trust the idiots who misplaced apostrophes to think size meant security.

Double ping.

Three of the garage's four hatches had been dogged down. Yet to be closed were the old loading doors behind the dais; the moment Varga noticed something was up, he'd be out them faster than Havarti through a H'san. Unfortunately, with the crowd staring directly at those doors, they had to be closed last.

Through speakers mounted along the roof of the tunnel, she could hear Varga listing everything Humans had been denied. Where *Humans* equaled Richard Varga. It was a long list. Sooner rather than later, one of his less reflective followers would get bored, decide it was a good time to hit the shitter, and discover they couldn't leave.

Torin raced for the fourth door, reached a T-junction, made a hard right . . .

Ten meters away, three men stood outside the big doors; three large men armed with black-market–acquired Marine Corps KC-7s. Guarding Varga's back.

The paranoid bastard.

Given the way they filled the space, she could hear more than she could see Binti Mashana charging in from the opposite end of the tunnel.

Two of the guards turned toward Torin, the third turned the other way. All three raised their weapons and the largest of the three, a man with his beard divided into two braids, barked, "Hold it right there! Both of you."

Torin smiled and kept running. At the other end of the tunnel, Mashona picked up speed.

"I said, hold it right there!"

When an approaching enemy declined to *hold it right there*, the correct response was to pull the trigger, not repeat a command already ignored. Of course, they couldn't be positive Torin was an enemy; she could have been one of Varga's people in a hurry to get somewhere, but it was still sloppy work. Torin decided to take that personally as the weapons raised the odds that all three of this lot were ex-Corps. Everyone in the Corps, regardless of specialty, trained first on the KC-7.

She ducked under the barrel of the raised KC without slowing and hit Bearded Guard at the waist, her shoulder driving deep into a layer of fat over muscle. He grunted, folded, and went down, crashing into the guard behind him hard enough to drop him to the floor as well. In her peripheral vision, she saw Mashona grab the muzzle of the third weapon, point it at the ceiling, and aim her knuckles at the windpipe of the man holding it.

Her weight on Bearded Guard's chest enough to keep him temporarily on the floor, Torin grabbed the barrel of his KC, yanked it out of his grip, and swung it one-handed at the second guard who'd made it back up onto his knees. The butt slammed into his jaw with a crack of metal against bone and he went down again.

She jerked back in time to avoid a fist aimed at her nose, the blow glancing off her mouth instead, hard enough to slam her lower lip into her teeth, splitting the soft flesh. Mouth filling with blood, Torin rose up, dropped, and felt a rib give way under her knee.

Bearded Guard bellowed. Torin spat blood in his face.

The crack of a fired KC echoed in the enclosed tunnel, overlapping the high-pitched buzz of two ricochets and a grunt of pain Torin barely heard over the ringing in her ears. Early on in the war, it had been discovered that the more complicated and high tech the weapon, the easier it was for the opposing side to fuk with it from a distance. A contained chemical explosion propelling a piece of metal at high speed out a rifled tube could only be fukked up by the person firing it.

She couldn't tell who'd been hit.

"Mashona?"

"Dipshit here had his finger on the trigger . . ." Mashona wrapped profanity around the muted thud of fist against softer flesh. " . . . and shot himself in the leg. Apparently, he slept through . . ." Two fast blows. " . . . Lieutenant Cole's lecture on trigger discipline."

Discipline dropped into silence. The list of Varga's grievances had stopped blaring out of the speaker over the door.

All five combatants froze for a single heartbeat.

Torin braced herself against the sudden roar of sound from inside the garage.

"Gunny, they heard the shot!"

"Lock it up, I'll deal with this." Torin blocked an elbow with her forearm and rolled up onto her feet as Mashona dove for the door. She kicked Bearded Guard just above the curve of his gut, hard enough he lost interest in anything but puking and choking on it, both arms holding his rib cage together.

Ignoring the blood soaking into his pant leg, Mashona's Dipshit pulled a knife from a boot sheath. Torin bent away from his first swing, spun around to his bad side . . .

"Gunny! Door's stuck!"

. . . then kicked him in the thigh, driving the toe of her boot into the bullet hole. He howled with pain as his leg collapsed under him and was smart enough to yell for backup before he lunged at her again.

This one was *definitely* ex-Corps.

Catching his blade in the trigger guard of the KC, Torin twisted it out of his hand, continued the movement around behind him, and got an arm around his neck and choked him out with the strap.

"Gunny!"

Rusted hinges had jammed one of the big double doors with twelve centimeters still to close. A scuffed boot stuck out through the space by the floor and two, no, three sets of fingers emerged farther up. Torin slammed the muzzle of the KC into the shin above the boot—hard enough to break the skin and invoke a stream of impressive profanity—then she used the butt of the weapon on the reaching fingers. As they disappeared to slightly less impressive profanity—probably ex-Navy—she threw her weight against the pitted steel, her shoulder next to Mashona's, and together they managed to move it far enough for the three big canted, coiled spring latches to finally snap into place.

The background roar from the speakers grew louder while over it a familiar voice demanded they open the doors immediately. Or else.

"Does he honestly think he's still in charge?" Mashona wondered.

"He thinks Human's First has an apostrophe." Torin spat out another mouthful of blood, checked the magazine of the weapon she held, tossed it to Mashona, and bent to pick up the other two as Varga began listing the ways they'd pay when he got out.

Lifting one of the second guard's arms into the air, her fingers dark bands around his pale, grubby wrist, Mashona shook her head. "Gunny, I don't think this one's going anywhere."

"Is he dead?" Varga had trusted these three with weapons at his back, so she'd be willing to bet they'd been among those who'd attacked the stations and killed noncombatants. Torin wouldn't mourn if she'd taken one out when taking him down, although the Wardens would be pissed. Again.

"No. But . . ."

"If he's alive, secure him. There's three of us against everyone else on this moon; if we sideline someone, I want them to stay out." She rolled Bearded Guard up onto his side so he could breathe, cracked ribs topside. Then, avoiding the spreading puddle of vomit, she got out the zip-ties.

A few moments later, after elevating Dipshit's leg on Bearded Guard's hip, they ran side by side up the tunnel, the extra gun slung across Torin's back and the knife filling the empty sheath in Mashona's boot. Retracing Torin's approach, they passed the first guard. She'd regained consciousness . . .

"You going to let her say that about your mother, Gunny?"

"I thought she was talking about your mother, Mashona."

. . . went through a hatch and up a level, boots ringing against metal treads. As they reached the top of the stairs, the upper hatch flew open and they came face-to-face with one of Varga's men heading down.

The anarchy symbol tattooed on his forehead dipped in and out of his frown, deep purple against the kind of pale, pink skin that could only have come from time spent behind insufficient shielding. His gaze locked on their weapons, not their faces. "What the hell . . . ?"

"Big hatch is jammed," Torin yelled without slowing. "We need the tools from the mechanic's locker."

"But that's empty."

"Let's hope not!"

As he turned to lead the way, Torin took him down and held him as Mashona applied the zip-ties.

"Okay, *that* . . ." She crossed his wrists and yanked the tie tight. " . . . was definitely about your mother."

"Next time, we bring gags." Torin led the way topside, guarding Mashona's back as she dogged the hatch shut behind them. Varga's increasingly hysterical orders blasted out of speakers at both ends of the corridor, the actual content lost under the fight going on in the background. "If I had to guess, I'd say Craig . . ."

Binti was Mashona on the job. Craig was always Craig. But then Craig hadn't been Corps.

" . . . hasn't found the override for the inter . . ."

Silence.

Broken by a snicker.

Torin shrugged. "Never mind." She could see the door to the control room and could hear . . . Boots. Pounding up metal stairs.

There were two open hatches between them and the control room and two beyond. With Varga quieted, the sound of the boots bounced off multiple hard surfaces, their source impossible to pinpoint.

The first hatch they passed had rusted open.

"We're in sealed tunnels under the desiccated surface of the dark side of an uninhabitable moon. How the hell is there enough moisture for all this rust?" Mashona snarled, misstepped, and lengthened her stride to catch up. "Gunny, that sounds like . . ."

"Like a benny charging." The bennies, BN-4s, were tight-band lasers that also contained a molecular disruption charge and, although they were susceptible to enemy EMPs while the KC-7s were not, they were a Marine's weapon of choice in places where a projectile weapon would be a bad idea. Places like stations and ships, where smart people thought twice about blowing a hole into vacuum. Or rock tunnels where ricochets were a given if the round fired didn't immediately hit a soft target. Given the presence of black-market KC-7s, it came as no surprise that Human's First had gotten hold of at least one benny. Torin tongued her implant and didn't bother subvocalizing. "Craig, we're five meters out. We're coming in hot."

The control room hatch unlocked as they reached it.

Mashona shouldered it open and Torin stepped through on her heels, slamming it behind them. Her hand still on the metal, she felt the buzz of an MDC impact. And then another, and another. "Idiot."

"Oh, yeah, and you're so smart. You're locked in here now, too."

Torin turned her head to see a young woman in her mid-twenties sitting on the floor in the corner, wrists and ankles secured. She wore a pair of deep green coveralls over a striped sweater and had shaved her head so a single ten-centimeter tuft of dark curly hair waved over her crown. She looked unharmed, but very pissed.

"The MDCs only work against organic material," Mashona snorted. "Your buddy's just decontaminated the other side of the hatch."

The next impact felt like a heavy body slamming against metal.

Torin exchanged a long look with Mashona that contained all the contempt she felt for anyone who felt they could shoulder their way through a pressure door, then she leaned both KC-7s she carried against the wall. "When I give the word, unlock the hatch and open it."

Two. Three.

Another slam.

"Now."

Two. Three.

Unable to stop in time, a middle-aged man with a red ponytail and a tiny silver ring in one nostril stumbled over the lip and right into Torin's hands. She dragged him clear and slammed him to the floor as Mashona re-secured the hatch. He whimpered continuously as she secured him and she fought the urge to ask him what he thought would happen when he joined a group that killed to support speciesist bullshit. He couldn't possibly have believed the Confederation would allow them to exist unopposed.

"You didn't have to hit him!" Tuft-girl protested, sliding her ass along the floor until she could support Whimpering-guy's head on her leg.

"Technically, the floor hit him." Torin straightened and walked over to the control panel where she leaned over the back of a chair so close to collapse that it made the duct taped pilot's chair in *Promise* look shiny and new. She dragged her thumb along the plastic trim. "So, how did you subdue Tufty over there?"

"Smiled." Craig grunted without taking his eyes off the board. "Flashed a bit of arm."

Both were admirable, Torin had to admit. The smile came with dimples and pale gray eyes that crinkled at the corners, and while she considered herself hard to distract, the heavily muscled arms had caught and held her attention more than once.

Craig's hands skimmed over the touch screen and froze in place. His left hand moved two centimeters to the right. His thumb tapped the screen twice, and he let out the lungful of air Torin hadn't been aware he'd been holding. "Okay. I think I've got control of the base sysop."

"You think?"

He snorted. "You want definite, you should've brought Ressk or Alamber."

"Because short and green or tall and blue would pass as Human."

"I've seen both."

"You've gotten around."

"I have that." He glanced back over his shoulder at her and

narrowed his eyes. "You're hurt."

She rubbed at her hands "It's rust."

"And the split lip?"

"Right." Torin touched her tongue to it, then bit his probing fingertip, ignoring Binti's comment about where the finger had likely been. "Forgot about that. It's nothing."

"Don't rubbish me. You're slurring your sibilants and there's blood on your boot."

"It's not mine. What about you?" She couldn't see any damage. They both knew that meant nothing.

"I got the drop on the kid Varga had standing security. She . . ." He nodded toward the corner without taking his eyes off Torin's face. " . . . didn't touch me."

"I wouldn't touch you if you were the last Human male in known space!" Tuft-girl sneered.

Craig rolled his eyes. Torin ignored her. "Are you okay? Not physically," she added before he could protest. She'd have never asked him for violence if they hadn't needed all three Humans on the team to complete the mission.

"Aces." His brows dipped in. "You?"

"Me?"

"You telling me you didn't enjoy yourself?"

She could see the concern, knew where it came from. He'd seen the way war twisted the survivors, seen the way *surviving* twisted the survivors. He'd seen what happened when someone got twisted all the way around until they broke. This time, though, he was seeing something that wasn't there. "Maybe I enjoyed myself a little," Torin admitted, licking blood off her lip. "These guys were just so straight line, fukking easy to beat. It's refreshing." When he looked dubious, she flicked her gaze past him to the board. "Should that light be red?"

"No, it should not." Facing the board again, he dragged the red light left until it shifted to green. "Okay. If Ressk's patch worked, and I'm reading this right, everything's locked down. Ships and shuttles both are nailed in until I release them. And, yeah, I can't believe they handed over their codes when the sysop asked," he added as the communications panel lit up. "I suppose mockery would be out of order?"

"They're spelling *Human's* with an apostrophe," Torin sighed. "They've gone past mockery and straight into derision."

"Maybe it's not a declaration. Maybe it's descriptive." The control chair screeched a protest as Craig spun it around. "Like baby's first solid food."

"Human's first post-Confederation revolution," Binti offered.

"Well, we're millennia late for it to be Human's first dumbass idea." Torin put her boot on the chair between Craig's legs and stopped both spin and screech.

Binti dropped into the other chair and nodded toward the speaker on the wall. "We should probably make sure they haven't gone anywhere."

They hadn't.

"What are they using against the doors?" she wondered over the clang of intermittent percussion.

"Each other?" Torin offered.

"Sounds like they've broken up the dais," Craig said thoughtfully. "They're using the structural pipes. Morons."

"Di'Taykan lovers!"

All three turned to look at their prisoners. "Well, duh," Binti responded.

Craig wrapped his hand around Torin's ankle, thumbnail flicking at the fasteners of the boot not sticky with blood. "So what do we do now?"

"We wait for the Navy."

The second chair screeched as Binti rocked back, propped her heels on the edge of the control panel, and sighed. "Who'd have thought going freelance would be so much like being in the Corps . . ."

"The boss wants to see you."

Jamers a Tur fenYenstrakin hunched her shoulders and kept her eyes on the cargo bay doors. "I are being busy . . ."

"You are being seen if she wants you to be seen. Come on."

She flinched as one of the Krai unloading water from the pen snickered, but fell in behind the big Human as he are leading the way down the cliff and into the structure. The light are being dim enough her lenses are lightening until they are being nearly clear.

"Given the speed we clocked you at, I'm impressed you got down without getting your ass kicked by the satellites."

He didn't expect her to answer and that was good, because at half his height she had to run to keep up and she was needing what air she had for breathing. She wasn't being young—as the graying skin on her hands and feet kept reminding her. Maybe that are being all it was. Maybe the boss are wanting to be giving her a bonus for landing the supplies in one piece. Maybe the boss are realizing she are having negotiated a better price for supplies so are having added an extra tenday before she are having to go out again.

Maybe.

She was panting by the time they are having reached the crypt the boss are using for an office. Panting and shedding, great clouds of underfur are being visible in her peripheral vision as she are stopping far enough away to leave an angle she are able to sight along. The boss, like all her species, are being too damned tall.

The boss' turquoise hair are lying flat against her head. The boss' hair are always flat. Motionless. Jamers are not having thought that possible with her species.

"You took something from a sarcophagus, Jamers. Several somethings. I want them back."

She are having thought the others were being busy searching at the long wall, but apparently not *all* the others and she are having been seen. Her luck are always being like that. Always. "You are having said your people are not to be taking them. You are making them be putting them back. You are having said you are only being interested in the weapons because that are what you are being paid for."

"I know what I said."

The boss' teeth were not being as pointed as Jamers' own, but her smile are being much more deadly. Jamers sighed. "I are not having them now."

"You destroyed them?"

Jamers wanted to say yes, but she are knowing that the boss are knowing it would be a lie. There are being many things this boss are not tolerating. Touching. Lying.

"You sold them, didn't you?"

She scratched at her arm where the fur are being so thin she are seeing the mottled pattern of the skin beneath. "Yes."

"Did you tell your buyers where you found them?"

"No!" She'd been hired to bring in the water because she are being able to buy in nearby systems unnoted if not unseen. Because she are not Younger Races. She are knowing better than to give away the compound's location. "I are being careful. There are being nothing to be connecting them to here."

"Nothing?"

"Nothing," Jamers repeated, willing the boss to believe it. Her mouth are being dry and she swallowed.

The boss' hair are remaining perfectly still. "Nothing but you."

"Yeah, yeah, it all worked out and the Navy actually came when they were called, but I don't like the kind of bullshit missions where half the team faces a bunch of crazy, militant fukwads and the other half sits on their collective asses doing sweet fuk all." Werst's bare feet slapped against the station floor, adding a fleshy emphasis to his words. "Look, we're good at what we do because of the way our strengths combine. The whole is greater than the sum of the parts and all that crap. And, yeah, it worked, fine, and these guys gave dumbasses a bad name, but they had live ammo they were willing to use and you got lucky. You shouldn't be facing those kinds of odds without me, Gunny. Mashona's learned a little meat to meat, but Ryder's fukking hopeless."

Torin grinned at Werst's disgruntled tone, secure in the knowledge that the significant difference in their height meant he wouldn't see it. "You're a meter two and greenish brown. You wouldn't have passed."

"Didn't say I would or that I wanted to, only that I'd rather you had better backup when it's three to however many *serley* idiots Human's First had managed to round up."

"They weren't exactly hard to beat."

"You didn't know that going in." Werst stepped into the vertical and grabbed a passing handhold. By the time Torin stepped in behind him, it had risen far enough that they hung eye to eye in the zero gravity. "And if you mention that fukking apostrophe, like it's the reason they were so easy to take down," he added, nostril ridges flared, "I'm going to inform your court-appointed therapist about your sudden grammar fixation."

"One apostrophe is not a fixation."

His lips pulled back off his teeth in what would have been a smile had he not been Krai. When Krai showed teeth, they weren't smiling. "You keep telling yourself that, Gunny."

Pointedly ignoring him, Torin exchanged a nod with a staff sergeant descending down the other side the vertical—he'd pulled three jacks to her trip tens on their last visit to Ventris Station—and silently acknowledged that Werst wasn't wrong. They *had* gotten lucky.

Binti had been a sniper back in the Corps and while she hadn't had the specialist training in unarmed combat both Torin and Werst had received, she at least had basic hand to hand to build on. Craig, however, had been a civilian salvage operator, arriving after the fight was over to mine the debris field. He was a big man with a heavy layer of working muscle, but like most people outside the military, he had no training in violence and little amateur experience. Occasionally, over the last year of dealing with messes the Justice Department couldn't—or wouldn't—clean up, he'd had to expand his skill set. Truth be told, Torin didn't like it when Craig was in the thick of the fight any more than Werst did. She wanted Craig safe on board ship, hands on the controls, ready to swoop in to save them using *his* training and experience rather than trying to fake hers. Or Werst's. Or Binti's. Or even Ressk's—who'd proven even more resistant to learning the dirtier tricks of unarmed combat than Craig. They were all ex-Corps, or as ex-Corps as anyone ever got, and her concerns for and about them were familiar—she'd had years of practice separating legitimate concern from speculation. But she didn't think she'd ever get used to the feeling of Craig in danger even if she had gotten good at repressing it.

If the guard on the hatch hadn't been young and stupid . . .

although his youth and stupidity had been why she'd sent Craig to that particular hatch. If Craig hadn't been able to bluff his way into the control room . . . although he'd bought a new converter for the *Promise* bluffing out a pair of eights so she didn't want to sell his skills short. Neither did she want to make him into something he wasn't. Nor did she want to insist he never change. She just wanted to keep him safe.

Without, of course, making her concern for his safety so blatant that he was insulted, hurt, or angered by it.

She worried about the team's young di'Taykan as well, but Alamber was an entirely different problem. Had the *vantru* who'd fukked him over still been alive, Torin would have happily put the boots to her. The relationship carried a lot more emotional weight than the translation of primary sex partner implied and Alamber had been almost obscenely young when she'd dragged him with her to Vrijheid Station and not significantly older when she'd gotten herself killed, abandoning him there. Unfortunately, while it helped that they all knew *why* he defaulted to manipulative self-centered shit under stress, it didn't change the fact he did it. Alamber's response to being left behind while the three Humans infiltrated Human's First had made Werst's look calm and measured. A lone di'Taykan among other species became the definition of codependent, and Torin needed to either find another di'Taykan for the team—and where the hell she'd find one who'd fit she had no idea—or cut Alamber loose. To do what? He'd been a career criminal, albeit a junior one when they'd adopted him—Craig's words and not entirely inaccurate even given that Alamber was legally an adult—and their position in the shadows where the law couldn't reach suited him perfectly. Or it did when he wasn't left behind to take out his frustration by rerouting drone shipping.

Fortunately, Ressk, just as frustrated but less likely to end up imprisoned for it, had spotted the hack.

Which brought her back around to Werst's point about bullshit assignments. It might be time to take another look at the parameters of their arrangement as independent contractors with the Justice Department.

A twitch in her peripheral vision caught her attention, and

she swung out into the level nine corridor before Werst had entirely released the handhold.

"Could've sworn you weren't paying attention," he grumbled as he dropped to the deck beside her. "Should've known better."

In too much of a hurry to say anything, a pair of captains settled for glaring disapprovingly at their civilian clothing as they pushed past and into the lift. Four meters down the corridor, a di'Taykan second lieutenant opened her mouth and snapped it shut again as Torin met her eyes. Bright green hair flattened against her head, and she nearly slammed her elbow into the bulkhead, putting distance between them as she passed.

Werst snickered.

In Torin's opinion, it was never too early to start training officers to recognize senior NCOs out of uniform. Or out of the Corps entirely. After a certain point, the rank and its ramifications remained.

The waiting room outside Dr. Ito's office was empty. As far as Torin knew, it was always empty. Over the last year, she'd never seen anyone sit in one of the three admittedly uncomfortable looking chairs. Never seen anyone pick up the slate on the small, round table. Never seen anyone put eyes on the vid screen that always showed the star field outside the station like it was a badly situated window.

When she mentioned the lack of any other patients to Werst, his shoulders lifted and fell in what was almost a shrug. The Krai had picked the motion up from Humans, but had never been able to entirely duplicate it. "Yeah, because you'd be such pleasant company sharing this shithole."

He had a point, Torin allowed as Master Corporal Tresk, Dr. Ito's current admin, looked up from her desk and stroked a document closed as she acknowledged them. "Gunnery Sergeant Kerr. Master Corporal Werst."

Torin had stopped reminding Tresk they were civilians three appointments ago. She had two brothers; the Corps hadn't needed to teach her to pick her battles.

Nostril ridges open, Werst spread his arms. "Sorry, Tresk, still happily taken."

"Sorry, Werst, still not interested."

Torin wouldn't have known Tresk was female had Werst not mentioned it. The Krai had so few secondary sexual characteristics, it was difficult for a Human to determine their gender. Torin liked to think that once she knew, she could spot the difference in the way the bristles grew on the mostly bare scalp or the subtle distinctions in the mottling, but the odds were high she was fooling herself. The di'Taykans, who relied on scent, had no difficulty telling male and female Krai apart— which was amusing as di'Taykans probably cared less about gender than any species in Confederation space.

"We'll be in Sutton's when you're done, Gunny."

"What, you're not going to wait here to escort me down?" Torin touched her slate to the desk with one hand and ran the fingertips of the other along the plastic trim.

"Yeah, funny thing, you never disappear on your way to the bar."

"Miss one appointment," Torin muttered as he went out the hatch.

"Seven," Tresk corrected. "Over the last six months. The doctor will see you now, Gunnery Sergeant Kerr."

Werst waited in the corridor outside Dr. Ito's until he heard Torin go into the inner office and the hatch close behind her. Then he exhaled, allowing his nostril ridges to flutter in relief. She'd never walked away from an appointment once she was in the office, and she always had a reason when she missed one—it wasn't like they kept to a regular schedule—but he preferred to be sure before he walked away.

And not only because of the "court appointed" part of the sessions. They all joked about it, sure, but Werst had seen the changes in Torin after Vrijheid Station, had seen the shadows behind her eyes, and, since she wouldn't talk about it with the team, Dr. Ito became a necessary evil.

Gunnery Sergeant Kerr had been one of the best Marines Werst had ever served with. With the weight of the Corps behind her, she'd been able to be as practical and as ruthless as needed to bring her people home alive. Leaving the Corps hadn't worked out quite the way she'd expected; the life she'd tried to build with Ryder had been kicked apart by some Grade A assholes—currently space particulate thanks to Mashona's aim. Without the weight of the Corps behind her, Torin had been searching for definition, and whatever had happened in the shuttle bay on Vrijheid, whatever made that fight, that death different, had skewed the way she saw herself.

Werst knew *not quite right* when he saw it.

The others didn't see it. Ryder, for all Werst generally approved of him, didn't have the context to see the differences. Mashona saw better from a distance. Ressk was better with code than people.

Gunny said she was fine.

For fuk's sake, she was Gunnery Sergeant Torin Kerr. Of course she was fine.

"She's fine," echoed Ryder and Binti and Ressk.

Alamber . . .

To give the little shit credit, Werst acknowledged, heading back toward the vertical, Alamber had noticed something was off. He was probably trying to take advantage of it, but at least he'd seen it.

"And you don't think it might be better if you made a clean break from the Corps?"

"And what exactly might be better, Doctor?" Torin raised a brow and the doctor smiled. Her first court appointed psychologist—after the exploded pirates and the destroyed station—had been brand new to the job and that had been a disaster. Dr. Ito, however, had a streak of cynicism Torin could relate to and he almost understood. About the war with the Primacy. About how the war had more or less ended once she'd discovered it had been a lab experiment run by sentient, polynumerous molecular polyhydroxide alcoholydes—hive-mind organic plastic. Granted, the war had "ended" more on some days, less on others. About what she'd done and what she'd been willing to do when Craig had been taken and tortured by pirates. About the weight of all the small metal cylinders she still carried, the ashes of all the Marines she hadn't been able to bring home alive, although the cylinders themselves had long since been returned to family and friends.

When she got around to mentioning it, he might even understand how it had felt as though she'd been fighting herself in that explosives locker.

"You haven't actually been a Gunnery Sergeant for some time now, Torin."

"You never stop being a Gunnery Sergeant, Major."

Dr. Ito's left eye twitched. He'd made it clear from the beginning that he preferred to be addressed by the medical honorific. "I think you've just made my point for me."

"I notice you don't have any visible plastic in your office." Torin smiled. In the year since the hyper-intelligent shape-shifting organic plastic had been exposed and had admitted to manipulating both the Confederation and the Primacy into a centuries-long war, natural fibers had started to make a comeback. "Is that for my benefit or for yours?"

"Are you still angry that you haven't been sent out to hunt for the plastic aliens?"

Torin stared across the room at the psychiatrist. Dr. Ito stared back at her. They'd spent one whole session like that, Dr. Ito silently waiting for Torin to answer, Torin wondering how long he'd wait. This time, they kept the dance short.

"Yes," she said. "I am still angry that we haven't been sent out to hunt for the plastic aliens. I am fully aware that no one has any idea of where to start looking. I know while the cellular marker they stuck in our heads means they occasionally respond to my touch or to Craig's, that means shit in the end given that I carried a plastic bowl for days without them giving themselves away. But I also know that people died— good people, mediocre people, bad people, *people*—because they were using us, all of us, Confederation and Primacy both, as subjects in a social science experiment. The war was their laboratory, our deaths were data, and they don't get to do that without consequences."

"And yet, because they've disappeared from known space, it appears they have indeed escaped without consequences."

Torin pushed both hands back through her hair and sighed. "Why do I think the word displacement is going to show up any minute now . . ."

On OutSector stations, the lowest two or three levels of the central core were set aside for off-duty and civilian personnel. On a MidSector station the size of Ventris, five broad concourses had been set aside for stores, bars, and cantinas. Although Sutton's on Concourse Two was a civilian bar, it seldom saw civilians; both officers and enlisted personnel gravitating there for the excellent beer, the first-class kitchen, and the enormous vid screen that showed a steady stream of the Confederation's more obscure sports. In spite of three solid days of cricket annually, it had been Torin's favorite bar when she'd served on Ventris and she saw no reason to find another just because she no longer wore a uniform.

The first time she'd sat down with her team in Sutton's after a Justice Department debrief—the debrief where Torin had picked up another dozen visits to the Corps psychologist for what the Wardens had called excessive violence while closing an orbital factory turning Katrien into coats—a brand new second lieutenant had made a comment about certain people not knowing where they were unwelcome. The comment had been intended to be overheard. Before Werst could do more than threaten further excessive violence, the lieutenant had been set straight by two captains, three NCOs, and Elliot Westbrook, the grandson of the original owners.

Staff Sergeant Kerr had fought a thousand Silsviss to a standstill, ripped off their leader's head, and brought the vicious reptilian race into the Confederation.

Staff Sergeant Kerr had outwitted a sentient alien ship and, unarmed and with only an HE suit between her and vacuum, stood between her people and enemy fighters.

Gunnery Sergeant Kerr had brought down Crucible when it turned against the Marines it was supposed to teach and by defeating it—with nothing more than a platoon of trainee Marines—had discovered the hyper-intelligent shape-shifting plastic aliens who'd been collecting data on the Confederation.

Gunnery Sergeant Kerr had survived the destruction of Sho'quo Company, escaped from an alien prison, and threatened the hyper-intelligent shape-shifting plastic until they admitted they'd nurtured the fight between the Primacy and the Confederation as a sort of social experiment, and then she'd ended the war.

The poor kid's hands had still been shaking when she downed the beer Torin had bought her as an apology for the exaggerations.

Unfortunately, although the war was over, the fighting had become a centuries-long habit and it hadn't entirely ended. The plastic aliens had been happy to explain; she hadn't had to threaten them. Much. The Crucible thing was essentially true, but, in all honesty, it had been an accident of placement as much as intent that had put her between her Marines and the enemy after leaving the alien ship in Craig's salvage pen. And she certainly hadn't fought a thousand Silsviss to a standstill by herself. There'd been a platoon of Marines with her. She did, however, acknowledge that the Silsviss skull in her old quarters had probably been how the "ripped off their leader's head" rumor had gotten started.

Because she'd been out of the Corps at the time, the destruction of a pirate fleet and the station they'd used as their base with three ex-Marines, a civilian salvage operator, and a morally flexible di'Taykan seldom got mentioned on military stations although it was the first topic of conversation on the small OutSector stations where they often ended up in the course of their deployments by the Justice Department.

"They're jobs, Torin," Craig had sighed. *"Can you try to call them jobs? For me?"*

They hadn't been back to Ventris in nearly two months, having bounced from their previous deploy . . . job to the takedown of Human's First, without a break. As *you are no longer a part of the military* had been explicitly mentioned in every Justice Department briefing they'd been to over the last year, the department sending them in to meet with Major di'Uninat Alie had come as a surprise. Major Alie had been Torin's Intelligence Service contact before Crucible, back when she'd been the Corps' best resource on the Silsviss. Fortunately for all concerned, her battle observations had been quickly replaced by a battery of reports from xeno-ists. Biologists. Psychologists. Sociologists. Hell, maybe even xenoherpetologists; the Silsviss *were* one of the Confederation's few reptilian races.

Given that the summons had been for the entire team, not for her alone, odds were the meeting had nothing to do with the Silsviss. Unless a few of the big lizards had gone rogue.

"Yeah, that'd be fun," Torin muttered, pausing just inside the door of Sutton's while her eyes adjusted to the lower light levels. She turned toward the sound of Craig's voice and spotted the team tucked back in the far corner near the doors to the kitchen. Exiting through the kitchen and out the staff entrance would take them to the service corridors and from the service corridors, they could get anywhere in the station. More importantly, they could get back to the *Promise*. Alamber and Ressk had hacked through the lowest levels of station security, pulled the schematics, and uploaded them to everyone's slate under a mask of false directories.

Back in the day, Ressk had made a game of getting through at least the basic security of every ship Sho'quo Company had been deployed on. Had Military Intelligence found proof, they'd have used that leverage to poach him from the infantry, but he'd always been able to cover his tracks—at least to the point of plausible deniability. Alamber, who'd spent his formative years learning how to cripple code for shits and giggles and profit, knew a number of very nasty tricks he was more than willing to apply. Torin had cut them off before they could go any deeper and had made it clear she expected Ressk to police the young di'Taykan.

"*Because, in this, you're the only one who can,*" she'd snapped when he'd protested. She didn't know how, she didn't need to know how, but he'd stopped Alamber before they crossed the line between too smart for their own good and treason.

Back in the day, when she'd had the weight of the Confederation Marine Corps behind her, she hadn't needed to know the alternative exits from her favorite bar. Times had changed.

She passed a table of three di'Taykan corporals in the midst of settling their bill and arguing about whose quarters had the largest bed; passed a table holding two glasses of wine where a lone Krai lieutenant sat watching the clock; passed an empty table—although a bowl holding the dregs of congealing curry suggested it hadn't been empty long—and finally dropped into the seat left for her, one hand on Craig's arm, the other reaching for a beer, muscles she hadn't realized were tense, relaxing.

"It wasn't my fault!" Alamber protested, acknowledging her arrival with a spear of pineapple, pale blue hair flying about his head as though it were being directed by the waving fruit. It wasn't actually hair, but protein-based sensors similar to cat whiskers that grew a uniform eight-to-ten–centimeters long, its motion a fairly good indication of a di'Taykan's emotional state. Given the flourishes, it looked like Alamber'd been impressed by whatever it was that hadn't been his fault—although it was more likely he was using those flourishes to draw attention and control his companions' reaction to him. He also looked like he'd had a few of his more obvious emotional edges blunted so he'd likely found a few di'Taykan and gotten laid. "If you'd seen it," he continued, with heavy emphasis on the pronoun, "you'd have asked if it was real, too."

"I wouldn't have been looking," Ressk muttered, eyes on his slate. "Some people like to piss in peace."

"I'd have looked," Werst said thoughtfully.

Alamber's eyes darkened as light receptors opened, and he snickered, one hand rising to the masker at his throat. "Not getting enough at home?"

Torin tapped her bottle on the table. His lower lip went out and he tossed his head dismissively, but he lowered his hand. When the di'Taykans discovered that their pheromones worked on all mammals and some nonmammals more powerfully than they worked on other di'Taykans, they took that to mean the universe intended them to have sex with most of known space. The maskers were Parliament's solution to the problem of biological consent. They could still have sex with most of known space, but now known space had a choice.

Under cover of Werst's snarled protest that he was getting quite enough at home and Alamber's insisting he be more specific about what exactly enough meant, Craig leaned in until his shoulder touched Torin's. "So, still sane?"

"Sane enough for government work." Torin nodded her thanks as Binti pushed a bowl of nuts closer to her hand. "Apparently, we need to take a break when the job conflicts with my appointments."

"I thought they scheduled your appointments between jobs?"

"Yeah, well, waste management is less flexible than they think."

"Waste management?"

"We take out the trash."

Craig snickered, the outer corners of his eyes crinkling, and Torin shifted her leg so their thighs pressed together under the table. "You use that line on Dr. Ito?" he asked.

"I did. Distracted him from a long discussion about my feelings. Which haven't changed since the last time," she added before Craig could speak. She believed in what they did and found a certain satisfaction in using her military training to clean up the broken pieces left behind after centuries of war. And she *hadn't* needed Dr. Ito to remind her that those broken pieces were people.

She'd washed enough blood off her hands; she couldn't forget.

Before the Justice Department had put their collective Elder Races' feet down, military brass had argued their team should be lumped in under the Special Forces' banner. But two of her people had never been military and, while he was no longer a CSO, Craig had no intention of ever *being* military and Torin had no intention of allowing the military too close a look at Alamber. The official belief was that she'd rescued the young di'Taykan before Vrijheid Station had blown and as that was within spitting distance of the truth, it was a belief Torin encouraged. Fortunately, the Wardens seemed willing to take her word for it.

"Gunny." Ressk waved his slate until he saw he had Torin's attention. "Major Alie's set our meeting with Intell for 0830 tomorrow morning."

"Is it a good thing or a bad thing that she wants it over early?" Alamber wondered, fingernails picking at the embroidery on his cuff.

"It's a thing," Torin sighed. "Although," she added setting her empty down on the table and tapping in an order for another, "the odds are good it's early because no one wants you lot wandering around unsupervised any longer than absolutely necessary. The sooner the major's done with us, the sooner we'll be redeployed . . . given a new job," she amended as Craig blew out an exaggerated sigh and the others laughed. "And when I say, you lot, I mean everyone but Binti who, so far, has managed to not get hauled in by the MPs."

"Hey!" Werst protested. "I didn't . . ."

"Depless Station. You kicked the shit out of that supply officer who suggested the vid of the plastic aliens had been faked." Werst's nostril ridges slowly shut, and he muttered something about the privileges of being a civilian Torin was just as glad she couldn't hear. "And you two . . ." She nodded at Ressk and Alamber. " . . . have little enough concept of personal privacy singly. Collectively, well, get caught here and you'll be contemplating the meaning of firewalls from inside a couple of tech free cells. And you . . ." A nudge against Craig's shoulder, rocked him sideways. " . . . were in a poker game with marked cards."

Looking smug, Binti raised her glass in a mocking toast.

"They weren't my cards," Craig protested. "I was an innocent bystander."

"You had most of the money piled in front of you when the MPs showed up."

"Not my fault that corporal couldn't cheat worth shite."

"You said no fighting or hacking deep on Ventris, Gunny." Ressk hung his slate back on his belt and waved a foot through the table's sensor field to summon a waiter. "We are therefore neither fighting nor hacking."

Ressk held out his bottle. Werst and Binti tapped theirs against it. Torin rolled her eyes as Craig added his.

"Yeah, but because you won't let me delve deep . . ."

Years of practice allowed them all to ignore the thick layer of innuendo.

" . . . I still can't find what the major wants us for." Alamber frowned down at his slate and looked up to find everyone staring at him. He took a moment to preen. "Nothing on official channels. Nothing on unofficial channels . . ."

Alamber's previous life on the other side of the line had given him access to some very unofficial channels.

". . . and, strangest of all, nothing on any of the social networks. The military's not even gossiping about it and you lot are worse than a group of *sheshan* at a family reunion."

"We don't gossip," Werst began.

Alamber cut him off. "Please, it's all stoic warrior shit in public, but on private forums you guys are all whine, whine, whine. The food sucks. I don't want to go to Caraba. The tracker at the range is busted, my score should be higher. The sergeant's picking on me."

"Enough." Torin's tone put Werst back into his seat. She let the rude gesture he flicked at Alamber as he sat go. They'd all been on edge since they'd received the summons. They'd been chewing over possible reasons for the last three days and the best they'd been able to come up with was the Intelligence Service needed information on one of their deployments firsthand, untainted by the Wardens' interpretation.

"We should've told them we don't take military jobs," Craig muttered, flicking the menu up, then down, then up again.

Torin shrugged. "They know that."

Up, then down. "I don't like jumping when the Corps says jump."

"We're not." He'd made his opinion on that very clear on their way to the station. "Our employer, the Justice Department, has informed us that Major Alie wants to speak with us. Speaking. That's all."

Turning far enough to meet her gaze, he sighed. "If that was all it was, they'd have told us what it was about, and if the Corps wasn't involved, you'd be all over the lack of information. You spent years obeying orders, Torin, you haven't shaken free of it yet."

She wanted to tell him she had, but way back when they'd first got together, back when she was still in uniform and she couldn't always tell him the truth, she'd promised she wouldn't lie to him. "We had to come back to Ventris anyway. Dr. Ito is my court appointed therapist of record."

Ressk swallowed a mouthful of nuts. "There is some talk about you being back, Gunny. A lot of Marines know you by sight thanks to the whole plastic aliens thing."

"And the Silsviss thing," Binti added. "And the Big Yellow thing. And the . . ."

"Yeah, I get it." Torin cut her off. "A lot of Marines know me by sight." Especially now that she'd lost the anonymity of the uniform. Hopefully, that was all that it was. "Is General Morris . . ."

Binti grinned. "General Morris isn't on station, I checked."

"Thank you. So it could be worse. Whatever *it* is." General Morris had been her own two star pain in the ass for years. He'd sent her to Silsvah, he'd sent her to Big Yellow. He hadn't sent her to Crucible, but he'd been around. If he was here, on Ventris, she could pretty much guarantee her life was about to hit the shitter.

Of course, his absence was no guarantee of *sah* and *kayti* either.

TWO

Intell took up Sections 23, 24, and 25 of Level 9 and, rumor had it, a Section or two off the public record in spite of stringent full disclosure laws. The vertical took Torin and her team as far as Section 22. A short walk down an empty corridor took them to a set of double hatches outside Section 23 that, when closed, would create an emergency air lock.

"I'm impressed by a paranoia that takes steps to avoid explosive decompression when they're nowhere near the outer wall of the station," Craig declared, touching the clear plastic cover on the emergency controls before stepping over the inner lip. Given his history—one man, working alone out of a small ship—Torin figured the odds were even that hadn't been sarcasm.

"We're in part of the station's original build," Ressk told him. "The tech in the walls is still self-contained enough . . ." He held up his slate as he crossed. " . . . to make sure nothing goes in or out that isn't filtered through Intell first."

Alamber's hair flattened and he froze. "We're locked?"

"We're filtered." Werst shoved him forward, then crowded him through the second hatch. "Everything you say can and likely will be used against you."

"Boss!" Twisting around, he shot a wide-eyed, unhappy look over Werst's head.

"It's just like being back on Vrijheid," she told him, "with Big Bill listening in."

"Only the part of Big Bill will be played by the Intelligence Service of the Confederation Marine Corps," Binti added before Alamber could respond. "So, on the one hand, they're the good guys."

"And on the other hand?" Alamber demanded when Binti stepped through the lock without saying anything further.

"On the other hand," Torin said dryly, "they're the Intelligence Service of the Confederation Marine Corps." She briefly rested her finger below the smudge Craig had left on the plastic cover, and stepped through into an area roughly three meters square that showed all the signs of having once been the decontamination chamber for the small lock. Currently, it was a security station, complete with two armed Marines and a lieutenant in a uniform so perfectly creased and boots, brass, and masker so perfectly shined, she found herself thinking of her first meeting with Lieutenant Stedrin, General Morris' aide. The lieutenant waiting here had fuchsia hair and eyes while Lieutenant Stedrin shared Alamber's pale blue coloring, but the "I'm making a point here" spit and polish were the same. The memory of Lieutenant—now Captain—Stedrin, who'd become an officer Torin would be honored to follow, smoothed out her reaction to being summarily lined up and scanned into the data stream even though anyone with half a brain knew the OS had registered them the moment they'd entered the Section.

She smiled, catching the lieutenant's gaze and holding it. "Thank you for meeting us, Lieutenant . . . ?"

"di'Miru Harym, Gu . . ." His hair flipped in choppy arcs and his eyes darkened as light receptors opened. "*Per* Kerr."

The civilian honorific as a reminder she was no longer in the Corps was the bald truth, not an insult no matter how unhappy Lieutenant Harym felt about his instinctive reaction to her tone. Given the faint growls she heard behind her, she needed to remind Werst of that. Again. She nodded, politely, and allowed him to look away.

Hair beginning to speed up, eyes darkening further as he glared past her, the lieutenant opened his mouth.

Torin cut him off before he could speak. "I have 0826, Lieutenant. If we're more than four minutes out from where

Major Alie wants us . . ." She left the statement hanging, allowing the lieutenant to fill in the consequences of a late arrival.

His hair flipped once, front to back, a final protest as he turned and snapped, "Follow me."

Although the Confederation had been nudging the Taykan toward an ability-based system, traditionally the upper classes carried shorter names. Four letters slotted in just below the aristocracy. Torin preferred to believe the Corps didn't give a H'san's ass about the background of its recruits, but the odds were high senior family members had arranged for di'Miru Harym to be posted to Intell where he could accumulate the political capital necessary for the eventual promotion to a flag position.

She had to admit, the lieutenant's ability to make it look like his presence was all that kept them from running wild through the Section impressed her.

"If he made a little effort, he could probably get some enjoyment out of that stick up his ass." Alamber seemed less impressed.

The corridor the lieutenant led them into stretched twenty meters in both directions and was empty except for a hurrying captain who shot them a disapproving look nearly identical to the one on the faces of the captains she and Werst had passed in the corridor by Dr. Ito's office. All but this last year of her adult life spent in the Corps, and Torin had never realized that captains were inherently against civilian clothing.

Not that they were exactly flamboyant; Craig wore blue trousers and a brown jacket over a yellow shirt, and Alamber had wrapped himself in flowing layers of ragged, deep purple fabric that covered everything except his head, his fingertips, and his platform boots, but the rest of them were squared away in black. Not in uniform, but not exactly out of it. The Corps had switched to black when the Elder Races added the di'Taykan to their military—it seemed agreeing to fight and die in an interstellar war was one thing, but multicolored pastels over the old camouflage crossed a line.

"You and your team can wait in here, Per Kerr." Lieutenant Harym gestured through an open hatch.

A rectangular black table and ten chairs nearly filled the small room. The long wall facing the hatch showed distant birds wheeling through a silver sky over turquoise waves that lapped gently against a sandy shore. Banal, but a pleasant enough change from the default starscapes. At least it wasn't pretending to be a window. The other three walls appeared to be pale gray, painted metal.

"Per Kerr?"

"Eyes before feet, Lieutenant." Senior NCOs made sure that junior officers survived long enough to learn how to lead. It was a hard habit to break. Torin stepped over the hatch and into the room.

The edge around the table's screen was gleaming black . . .

"Lacquered wood." Werst caressed the sleek surface. "Krai work, definitely."

The room was empty of visible plastic. The chairs were the same black lacquer; the seats unpadded, but then this wasn't a room designed for comfort. It smelled faintly of cleanser, all evidence of the last people to use it wiped clear.

"You think Intell's dumped the plastic out of their entire sector?" Binti wondered.

"If anyone has." Torin walked to the far end of the table. Her jaw implant chimed 0830 as her ass hit the chair.

Craig sat to her right. "So they're making us wait. Because we're less important than anything else they could be doing?"

"Or something came up. I doubt we're the most important item on today's agenda." Torin hid a smile when Craig seemed determined to remain annoyed. The Wardens they dealt with recognized the need for their combined skill sets while simultaneously disapproving of how those skills were applied. Given that the Elder Races tied themselves in knots over the need for a military at all, let alone the less savory needs that violence as a career had created, Torin had gotten into the habit of ensuring no one on the team took that disapproval personally. The Elder Races needed to own their shit.

"I don't like going in blind." Craig tipped his chair back and braced a knee against the table. "Is it against protocol to give us a heads-up? Let us know what they want us flapping about?"

"Yes."

"Yes?"

"Yes, it's against protocol. They'll get more detail if they don't give us a chance to compare stories."

"Sneaky bastards."

"True that." Binti sat on Torin's left, having beaten a scowling Werst to the chair. "But marketing thought Intelligence Service sounded better and the Elder Races weren't familiar with the term oxymoron."

At 0837, the glossy black tabletop turned pink, the color surging through the glass in a virulent wave.

"Alamber."

Eyes on the vertical lines of a Taykan keyboard he'd called up amid the pink, he waved her off. "Not hurting anything, Boss."

"Reset the defaults."

"Oh, come on, Boss." His voice dropped into a seductive purr. "Let me play for a while."

"No."

"But . . ."

"Defaults. Now."

"Told you," Ressk murmured as the pink disappeared.

At 0839 a Krai colonel stepped through the hatch followed by a di'Taykan major, bringing the four ex-Marines to their feet. Torin didn't recognize the colonel, but Major Alie hadn't changed. Being Taykan, when she finally did change she'd move from di' to qui' and out of the Corps. None of the Taykan served during the brief years they were breeders although a few returned when they changed again.

"As you were, people." The colonel took the seat at the other end of the table, the chair automatically compensating for his height. In the beginning, trying to merge their three new species into a cohesive military, the Elder Races had attempted a compromise—the Krai were to sit a little too far from the floor, di'Taykans and Humans a little too close, and everyone would be equally uncomfortable. The Krai, born and raised in arboreal cities, had headed immediately for the highest chairs available and the whole idea had been filed under *nice try, next time ask.*

Major Alie nodded at Torin as she sat. The ends of her deep orange hair barely moving, she swept a level gaze around the room. "I am Major di'Uninat Alie. This is Colonel Hurrs."

Ressk gripped the edge of the table, and Torin assumed he'd placed the colonel as well. Unless there'd been layers under the surface she'd missed, nothing they'd done in the last year should have brought out the Intelligence Chief of Staff. And Torin didn't like the implication that there'd been layers she'd missed.

Nor did she like how comfortable she felt being in a room with an officer in charge. Over the years she'd had more good officers than bad but, good or bad, an officer gave her a point of reference. The freedom to look after the details, to do her job and not have to worry about the big picture. Although as the big picture had turned out to be plastic aliens provoking and extending a war as a social science experiment, resulting in millions dead, maybe she should've worried a bit more.

"As we have information on all of you . . ." Major Alie touched the table with two fingers. The full surface lit up, showing multiple files.

Alamber stood and leaned out over the table, trying to read his, twisted far enough around Torin's spine hurt just watching him. She glared him back into his seat.

". . . as well as the reports filed with and by the Justice Department concerning your previous missions, we'll forgo further introductions and proceed directly to the reason you were called in. Colonel."

Colonel Hurrs tapped a file from the table up onto the big screen. "This is a H'san grave good from the Bertan'sh dynasty—some two hundred and ten years postConfederation. It was purchased in a market on Abalae and sold to a wealthy Human collector. This collector is known to one of our retired specialists who brought it to the major's attention. Major Alie brought it to me."

If her team had been in contact with H'san grave goods over the last year, this was the first Torin had heard of it. Alamber, the best bet for having been running an illicit antiquities business on the side, had his head slightly cocked to the right, a clear tell that he was processing new information. From the collection of ticks and tells around the table—and Craig's overtly irritated confusion—the image was new to everyone.

"Excuse me, sir, but what is it?" It looked a little like a hollow, ceramic fish with a metal interior—if fish were pale pink, slightly squashed half circles with blue spines and, for all Torin knew, some were.

"As near as we can determine without consulting the H'san, it's a biscuit warmer."

Alamber opened his mouth, then gasped and closed it. Given the minimal shifting above the table, Torin assumed Ressk had squeezed Alamber's leg with a foot.

Binti leaned closer to Torin. "Why would a H'san be buried with a biscuit warmer?" she asked quietly.

"The H'san prefer warm biscuits in the afterlife." Gunnery sergeants always knew. It was part of the job description.

"Bullshit," Binti muttered.

The last year as an ex-gunnery sergeant had worn a bit of shine off the brass.

"And this . . ." The colonel touched the table again, and the image changed. " . . . is a H'san grave good from the early Bertan'sh dynasty, roughly one hundred and fifty years postConfederation, purchased on 3Bortan." And again. "As is this, but purchased on Darquen Bi."

As she hadn't heard of either planet, Torin assumed neither had been attacked by the Primacy. Her best shot at identifying the first artifact was that it was a coil of irrigation tubing. The second might have been a shoe. It might have been another biscuit warmer.

"And this, purchased on Sarvai or Minout or whatever they're calling it now." He squinted at the piece of flattened metal, covered in strapping. "Although our expert suggests this is closer to one hundred years postConfederation."

Definitely not a biscuit warmer. Possibly, given what looked like hinges, it was the door off a small cupboard. Or the H'san version of a baby carrier. Or a cheese tray. Who knew with the H'san?

"I'm sure that's made a few archaeologists shit happy bricks, Colonel." Craig laid both hands flat on the table. "But what do photos of ancient naff have to do with us?"

Colonel Hurrs glanced at Torin, who looked politely attentive. When it became obvious that was all she was going to do, he frowned, shifted his attention to Craig, and answered the question. "The H'san do not sell their grave goods. These items were looted from H'san graves and sold. We're not certain how many items these grave robbers have taken, but that's of less interest to us than the era they were taken from. The H'san are a very old race. The Eldest of the Elder Races." A faded photo of a shattered building surrounded by bodies and body parts appeared on the screen. "And a very long time ago, they were a very violent race. After a war that went on for centuries, killing billions of their people and reducing a colony planet to a smoking ruin, they achieved enlightenment, pledged themselves to peace, founded the Confederation, and turned the planet they'd recently destroyed into a memorial slash cemetery. For more than a millennia they fetishized their dead and . . ."

Grave goods. Torin's hands curled into fists. "And having given up war, they buried their weapons. These grave robbers are looking for H'san weapons and they're only a hundred years away from finding them."

"That's the conclusion we have also arrived at, Gunnery Sergeant." Colonel Hurrs drummed the toes of his right foot against the edge of the table. Torin doubted he knew he was doing it. "While the H'san themselves might, and I stress 'might,' forgive the desecration, others will not. The discovery that members of the Younger Races are grave robbing for ancient weapons is the kind of information that could be used to convince Parliament the Younger Races are not ready for civilized society. Now that you've ended the war, there's a certain powerful faction in Parliament who believe that as soon as the fighting actually stops, we will no longer be needed. That the Younger Races' capacity—some say, affinity—for violence means we should be restricted to our own sections of space, locked in until we become better socialized. They're looking for an excuse, and this could give it to them."

Restrictions would label the Younger Races as *lesser*. Maybe the Elder Races had the technology to enforce it—they hadn't shared all they knew, that was a given—maybe they didn't, but in the end it would mean civil war. Torin only barely managed to stop herself from touching the bulge of cylinders, of dead Marines, she wasn't actually wearing—a tell she had no intention of gifting to Colonel Hurrs. Dr. Ito thought it was time she put down her dead. And he wondered why she missed appointments.

"Should the weapons be found, and they're clearly heading for the correct era . . ." The colonel's bristles made a soft shoosh as he rubbed his head. ". . . we will lose any hope of keeping this quiet. We have to shut them down quickly and quietly."

Craig leaned forward, leg pressed against hers under the table. "When you say *we*, who exactly are you referring to?"

"This problem cannot have a military solution." Colonel Hurrs sounded calm enough, but his nose ridges kept opening and closing slightly, the movement not entirely under his conscious control. "The laws of full disclosure," he continued, "would require the military—Corps or Navy—to file a battle plan with Parliament and make all files available to the press. Involve the military, and we might as well hand that faction . . ."

Torin appreciated the way he made *faction* sound like profanity.

". . . an annotated report. This problem must be solved with no official military involvement."

"Nothing official, right." Craig maintained the pressure against her leg, and Torin remained silent. "To be clear, these *galahs* have to be stopped before they reach a buried cache of H'san weapons and announce their find by blowing shit up. Ignoring, for the moment, the effect on the shit—where shit generally means persons and property—this'll open the door on what the bastards have been up to and give certain politicians exactly what they need to convince Parliament that the Younger Races should be *restricted*. You can't do anything about it because you've got eyes on you twenty-seven/ten, so you need a team you can send in on the down low."

Major Alie opened her mouth, but Werst cut her off. "A team you can count on to keep their mouths shut."

"A team," Binti said thoughtfully, "that does the impossible every morning before breakfast."

"A team with a clear and distinct disconnect from the military so you can maintain plausible deniability if it goes *revenk*. We have two civilians and, thanks to Gunny's very visible trial after the incident on Vrijheid Station, everyone knows we work for the Justice Department." Ressk's nostril ridges very slowly closed. "Except we won't be working for the Justice Department . . ."

"Because Justice is stuffed with the Elder Races," Werst interjected.

". . . and if this goes *revenk*, we're fukked."

"If this goes *revenk*," Colonel Hurrs repeated, "we're all fukked."

The colonel hadn't observed these Parliamentarians from afar, Torin realized; he'd gotten up close and personal and they scared the shit out of him. And he was allowing her to see they'd scared the shit out of him. She moistened a mouth gone suddenly dry, and asked, "What reason did you give Justice when you requested they call us in?"

"They were informed we needed to go over your recent successes in detail, in the hope of identifying certain asocial factors and preventing further violence before it can occur."

Werst snorted. "Oh, they must've loved the idea of stopping the bad guys with flow charts."

"They did," Major Alie agreed. "As a result, you've been loaned to us for as long as we need you. If you accept the mission, we'll provide the *Promise* with new codes and keep the old codes registered here."

"So if Justice checks?" Craig prodded.

"If Justice checks, you're still at Ventris."

Ressk answered Torin's silent question with a bored eye roll. Not only doable then, but simple.

"How much backup can we count on, sir?"

"From the military? None. We'll provide you with all the intelligence we have, but that's all we can risk. If even the smallest hint of this reaches the press, it'll be enough to open an official investigation."

"Of the grave robberies or of the Intelligence Service hiding the grave robberies?"

"I can't see how it would matter," the colonel snorted. "Other than on a personal level, the results would be the same."

Torin met his gaze for a long moment, then she showed teeth. Humans were nearly unique among mammalian species in considering bared teeth an expression of joy. The colonel was Krai, the major di'Taykan; they understand what she meant. "If something does go wrong, wrong enough to be noticed, with us involved you might be able to spin it away from the Younger Races. The recordings from the prison planet still get shown." She leaned back in the chair and spread her hands. "I've been under mandatory psychiatric observation. All six of us could be used as a textbook example of survivor guilt. Two of us had those aliens in our head."

Colonel Hurrs mirrored her expression. "I'd forgotten you played host to the aliens. If we have to remind the press of that, we win the blame game."

"You're welcome." She closed her teeth on the *sir*. He'd clearly considered the first two points. "Consider it a freebie."

"Speaking of freebies." Alamber leaned in, both hands flat on the table. "Who's paying us?"

Major Alie's hair lifted, not so much surprised by Alamber's question, Torin suspected, as by him speaking at all. If the major had given it a moment's thought, she'd have realized only Alamber or Craig could've been put in charge of the team's finances. The rest of them had only ever been paid by the Corps. "Paying you?"

"Paying us." *His* hair fanned out in a pale blue corona. "We're not working for Justice, we're not working for the military—so who's paying us? Saving the future is all well and good, but air isn't free, the ship needs fuel, and I refuse to wear this outfit more than once."

"Once is enough," Werst growled.

"Take it off me if you . . ."

Torin rapped the edge of the table. Both Alamber and Werst fell silent.

After a moment of increasingly uncomfortable quiet, the major realized Torin expected her to answer the question. "The Intelligence Service has certain discretionary funds we'll shift into your ship's account."

Discretionary? It sounded as though Intell hid operating funds from the Parliamentary budget committees. Fully aware that at least three members of the team had filed the information away for later use, Torin let it go. "To be clear . . ." she deliberately echoed Craig's words. ". . . the mission, should we accept it, involves us taking out an unknown number of grave robbers who may or may not be ex-military on a H'san cemetery planet before they can use the weapons they're searching for, while maintaining an information blackout on both the problem and the solution. If we get into trouble we can't handle, we're on our own."

"Is there trouble you can't handle?" Major Alie asked, hair out.

"No, sir. Not so far." Torin refused to be baited. "But so far, we've been asked to bring certain persons to justice, not to dispense it."

"We haven't been judge, jury, and executioner," Craig pointed out.

"You're setting a dangerous precedent," Torin added flatly.

"We're aware of that." The colonel shifted and his nostril ridges slowly flared open. *Trust me*, the vulnerable position declared, *because I trust you*. Considering the information he'd already shared, there was a chance he did. "That precedent is why we want you. As the major said at the top of this meeting, we've seen the reports filed with and by the Wardens concerning your previous missions. We saw the recordings made when you apprehended the furrier."

Katrien in cages, chemically silenced, watching friends and family secured to a metal lattice . . .

Torin jerked out of memory as the table in front of Werst cracked. The two of them had gone alone into that final room. They had the most experience with the worst people were capable of and, at that point, they'd had a pretty good idea of what they'd find.

"If those . . . *people* made it to trial," Colonel Hurrs continued, his voice so neutral Torin knew the Chief of Staff had seen a battlefield or two in his day, "then I, personally, have no fear you—any of you—can be driven to take advantage of this dangerous precedent we are, indeed, setting. If those weapons are found and used, there is a very good chance they could be the first shots in a civil war. Do what you must to stop the grave robbers. To stop a war. We've all seen too much war. That, Gunnery Sergeant Kerr, is the mission should you choose to accept it."

Torin considered asking what would happen if they didn't accept, but everyone from Colonel Hurrs to Alamber knew they wouldn't be sitting here if there'd been a H'san's chance in hell of them turning it down. She swept a glance around her people, holding each gaze for a moment. Alamber was the last to agree, his nod weighted with disinterest Torin knew was mostly for show. "We're in."

Colonel Hurrs nodded, nostril ridges half closing.

Major Alie looked as though she'd only barely stopped herself from saying, *of course you're in, stop wasting my time.* "Keep a low profile on the way back to your ship. We'll clear as much of the docking arm as we can without rousing suspicions, but try not to be seen. You'll carry the information out of here locked down on your slates. It won't release until you're in Susumi and it can't be tapped."

"We'll need a destination in order to create the Susumi equations," Craig pointed out. He'd shifted closer at the mention of the furrier, his shoulder a warm point of support against Torin's.

"We'll give you . . ."

"Yeah, well, not to be all big note about it, but there's not a chance I'll use an equation I don't work out myself."

The colonel raised a hand, cutting off the major's reply. "Start at one of the planets where the grave goods were bought. Backtrack the seller."

"Backtrack the seller?" Craig repeated. "Are you shitting me?"

"You don't know where the H'san cemetery planet is," Torin said before either officer could answer. "You have stories and a few old photographs, but no actual coordinates."

Werst's snort managed to express both disbelief and derision.

"The story of how the H'san emerged from war into peace is one of the founding narratives of the Confederation." Major Alie leaned forward, fingers laced so tightly together Torin could see the strain even from the other end of the table. "We know the cemetery planet is in the H'san's system of origin, we know that system was abandoned just prior to their sun becoming a red giant, but the H'san have buried the coordinates of the system. Our search for it set off flares and we started attracting some of the wrong kind of attention. We barely managed to cover our tracks."

"So . . ." Craig began to draw the vowel out. Torin's elbow cut it short. ". . . in order to stop this potential war of yours, we don't only have to stop people from robbing H'san graves, but we have to find the graves first."

"Yes."

"You'd better be freeing up a boatload of discretionary funding, Major." Craig slouched back in the chair. "Just one more thing: the H'san have been peaceful for millennia."

Major Alie speared him with a glance. "Your point?"

"I've pulled weapons out of significantly more recent battlefields and there's sweet fuk all that still fires."

The major's hair twitched. "We know the weapons weren't destroyed before they were buried, but we can't exactly ask the H'san for information about their condition." She touched the table and the first image, the might-be-a-ceramic-fish reappeared on the screen. "We do know they've never heard of built-in obsolescence. This still heats biscuits."

"And we head out to save the day with a picture of a biscuit warmer and the unsupported assumption we're stopping a potential warlord and not a rogue archaeologist." Craig leaned back in the pilot's chair and scowled out the front port as the last three berths on delta arm passed by. He hated giving over control of his ship to the Docking Master, but he had no choice within the Ventris perimeter. Although, this time, he supposed he'd given control to the Intelligence Service. Because that made it so much better.

"There's also the irrigation tubing and the cheese tray," Torin pointed out.

"I can see why they called us in."

"Rogue archeologists?"

"Mad scientist subset."

"I see." She turned the copilot's chair until she could rest her bare feet on his leg.

"*Private vessel* Commitment, *this is Ventris perimeter. Control will be returned to your board in fifteen seconds.*"

Dumbass name for a ship, but no one had asked him. He faced the board, hands above the screens, Torin's feet still on his lap. "Once I've got the course to the traffic buoy locked in, we could . . ."

She dug her toes back into his thigh. "We have the watch in the control room until we jump."

"We used to have sex in the control room."

"It used to be the only room on the ship."

Back before the refit, when it was just him and Torin on the *Promise*, they'd have only had to cover four meters to make it to the bunk. If they'd bothered. Both pilot's chairs were a lot sturdier than they looked. Now, a row of suit lockers filled the bulkhead where the bunk had been and four other seats had been bolted into what had been open floor—albeit not a lot of it. The payout from the mining cartels for taking down the pirate fleet had attached an actual galley and a full-sized head as well as crew quarters and a small gym. From the outside, the added units looked like miniature versions of the Marine packets the Corps attached to Navy cruisers; boxes grouped around an engine, aerodynamics irrelevant in vacuum. Their Navy surplus shuttle was small and heavy and dropped through atmosphere like a rock, but, so far, the heat shields had held and the way she threw herself back up into the air—seemed the Navy disliked being dirtside as much as he did—had endeared her to him. He'd called her *Glee* and, in spite of protests, it had stuck.

He still had the occasional moment where the thought of sharing his ship and her limited resources with five other people tightened his sphincter and backed the shit up to his brain, but they had room enough he could convince himself during those occasional moments that it was still just him and Torin.

"*Private vessel* Commitment, *this is Ventris perimeter. Control will be returned to your board in three, two, one. You have control.*"

"Roger, Ventris perimeter, I have control. Pr . . . *Commitment,* out." A two-second burst from one of the port lateral thrusters moved them onto the correct heading. Jumping OutSector was point and shoot and pray the math had been dummied out to the necessary decimal point. Jumping toward the Core meant a three-hour registered burn from Ventris and an assigned jump time issued from the traffic buoy. He double-checked the numbers to the buoy, locked them in, and sat back working the tension out of his shoulders.

"This isn't the life you expected to be living."

It wasn't and Torin knew that as well as he did; thus the complete lack of a question in that statement. He'd assumed . . . he'd *expected* that the two of them would make a success of salvage, build a home on one of the salvage stations, have a family. "True that. But then who actually expects they'll end up buzzing around known space doing the Justice Department's dirty work?"

"Or the Corps'?"

"No, that you expected."

He laughed when she shrugged. Of course she had. Stopped laughing when she asked, "Do you mind?"

"Honestly?"

"Please."

He turned, looked her in the eye, and said, "I don't really care what I'm doing as long as I'm doing it with you."

Her gaze sharpened, looking for the lie.

After a long moment, as she relaxed, he added, "There's things we do that I hate, not denying it, but they're necessary and, truth, I hate that they're necessary, but as long as we're doing it together, I don't *mind*."

The corners of Torin's mouth lifted in the soft almost-smile only he got to see. "Good."

"Yeah." As there were now rules about having sex in the control room and he was an adult, God damn it, he tapped down the rising heat. "Tell you what I do mind. I mind the nasty feeling that we're making this job up as we go because the Intelligence Service has fuk all in the way of intelligence and hey—surprise, surprise—we're making it up as we go."

Her smile twisted into the more familiar, weaponized curve.

"Doesn't matter. What matters is that a lot of people who might die, don't."

"It's that simple?"

"Sure." She dug her toes into his thigh. "Simple's best. Just don't mistake it for easy."

"I can't decide whether to be flattered at Intell's opinion of our ability to make *mertain* out of a single leaf or astounded at their tenuous grasp on reality." Ressk set his slate down on the galley's small round table and sat back, reaching for his half-empty pouch of *sah*. "We've got the name of the Rakva who sold the artifacts to the collector. We've got the names of the planets where he bought them and the names of the intermediaries he bought them from, but we don't have anything on who sold them to the intermediaries, which is, of course, the information we actually need because that's who knows where the fuk the dig site is because everything they sent us about the H'san is myth or hyperbole and in the entire visual history of dead H'san and the planet they destroyed and the system of origin they buggered off from, there isn't one single record of the night sky we could match to current star charts."

"After sifting through two millennia of variables," Werst grumbled, eyes half closed.

Forehead on the table, Alamber poked at an empty pouch without looking up. "Data crunching. We just set up the parameters."

"Except . . ." Ressk raised his *sah* in a derisive salute. ". . . we don't have the parameters."

"We know that almost immediately after they'd formed the Confederation, the H'san abandoned their world of origin before it was engulfed by the spreading photosphere of a star phasing red." Torin's shoulders cracked as she rolled them back. Three days of combing the Intell upload had left her stiffer than three days of combat. "The timing confirms the cemetery planet was in that same system, only orbiting far enough out to have avoided destruction."

"No offense, Gunny, but do you know how many red giants there are in known space?"

"Not a clue."

"And there we have it. Where *it* stands for nothing at all."

"Yeah, because it's not like we were fighting a war or anything." Binti tossed her own slate down. "Where a shitload of buried weapons might've come in handy."

Alamber poked at the empty pouch again. "I've got a question . . ."

"I've got nothing but questions," Ressk muttered.

". . . How do we know it's the Younger Races doing the grave robbing?"

"The colonel said . . ."

"Yeah, but how does *he* know?" Alamber sat up and slid immediately into a boneless slouch, the graceful transition as much age as species. "I mean, we've spent three days establishing that the Intelligence Service of the Confederation Marine Corps knows sweet fuk all. Why blame the Younger Races for stealing a biscuit warmer? Because we're violently antisocial? Isn't that why Parliament wants to lock us away? And it's a bad thing when Parliament believes it, but it's business as usual when it's all the Corps' got? Or is because the Elder Races fart rainbows? Because I've got to tell you, there was a Ciptran on Vrijheid and that bug was a total *senak*. Elder Race." One hand rose, one fell, sketching out a scale. "Total *senak*. Not mutually exclusive."

Torin ignored the argument—the staccato spill of words coming from five different sides with the sides in constant flux—and went over everything Major Alie and Colonel Hurrs had said at the briefing. H'san grave goods had been found, the trail leading toward a weapon cache. Clearly the Younger Races were responsible. Because the Younger Races were inherently violent? And if they believed that, what was the difference between them—the major, the colonel, and the ex-gunnery sergeant who'd accepted every word out of their mouths without question for no better reason than rank and a uniform—and those members of the Elder Races who declaimed they should be locked up until they become better socialized?

Was there a difference?

Yes.

"He has a point." Torin pitched her voice to cut through

the shouting. Finished her coffee as it died down, then let the silence settle for a moment before continuing. "Members of the Elder Races can be assholes. They can be pompous, greedy, self-righteous pains in the collective ass, but they'd moved far enough away from institutionalized violence that when it was fight back or die, they couldn't figure out how to fight back. They had to come to us."

"Could be they've learned from us," Craig offered.

All three ex-Marines looked a little sick at the thought. Even Alamber who, for all the violence in his life had never seen a battlefield, was slowly shaking his head in denial.

"Do of any of you honestly believe that the Elder Races took a look at the shitstorm we got called in to deal with, looked at the dead and the damaged, and thought, damn, we were wrong, looks like war is the answer after all? Because I don't." She crushed her empty coffee pouch. "Cards on the table: the H'san weapons are weapons of war. Place your bets on who you think would want to put them back into play, us or them."

"Us," Werst growled. Four nods of agreement.

"Assumption," Alamber began.

Torin cut him off. "There's nothing wrong with the assumption. The assumption's justified."

"And the difference?"

"Is them assuming we're incapable of policing ourselves. And assuming we're incapable of learning from them. And assuming we won't take a swing if they push us into a corner. You can assume they fart rainbows, I don't care. I care about preventing a civil war. Which, by a happy coincidence, is also the job they're paying us to do. So we talk to this . . ." She glanced down at her slate. ". . . Bufush on Abalae who sold the biscuit maker and we find out who sold it to them and . . . Did you have something to add, Alamber?"

He grinned. "I was just going to ask what we do when the dealer won't talk to us."

"When?"

"Strangers asking about the sale of illegal artifacts? Oh, yeah. That'll lead to a happy discussion of provenance and origins over tea and cakes."

"Patronizing *serley chrika*," Werst muttered.

"They'll shut up tighter than Werst's asshole," Alamber continued, ducking Werst's swing. "Best we'll get is an offer to exchange contact information in case something comes up and they'll back run that to find out who's asking. They don't find what they like, they'll drop a worm to scrub us or they'll load incriminating data and tip the Wardens."

The voice of experience, Torin acknowledged. Perhaps a little too experienced. "Ressk?"

He jerked, his gaze flicking up from his slate. "You asking about Werst's ass . . . *Chreen!*"

Torin got another coffee during the digression. "Can you deal with a potential information hack?" she asked, when both Krai were back in their seats.

"When you say deal, you mean back hack it, right? Use their hack to slip into their system?"

She did now. "Yeah, that's what I mean. If we can get a name on Abalae, we can get a ship. If we can't get enough for a ship, we get what we can and head for the next dealer. But *when* we get a ship . . ." Because there was no point in assuming they wouldn't, and fukking hell that word wouldn't quit. ". . . Ressk and Alamber can trace how it came into the system through the traffic buoys."

Ressk swept both hands back over the bristles on his skull and down to cup the back of his neck. "You know that's illegal, right, Gunny? Not sliding through a battleship's firewall to mock the feed from the Wardroom illegal but the kind of illegal the Wardens understand. This is . . ."

"What it'll take to stop a war."

Torin saluted Werst with her coffee . . . "That's exactly what it is." . . . and turned her attention back to Ressk. "Can you get in and out of the traffic buoys without getting caught?"

"Probably?" He leaned in to catch Alamber's gaze. "This is more you."

"I was working a program to crack the buoys for Big Bill, but I needed a working buoy to finish." He glanced around the table and added, "You have to race the security resets." When Ressk snorted, his hair flattened. "I was simplifying for my audience."

"And your audience appreciates it," Binti told him. "How far did you get?"

"I told you." His shoulders began to rise. "I needed a buoy to finish. I didn't have one."

Torin could read Big Bill's response in the lines of Alamber's body. *Worthless* had probably been the kindest word used. She caught Craig's eye, and the two of them had a silent conversation about how unfortunate it was that Justice had the former crime lord tucked away out of reach.

"Got it with you?" When Alamber nodded, Ressk pushed his slate over. "Share up."

"Because you're just that good?"

Ressk showed a bit of teeth. "No complaints so far."

"Three more days in Susumi to work it out, gentlemen. Will that be long enough or should we have Craig jump us in and out of the Core a few more times?" Torin smiled as they turned identical expressions of pique on her, equally annoyed by her lack of faith in their combined abilities.

"In three days we'll own those buoys," Alamber declared.

"In three days," Ressk snorted, "the horse might talk."

Alamber's eyes darkened so quickly he had to catch hold of the table as he turned. "Are you mocking me, *trin*?"

"It's an oldEarth saying he got off a guy we used to serve with," Binti explained, wrapping a hand around Alamber's forearm, loose enough he could pull away easily if he wanted to, her thumb stroking small circles on the soft inner skin of his wrist. "Guy named Hollice. He had a million of them. Half of them made no sense and the other half were too stupid to repeat."

Sergeant Adrian Hollice had died with the rest of the Sh'quo Company on ST7/45T2. His remains, and the remains of most of a ground expeditionary force had been fused permanently into the planet's surface by a Primacy weapon. The toes of Ressk's right foot drummed against the table until Werst, who'd been Recon with Bravo Company—also lost in the glass—reached out and gripped the back of his neck. Teeth gritted against the sudden spill of hot liquid over her hand, Torin set her coffee carefully down on the table. Hollice had been in her squad when she was a sergeant and then, when she made staff sergeant, her platoon. She'd fast tracked him for his SLC, but had been tanked, regrowing her jaw, when he got his third chevron.

"Torin?" Tipping his chair back, Craig snagged a damp cloth from the galley's half meter of counter.

"It's okay." She pulled the cloth out of his grip before he could clean either the table or her. "Sometimes," she said, eyes locked on the skim of moisture trailing behind the cloth, "talking to Hollice was like talking to a Katrien. It was definitely Federate and, given the context, you thought you knew what he was saying, but I never did find out what a rubber stamp was."

"Or how shit got on the stick," Ressk added.

As she listened to the other two surviving members of Sh'quo Company dig out what they remembered from Hollice's love of oldEarth idioms, Torin realized she was smiling. She tossed the cloth over her shoulder into the tiny sink.

"Two points!" Binti and Ressk called together, slapping palms over the table.

"No idea," Torin admitted when Craig's brows rose. "Hollice used to yell it. He yelled it once when the artillery actually nailed the coordinates we called in."

Binti took a deep breath and let it out slowly. "I heard he aced his sergeant's exam."

"Yeah." Ressk raised his pouch of *sah*. "I heard that, too."

Alamber turned from rummaging through one of the upper cupboards. "My *yasha* told me that when you remember someone they never really die."

"Yeah?" Werst snorted. "My *jernil* said my *jernine* repeated on her for days."

"Touching." Binti beckoned Alamber over and plunged a hand into the bag of cookies he'd found. "*My* grandmother never talked about eating dead people because in her house, that would have been a fukking creepy dinner table conversation."

"Yeah, well I find it shonky that the H'san bury their dead with biscuit warmers," Craig said. "Why waste gear on the dead that the living can use?"

Ressk's nostril ridges opened and shut. "Like a biscuit warmer and enough weapons to rebang the big one?"

"Given how long it's taking the grave robbers to find the

weapons, seems the H'san object to coordinates in general," Alamber pointed out, reclaiming the bag, the cookies, and his seat.

Werst rolled his eyes. "Yeah. Well, when we find the planet, it won't be hard to find the only living people on it." With both hands wrapped around his *sah*, he grabbed the bag with a foot.

"*Ablin gon savit!*" Alamber grabbed it back. "How many times do I have to tell you, no feet in the communal food! I don't care what they let you do in the Marines!"

"He was Recon," Binti sighed, as though that explained everything.

"Then he can go find the planet." Alamber held the bag over his head. "We'll find a *mirin* with deep baths and large beds and wait."

Torin figured Werst was about half a second away from climbing the much taller di'Taykan like a tree—which was exactly what Alamber wanted. She caught Alamber's gaze and he sighed, set the bag on the table, reached into it, and, their eyes still locked, licked the icing out from between two wafers. Torin maintained zero reaction until Alamber looked away, his hair flattening, as he ate the damned cookie.

"Look, most people are shit at keeping secrets." She finished the dregs of her coffee. "The odds are in our favor that the grave robber who's been selling the artifacts will be *most people*. Odds are higher they're not using more than the four Susumi equations we have evidence of. Every new jump's a chance to drop a decimal and die horribly, so why risk it? Alamber's right, it's taking them time to find the weapons; they'll be picking up supplies for the dig on those jumps, not just selling grave goods. The dealers won't be our only source."

"Smart people would want to spread the jumps out as much as possible," Craig protested. "Keep from establishing a pattern."

"Smart people," Werst snorted, spraying crumbs, "wouldn't have sent up flares by selling the artifacts. These are not smart people."

"Major Sujuno?"

She looked up from entering the day's notes into her slate.

H'san security had wiped out all conductivity, reducing them to isolated programming, no scanners of any kind, no coms. Her jaw unit hadn't been this silent since she'd gone home on leave and . . . Her slate creaked as her grip tightened, and she forced her hand to relax. Took a deep breath, banished the memories, and beckoned Toporov into the crypt. He moved quickly for such a large man, but not quickly enough to prevent a swirl of red dust from following him through the overlap in the clear plastic sheeting.

Half a meter from the enormous stone sarcophagus she was using as a standing desk, he fell into a reasonable approximation of at ease—learned behaviors made it easier to maintain order, so from the beginning she'd run the dig as close to a military maneuver as she could stomach. "Dion's found the next symbol."

"Is he certain, Sergeant? Because I seem to recall that the mark he found the day before yesterday went absolutely nowhere." Dion's information, the information he'd pulled from an ancient crystal allegedly found discarded in the Central Library's trash, was more a suggestion than an actual map. The degenerating, millennia-old memories of the last H'san who'd seen the weapons cache had contained nothing as useful as directions, but rather a blank verse ode to symbols scratched throughout a city of the dead. Dion, who had an annoying habit of randomly announcing he was an expert in ancient H'san, remained convinced the symbols marked the route to the weapons. He'd been right about the location of the planet as well as about the planetary security, so Sujuno was giving him the benefit of the doubt on the symbols. She didn't know if Dion had found their backer or if his bragging had led their backer to him. Nor did she care. The only thing that mattered was that her payment, upon delivery of the weapons, would be enough to register a progenitor and begin her family line again.

"He's pretty certain, Major. He found another control panel behind it."

"Behind the symbol?"

"Yeah, tucked inside the block of stone. The front face sheared off, pretty as anything." One huge hand sketched the fall in the air. "And there it was."

"And what does it do?"

Toporov began to shrug, caught her eye, and turned it into an uncomfortable twitch. "Can't say yet, sir. Pirate doesn't want to crack the case without an air lock to keep the dust out."

In spite of her best efforts to keep it still, her hair flicked back behind her ears. She hated the dust. Suspected it was actually one of the H'san's subtler traps. The fine, red grit got in everywhere, adhered to moisture, and, eventually, created an impenetrable barrier. Katherine McKenna, out front when they'd breached this sector, had breathed deep in the initial release and suffocated before any of them had realized the problem. McKenna had been Corps of Engineers and the team's medic. Sujuno had been furious about losing another one of her people to carelessness.

She was still angry about the loss of Timin di'Geirah, and that disaster had occurred back on the first day they'd breached the tombs. Along with the progenitor price, she had to provide proof there'd be sufficient gender divergences after the change to qui. Timin hadn't yet agreed to sign on, but she was certain he would have by the end of the mission. His carelessness had cost her.

In comparison, all McKenna's death had cost was comfort; the whole team had been living in filters and would have to remain in filters until they cleared the dust.

Her hair tried to flick forward again when Toporov held out a piece of paper—two-millennia–old paper pulled from one the first tombs they'd opened—but she held it still and waited until he set it on the tomb to pick it up. "I see he's drawn up a plan." A double air lock, each section only large enough for one person and both set up with six point four nine minutes of air exchange. "That's . . . precise."

"The math is on the back. Pirate says he'll need to rework it if anyone else goes in."

She didn't flip the page, trusting the math if not the pirate himself. Although, credit where due, she'd only had to correct his assumptions once and he'd been careful not to touch her since, his response significantly better than most others of their ridiculously tactile species. "Build it. And tell him to take food, water, and a bucket in with him. We've a finite supply of filters and there's no telling how long this dust will be with us."

"About that, Major, Verr says she can fly the Katrien's ship if we need . . ."

"No." She wasn't denying that Verr could fly the ship—a Marine pilot, the ex-lieutenant had flown them through Susumi space and then switched to the Taykan VTA they'd taken down to the landing site. Verr could fly anything she could get into the air. Had her bonded's temper not gotten him discharged, had she not followed Wen into a civilian life they were both ill-suited to, Verr would have continued flying M74s until the final moment of the war. Sujuno was casting no doubt on Verr's ability to fly the Katrien ship, merely on the necessity.

Showing more perception than usual, Toporov seemed to take her meaning from the single syllable. He nodded, spun on one heel, and slipped back through the overlap, calling for Verr and Wen to bring the construction materials before he'd cleared the plastic.

If this was the correct control panel, and not another dummy or another trap, then they were close. Close enough they had no need to risk a supply run.

Because ships emerged from Susumi space minutes after they entered, regardless of distance traveled, there were academics who claimed the time spent within a mathematical construct was irrelevant. Those people were idiots. In Susumi space, the ship and those she carried defined their own reality and with reality so tightly defined, relevant things were inevitably squeezed out of dark corners.

Torin knew how to deal with Marines and a Marine's problems. Mission prep helped, but this time there wasn't much of it. Not yet. So when Werst needed to fight, she stepped in and called it training. When Ressk wielded code like a weapon, she minimized collateral damage and calibrated his sights. On day three, after a night when her dead died again while she fought against the drag of melted glass, unable to get to them, she sat shoulder to shoulder with Binti in the darkened galley and watched recordings of a Rakva soap opera with the translator off, adding their own dialogue to the ruffled feathers and high drama. She didn't need to ask why Binti was there. She didn't need to explain why she was.

Marines, she understood.

Craig's demons were remarkably similar.

On day two, Torin woke with Craig's arms wrapped tightly around her, his heart racing, his breath huffing out hard and hot against the top of her head. On day four, she woke crouched on the deck ready to fight—thrown out of bed by his old panic of too many people and too little air. In the first case, she was there for him to hold as long as he needed to. In the second, her reassurances were less passive and, counterintuitively, used up a fair bit of air.

Alamber . . .

He'd done what he had to in order to survive in Big Bill's criminal organization after his *vantru* died. Torin appreciated his competence, admired his courage, and acknowledged his *vantru* had been a viciously twisted excuse for sentience who'd thoroughly screwed him over. At an age when sex should have been play and exploration, he'd been taught to use it, and the touch di'Taykans needed, as a means to an end. He was brilliant and screamingly insecure and, in spite of the certain knowledge that he'd broken any number of laws, Torin had no intention of turning him over to the authorities even though she suspected she should. Suspected it might be better for him to get his shit straightened out by professionals during an official rehabilitation. But he had no family to stand for him and, given a choice, he'd chosen to stay. She wouldn't be another person who held power over him and abandoned him.

After a year, he still doubted Torin wanted him there because she wouldn't have sex with him.

He was an adult. Old enough to die for the Confederation. Older than many of the Corps' new recruits.

Taykans were a communal species. If they could help it, they never slept alone. Most often, Alamber slept with Binti, sometimes he slept with Werst and Ressk, and . . .

. . . on day five . . .

"Boss?"

"All right, come on." She slid back against Craig and lifted the covers so Alamber could crawl in beside her. He squirmed around until she swatted him, then settled with his head on her shoulder, legs long enough to wrap around hers and Craig's, his skin cool and soft, his hair slowly stilling, the metal of the masker warming between them.

This wasn't sex. It was comfort. Family. Needing to know he belonged. It happened most often while they were in Susumi space—Binti had a theory it was tied to the distinctive hum of the Susumi engines and they'd shared a silent agreement not to speculate on what had caused it. His scars were layered and deep, but every now and then he let her give him a few hours of peace. By morning, he'd be back to insecurity and innuendo.

"We have *got* to get another di'Taykan in this crew," she murmured when Alamber's breathing slowed and the grip on her arm finally eased.

Craig kissed the back of her neck, his arm wrapped around her, one big hand cupping Alamber's hip. "Not arguing."

"What do you want?" With only one other di'Taykan on the entire planet, Sujuno hadn't needed to look up from her slate when she'd heard the rustle of the plastic sheeting being moved aside. The scent was unmistakable. "Turn your masker back up," she snapped before he could get any closer. Most di'Taykan commanders allowed maskers to be removed when there were only di'Taykan, present but *most* did not mean *all*; her vows kept her from indulging in such pointless excesses. If he chose to remove it among the Humans and Krai, well, that had nothing to do with her.

"They've almost got the air lock built."

"Good."

"I could be in there for a couple of days. Or longer."

She looked up then to see his lime-green eyes darken as more and more light receptors opened.

He shuffled his feet, his hair flicked around his head in small arrhythmic arcs, and, when he finally realized she wasn't going to fill in the blanks, sighed. "I thought we should spend some time together before I got sealed in."

"Why would you think that?"

"Because . . ." His fingertip traced a pattern she didn't understand on the lid of the sarcophagus. ". . . I'll be alone in there and you'll be alone out here and Humans and Krai are all very well for a while when you're not about to be alone and Timin's dead."

"Major, I may have found something."

The others were searching the crypts, searching the sarcophagi, searching the bodies, but Timin had remained in the main hall of the necropolis, frowning down at his slate and then up at the symbols that made up the balusters of the balcony railing. As Lieutenant di'Geirah had been a linguist within the Intelligence Service, Sujuno had kept the greater part of her attention on him.

"There," he said, as she joined him in the center of the hall. "If Dion's right, then that sequence ends in the symbol we need."

She could barely see the difference between the symbols he pointed at, but then, she didn't need to.

"Logically," Timin continued, moving toward the far wall, "the door, exit, opening, govian, should be under the symbol."

Sujuno fell into step beside him. "I don't see it."

"The H'san know how to . . ."

The floor fell out from under him, what had looked like solid stone shattering into hundreds, thousands of tiny pieces. She felt the side of her foot begin to dip, and time fractured as she jumped away. She saw Timin throw out a hand, reaching, his eyes black, his hair clamped tight to his head. She knew where the edge was. She could step forward enough to grab his hand. To yank him to safety. To save him. To touch him. Hand to hand. Skin to skin.

No.

Time pieced itself together.

Timin disappeared, screaming. The fingers of one hand slapped the edge, but gravity gave him no chance to hang on.

By the time he hit the bottom and the soft/hard, wet impact cut off the scream, the others had gathered.

"Should we . . ." Toporov began.

Sujuno cut him off. "Lieutenant di'Geirah is dead. We would be of as little assistance to him as he now will be to us. We should check that section of wall for an exit to the weapons cache."

"Major?"

He'd moved closer. She stared at his reaching hand until he lowered it then nodded, once, and said, "Get out."

"Jump ends in three. Two. One. And we're out."

The song *Promise* sang to keep them moving, to keep them safe, chased away the hum of Susumi, and Craig felt his shoulder muscles relax.

"Coreward buoy, registered." Sitting second, Werst enlarged the pertinent screens. "We're not only alive, we're right where we're supposed to be, three and a half minutes after we left."

As a hundred kilometers of translucent netting harvested the energy of their Susumi wave, the buoy brought *Promise's* front thrusters on to slow their emergent speed. "You know," Craig growled, hands held above the board, "I only thought I hated giving over control to the docking master. That's all over soft compared to how I feel about handing her over to a buoy."

"*Garn chreen,*" Ressk breathed from the second row of jump seats. "I've never seen so many stars."

Craig hadn't either. Facing into the heart of the galaxy, even as far out as they still were, meant facing into a blaze of light, individual stars lost in the center of the display.

"I've heard that the Mictok homeworld never gets dark," Binti said from directly behind him.

"Yeah, and that's why evolution went with the exoskeleton." Twisting slightly, Craig could see Alamber in the seat beside Torin, his legs crossed, his pale feet bare. "All the bugs are from farther in. Ow. What?"

He saw the corner of Torin's mouth twitch when Binti leaned over and flicked the di'Taykan on the ear. "We don't say bugs."

"So we say what?" Alamber sneered. "Evolved insectoid species?"

"We say Mictok. Or Ciptran," Torin told him, eyes on the stars. "The same way we say di'Taykan or Krai or Human."

"Yeah, but, Boss, that net out there? Probably extruded from Mictok ass."

"Your point?"

"They creep me the *sanLi* out."

"They creep everyone the hell out, Alamber. They're giant spiders. Suck it up, be polite."

"Get it off me. Get it off me," Binti said quietly.

"Hollice?" Craig asked as Torin's left hand twitched toward her torso.

"Glicksohn."

He liked to think it was progress that the names of the dead were being spoken. Sliding the incoming data into a temporary file, he tossed her a grin. With nothing to choose between the three dealers, they'd gone with a random draw and Torin's expression when it turned out they were chasing the biscuit warmer had been aces. "The buoy's cleared us for Abalae." The codes tapped in, he felt *Promise* alter her course. Even a million point six kilometers out from the planet—no one jumped close in the Core—space didn't seem as big in here.

He already missed the dark.

Their new registry raised no alarms when *Commitment* docked as an independent trader on the most stripped down of Abalae's three stations.

"If I hack the sysop, I could narrow our target." Irritation added volume to the slap of Ressk's feet against the deck as all six of them made their way along the docking arm toward the main bulk of the station. "Once I'm in this station, I can squirt over to the others . . ."

"Never going to unhear that," Binti muttered.

". . . and amalgamate the data before I sift it. Give me a couple of hours and I can come up with the registry number of every ship that makes regular runs. A few hours more and I can hand over a list of their crews."

"We don't need a list of their crews."

"Yeah, but I could still give you one."

"You'll dux out the ship we need faster if we can narrow the parameters before you start," Craig told him. "Faster you're in and out, less likely you are to end up with your balls in a vise."

"And it's been a while since any of us have been dirtside," Torin added. Most of them had taken personal time during the ship's refit—Craig had refused to leave the dockyard, Alamber had stayed with Craig, the rest of them had visited family, Torin had caught hell for not bringing Craig with her—but they'd had very little down time since the team had gone active. "We could use the break."

"We're lucky they had seats for all of us," Alamber said as they entered the waiting area outside the tether's boarding gate. "We were looking at four days of total boredom if we'd had to wait for the next drop. As it is, we won't be here long enough to overhaul the station's entirely out-of-date entertainment options. They'd have thanked us," he added when Torin's eyebrow rose.

"You know, we have a shuttle," Craig began, but Alamber cut him off.

"Landing fees are stupidly expensive on any planet with an elevator system and this one's got three."

"All extruded out of Mictok ass," Werst noted.

Torin crossed to look out the nearer of the two, meter-high, concave ports that broke up the outer bulkhead. The surface was smudged and pitted, but it looked structurally sound with no weak points an assault team could take advantage of. She leaned forward, one hand against the glass, weight shifting to account for the duffel bag hung over her shoulder, and counted nine moving lights. Nine ships, too many stars to count.

"Station maintenance could use a kick in what serves them for nuts," Craig muttered from behind her. "You see bolts loose in the public areas, you wonder what upkeep on the important part of the structure's been like. What are you looking at?"

"A casualty list in the billions had Primacy jumped this far in."

"Yeah. Well, stop. If they'd jumped this far in without the buoys, they'd have carked it trying to occupy a space already filled with a ship or a planet or a moon or a . . ."

"I get it."

He kissed the top of her head. "Losses sure, but not billions."

"That's strangely reassuring."

"It's what I do. Strange reassurance."

She smiled as she turned toward him, but the smile slipped as she caught sight of three Trun, clearly security of some sort given the uniforms provided by the company that ran the tether. Talking among themselves, hands and tails waving, they were clearly discussing her team, ignoring a family of Rakva, the adults being driven to distraction by a four-egg clutch, as well as half a dozen Niln wearing the same symbol on their vests, who stood nose to nose shouting at each other and waving their slates.

Craig turned just far enough to follow her gaze, then turned back to face her. "They don't look a whole lot different than the security at the shuttle heading down to Paradise. Except for the tails. And the entirely unsubtle way they're looking us over."

"We're making them nervous."

"We're twice their size."

"So are the Rakva."

"True enough, but the Rakva are half their weight." He leaned in and pressed his shoulder to hers. "No one gets nervous about a species that has to fill their pockets with rocks so they don't blow away in a high wind."

"Still . . ." The actual security had been automatic; hand in a scanner to confirm commerce was, indeed, the purpose of their visit, then a blood test to ensure no one carried anything that could affect the indigenous population, flora, and fauna. "Both the Rakva and the Niln used the scanner first." She rubbed the tip of her finger where the trio of needles had punctured the skin. "Maybe it didn't recalibrate properly."

"Torin." She could hear the smile in his voice. "Not your job to worry about their ability to do their job."

"I know."

"What's really bothering you?"

The boarding klaxon rang before she could answer.

"Hold that thought. I'm going to grab us coffees for the trip."

She watched him cross to join Binti at the vending machines—watching Craig walk was always worthwhile—shifted the strap of her duffel bag higher, and joined Ressk and Werst. Alamber, for reasons of his own she couldn't hope to understand, had decided to amuse the hatchlings as they lined up at the scales.

For the first time in her life, she was unarmed while landing on a new planet.

Craig would probably think that was sad.

Torin rubbed her palms against her thighs and wished she had a weapon.

THREE

Torin had never ridden a tether. Paradise had a regular shuttle service, a maglev track up the side of Mount Bliss, and the Corps preferred a quick and dirty VTA drop rather than load the taxpayers' credits into a vehicle dependent on a string a child could cut—albeit a child with a high-powered cutting tool. Even if there'd been one in place, a tether would have been far too vulnerable to exactly the kinds of things the Corps would have been heading dirtside to deal with. Not to mention vulnerable to battle debris. And the weather.

"Remember how you were wondering about station maintenance?" she asked, leaning a little more weight against Craig's shoulder. "Next time we're about to plummet four hundred kilometers down a braided strand of Mictok webbing at 200 kilometers an hour, you can keep those questions to yourself."

He paused his game and turned toward her. "Worried about the brakes?"

"I don't worry about things I can't affect."

A dimple flashed. "And you hate having no effect. If it comes to it, how long to get the emergency pods from here?"

"We can have pods locked and launched in six point two seconds if we don't stop to assist the civilians. If they need help, given that all but two of the civilians are small enough to be grabbed and tossed and the adults, being Rakva are lighter than most bipeds their size, fifteen point two seconds, give or take a tenth of a second. Slightly more time if all four hatchlings have to be in a pod with their parents. Slightly less if more than one of the hatchlings is in arms when the abandon ship is given."

"You didn't even look at the pods."

"You mean just now?" She frowned. The pods were lined up in the bulkhead to her left. There were eight, each rated for nine hundred kilos, emergency access code in bright yellow across each hatch. "I worked the timing out before we started to move."

"Of course you did."

Torin wondered what he found so funny when she knew he'd done similar calculations. He had a lot more trouble relinquishing control in moving vehicles than she did and the game he had up on his slate was a distraction from the unpleasant reality of entering the atmosphere in a can on a string. A string extruded from a Mictok's ass.

"I look at it this way, Torin; the company may not care about the cheap seats, but this tether's mostly freight and there's about fifteen tons plummeting with us. They'll want to minimize the odds of company profits vaporizing on impact."

"And that helps?"

He grinned, grip white-knuckled around his slate. "Not really, no."

"All right, then." She nodded at the screen. "Red durr on green banon."

"Not yet. I have a strategy."

"For losing?" Craig had acquired a fairly extensive game library while working alone as a Civilian Salvage Operator; the addition of four ex-Marines and one ex petty criminal had removed the qualifier. "You've never gotten above shield level seven."

"Yeah, well, welcome to level ei . . ." The screen flashed red then yellow then black. "Fuk me sideways!"

The male Rakva turned toward them, crest up. Hands over the bright green auriculars covering a hatchling's ear openings, he snapped his rudimentary beak. It would have been more effective had the beak been less rudimentary, but he made his disapproval clear.

Craig, who'd had more experience with children—and their parents' expectations—than Torin, clicked what she assumed was an apology. Crest fully extended, the male pointedly turned his back. The female dragged the smallest and downiest of the hatchlings onto her lap. "What did you say?"

He shrugged. "This one is sorry for any offense. Could be a dialect problem."

"Could be." But she doubted it. She remembered her first trip to Ventris Station, standing in the docking bay with sixty other raw recruits, many of them meeting a new species for the first time and seeing only that di'Taykan were too colorful and their eyes were weird and Krai were too short and their feet were weird and Humans were too soft and their noses were weird. Finding the similarities came later. But without the Corps to emphasize a Marine is a Marine, how long did it take civilians to get to the point where they realized the similarities far outweighed the differences? Or, she wondered, watching the adult Rakva shift around until their bodies blocked their hatchling's view of the Younger Races, was it a realization not everyone bothered to reach?

During boarding, the Rakva had taken seats as far from Torin and her team as possible, even though it put them closer to the half dozen Niln who'd clearly been drinking and were skirting the obnoxious edge of boisterous. If it came to the vote Colonel Hurrs feared, would the Rakva vote to turf the Younger Races out of the Confederation?

Dragging her hands back through her hair, she exhaled and cursed the colonel. This was why she never bothered with politics. Even if these particular Rakva never managed to get past the differences, they didn't speak for their entire species.

"Deep thoughts?" Craig asked, bouncing his shoulder off hers.

"I'm remembering the doctor who was with us on Silsvah." An environmental research physician thrown into combat, Dr. Leor had done everything possible to keep her Marines alive. "He had the same coloring as mama bird over there."

"Could be related. You should go ask."

"No."

"Because you don't care?"

"Because there's a billion Rakva with the same coloring and

the odds are very high they're no relation."

"Never change." He leaned in, aiming for her mouth—she assumed—kissed the side of her nose, and went back to his game.

"So, Boss, if you and Craig aren't going to play," Alamber began, dropping into the seat on her right. "You and I could . . . Kidding!" he assured her when she turned to face him, waving off any reply she might have made, the other hand dramatically clutching his masker. "You have made your opinion on sexing up the subordinates absolutely clear. Besides," he added, hair moving in a self-satisfied arc, "I don't need you; the Niln offered."

"All six . . . five of them?" The sixth was framed in the open hatch of a species neutral refresher, puking into what Torin hoped was a toilet.

"I think they wanted research sex." When Torin turned to face him . . .

"Hey, I was leaning on that shoulder," Craig muttered, shifting his weight without looking up.

. . . Alamber grinned. "See, this whole group of short and scaly are grad students heading back after a break. I think they said they're studying cultural anthropology, but that sparkly red-and-gold one, she's got an accent I can barely get my head around." Stretching out long legs, he admired the *fragile* stickers on the toes of his boots. They'd been free at check-in and Alamber had happily taken a couple. "Anyway, they've studied up on members of the Confederation and a couple of them have heard things from a friend who knew someone who'd gone out of the Core, but they've never seen a di'Taykan before. Or a Krai for that matter." He snickered, eyes lightening. "Actually, for an entirely different matter as having research sex with short, cranky, and disproportionate never came up."

Torin had no intention of asking him to clarify what he meant by disproportionate.

After a moment, he realized that, shrugged, and continued. "Your lot, they've seen. But only because there were two Human crew on the cheap holiday boat they just left. The Trun checking us out up in the station? We were firsts across the board for them and they're out of the gravity well, so I think it's fair to assume they're going to be a bit more exposed than their buddies on the ground."

That explained the attention. They were new. Different. "So, when our antique hunters . . ." Grave robber was not a designation Torin wanted overheard. ". . . came in for supplies, they didn't use this tether."

"Or they didn't use it when those two were on," Alamber pointed out. "There's three crews on a ten-day up/twenty-day down rotation, but I didn't get a chance to delve for details because they were all . . ." He waved a hand gracefully between them. ". . . hurry, hurry, no time, schedule to keep. But this is the cheapest of the three ways down, not to mention back up again, so unless our antique hunters have found a backer with deep pockets, this had to have been their ride."

Unfortunately, they had no idea of how well-funded the grave robbers were, and if Big Bill's operation on Vrijheid had taught her anything, it was that crime didn't have to be petty. Big Bill had taken a percentage off every pirate in two sectors as well as off the merchants who supplied them with food, fuel, and entertainment. But if these particular criminals were well-funded, would they have needed to sell an artifact to make a little extra on the side? Not necessarily *need*, she reminded herself. Greed was a much more likely motivator.

How much would a dealer pay for an illegal biscuit maker?

"You're thinking about the biscuit maker, aren't you, Boss? You've got a little line . . ." Alamber touched her forehead with a cool fingertip. ". . . here. Happens every time."

Torin bit back the urge to deny it and glared past his hand until he removed it.

"I'm just saying."

"Don't."

"Okay, then. So, data point on the Trun; they weren't at all interested in figuring out if the parts fit. I was crushed. Prehensile tails," he expanded when Torin's brow rose.

"I thought you didn't have time to delve? Schedules to keep?"

He frowned thoughtfully. "Yeah, that could've been why."

Torin opened her mouth, and closed it again. Those were the first Trun Alamber had ever seen; of course he was going to ask. They were the first Trun Torin had ever seen. According to the information in Intell's packet, which she suspected had been heavily cribbed from *Races of the Confederation*, a book every schoolkid was familiar with, the Trun were hermaphroditic, all of them able to produce viable sperm and carry young. They preferred to live in large family groups. Having colonized four planets, they'd decided that was enough of that and, for the most part, left their home planet only to visit one of the other three. Having spent the last sixteen years jumping from battle to battle all through the OutSectors, Torin had to remind herself that most people never left the gravity well they'd been born in.

Last of the four planets settled, only sixty percent of Abalae's population were permanent residents, the other forty percent held short-term visas and attended one of the five Centers of Learning or two Centers of Discovery, or were visitors at one of the four Centers of Commerce or the seven Centers of Nature. Given the split, Torin had assumed they'd go unnoticed. It hadn't occurred to her that the Younger Races in general didn't frequent this part of the Core. Why would they? The military had always been pointed in the other direction.

"Nice bit of recon, Alamber. Thank you."

His eyes darkened to let in more light—checking her face for sincerity. After a moment, his hair fanned out and he smiled, not his usual cocky grin but a younger, softer expression that hinted at a desperate need for approval and made Torin want to shoot his *vantru* every time she saw it. "You think we should we talk about it, Boss? I could wake the others."

"No. Let them sleep." Binti and Ressk had stretched out, foot to foot, over a row of empty seats, Ressk's head in Werst's lap. Werst was reading, probably a Krai romance if only because it was usually a Krai romance. He had his free hand wrapped loosely around the back of Ressk's neck. "Give them a heads-up before we leave the pod."

"And this had been such a simple straight-on job," Craig said quietly as Alamber disappeared with three of the Niln. "Slide in, find out who sold the biscuit maker, crack a little code. Harder to slide if we're going to be exotic visitors from the OutSectors. I'd ask if you think there might be trouble, but that's pretty much your default setting."

"You know me so well." She dug an elbow into his side when

he smirked. "It's still a straight-on job. If the Younger Races are rare on the ground, odds are higher the dealer will remember who sold them the artifact."

"But?"

Stretching out her legs, she tapped her right boot against her left. "But why would they come here if they knew they were going to be noticed?"

"Who says they knew?" He shrugged broad shoulders. "They wanted to unload a biscuit warmer, thought Commerce would be a good place to do it. Felt exposed, never came back."

Torin turned that over. Examined it from all sides. "Makes sense. Doesn't feel right."

"A gut feeling, then?" He was smirking again.

"Shut up."

A glance down at his game, then back up at her. "We're not supposed to be noticed either. What do we tell the locals if they're all about why we've visited their lovely planet?"

Torin sighed. "I miss not having to explain myself."

We're the Marines, we're here to save you. It had never descended quite that far into bad vid territory—uniforms and weapons made the announcement redundant. "Confederation citizens," she said after a moment, "have the right to travel freely within the Confederation. We are Confederation citizens. Abalae is part of the Confederation. We have the right to travel freely here. And," she added, not bothering to soften the edge, "we could always mention how, now the war is over, we thought we might like to see what we've been dying for."

"Guilt." He cocked his head. "That could work."

Then the greenest of the hatchlings shrieked. Torin glanced over as Craig jerked forward and caught his slate as it slipped from his hand.

"I can't believe you didn't react to that." He had to raise his voice to be heard over the undulating, high-pitched noise.

She shrugged; it wasn't a sound they'd been conditioned to, there weren't a lot of angry kids on a battlefield. Across the cabin, Binti pulled her jacket over her head. "He's tired, that's all." A bit of emerald fluff flattened against the screen over the air purifiers. "And I think the yellow-and-blue one plucked a feather."

* * *

The tether dropped them on a constructed island in an equatorial sea. A boat to take them to a transport station on the closest continent, visible as a green-blue smudge against the horizon, had been covered in the drop ticket.

When the boat rose out of the water on what looked like skis, Torin tightened her grip on the railing.

"They're called hydrofoils. They lessen friction and allow the boat to move faster while using less fuel."

Torin turned to Ressk, his face lifted into the wind, eyes and nostril ridges slitted nearly shut.

"What?" he asked. "You think we only have trees on Harask, Gunny? We have oceans. Four of them. And rivers. And lakes."

She knew that.

"Look, Yeen!" Binti pointed at long, lithe shapes moving parallel to the ship just under the surface of the water, rounded curves and translucent flukes rising and falling amidst the waves.

Squinting, trying to pick out a definitive feature, Torin decided to take Binti's word on the species. Three members of the Confederation were water breathers, but the Primacy had never attacked a wet world, so the Corps had never deployed to one and Paradise had been rejected after offering her seas for colonies. Before Colonel Hurrs, Torin had believed the water breathers had rejected Paradise because her seas had been too cold or too salty or too warm or not salty enough. Now, she suspected it had more to do with the 2.8 billion Human inhabitants.

"I bet they let the Yeen land in a shuttle," Craig muttered.

"Or they filled the tether with water. It's waterproof," Alamber added.

"Do I want to know how you know that?"

"If you can't figure it out, I have serious concerns about your ability to extrapolate from known data." He laughed when Craig flipped him off. "I checked before we docked." The wind moved Alamber's ribbons in long sinuous arcs his hair tried to copy. "There's always seats on the freight tether."

"I don't like being dependent on someone else's schedule."

"What's the difference between that and taking the shuttle to and from Paradise?" Torin wondered.

He braced his forearms on the railing. "We weren't working on Paradise."

Although they *were* working here on Abalae, there should be nothing in this part of the job that would require them to leave suddenly, on their own schedule. Of course, *should* was one of those words that got people killed, Torin acknowledged, watching a huge white sea bird dip down to touch the crest of a wave.

A spear thrust up out of the water and red bloomed against the white. The bird hit the water, floated for a moment on the surface, and then abruptly disappeared.

"Seriously?" Alamber snorted. "You know their interstellar craft use an independently developed version of the Susumi drive, right? They can bend space and they hunt with a spear. That's just wrong."

"That was a sport hunter, nothing to do with tech level. Or don't your people fish?" Werst asked when Alamber made a disgusted noise.

"Kill for fun?" His eyes were so light Torin wondered if he could see, and his hair flattened so tightly against his head she could see the curve of his skull. "That's barbaric!"

"You know, for an ex-criminal . . ." Torin moved away from the railing and tucked him into the circle of her arms. ". . . you have a number of interesting blind spots."

"I never killed anyone," he protested, the fine tremors shaking his body beginning to ease with physical contact. "And even Big Bill didn't kill for fun."

Torin had her doubts about that, but decided to keep them to herself.

"You know what would make me feel better?" he asked after a few minutes.

"Yes." She shifted Alamber into Craig's arms and checked his masker. "But Binti's gone to find food, so you'll have to settle for that."

The transport station had been built over the end of the dock, a sturdy structure covered in photovoltaic panels, large enough for passengers to disembark inside. While the station could have easily been automated, a dozen Trun in transport uniforms stopped working and watched as they crossed from the landing to the ticket counter. At a glance from Torin, Alamber peeled off and advanced toward them, smiling his most distracting smile, one hand at the pheromone masker at his throat.

"*Lower it one mark only,*" she'd told him. "*We have no idea how the Trun will react . . .*" All mammals reacted. "*. . . and we only want them happy enough to answer a few questions.*"

"*Maybe that's all you want,*" he'd sighed.

"Six seats." Craig touched his slate to the counter and two fingers to the plastic casing around the edge of the screen. "Commerce Three, Section Eighteen."

The Trun who ran the transaction slid six pieces of actual paper across the counter, half turned, and murmured something that sounded distinctly uncomplimentary to zir companion. When zi looked back, Torin met zir eyes. And smiled.

Zir eyes widened. "Details . . ." Zi swallowed and tried again. "Details have been sent to your slates, Visitor."

"Thank you."

"Sure." Zir tail wound around the other Trun's. "I mean, you're welcome, Visitor."

"Letting them know they can't trash talk Humans?" Craig asked as they walked away.

"Letting them know they can't trash talk us," Torin snorted. "Humanity's on its own."

Transport turned out to be a maglev train, much like the ones on the stations and the larger of the Navy's destroyers. The trains, like the tether, were set up predominately to carry freight, the four-link trains tagged Learning, Discovery, Commerce, and Nature, looking distinctly second class beside the sleek metal platforms being loaded with crates. Arguing about their baggage, the Niln climbed into Learning, the Rakva family boarded Nature. The team had Commerce to themselves.

The link's seats had been designed for tails, but were comfortable enough for those species without. Everything was worn, rubbed smooth by use. In spite of the lingering scent of powerful cleansers, the interior had the grubby patina of a link too long in service. Torin touched one of the faded red plastic seats that made up a row of four along one outside wall before she sat, her back to the window, her reflection in the window across the car.

"They really don't like anything in the air, do they?" Craig touched and sat on her right.

"Ground transport allows greater control of visitors." She touched the seat to her left and silently acknowledged that touching every seat would border on obsessive. "We're confined, at their discretion, to a five-by-three–meter compartment."

"And that doesn't sound at all ominous," Werst muttered as he and Ressk sat in the two seats at the end of their row facing the direction of travel.

Binti took a seat across the aisle. "At least we're not heading into a war zone."

Torin had led them to the middle of the car so they couldn't be cornered, movement preferable even over the possibility of being surrounded. Without a heavy gunner, it was easier to fight through flesh than a solid wall. Not that they'd have to.

"Did I mention those tails are fully prehensile?" Alamber reached up and pressed his palms flat against the ceiling. The Trun, while not as short as the Krai, weren't tall. "I am *really* looking forward to a test drive. What?" he demanded when Werst snorted. "Plenty of people spill secrets after sex."

"He has a point." Ressk admitted. "You told him about our . . ."

Werst's nostril ridges flared. "That was *not* a secret."

None of Torin's business. "Have the workers at the terminal seen any . . ."

"Of us?" Alamber's head moved one way, his hair moved another. "No. Looks more and more like they spent the lolly to take another tether."

"Lolly?" Torin asked.

Alamber nodded at Craig. "He says it."

"And you're working on a new dialect?"

"Might come in handy."

Torin couldn't argue with that.

As a bland, species-nonspecific voice began listing the

behavior expected while the train was in motion, Binti shook her head. "Low rent tether aside, this is not the rough and ready free trade sort of place you'd expect grave . . . antique hunters to resupply at."

"Maybe that's why they came." Torin frowned up at an ad for a spa on its second loop through a dozen static-filled images. "No chance of being caught up in a sweep by the Wardens. Or maybe this is rough and ready for the Core worlds. How would we know?"

At almost five hundred kilometers an hour . . .

"This train is moving faster than the tether." Ressk glanced up from his slate. "Does no one else find that strange?"

. . . the windows were opaque unless specifically touched transparent. Werst tapped the glass clear, dark, clear, dark, clear, dark until Torin reached over and grabbed his wrist.

"Stop that, or I'll puke in your lap."

Krai didn't get motion sick. Or space sick. Or, apparently flickering images going by too fast to really focus on, sick. Neither did gunnery sergeants, but Torin wasn't willing to completely discount the possibility.

At the first station, they were instructed to remain seated while five people entered the link. Two Trun. Three Katrien. The Katrien Torin saw OutSector were plush, their fur thick and dark with silver tips, their hands and feet glossy black. These three had sleeker fur without the silver, their hands and feet a deep brown, the darker masks around their eyes and muzzle less distinctive. The glasses protecting their sensitive eyes from the light weren't mirrored but after a moment's thought Torin realized that might be one of Presit's affectations rather than a species imperative. The Katrien reporter liked to make an impression. All three fell silent as they realized who they were about to share the link with, then turning their backs, began talking at once, their voices rising quickly into the cat fight range. The Trun, however, huddled silently at the far left of the link, tails entwined.

Binti flicked her eyes in their direction. Torin shook her head, willing to bet, in spite of unfamiliar physiognomy, the Trun looked wary, not threatening.

At the next stop, two adults and a juvenile Trun stepped on at the far right end of the link, looked around, and, hair up and ears flat, froze in place. They jerked as the doors shut and finally sat as the train started to move. Before the train was fully out of the station, the youngster knelt on the seat and stared over the back. When Torin smiled, without showing teeth, zir eyes widened but before any further contact could be made, a tail dragged zir down into the seat.

The next stop was close enough the train hadn't time to reach full speed and the car was three quarters full when they pulled away. They were still the only members of the Younger Races present and the seats around them remained empty.

"Are you a Marine?"

Torin looked up from her slate. She'd been watching the youngster approach, wondering how far zi'd make it before the adults noticed zi was gone. "I was."

"Was it scary?"

"Sometimes."

"Oh." Holding zir tail in one hand, zi stroked the orange tip with the other. "My kada says there wasn't no reason for there to be a war."

"There wasn't."

Zi cocked zir head, golden eyes wide. "Then why did you go and fight?"

"We thought there was a reason."

"Were you wrong?"

Sliding through the spectrum and then fading back into gray, the alien mass rose in the middle, rounded the crest, extruded two short arms, and created a vaguely bipedal shape. It turned its minimal face toward the camera and blinked gray on gray eyes. "It takes time to collect sufficient data on new species. Creating extreme situations erases all but essential behaviors and shortens the duration of the study."

"Yes." Torin dried her palms against her thighs. "We were wrong."

"My kada says your kind can't stop fighting. My kada says you fight like nunnurs in spring."

The rest of the team was listening in. She could feel their attention. "And what are my kind?"

"Like you. Big with boots." Zi pointed at the Krai's bare feet. "And like them. Littler with no big boots. Or hair."

"And what's a nunnur?"

Zi cocked zir head, the markings on zir brow folding into a double-u. "You don't know?"

"I've never been to Abalae before."

"Oh. Nunnurs are little." Zi dropped zir tail and brought zir cupped hands close together. "And soft. With short puffy tails and big, big feet."

"That doesn't sound so bad."

Zi leaned closer. "I petted one once. Zi tried to bite me. They have lots of pointy teeth. Your boots are very shiny."

"Thank you."

"Do you have toes?"

All members of the Confederation spoke Federate. Most also spoke another, species-determinate language. Trun was a deep bass line, languidly rhythmic even when being growled at a protesting child scooped up by arms and tail and returned very quickly back to the other end of the car.

"Cute kid." Craig pressed his shoulder against Torin's. "Don't think I like zir kada, though."

"I'm more than my boots," Alamber grumbled.

"This is not what I expected."

The station at Commerce Three, Section Eighteen was a larger copy of the oceanfront station. Grubbier, smellier—both Krai had their nostril ridges nearly shut and Alamber's hair had begun to flip back and forth in small, jerky arcs—but essentially the same. A crowd of several species surged past them to get onto the car, the barriers that had once kept the arriving and departing apart having been snapped off, leaving nothing but jagged ridges on the floor.

"They're not all going to fit," Werst grumbled, glaring a Trun out of his way.

"Not our problem," Torin told him. It wasn't an evacuation, people fighting their way onto the last ship out of a burning port. They'd be fine. "If you want to worry about something, worry about how far we are from the tether and how we're dependent on the links to get back."

"Thanks a fukking lot, Gunny."

She grinned. "No problem." But now he'd be keeping an eye out for a vehicle they could commandeer if things went down the shitter. Not that things should. And there was that word again.

The early evening air outside the station was warm and humid under a low, gray cloud cover.

"Fukking hell." Werst snapped his nose ridges shut as Ressk began to sneeze.

Breathing through her mouth, Torin grabbed one of Alamber's ribbons, dragged him back out of the station, and led the way down the stained stairs. "We'll get used to it."

He had a hand clamped over his mouth and nose. "I don't want to get used to it, Boss."

Three roads that began at the half circle below the station divided Section Eighteen into thirds. The roads had originally been broad avenues but had been divided in turn by stalls and carts, a jumbled mass of wood and plastic and metal that may have started out mobile, but over time had become permanent. It reminded Torin of the ships that made up the structure of the salvage station Craig used to call home and, from his expression, she'd bet he was thinking the same.

The prevailing smell—although by no means the only smell—was hot oil and frying meat. The stalls and carts selling food were surrounded by harried looking people—mostly Trun but some Katrien and Niln—pushing forward, yelling out their orders, and making it clear they had no time to waste. Given the scrum, Torin was impressed the Truns' tails didn't knot with their neighbors. Most wore the minimal harness of Commerce workers and the steady stream of snacking Trun heading for the train suggested they'd arrived at a shift change.

The three- and four-story buildings lining the roads were made of stone and wood—both probably harvested to create the section's plateau. On the other side of the station, great rocky ridges rose to the sky fringed with trees that caused the Krai's eyes to widen.

"If we have time and there's a nature sector close enough . . ." Werst's voice was as close to awe as Torin had ever heard it.

"... I wouldn't mind a closer look at those trees."

"With luck, we'll get some down time when we're done."

"Yeah, but, Gunny ..." Ressk paused to sneeze. "... we're here now."

"Here and now, we're working."

It was late enough the lights had begun to come on, breaking the chaos into even smaller pieces. This looked more like the sort of place an illegal artifact might be sold, although Torin still had a problem getting around the distance from the tether. It was the closest Commerce Sector to the tether, however, so she would have to be satisfied with that.

"Room first," she decided. "Then food. Then we find out who blew into town with the biscuit warmer." Which continued to sound ridiculous.

Ressk sneezed twice. "Who'd look for a high-end preConfederation piece in this?"

"The best pieces are found at the worst stores. Because," Alamber continued before anyone could ask, "most of them are acquired illegally, so it's not like they're going to be sold at high-end, squeaky clean places, are they?"

"How do you know?" Werst asked.

"Hello? Big Bill? Vrijheid Station? Illicit gains?" Alamber's hair spread out and settled as he sighed. "You people are so sheltered."

There were three Trun waiting for them at the edge of the plaza. Not Wardens. Wardens maintained the law between the worlds—until they couldn't; then they called in Torin and her team. These were quite obviously the local equivalent. Someone at the station had called ahead and this was what the bargain basement Commerce Sector could field at short notice.

When they moved to block the way, Ressk murmured, "They're called facilitators. The baton on their belt is a stun gun."

"Visitors." The shortest of the three stepped forward. Torin stopped about three meters away, heard the others spread out behind her. "Welcome to Section Eighteen, Commerce Three." The voice was unexpectedly deep for zir size. Torin touched the place where the cylinders of ash should be. The facilitator reminded her of Captain Rose. "What," zi continued, tail tip lashing, "brings you here?"

"Ship. Tether. Boat. Train." Werst growled the list just loudly enough to be heard, softly enough to be ignored.

Torin smiled, keeping her teeth mostly covered. "We came to shop."

The facilitator blinked. "Shop?"

"We were told about your commerce sectors, thought we'd check one out. Is there a problem?"

"No . . ." Zi visibly shook off zir confusion. Her response had clearly been unexpected, but zi was just as clearly determined to stay on script. "No," zi repeated, leaning forward slightly, ears flattening. "And we don't want problems."

Zi had a little power over zir lower-ranked companions, a little more over shoplifters, drunks, and vandals and none at all over her. Torin swept an assessing gaze over the three of them, frowned slightly at a sloppy twist in the tallest facilitator's harness that had tri-colored hair stuck up in tufts around it, finally met the shortest's gaze, and, after a moment said, "Good."

"Good?" Zi sounded unsure.

"We don't want problems either." Torin pitched her voice to support a corporal under her command.

Zi nodded, posture relaxing. "Good," zi repeated. "Have a pleasant evening, Visitors."

Torin returned the nod, zi barked an order—which caused one of zir companion's ears to lift—and the three of them strutted away. Given the way their legs bent, she gave the strut the benefit of the doubt.

"You need to promise me you'll only use your powers for good," Craig said softly at her right side.

"Police forces are hierarchical." Torin watched zi reach over to tug at the twisted strap, chewing out the other facilitator in a low rhythmic burr. "If the military teaches you one thing, it's how to spot your place in the hierarchy."

Craig made a noise that might've been disbelief, might've been derision. "*That's* the one thing?"

"We don't give them live rounds until we're sure they'll only shoot what we tell them to shoot," Torin answered absently. The crowds streaming past on their way to the train, anxious to get home at the end of shift, had been ignoring them. Unfortunately, that had changed the moment they'd been stopped by the facilitators, and now she'd bet that a high fraction of the noise surrounding them concerned them. She could feel the weight of multiple gazes. "This is a stupid place to sell a biscuit warmer."

They rented a large room above the bar closest to the station. The room was clean, reasonably priced, and the only one in the establishment designed for the taller members of the Confederation. Unfortunately, the room and contents had been constructed entirely of molded plastic.

"That's one fuk of a lot of potential hyper-intelligent, polynumerous molecular polyhydroxide alcoholydes," Torin muttered from the threshold. It was one thing to refuse to allow the little plastic bastards to dictate any more of her life and another thing entirely to walk into the belly of the beast.

"Your call, Gunny." Werst stood a little too close behind her, but she couldn't tell if that was due to her shit or his own. He'd been on Big Yellow and in the prison. Out of her personal triumvirate, he'd only missed having a conversation about context with Major Svenson's arm.

"We're out of here."

They rented a second, more expensive room a half block away, the visible plastic unobtrusive enough to ignore. The room had clearly been designed for Rakva—so had the other, Torin realized, forcing herself to look past the memory of the plastic—but they could all work around that.

"Why not get the information we need and sleep on the train on the way back to the tether?" Werst demanded.

"Because then it'll look like we were here to get information," Alamber sighed from the larger of the two nests. "No tourist would come this far and not stay the night. You guys really suck at directing attention. And if *I'm* using suck in a derogatory way . . ." A rude gesture completed the observation.

"Don't you mean redirect?" Craig asked, opaquing the windows.

"Yeah, no. In order to redirect, you have to direct, and I was serious about the *really* sucking."

By the time they emerged back onto the street, it was full dark. Under low, yellow-white lights, the buying and selling went on. Waiting for her vision to acclimatize, Torin paused on the bottom of the three broad steps leading into the inn.

"Commerce," Alamber said, sounding satisfied, "never closes."

"You learn that from Big Bill, too?" Binti asked.

"Well, yeah . . ." They were behind her, but Torin could hear the shrug in the di'Taykan's voice. ". . . but I also read it in one of the brochures I picked up on the tether. Commerce never closes! It's a thing."

The crowds had cleared from around the carts, leaving only a few people hunched over mugs or bowls or meat on sticks. The scent of grain toasted with peppers suggested that at least one of the carts sold Rakva *arliy* and she could hear Katrien in the distance, but the only race Torin could see were Trun.

"My kada says there wasn't no reason for there to be a war. My kada says your kind can't stop fighting. My kada says you fight like nunnurs in spring."

Your kind.

Torin shifted her shoulders, a year later still checking for the weight of her KC.

"Torin." Beside her, Craig's voice held a familiar mix of impatience and affection. When she turned toward him, he smiled. "They're not the enemy."

"I know." Everyone she could see moved like a civilian, only marginally aware of their surroundings. If they'd seen anything of the war, it had been on vid screens. The Trun throwing zir cup into the recycler had watched news clips of battles happening far away and had never been told those battles were happening far away in order to prevent battles from happening up close and personal. The pair of Trun arguing as they ate had never dropped dirtside through heavy fire, looking faintly bored while metal shrieked and the VTA bucked and pitched because every eye was on zir. The Trun buzzing by on . . . actually Torin had no idea what the fuk zi was riding. A metal rectangle about twenty centimeters by ten, maybe six centimeters thick with a meter-high control stick extending from one narrow end, provided barely enough space for the Trun to stand sideways. It moved quickly, about three centimeters off the ground, and it didn't look like it had wheels. Tail extended for balance, one hand on the stick, the other holding a bag of vegetables, zi sped nonchalantly around carts and people and disappeared into the night.

"I want one," Ressk announced.

"Looks like fun," Alamber agreed.

"You okay?" Binti asked over the discussion, quickly growing heated, that Alamber was too tall for the vehicle.

Torin stepped aside as Craig moved past to throw a pilot's perspective into the argument. "I'm fine."

"It's just that you'd shifted into kickass posture."

Kickass posture? "I didn't . . ."

When Binti's brows rose, Torin shook her head. "I'm fine," she repeated, forcing herself to relax. They were attracting a certain amount of attention; a couple of people stared openly, most glanced over and away, and over and away, radiating a studied nonchalance that said, *Yeah, so what, Younger Races. Why should I care?* She didn't see any slates up, although she assumed that unless the Trun were significantly different than every other sentient species in known space, pictures had been taken. Curiosity was what had dragged sentience out of the muck, after all. And Marines had their pictures taken all the time. They weren't covert . . . hadn't been covert. "Though I could be thinking too much," she admitted after a moment.

"Yeah, well, fuk Colonel Hurrs, right?" Binti's smile twisted. "I never thought about it in terms of us and them until that bastard brought it up."

"I'm not sure if I should be glad it's not just me," Torin muttered.

Binti's smile twisted further. "Me either."

"Lengthen the stick?" Craig raised both hands in a plea to the divine. "How the hell can you suggest lengthening the stick when you don't know what the stick does?"

"I know what my stick does when you lengthen it," Alamber muttered.

"All right, people." Werst's mouth closed with a snap of teeth and Torin knew with a comforting certainty, he'd been about to say, *"We all know what your stick does when you lengthen it."*

"Come on." She stepped down onto the street. "Let's eat."

A good portion of the local food shorted all three species of necessary amino acids, although, for a change, the Humans would be in the best shape should they run out of supplements.

"We eating singly or collectively, Gunny?"

"Let's stay together for now."

The Krai led the way to one of the larger stalls with counter seating. The stools were not only low but made for multiple users—three, maybe four Trun curled up together.

Binti took one look at them and snorted. "I'm sharing with the skinny ass," she declared, pulling Alamber down beside her.

Torin and Craig arranged themselves into a semifunctional position, and the four of them settled in to watch Werst and Ressk do what the Krai did.

The cook had clearly heard the stories that the Krai could and would eat anything organic—the Krai had fully committed to omnivores having better odds of achieving sentience—and, like every cook in known space, this Trun had to take up the challenge. The Krai always won.

Back on Big Yellow, Werst had eaten a piece of fake fruit. Which, as it happened, meant he'd eaten a piece of Big Yellow. Given that Big Yellow had been an organic plastic construct, that meant he'd eaten a piece of sentient, polynumerous molecular polyhydroxide alcoholyde with no ill effect.

Krai digestion was Torin's ace up the sleeve should the little gray fukkers return.

On the other side of the open kitchen, three Trun sharing a stool lifted bowls to their mouths and watched them over the edges.

The meat on a stick laid the unmistakable film that came from vat-grown food on Torin's hard palate. Fortunately the vegetable mash tasted like it had been grown in actual dirt. She cleaned her bowl with one of the shallow wooden spoons, half her attention on Werst eating a pale green gelatinous mass with every indication of enjoyment.

"What the hell was that?" Craig muttered, leaning past her to watch the last wobbly bit disappear.

"Don't know." She passed him her second stick of meat; he preferred vat over live. "Don't need nor want to know."

When Ressk ate a spoon, Torin put a stop to the challenges

before the Trun connected the dots. It was all fun and games until someone in the crowd realized they could be next on the menu.

"If I was in charge," the cook grinned as Werst touched his slate to the counter, "I'd comp you both, *kir survilav*."

::*Kir survilav*: dialect, Hurlarnir Islands. Little furless ones,:: Torin's jaw implant translated. Although Justice had provided the entire team with implants, only Torin and Alamber had more than basic communications. The Corps upgraded gunnery sergeants to the top of the line and the degenerate who'd called herself Alamber's *vantru* had his jaw cracked the moment she could find a tech who'd take her money, everyone involved ignoring the high possibility of bone deformities as his jaw continued to grow. Not long before the shit hit the fan on Vrijheid, Alamber had that first unit replaced with the best tech pirates could steal. When he'd matter-of-factly explained how he'd paid for it, Torin had beat the crap out of a punching plate. Craig's old implant, described as *"like a can on a string"* by Justice techs, had been replaced while the other three had their units installed.

"I think he likes you," Alamber purred as they moved away from the stall.

Werst belched.

"At least he likes your little furless ones; right, Boss?"

"Leave me out of this," Torin told him, indicating they should huddle up. With any luck, they'd appear to be a group of friends deciding to part ways for the evening. "Back at the room by local 01:30, unless you've cleared your absence in advance," she added as Alamber opened his mouth. It seemed unlikely, but if there were di'Taykan in Sector Eighteen, Alamber would find them. "Share intell as you get it—if we can ask about specifics, it can only help, but there's no need for regular contact."

Ressk looked up from his slate, nostril ridges half closed. "Socially evolved beyond warfare doesn't mean evolved beyond individual stupidity. One of the Trun sitting across from us had notched ears and a patch of fur missing from zir tail."

"The big orange one." Werst nodded, shifting his weight back and forth, toes spread against the pavement. "And all three had a pattern clipped into the fur of their forearms." Arboreal, the Krai had excellent vision in flickering light. "Could be a gang sign. Could be a symbol of their connection to their divine. Could be they go to the same crappy barber. If we see them again, we'll ask."

Tough guys—if they were tough guys—had to keep proving they were tough. Although, Torin acknowledged, they made good Marines if they could overcome that basic insecurity. "If they try something stupid, we don't engage. If they force the issue, minimum effective response." She swept a gaze around the team. "Mission objective is the identity of that supply ship. Maintain a low profile."

"A low profile?" Binti shook her head. "Gunny, they're watching us like they expect us to start shooting any minute."

Looking beyond Binti's shoulder, Torin could see the group around the food stall arguing with the cook. Beyond that, a facilitator stared across the promenade at them from the steps of their inn. When zi realized Torin had spotted zir, zir tail began to lash and zi raised two fingers to zir eyes, making a gesture universal among biocular species.

"No one actually likes tourists," Alamber pointed out. He tucked his hand in the crook of Binti's arm. "Come on, let's go buy crap, ask naive questions, and I'll show you how to have a good time in a strange place."

"His good time's been in some pretty fukking strange places," Werst muttered as they walked away.

"Binti can handle him. Shut up," Ressk added before Werst could comment. "Alamber has been a bad influence on you." He snapped his slate back onto his belt. "Let's go play quartermaster."

Werst waited for Torin's nod before falling into step beside his bonded. "You sure you know where we're going?"

"We follow the tracks to the warehouse district. I thought you were Recon . . ."

"And then there were two." Craig held out his hand. "Come on, let's go stop a war with a biscuit warmer."

The directions to Bufush's shop, while available, wouldn't download onto either slate.

"You think it's because we're bouncing off the ship and not fully integrated into their system?" Torin tapped the screen a few more times, unable to stop herself, knowing full well repetition wouldn't solve the problem.

"Could be. But if I had to guess, I'd say they prefer we do this the hard way." Craig pulled the slate out of her hand. "They want tourists to wander, get a little lost, spend more."

"On what?" The expression he turned on her was so incredulous she had to smile. "Okay, granted, there's a million things to buy, but I don't recognize half of them." The directions they'd managed to decode from the scramble had taken them to a narrow road of small, open-fronted shops under what were probably two or three stories of living quarters. Most of the shops sold a variation on a theme—harnesses, jewelry, small electronics, items that might've been toys or sex aids, Torin honestly didn't know.

It looked a lot like the concourses on the stations or the markets back home on Paradise, but . . .

The heavy bass drone under every piece of music was setting her teeth on edge. There was no smell of di'Taykan spices. No Krai ropework. Fabric, but almost no clothes.

"Do you ever wonder if our lack of fur is what kept the Younger Races so aggressive?" she asked glancing at a bin of unfamiliar fruit.

"I hadn't." Craig pulled her to a halt as the street split around an enormous tree that smelled faintly of dill. "We need to ask for directions."

Torin smiled at a Trun who scowled suspiciously and stepped back into zir shop. "Yeah, that'll go well."

"Shopkeepers'll be more friendly if we hand over the lolly."

"You want us to buy their tolerance?"

He shrugged. "You'd rather wander randomly?"

Now they were standing still, the number of Trun watching them had grown. The four who'd been following them from the far end of the street had gathered another two and all six were standing, tails lashing, exuding a combination of warning and fear.

Torin had been feared before. Just not generally while she was shopping.

"All right," she sighed. "Let's try it."

Three of the six scattered as she headed directly for them. The other three held their ground, radiating *you'll have to go through us*. Torin stepped around them to a display of iridescent scarves that reminded her a little of the saris an old girlfriend had worn. Every possible color combination, the scarves were decorative rather than insulating unless the metallic threads flickering in and out of sight as the translucent fabric rippled in the warm breeze indicated built-in tech.

"You have to pay for that." The young shopkeeper glared up at her, the row of tiny pink rings in zir ears quivering, a double loop of gauzy pink around her neck. "You can't just take it."

Torin pulled another scarf off the rack. "I know."

"You know? Sure you do."

"We need . . ."

Craig cut her off, leaning around her and lifting the spill of blue fabric off out of her hand. "We need your opinion. Blue for her?"

"Seriously?" The tiny pink rings flicked forward and back. "Blue for you. Blue'd make her look all gray and bleh. She should wear the brown and orange." Zi reached for the green scarf Torin still held, realized what zi'd done and froze, eyes wide, zir expression a clear *don't hurt me.*

Torin draped the green scarf over zir hand. "Brown and orange? Together?"

"Brown to anchor." Zir tongue moistened both halves of zir bifurcated upper lip. "Orange to warm. Here." Zi stepped back and shoved the scarf in question toward Torin, but before she could take it, Craig grabbed it and draped it around Torin's neck in a twisted mess.

"Oh, for . . ." The height difference was too great for her to fix it herself, but by the time zir impatient instructions had both scarves arranged to zir satisfaction, the fear had disappeared. By the time payment had been settled and zi'd explained how to reclaim the taxes using small words and short sentences, directions were no big deal.

"Okay, look . . ." The young shopkeeper waved zir tail to get their attention. ". . . you want Bufush's . . ." Zir voice dropped and lengthened the vowels into what sounded like a low moan punctuated with an exhalation. ". . . you have to go all the way to where Cariberry cuts across Nult Way. This is Cariberry." Zi waved a hand at the street. "Okay, so and then you go left on Nult . . . no, wait, right, go right on Nult until the *casatrai* shop, you'll know it when you see it, it has a big *casatrai* in the window and it's across from a row of three trim chairs under a canopy, but they'll be closed because it's nighttime and Mirlish won't hire night help because zi says a good trim needs natural light, right? Anyway, go past the *casatrai* shop to the next corner and then go left until you get to where Sound and Fury used to be, it's empty now, stupid building codes, then turn left again and that's where the seconds start. I don't know how far you have to go into the seconds because I don't go into the seconds, do I? But Bufush's is there. Somewhere."

"Reminded me of Helena." Craig threw an arm across Torin's shoulders as they headed toward Nult.

"Pedro Buckner's daughter?" Pedro was a friend of Craig's. Another CSO. Actually, given the whole pirate incident, Torin amended, forcibly relaxing her jaw before her implant went off, probably not a friend anymore.

"Yeah, her." The tension in his arm suggested his thoughts had gone the same way. When he laughed, Torin didn't believe it, but she didn't call him on it. "Teenagers are surprisingly species nonspecific."

"Zi was afraid of me."

"That's new?"

"It is when I'm not trying to be frightening." Zi was afraid and suspicious then dismissive and the other six were afraid and suspicious and Torin was used to being *other*—her career had involved being shot at after all—but this was different. She couldn't fight back.

The metallic threads in the scarves were data storage, sound files that complimented the color scheme. The brown and orange looped loosely around Torin's neck played a quiet rustle of wind through leaves that reminded her of home while Craig's blue and gray came with a soft shush shush of waves against a shore.

Given the greater number of people, Nult Way was a popular

boulevard. The open air cafes running down the center of the wide pavement served as many Niln and Katrien as Trun. Although Torin and Craig were taller than all three species, the overhanging signs, protruding second-floor additions, circles of overlapping yellow light, and the crowding of stalls made it difficult to get a line of sight on the *casatrai* shop.

::*Casatrai*: Trun basic, hanging bed large enough for family sleeping.::

"Like a hammock." Craig sketched a half circle in the air. "People live tight on salvage stations; they're useful."

The two of them were attracting attention, the Katrien more obvious about their interest than the Trun or the Niln. The hair lifted off the back of Torin's neck. She tabbed off her scarf as the whispers jumped ahead to a clump of all three races standing by a stall selling unidentifiable sticks and wire, furred and scaled tails in motion.

They were complaining about cost, Torin realized as they drew closer. Complaining about the taxes on what they sold. On what they bought. Complaining about the cost of waging a war.

"I hear wasn't about anything in the end. Don't know why we had to pay for it," an elderly Niln muttered as they passed, blunt muzzle thrust toward them.

"Torin . . ."

She shook off Craig's hand and faced the eight, no, nine noncombatants. Drew herself up to her full height, shoulders squared, and looked down on them. "You paid in taxes," she said, her voice parade ground clear. "We paid in lives."

They were past the *casatrai* shop before the whispers started again.

Craig stayed close and kept silent.

The Katrien and the Niln weren't even Elder Races. They were Mid Races, like the Rakva, joining the Confederation after it had been established but before the war. Torin had . . . well, Craig had . . . Fuk it. As irritating as the Katrien reporter was, Presit was a friend. How would the Katrien vote if it came to it?

"You can't fix this, Torin."

"I *know*."

"Pisses you right off, doesn't it?"

"Shut up." She moved closer until their hands brushed together as they walked. "Let's go recon the shit out of Bufush."

The left turn at Sound and Fury—windows boarded shut with actual boards, the door sealed with liquid lock—took them onto a street too narrow for stalls and carts, the pavement a uniform gray without lines of random color. Although all the overhead lights were working, they didn't seem as bright. After a moment, Torin realized that was because the surfaces were streaked with bird shit.

Seconds as per the young scarf seller, meant secondhand. Clothes. Furnishings. Toys. Tech. Why not grave goods stolen from a H'san cemetery that could start another war?

Bufush's lights were on, the door was open, and security eyes compensated for the absence of the shopkeeper.

"Hello?" Craig's voice got lost among the floor-to-ceiling shelves, piled high with junk. The good news was that the ceiling was about four meters up and they could stand inside the shop. Not always a given with the shorter races. Torin's ride in a Katrien ship had given her a choice between sore knees and a cracked skull.

She glared up at one of the eyes. "We'd like to speak with the proprietor."

"We'd like to give the proprietor an opportunity to fill zir pockets," Craig added, tucking his chin over her shoulder. He shrugged when she ducked out from under him. "Zi might be more chuffed to see us if zi knew why." Then he tucked his mouth up by her ear and breathed, "And you sound like a Warden."

She wanted to snarl that she'd sounded like a Marine, but Craig wasn't responsible for her mood, so she took a deep breath instead, let it out, and got her head back in the game. Sounding like a Warden in a shop that sold illegal artifacts wouldn't get them the information they needed. She touched his chest lightly in thanks before turning and scanning the shop.

Two minutes. Three. No answer, no proprietor.

"Zi's likely at the back. With the good stuff."

A nod to acknowledge Craig's experience in resale, and she stepped between the first set of shelves. "What keeps people from stealing the stuff at the front?"

"Other than the eyes?" She could hear the shrug in his voice. "Could have something to do with how much of it's crap."

About six meters in, the shop spread out, using the space behind the neighboring storefronts, although the floor-to-ceiling shelves made it impossible to get a line of sight and determine the exact parameters. Reaching up, Torin tugged on one of the protruding metal loops and, when it held her weight, went up three. At a meter five off the floor, she dropped, landing as lightly as boots allowed.

"Go back far enough," she said in answer to Craig's raised brows, "we're arboreal, too." If it came to a fight, she needed to know she could access the high ground. Torin unhooked a protruding wire from her sleeve and tucked it back into the tangle on the overloaded shelf. "I've been on stations that looked less chaotic after having been taken by the Primacy and then retaken by the Corps."

Craig flicked his thumb over the ridges in a piece of plastic pipe and frowned at the line of black under his nail. "How badly do you want to yell at someone to clean this up?"

"Pretty badly." It smelled of mold and dust and probably sweaty Trun. Closing thumb and forefinger around the plastic handle on a metal drawer, she half hoped for a reaction. The little gray fukkers deserved to spend time in the midst of such useless debris. "I'm impressed anyone found the biscuit warmer in this."

They passed groaning shelves and thematic piles. They doubled back twice, then cut through a long rack of funky smelling fabric. About the time Torin began indulging in fond memories of calling in air strikes, they finally emerged into an area better lit and visibly organized. The shelves were now about a meter and a half high, still taller than the locals, but no longer out of reach. Glancing up, she noted the security eyes were both more numerous and more obvious.

"I wonder how much of this is illegal." Craig poked at a ceramic cylinder.

Torin grabbed it before it could fall off the shelf. "As long as they're not selling weapons, I don't really care." She'd been scanning the shelves for familiar shapes, in whole or in part from the moment they'd entered the shop.

"Little chance of that this far into the Core . . ."

He fell silent on her signal and they retreated behind the last of the higher shelves. She cocked her head, straining to target the muffled noises. Not random . . . a voice. High-pitched. And furious. When Craig leaned out and pointing toward a closed door in the far wall, she nodded. The voice was coming from behind the door and getting louder. Closer. Close enough for the occasional word.

". . . fool . . . being . . . don't . . . here!"

"Katrien," Craig murmured. "Sounds pissed."

"Don't they usually?"

The argument had come close enough they could hear the low thrum of a Trun, also angry but unable to get much of a word in edgewise—pretty much the default in Torin's experience with the Katrien.

Then the door Craig had pointed out opened just far enough for an elderly Trun to slip through, followed by a loud and distinct, "Liar!"

Zi slammed the door shut, thumbed over the lock, and sagged against the painted wood while small fists banged on the other side. When the banging finally stopped, zi straightened, stared out over the long wooden counter in their general direction, and said, "How may I help you, Visitors?"

The Trun's lips pulled off zir teeth as they emerged, head and shoulders higher than the shelves now between them. Someone who hadn't served with the Krai might even think it was a welcoming smile.

Torin didn't.

FOUR

The Trun's fur was a short, dusty brown, with gray streaking zir square muzzle and tail. Zi wore a long, faded blue vest with an eclectic arrangement of pockets, some visibly bulging, and a single plastic ring in one ear. Beckoning them forward, zi looked like every bad cliché of a potty old junk dealer, but zir gaze never left them and Torin knew a threat assessment when she saw one.

"Please, Visitors, come closer."

Craig laughed his bullshit laugh. He was the sales, she was the muscle. "Come closer, you don't bite?"

"That has yet to be established." The old Trun's smile was blandly sincere.

Given the security, zi'd been aware of them since they'd entered, had made assumptions watching them navigate the maze, and was now in the process of adjusting those assumptions based on actual interaction. Zi was the first Trun Torin felt she understood. Zi might be as speciesist as those fukheads on the street, but zi wouldn't let it show unless it served zir purposes.

The path around the shelves was less maze-like but still convoluted enough that it took three, maybe four, minutes to walk to the counter. Sized for the Trun, the shelves were approximately hip-high on them both and seemed shorter given the height of the ceiling. A hard shove proved them secure enough to go over if it came to it—four to seven seconds from the counter to the less exposed part of the shop when taking the direct route. They'd be no protection against even small arms fire, but there were enough of them a shooter would need to be up close and personal.

Core planet or not, zir smile was bland enough that Torin wasn't ruling out shooters. Varga had been able to get his hands on black market weapons and he was an idiot. More to the point, she'd never believed thieves had any honor at all.

"So . . ." Zi spread zir hands, stopping their advance before zi had to crane zir head back to meet their eyes. ". . . I am Bufush." Trun pronunciation drew the vowels out. "How may I help you, Visitors?"

Torin remained just back of Craig's left shoulder, weight on the balls of her feet, hands loose at her sides.

Craig mirrored Bufush's position. According to the Justice briefings they'd been forced to sit through, it made people subconsciously feel more at ease. As maneuvering officers toward the required response was one of the jobs of the senior NCO, Torin had found that particular briefing a strange combination of fascinating and redundant. "My employer is interested in purchasing rare antiquities. She saw a ceramic piece in a . . . friend's collection and discovered it had been purchased originally from you."

The short pause Craig tucked in before *friend* was genius, Torin realized. Competing collectors would pay a lot more.

Bufush cocked zir head. Mild interest at best. "Discovered?"

"Eventually."

Veiled threat with full deniability. Torin was impressed. In a just universe, she'd have had more chances to see Craig negotiate while he was still a CSO. The thought of watching him go toe-to-toe against Staff Sergeant Bouyer at salvage acquisition was . . . distracting. She couldn't afford to be distracted. Not with a large area they didn't control not only behind them but between them and the exit. Not when they were speaking with someone who'd had eyes on them since they'd entered the shop. Someone who they knew had broken at least one law.

"I sell many pieces of collectible ceramics," zi said. "What specifically is your employer looking for?"

"Specifically?"

Both ears twitched. "Specifically."

"H'san."

And both ears stilled.

"H'san antiquities," Craig expanded. "Grave goods."

Zi spread zir hands, palms up, keeping the backs in contact with the countertop—to keep them from visibly shaking, Torin assumed. Clever. This was not, as Hollice would have said, zir first rodeo. "It is illegal to sell H'san grave goods."

"My employer is aware of that and is willing to pay for the inconvenience."

"Illegal, not inconvenient, Visitor."

"My employer will pay a significant amount . . ." Craig held up his slate, screen toward the Trun. ". . . for a more impressive piece."

Zir left ear twitched. Zi recognized the biscuit warmer.

"She's willing to pay enough for her piece to be the last piece you sell."

"That would be . . ."

Craig moved his thumb, and Torin knew the image of the biscuit warmer had been replaced by a large number.

Both ears twitched.

"That would be a very . . ." Zir tongue, like the lips just visible under the edge of zir fur, was purple. ". . . fair price, Visitor. But it doesn't make selling such items less illegal."

"Ah." Eyes on Bufush, Torin couldn't see Craig's smile, but she could hear it in his voice. "We're not Wardens."

If asked, the Wardens would support the denial. Vehemently.

"So you say, Visitors." Behind that entirely neutral response, Torin knew Bufush weighed the chance they were lying against the size of the number Craig had shown him. The number won. Hands still on the counter, zi shifted, mouth half open so only zir bottom teeth showed. "Unfortunately, I have nothing in stock. But, if you'll give me your contact information, I could inform you if a piece came in that would suit your employer."

"Excellent." Craig held out his slate.

And waited.

At the point where Torin had begun to worry they'd missed a cultural cue, Bufush finally blinked. "Oh. Of course." After an

I'm just a harmless old being pantomime of muttering and patting zir pockets, zi pulled out the smallest slate Torin had ever seen. Zi tapped the longer side, muttered something she didn't catch, and held it out as a pale purple, three-dimensional geometric image rose above the screen. "Touch your device to the matrix, Visitor. They should sync. Should," zi repeated a little dubiously.

She'd seen the hard light slates advertised, but even Ressk and Alamber had shied away from the cost. However, Bufush's didn't exactly cater to a luxury clientele and, from what she could see, this particular slate looked like a tool rather than an expensive toy. Another reminder that life was different in the Core.

The pattern flicked blue, then red, then purple again.

"Surprised that worked," zi admitted, returning the slate to a bulging pocket. "I'll message you the moment a new piece comes in. I can't promise when that'll be; I have no control over the supply." Zi rubbed a finger against the zir muzzle, pulling one side of zir bifurcated upper lip far enough to expose the points of yellowing teeth. "It might be better if you wait somewhere where you're less visible."

Craig snapped his slate back onto his belt. "We'll be ass in the air tomorrow. Maybe the day after. My employer appreciates your discretion."

"As I do yours, Visitor. If ceramics are the extent of your employer's interest . . ."

"Currently."

"Then may I show you the way out."

It wasn't a question.

Bufush led the way back through the maze of shelves, Craig following, Torin bringing up the rear, matching their route to the map in her head. Fingertips trailing over the plastic housing on a grubby solar battery, she noted all visible security eyes following their progress. It could be because they were the only people moving in the shop, but she suspected it was Bufush's reserves keeping a close eye on them until they were out of the building.

With the door shut behind them.

And the interior lights immediately turned off.

"Seems like zi doesn't want our kind hanging around." The street was nearly empty. Torin could see only a single pair of Trun in the distance, appearing and disappearing as they crossed the stationary circles of light until they finally disappeared for good.

"Zi doesn't want our kind to attract the wrong kind of attention because zi doesn't want that attention to be turned on zir. It's not speciesist, it's a criminal thing. You have to control the attention you're getting."

"Alamber?" she asked, as they headed back toward the distant corner and out of the seconds.

Craig's shrug said *who else* as eloquently as if he'd said it aloud. "Now that we've finished our business and are heading home—for variable definitions of home—we keep it casual. If we walk purposefully, everyone will know we've wrapped things up. We don't want people to know that. We've got four jacks and a lady and we're bluffing the table."

Made sense. One of the most dangerous parts of Recon was getting out, getting to the extraction point. It was easy to get careless with the information in hand. This trip to Abalae, to Bufush, was recon to stop a war; she needed to treat it as such. Torin slowed her pace.

"Not so slow as an amble." Craig pulled ahead. "More of a saunter."

She stepped close enough to shove him sideways, froze at a skittering sound from the narrow alley they were passing, realized it was local vermin in retreat, and returned to sauntering.

It felt like a poor neighborhood, not a dangerous one. If people watched unseen behind the dark surfaces of the upper windows, well, it made perfect sense they'd be curious. She could guarantee that the first Trun who moved to any of the OutSector planets would get tired of stupid questions long before everyone got tired of asking them.

When she mentioned that to Craig, he laughed. "They'd be fukking swarmed on a salvage station. Fur and a tail? Every kid who could walk would be up close and personal, making grabby hands. Human kid," he corrected. "We're a handsy species and when we're twice the size . . ."

Torin raised a hand and cut him off. "You're right."

"Often. About what, currently?"

"We're twice the size of the Trun." Pieces began slotting

into place. "We stick out here like a H'san in a . . ." All things considered, H'san comparisons had stopped working for her. "If the antique dealers we're looking for are Human or di'Taykan, they'd never use Abalae given any other choice. If successful criminals control the attention they receive—and these assholes are bare minimum good enough to involve us—walking around on Abalae when you're twice the size of the native population is the exact opposite of being able to control the attention."

"So . . . ?"

"So we know they had three other choices, three places we could have gone *rather* than Abalae."

"So here . . ." His gesture, while truncated, still defined *here* as Abalae. ". . . we're looking for Krai, then. They're about the same size as the Trun."

"Still Younger Race, still furless, still the wrong kind of attention." She frowned. "Alamber wondered why the person supplying the ceramics had to be one of the Younger Races and while my argument for the Younger Races being involved still stands, there's nothing that says they're the only ones involved. We've just proven the Trun can be bought."

"We've proven one Trun can be bought," Craig pointed out. "But, yeah, money talks. You think a Trun's involved, then?"

Torin glanced up at the night sky. The stars of the Core burned bright, even through the impressive amount of light pollution thrown up by the Commerce Center. "No, but there was a Katrien arguing with Bufush in the backroom." While the Katrien wouldn't agree with the wholesale violence of a H'san weapons cache, they could always be paid off before the weapons were found. "We've both had enough experience with them to know they can be opportunistic little shits." She tapped her implant on. "New data, people. Expand the search parameters . . ."

There were, Binti admitted, plenty of Katrien in Commerce Sector Three both buying and selling, their numbers owing more to the hour than the quality of the crap being bought and sold. Anchoring an elbow on the bar, she covered a yawn. She didn't think the fuzzballs were entirely nocturnal, but their eyes were definitely sensitive to light, and the weirdest thing about seeing them dirtside was neither the buying nor the selling, but the absence of dark glasses. This was the first time she'd seen them in a place where day and night hadn't been defined by the station or ship sysop.

There'd been Katrien in the last bar she'd followed Alamber into, half a dozen around an actual table, loudly defying the Trun's communal seating. Well, being loud anyway. In this bar, not so many Katrien. Actually, none at all.

It had taken them a while, moving down progressively darker side streets, but they'd finally found their way to a place where the people who might—or might not—ignore certain laws went looking for work. She hadn't needed Alamber's confirmation. The bar spoke for itself. It said, *Fuk off.*

A big bi-colored Trun glared at her from within the cupped curve of a platform about two meters up. She glared back and zi slid down out of sight. Seemed that being an ex-Marine gave her the kind of dangerous patina that counted coup on petty criminals—even if she'd only ever been dangerous within the confines of the Corps and orders given. Hadn't even been much of a troublemaker. Lifting her glass, she gave a silent salute to Haysole, the gorgeous little shit, tossed back the fermented whatever, and tapped the heavy base down on the bar for another.

Social species gathered socially, and this might not be a bar like any bar she'd ever been in before, but the Corps had taught her how to adapt. And see things a long way away. And then shoot them. Although technically, she could see a long way before the Corps. But right now, she had to adapt. That was the main thing. Adapt to tiny, little, itty-bitty glasses. And to the bartender, who had the cutest tufts on zir ears. No way they could be as soft as they looked.

Binti blinked and exhaled as the fizz faded out of her brain. Turned out, Humans metabolized Trun alcohol almost instantly. Thank fuk for the almost; kept it interesting. She tapped her glass with a fingernail, tapped her slate to the side of the offered blue glass bottle to pay for the refill, and nodded her thanks to the bartender.

Alamber's laugh drew her attention up to the platform he

shared with a pair of Trun. They'd seemed surprised at his climbing ability. It was unlikely that was all he'd surprise them with. She flicked her gaze past him without moving her head, searching the shadows for threats, saw none, and returned to faking interest in what might've been sports scores and might've been election results scrolling past on the grimy interior of the bar's one window.

The bar had minimal floor space, maybe five by eight meters, but the seating extended through the full three stories. Not nets and ropes like in a Krai bar, but ramps and shelves and platforms. Not all of them were connected and she'd been impressed to see the pair of servers—who matched the edged *don't fuk with me* attitude of every server in every other bar like this Binti'd ever been in—leaping, tails extended for balance, with full trays of drinks and not spilling. . . . well, much. The sucking noise the soles of her boots made leaving the floor suggested they'd spilled some.

The air smelled a bit like licorice, but she wasn't sure if that was the spilled drinks or the Trun. She licked her lips. Didn't taste like licorice. The drink didn't taste like licorice. She hadn't tasted a Trun though Alamber might've by now. Katrien didn't taste like licorice, but that was okay. They didn't need an actual Katrien, only the possibility of one. A possible Katrien. If their grave robber slash illicit antiquities dealer worked off Abalae, this was the sort of place they worked out of. Unless they didn't like licorice.

As the fizz faded again, Binti ate a few corn chips—it tasted like a corn chip, she was calling it a corn chip—and wondered if the Trun who owned the links ran the government because these sorts of bars were usually found in the seedier neighborhoods around spaceports and the whole anchored at the equator in the middle of the ocean thing had nothing to do with the Trun keeping buildings away from the bases of the tethers. Whole civilizations had been built in the middle of oceans. The cheapest of the commerce sectors nearest the cheapest of the tethers became the logical alternative, but the links, they were the only way in.

Objectively, it was such a stupidly inconvenient system, she was willing to call the Trun, in spite of the whole no-single-ass-in-a-chair seating arrangements, unsocial as a species.

And ex-Lance Corporal Binti Mashona knew social. Next to Alamber, she was the most social member of the team.

Although Alamber was social in more specific ways.

She was a sniper, she saw better from a distance. Alamber was all about the up close and personal.

"Another?" The bartender spoke Federate with a heavy Trun accent, extending every vowel almost to a moan. At least she fukking hoped it was zir accent. When there was moaning happening around her, she preferred to be part of it.

"Why not?" The fuzz had started lingering, sort of a low-grade buzz between drinks. Nothing she couldn't handle.

Alamber had been joined by a third Trun. Unless that new waving appendage wasn't a tail; Binti couldn't be certain given the angle. She wondered how low he had his masker turned down and made a mental note to have him turn it up again when he rejoined her. They'd need time for the pheromones to dissipate before they returned to the room.

There was no group sex in *team*.

Although Alamber cuddled up with both couples, Binti felt no attraction to the Krai, and while she'd happily tap both Torin and Craig, they were all still working past the whole gunny thing. Lance corporals didn't sleep with gunnery sergeants nor with those civilians gunnery sergeants were sleeping with. Ex-lance corporals could sleep with whoever the fuk they wanted and she'd shared a bed with Torin because she'd shared a past with Torin and sometimes that past came visiting in the night, but Craig couldn't really give her anything Alamber couldn't. And she had plenty of that.

In her opinion, and she was the closest to the problem, they needed another di'Taykan in the crew.

She needed another drink.

"So it's true what they say."

"Depends . . ." She tapped her glass against the bar. ". . . on who's saying it and what the fuk they're saying."

Zi nodded toward the platform where the moaning may or may not have been extended vowels.

"Oh, yeah, that's true. Pretty much whatever they're saying." It was Alamber's job to be talked about. Break the ice. Her dark skin made her blend better than his pale, pale pink. At least in this part of the world. Probably lighter fur in colder climates. She slid her glass away from another refill, and the bartender smiled. Probably. Gunny had a whole extended theory about teeth. "It's true," she added, tapping the side of her nose, "right up until it isn't. Biology. But right now, he's all up in your face." She could just see into the platform if she balanced on the upper rung of her stool but couldn't quite make out faces. "People remember him."

"No shit," the bartender muttered.

Binti leaned closer. "We need," she murmured, "a small ship. Susumi ship. Need it to run supplies further into the Core where we might be too noticeable."

Someone new moaned. Definitely a moan this time.

"More noticeable?" the bartender asked.

Binti sighed. "You have no fukking idea."

"True."

She tapped her slate against the bottle, ringing up ten times the cost of a single drink. "We pay well."

Zi looked at the number, pulled out zir personal slate, cleared the payment into it, and laid it on the bar where purple lines of light rose up from the screen. After a short give and take, zi slid Binti's slate from her fingers and passed it through the light. Zir ears flicked, once, when zi handed it back.

Code? Who the hell knew.

"Alamber!" She flicked a corn chip up into his platform. "We're done here!"

He joined her by the door. To her surprise, his masker was all the way up—full pheromone blocking. "They didn't want it. Or need it. They took . . ." He shook his head, pale blue hair the lightest thing in the bar.

Before he could continue, a striped body rose up out of a tangle of three or four Trun in one of the lowest platforms, pointed an arm only half covered in fur in their general direction, and bellowed, "Murderers!"

Binti turned toward him, leaned close enough he could read the memory of a long shot with an impact boomer, of a Silsviss head exploding, spraying everyone within three or four meters with blood and bone and brains. Then she smiled. The way Gunny would've.

Zi might've pissed zirself.

It might've just been the ambiance of the bar.

"Fukker," she muttered as Alamber tugged her out the door and onto the street. "There's a difference between murdering and killing."

"I know."

"Course you do. You said they took?" She tucked her arm in his, the fresh air clearing the last of the buzz from her brain. "What did they take?"

"Me. Sort of. This way." He nudged her around in the opposite direction. Narrow streets and bars and crap shops all looked the same to her. "It was like I was . . . I don't know, an experiment. Not a person."

"Oh, baby." Some people said di'Taykans couldn't be taken advantage of. Some people were assholes. She stopped and turned far enough to cup his jaw with her free hand. "Do I have to kick the shit out of someone? Are you okay?"

"Okay?" His eyes lightened. "Fukking hell, Binti. Prehensiled tails—it was almost everything I imagined!"

"But you said they . . ."

"Oh, *them*. Who gives a fuk about them?"

"Okay." Alamber was an adult di'Taykan with almost Ressk-level smarts who hadn't been through the training that allowed different species to find a common ground in the Corps. The last thing he needed was her second-guessing his reactions. "Come on, then, let's find another bar and gather more data points. There's got to be some lower class Katrien out drinking somewhere in this sector."

"Katrien," Alamber said, patting her hand and leading the way down the dry cobblestones in the center of the street, "have no tails."

Werst grabbed a fistful of fabric and steered Ressk around a puddle as they headed back toward the inn. It hadn't rained while they were in talking to the agents responsible for the supplies sent to the freight tether, so he figured it was safer not to speculate about the liquid filling the pothole. "We're going to have to secure the *seleeamir*." His mouth watered just saying the word. The small, organ-meat sausages were seldom found anywhere but in Katrien-dominated space. They weren't Katrien organs, so he wasn't sure why.

"We have to secure it because it's so *chrick* you can't keep it out of your mouth?"

"Nothing to do with my mouth," Werst snorted. "Two of the ingredients are toxic to Humans."

That pulled Ressk's gaze off his slate. "I didn't know that. How did you know that?"

"More than just a pretty face, *churick*." He ran a hand over Ressk's head, bristles stiff against his palm, and used the motion to hide a quick examination of the upper edges of the warehouses lining the far side of the road. Unfortunately, the far side of the road was downwind, and the position of the streetlights created shadows deep enough to hide the source of the noises that had drawn his attention.

Ressk nudged up into Werst's palm, then dropped his gaze back to the numbers running across the screen. "Gunny's going to be pleased. We've restocked supplies *and* scooped three sets of data."

"Scooped?" It could be one of Abalae's small scavengers using the rooftops as safe passage, but instincts and training both said that whatever was moving up there was moving with intent.

"Yeah, scooped. We bump tech and it slides a hack into their system, pulling any data they have relevant to our interests while redirecting their sniffers into dead-end files. I told you all this back on the ship."

"I remember. I'm questioning scooped." Another tug around another puddle. "Sounds like you're cleaning the *berrin* box."

"Given the amount of crap we likely got, you're not wrong."

"You'll sort it out." He always did. "And that Trun with the pale fur around zir eyes . . ."

"Maloniay?"

Werst shrugged. He hadn't been paying a lot of attention to names. ". . . gave you the name of the ship and half the name of the pilot when we cleaned zir out of *seleeamir*."

"A ship," Ressk corrected. "Not necessarily *the* ship."

"Oh, yeah, because leave your ship in orbit, drop down the freight tether, travel hundreds of kilometers to a crap Commerce Sector, then take the same pissant trip back when you leave is the smart choice for multiple ships to make."

"Except that Katrien ships clearly do it. They can't grow *selee* here. No *selee*, no *seleeamir*. I need to match cargoes in and out, narrow it down using info Binti and Alamber get from the bars, then seal it with what Gunny gets from Bufush."

Watching Ressk's fingertips tap against the screen in a sequence Werst saw as completely random made him wonder, not for the first time, how he'd gotten so fukking lucky. He'd grown up on the lower branches, barely off the ground, worked his ass off to reach the Corps' minimum academic requirement and joined the moment he could. The Corps had been good to him, Recon like coming home, and he'd have been career if not for the plastic aliens. He knew he wasn't stupid—stupid didn't survive Recon—and he had complete confidence in his ability to come out on top in any shit situation he got thrown into.

He looked at Gunny and saw what he could've been. Right up to and including the cracks. He respected the crap out of her. More than that, he liked her.

He looked at Ressk and saw a diplomat's son, best schools, top of the tree. Someone so *chrick*, so out of his league he thanked Turrist every day they'd ended up in that prison together. Except he didn't believe in Turrist and considering how it had turned out, he should be thanking the plastic aliens except he wouldn't give those fukkers credit for shit if they were holding a laxative.

He looked at the rest of the team and he saw where they fit, strengths and weaknesses linked together like the nets that kept his people safe. Krai people. Not Corps people.

Metal scraped against stone, and he looked up at the roof of the last warehouse in the row to see five Trun swarming over the edge.

On the one hand, it was about fukking time all the muttering and the finger pointing turned to violence. On the other hand . . .

"Why us?" he snarled, grabbing Ressk and dragging him back half a dozen steps until they were in the gray area between the overlapping circles of light that best suited their eyesight, backs against the wall of the warehouse on the far side of the street from their attackers.

"Probably because they're not entirely stupid. Appearances to the contrary." Ressk snapped his slate back onto his belt, gave it a tug to check it had locked in, and hit record. The chime, required by law, bounced between the buildings. "We're about the same size, so we're their best bet to prove a point."

"They think we're easier to beat than Ryder or Alamber?" Werst watched the five descend down the pipes and narrow platforms used for paths on most of the walls they'd passed and decided to be insulted. Ryder had some solid muscle on him, but for all his smarts, the kid would blow away in a strong wind.

"We're smaller. And they're extrapolating from sweet fuk all."

Tails extended, the Trun made jumps Werst wasn't sure he'd try, not at those light levels, but their feet, while flexible and not as limited as a Human's or a Taykan's, were still limited. When all five reached the road, they advanced slowly in a half crouch, hands at shoulder height, expressions . . .

Confused, if Werst had to guess. They looked confused.

"We're outnumbered. They expected us to run." Ressk's nostril ridges closed. "So they could chase us."

"Okay, they're not entirely stupid, but they're a little stupid." They'd heard him, as intended. Ears flattened. Eyes narrowed. Not a lot of teeth visible. Werst showed his.

"Organs are in the torso—ribs up top, soft tissue below, pretty much the usual for bipeds."

"Bad time to point out I find you prepped for a fight hot as *nerser*?"

"Little bit." He could hear the grin in Ressk's voice. "Throat and joints are weaknesses. Genitals are internal. Tails are used for balance; prehensile, but not strong enough to do much."

"Yeah, I'm so looking forward to Alamber complaining about that." Werst stepped forward, toes spread.

The large, orange Trun leading the pack snarled.

"Go home." Werst spread his hands in the universal symbol for *Seriously? We have to do this now?* "Have a drink. No one has to get hurt tonight."

"You're not so fukking tough!"

Ressk sighed. "Don't kill anyone."

"They're civilians!" Werst ducked under the orange Trun's charge . . . "Why would I kill them?" . . . rolled zir over his shoulder, and slammed zir into the ground. "See? Not dead!"

All five were street fighters and if they'd put together any kind of a coordinated attack, the numbers might've been a problem. But street fighting was as much posturing as making contact.

The Corps stamped out the need to posture early on.

He took a moment to admire Ressk leaping off the lamppost and flattening the largest of the Trun. Krai bones were heavy. Trun, not so much.

When the fight ended, in the interest of preventing any further negative opinions about the Younger Races, Werst spit out the piece of tail he'd bit off.

"Waste of food." Ressk turned off the recording as they walked away from the stains and the tufts of fur on the road, the Trun having staggered off in the opposite direction. "I swallowed."

Torin wasn't surprised to find Ressk sitting up in the other nest, already intent on his slate when she woke. He didn't acknowledge her as she slid out from under Craig's arm and padded across the room into the . . . facilities, she was going to stick with facilities. Turned out there was a lot she didn't know about the Rakva digestive system. She was good with that.

Werst and Craig were up when she returned. The former pushed past her into the facilities, the latter tucked his face into the curve of her neck, head resting on her shoulder. "What flaming bastard left the lights on?"

"It's artificial sunlight. Automatic." Light levels said it was about midmorning. Her internal clock, still working on ship's time, said about six. "I assume it's a Rakva preference."

"Any chance of coffee?"

"No idea." She stroked the warm length of his back, her thumb sliding along the dip between heavy muscle that followed his spine. "Ressk?"

He glanced up. "Coffee didn't catch on with the Trun, but there's a local stimulant that should work almost as well. Oh, and I have the ship."

"Good work."

Craig lifted his head and asked the question she couldn't. "Already?"

He shrugged. "Ran a search algorithm overnight. It sifted the bits and pieces we all brought in and spat out a registration number at about dawn." Eyes narrowed, he peered at the light emanating from the ceiling. "Local time."

"So you're saying we don't have to go to another planet?" Binti dragged herself up and flopped one bare arm over the edge of the nest.

"What part of *I have the ship* did you miss? Gunny was right, it's registered to a Katrien. No one we know," he added before Torin could ask. Odds would be astronomical that Presit had begun flying supply ships for grave robbers, but it wouldn't have been the first time the fuzzball had shown up uninvited. "*Seelinkjer Cer Pen* registered to Jamers a Tur fenYenstrakin. So yeah, I'm saying we don't have to go to another planet."

"Fukking yay." Binti's head dropped onto her arm like her neck had been broken. "My brain is still buzzing and my mouth tastes like socks and our antiintoxicants are shit up against Trun alcohol."

"Good to know," Torin murmured. Frowned. And leaned over the edge of the nest, attention draw by a sleek brown-and-green–feathered curve tucked along the side of Binti's body. "What the hell is that?"

Muttering a protest, Binti leaned back. "It's a stuffed waterfowl."

"Where did it come from?"

"I think I remember buying it." She balanced it on the edge of the nest. "Of course, I think I remember peeing liquid nitrogen, so who knows."

The beak felt enough like plastic that Torin shook it gently back and forth. No visible alien reaction, but the motion rocked the entire bird.

Pale fingers wrapped around Binti's shoulder, closely followed by Alamber's face, the dark makeup he wore around his eyes smeared enough it looked like a Katrien mask. "You're holding the corpse of a living creature!"

Binti winced. "Thank you, Alamber, we've covered that. It's been stuffed. Also, stop fukking yelling."

"I can't believe you'd be a part of something so barbaric!" Hair clamped to his head, he scrambled out of the nest, slipping into the facilities as Werst exited.

"Hey, a duck. Where'd you get it?"

Binti cuddled it in both arms. "No idea."

"I want everyone ready to go in ten." Local stimulants, Torin decided, seemed like a very good idea.

"Visitors."

These were not the three facilitators who'd stopped them the day before. Attitude and the amount of salad on the uniform announced the tri-colored Trun standing out front was of significantly higher rank and the two Trun flanking zir were close behind. Maybe yesterday had been their day off. Maybe they'd been brought in from a more affluent sector to deal with the situation. Torin neither knew nor cared.

The facilitators in the background, moving the crowd along, they were locals.

One of the great things about interacting with a species she didn't know well was that she could ignore what she saw as blatant contempt, secure in the knowledge that it *could* be admiration and she was merely misinterpreting an unknown physiognomy.

Facilities. Facilitators.

So many parallels.

Long years of practice standing in front of shiny new second lieutenants and senior staff officers with the shine long since worn off kept the amusement from showing on her face. She descended the inn's three steps to the street, putting her feet, at least, level with the facilitators. "How can we help you?"

Forced to crane zir head back to meet her eyes, zir tail tip flicked back and forth. "We've had reports of fighting, Visitors. This is not an OutSector station. This is Abalae. This is the Core."

Torin smiled. "Yes, it is. The fight was recorded." She snapped her slate off her belt. "Ressk."

"File's up, Gunnery Sergeant."

"That's not . . ." one of the backup facilitators began.

Cutting zir off with a glance, Torin thumbed the file open, let it run until the first Trun hit the cobblestones, then thumbed it off. "Did you need us to press charges?"

"Charges?"

"Against the Trun who attacked my people. We will if it's required, but I don't see the point. Do you?"

"Do I?"

"See the point."

Zi snapped zir tail back up as it began to lower, and Torin could almost see the effort it took to keep zir hands by zir waist. According to Werst's sitrep, raised hands indicated a Trun fighting stance. "You informed us you came to shop. I see no evidence of this."

Binti held up the duck. Torin reached back, pushed it down, and said, "The day's young and the Commerce Sector is large."

"No."

"That was definitive," Alamber murmured.

"We would appreciate it, Visitors, if you were on the next link back to the tether."

"The next link?"

"And in the next rise off Abalae."

"You're telling us to leave?"

"No." Zir took a deep breath, took a long step back, and locked an expression so neutral on Torin's face she found herself respecting the ability if not the Trun. "We have no reason to tell you to leave." *Although we both know I could come up with reasons if I wanted to.* "I clearly said, we would appreciate it if you would leave."

"Of course. Let's go, people."

"Thank you, Visitors." Zi took another step back and pointed, the metallic tips on the fur of zir arm gleaming in the sunlight. "The link is that way."

"We know where the fu . . ." Werst's mutter cut off so suddenly, Ressk's elbow had clearly been applied.

As they stepped into the open area, the half circle in front of the station where the three roads met and where there was no possible way to cover every defensive angle, Alamber moved up beside her and said quietly, "You made them think we were leaving because they wanted us to."

The facilitators were watching from the edge of the curve. She could feel the weight of their regard. "Yes, I did."

"But we have what we need. We were already leaving. Why play the game?"

"They could have prevented us from leaving. You don't piss those people off. You should know that."

"Prevented us? Boss, they wanted us to leave."

"Not the point. Keep walking."

The link back to the tether was empty of everyone but three Trun who kept to themselves by the door and tried unsuccessfully to look like they weren't facilitators. Binti, Ressk, and Craig slept. Werst finally closed his eyes when Torin made it clear she'd take first watch. Alamber sat close beside her, as far from the duck as possible.

"So, Boss," he leaned against her side, "I'm a little confused."

"About?"

"Well, I had a lot of on the job training rather than actual schooling, so there might, possibly, be the chance of a few small holes in my understanding of interspecies relationships."

Torin hid a smile. "I somehow doubt that."

The ends of his hair traced short lines against her cheek as he grinned. "Not those kind of relationships. Political ones. The Trun are one of the Elder Races, right?"

"Yes."

"And they live in the Core."

"Obviously."

"And they don't seem to like us Younger Race types very much."

She thought about telling him to get to the point, but even without the frequent stops, it was a long enough trip she was happy to have the diversion. "Also obviously."

"But there were Niln and Rakva and Katrien all over the place, just like they're all over the place in the MidSectors and OutSectors. I mean, we found three Katrien-only bars last night and we weren't even looking that hard. None of them are Elder Race species, are they?"

"No."

"So why are the Trun willing to be all buddy buddy with the Niln and the Rakva and the Katrien when we're getting an escort back to the tether?" He leaned around her and languidly waved a pale hand at the three facilitators—who managed to simultaneously ignore him and record the gesture.

"The Niln, Rakva, and Katrien all joined the Confederation after it was formed. Some people call them the Mid Races, most don't bother. Their homeworlds are on the edge of the Core so if they want to expand, they have to head out, that's why we see so much of them." Had she been talking with Craig or Werst, she'd have added that they saw more than they needed to of some Katrien. "The Trun want nothing to do with us . . ." She raised her voice enough to carry to the far end of the link. ". . . because the Younger Races were brought into the Confederation to fight a war. The war got us in before we overcame the societal impulse toward violence . . . Societal," she repeated raising a hand and cutting off Alamber's protest about the gang who'd jumped Werst and Ressk. "There's assholes in every species. But a *societal* impulse toward violence makes us at best uncivilized."

Alamber nodded. "And at worst, murderers. That got shouted at us last night," he continued in response to Torin's raised brow. "Binti dealt with it; no one died. The shouter, though, didn't even care that not all of us fought."

"Why should they?" Werst growled without opening his eyes. "They don't care that if we hadn't fought they'd have died under a Primacy bombardment, blown to bleeding bits. Weeping and wailing and not enough left living to take care of the dead who'd begin to rot and bloat and stink and . . ."

"Enough." Torin could see the tip of a tale lashing in the aisle. A fight would be in no one's best interest. Confident in Werst's compliance, she turned her attention back to Alamber. "Abalae is designed for off-worlders and its commercial sectors need a variety of goods, so why not allow the Mid Races access to a Core market. Of course, Commerce Three, Sector Eighteen wasn't exactly high end, and I have to wonder how many Mid Races you'd find in the pricier sectors."

"Harsh, Boss."

"Those Trun bars you and Binti went drinking in last night, any Katrien drinking in them?"

"No, but . . ."

"Any Trun drinking in the Katrien bars you found?"

"No, but . . ." Alamber's hair flipped up.

Torin swept it away from her eye. "People work together because of the demands of the job, but they socialize because they want to. Question becomes, why don't they want to?"

After a moment, Alamber nudged her with a pointy elbow. "Well, Boss? Why don't they?"

"How the hell should I know? We were only here for . . ." She glanced at her slate. ". . . just over thirty-one hours. I can't work out the problems with an entire species in . . ."

"Less than three days," Craig said on her other side.

"Oh." She felt Alamber nod against her shoulder, accepting the comment at face value. "That's fair."

They were the only passengers on the tether's rise. The rest was freight.

Station security met them as they exited and escorted them to the docking arm. Which would have been incredibly stupid had they actually wanted to cause problems since, had it come to a fight, Craig and Alamber could have taken them.

From the way their fur had puffed out, doubling the size of their tails, it seemed they knew that.

"Your supplies will be transferred from the freight compartment the instant the drones are available, Visitors." Zi didn't sound happy about the delay. Gesturing zir companion to the left, zi stood at the right of the pressure hatch, counting the six of them off as they stepped into the docking arm. "You will be detaching immediately after?" It was only just barely a question.

"We will."

"Thank you, Visitors."

Visitor, Torin realized following her team down the dockway, was not an honorific. It meant, *you don't belong here*. She caught Binti's eye and realized the other woman had realized the same thing.

And they *didn't* belong here.

Not when here had never been touched by war.

But they could. They could shop or learn or look at trees.

Would the Trun give them the chance, now the war was over?

Fukking Colonel Hurrs . . .

"Major Sujuno?" Verr stuck her head into the tomb, air filter glistening over her mouth and nostril ridges. "Pirate says he's through any minute now."

"He's sure this time?"

Verr shrugged, Krai muscles and joints warping the motion just enough to be annoying. "He says he is, but I don't know— maybe he just wants out of the air lock."

That was likely, Sujuno admitted, following Verr out into the catacombs' broad, central corridor. Most di'Taykan, di'Berinango Nadayki among them, didn't do well without physical contact. Unfortunately for him, it had been more important to keep the omnipresent dust out of the control panel than to cater to his needs. Personally, she'd have been thrilled to have been behind plastic for a few days, locked away from expectations.

A raised hand held Verr in place for the moment it took for her vision to adjust to the lower light levels. Because the Krai, with their long, spreading toes, hadn't quite caught on to the half glide, half stride that allowed the air to flow from the front of the boot to the back, creating eddies of fine particulate and throwing a minimal amount of dust up into the air, they walked a half a dozen paces behind both Humans and di'Taykan. As she led the way down the corridor, Sujuno wondered why Sergeant Toporov had sent Verr with the message. It had been a truism in the Corps that an officer was only as good as their NCO and with Toporov, she was operating at a disadvantage. He was solid and dependable, but there were days when she'd give her right arm—or possibly his—for solid, dependable, and *clever*.

The faint hum of the compressors sounded louder than usual

in the absolute silence waiting at the corridor's end. The security system the H'san had left behind reacted to noise above 45 decibels and a di'Taykan spice mix carried to make field rations palatable, and the zones it covered appeared entirely random. She doubted they were, but hadn't the time to waste on deriving an alien pattern from limited data. Quiet and bland had become the order of the day.

Toporov nodded as she arrived and stepped aside.

She moved up close to the wall they needed to breach, turned, and peered through into the air lock. Nadayki's lime-green hair lay flat against his head and he had so many light receptors open his eyes were nearly black, lid to lid. Smears on the clear plastic sheeting suggested he'd been rubbing against the barrier. Hopefully, only his hands and face. "Well?"

He leaned toward her, licked his lips, and that might have been because they were chapped although the odds were higher he was flaunting his lack of personal filter. "I'm sure this time."

"Good. Put on the glasses. I don't want to lose you again if the H'san set up another flash bang." Cracking the control panel had taken longer than any of them had anticipated although she assumed sharing the air lock with a bucket of his own waste had kept Nadayki's wandering attention on the job. Although, given the nine letters in his family name, he'd likely spent a good part of his life in filth. Being alone and untouched for those same days had probably provided a greater incentive.

"It won't happen this time, I know what I did wrong." Slender fingers sketched abstract lines in the air. "I know why the flash bang went off."

"Don't make me repeat myself." She'd allow him a little leeway in response to the cramped quarters he'd been living in for the last few days, but only a little. The three days she'd lost to temporary blindness at the second panel were not to be repeated.

He licked his lips again and put the glasses on, ears twitching through his hair as he settled the arms.

"Start a ten count," she told him. "Then open it up."

Toporov fell into step beside her as they walked back to the nearest tomb. "Pirate's looking a little twitchy, sir."

". . . nine, eight . . ."

"He has a name, Sergeant."

"Nadayki's looking a little twitchy, sir."

". . . seven, six . . ."

"Then let's hope this works." She glanced into the tomb, the spaces around the huge sarcophagus filled with the remaining eight of her ten-person crew.

Keo and Broadbent stood ready to rush the door when it opened, the stone they'd use to block it already in place by the air lock. A nod of her head moved them both a step to the left, and she slipped past without contact, the sergeant a solid barrier at her heels. She'd know soon enough if Nadayki was successful; she didn't need to put herself at risk watching it happen.

". . . two, one."

The silence extended. Then . . .

"It's opening."

The two ex-Marines raced for the door. Toporov moved just far enough forward to be able to lean out into the corridor and report, his left arm still wrapped, skin red and inflamed, from the unexpected blowback during the last attempt. The scorch marks on the stone walls continued down the corridor for another three tombs.

"Block's in, Major."

Broadbent was big and strong, and almost stereotypically stupid. Fortunately, his years in the Corps had taught him to follow orders.

"Keo's moving forward; she's over the threshold."

Keo was fearless. Which also made her stupid as far as Sujuno was concerned, but she could work with that. The heavy gunner carried the best black market exoskeleton money could buy along with a KC-12 and an obscene amount of ammunition. Her willingness to leap before she looked had saved their lives once already—where the definition of leap included firing impact boomers into irreplaceable H'san antiquities, destroying the weapons built into the wall behind them.

Toporov walked toward the door so he could pass on Keo's report to Broadbent without the volume of their voices setting off the security system.

"Spiral stairs, made of stone, descending only." His voice was a low, bass rumble. "The lights have come up in the stairwell . . ."

Most of the necropolis had automatic lighting, glass ovals set into the walls that they could only assume continued to work as designed, the power source as unknown as the reason for matching the days and nights on the planet above. The ancient H'san, Sujuno had concluded pretty much immediately after landing, were more than a little strange.

". . . and Keo's descending. Five steps. Ten. Fifteen. Halt!" Toporov's last word had been a command, not a repetition. "Major, we have to extend."

She sent Verr out into the corridor, allowing Toporov to move closer to the stairs, then she stepped into the corridor herself. Verr five feet away, Toporov five feet from him, Broadbent through the door and down the stairs, the top of his very blond head just visible at floor level. In the end, she had to add Wen, Nadayki, and Dion to the line—although Dion bitched and complained about how he was an expert and this was beneath him the whole time. He'd become skilled at keeping his voice just under the level that set off the sensors. If she'd given some serious thought to shooting him when he was no longer needed, it was his own fault.

The team descended the stairs as a unit until she stood alone in the catacombs.

The stairs went down sixty feet and ended in an enormous cave.

"A natural cave?"

"No idea, Major. I've never been in a cave before, natural or otherwise. But it's got plenty of ambient lighting. Pink stone, like the first hall. It's pretty."

"Less opinion, Keo."

In the center of the cave was a small lake, surrounded by stone benches and short pillars . . .

"Plinths," Dion sniffed.

"Seriously? That's a word?"

"Focus, people!"

Toporov's bark froze Sujuno in place. The energy beams fired by the noise sensors hadn't been fatal yet, but they hurt. If Toporov was going to be hit, best only he was hit.

"Smooth move, jarhead," Nadayki muttered.

"Silence," Sujuno hissed, the sibilants sliding past the sensors even at volume. At a sixty count, it became clear the stairs weren't a zone the sensors covered, but she counted twenty more before she gave the order to continue exploring.

"Okay, the things on the *plinths*, they're not statues. I think they're bodies." The sense of Keo's lip curl made it undiluted through all seven repetitions. "All different kinds of bodies. They're kind of, I don't know, preserved. And they're really fukking creepy. No visible weapons. No apparent security. Cavern is visually clear, floor is physically clear to six meters out from base of stairs where water begins. It's safe to send Dion down."

Dion, with little interest in the chain of command, started moving before Sujuno could give the order. "This is the bowl in the earth," he said, his statement passed up to her through Verr and Wen and Nadayki. "The text reads that the bowl has been upturned over secrets. We should be close."

Should be? Their intell was imprecise at best, poetry at worst, and the necropolis was significantly larger than expected. "Close is relative down here," she said. And *should* meant nothing at all.

"The station sysop will be watching our signals." Hands resting on the worn duct tape that held a split seam on the top of the pilot's chair together, Torin watched Ressk slave his slate to *Promise*'s computer. "Shouldn't you wait until we've detached?"

"No time to waste," Ressk grunted, curled into a half circle on the second chair, fingers and toes flying over the control board. "Sliding into the traffic buoy's more complicated than going to the JRM for a beer."

"Yeah, but we can't leave until the supplies are loaded," Werst reminded him, popping open the panel that hid the coffeemaker—one of the few remaining pieces of the original ship. "Supplies," he added, voice muffled by the sound of the reservoir filling, "that you bought."

"Point of interest . . ." Craig nodded toward a red light flashing on the upper left corner of the board. ". . . that's the docking master. The Trun want us gone, but we can't blow until we can file coordinates with the traffic buoy and we can't file coordinates until we . . . What's that?" He spread his hands. "Have coordinates to file. We don't even know if we're heading in or out. Ressk's right, he's got no time to toss. We need to know where the *Seelinkjer Cer Pen* went."

"Okay, first, let's shorten that to *Seeli*. And second, why? We can always refile and change course." Alamber leaned over the top of the second chair, eyes dark, head moving up and down as he scanned the streaming code, slate cradled in one hand.

Craig stroked yellow onto the board near the light, indicating a delay. "Given the density in the core, if we file one plan then switch, we'll ping an inquiry. Usually not a problem, free Confederation and all, but we're flying with a fake registration."

"And under orders to remain unnoticed," Binti put in.

"I don't take orders from the military." Craig slapped his fingers against the board with more force than necessary.

Alamber's gesture might've been dismissal, might've been agreement. "Yeah, and those would be the same orders that sent us to Abalae. Fail on the low profile." He rested enough weight on the chair that it creaked and bent forward. "You're doing support with your feet, right?" He poked Ressk in the shoulder. "Nothing original? Because if you are, that puts an ability to walk and fuk at the same time into a kind of pathetic perspective."

"Alamber."

He straightened, fully aware of what Torin had intended his name to represent. "Yeah, well, I suppose I'll just wait here until I'm needed."

"You do that. Werst . . ."

"It's brewing, Gunny."

It was taking too damned long. She pointed at the board. "The red light's flashing faster."

"Because the docking master's knickers are in a knot."

"I have no idea what that means."

Craig turned enough to grin up at her. "Yeah, you do."

"I'm in," Ressk announced before she could respond.

"How are you hiding the signal from the station?"

"They're reading it as a traffic inquiry." Right foot tapping a complex pattern across the bottom of the board, Ressk rubbed his hands together. "Because I'm just that good. Although, it helps that's what they're expecting to read. Give people what they expect and they get kind of stupid."

"So it's safe?" Torin nodded her thanks as Werst handed her a pouch of coffee, feeling muscles across her back relax as she breathed in the fragrant steam. Next time they went dirtside she was throwing half a dozen pouches into her duffel.

"No, not entirely safe. Not if someone actually takes a look at the code, then it's pretty fukking obvious what we're trying to do."

"Someone like the facilitators?" Binti wondered, accepting a pouch.

"No, we're off the planet." Torin took a long swallow. "That's all the facilitators care about."

"*Attention,* Commitment . . ."

It took them all a moment to remember that was them.

". . . *this is Drone Control. Drone 77A is approaching* Commitment's *cargo lock with container 12-8. Stand by to open lock.*"

"Werst. Mashona. Delay them as long as you can."

"On it, Gunny." Binti drained her pouch and tossed it into the recycler on her way out the hatch.

"Why isn't your throat entirely covered in fukking scar tissue?" Werst muttered, clutching his pouch of *sah* as he followed her out of the room.

The small cargo bay was, like the control room and the Susumi engine, part of the original *Promise.* Craig had used it more for salvage too delicate for the exterior pens than for supplies. Torin felt the deck shudder as the outer lock opened "It won't take them long to unload one container."

"It's a big container, Gunny, and they're not shoving it into an empty bay. It'll be a tight fit, and Werst may have to suit up and clear out the old crap."

"How much new crap did you buy?"

Ressk shrugged. "As much as would require a container as close to the dimensions of the bay as I could find. Don't worry, Intell paid." He leaned back, eyes locked on the board, nostril ridges half opening, half closing, not quite fast enough for Torin to call it a flutter. "It's a good thing the traffic buoys are old tech."

The answering silence evoked a snort. "You must've noticed that the tech dirtside was way above the shit we see every day."

Torin nodded, remembering the hard light. "The slates . . ."

"Everything," Ressk interrupted. "And it's all worn in enough that it's clearly not new tech to the people of Commerce Three, Sector Eighteen, even if they're on the lower branches of the local economic tree."

"So we've been getting Granddad's hand-me-downs from the Elder Races," Torin said softly. She wasn't sure how she felt about that. Maybe they wanted the Younger Races to advance on their own, to move forward independently instead of sitting around with their hands out in one of the displays of entitlement that Humans, at least, were prone to. Or, maybe, they didn't trust the Younger Races with anything too sharp.

"Well, they're not handing over the recent shit, that's for sure. But the buoys, these things have been around for a while. Alamber's program combined with my genius . . ."

Alamber flicked the top of his head.

"Ow. Fukker. Anyway, we should own this old sh . . ." The entire board flashed orange. "We have the buoy. And security's spotted me! Go!"

The di'Taykan were graceful. It was part of the Taykan default—tall, brightly colored, enthusiastically sexually indiscriminate, graceful. That said, it had never occurred to Torin to think a di'Taykan could hack a traffic buoy gracefully, but where Ressk looked efficient and in command of the board, Alamber's fingers danced over the screen of his slate, his body rolling back and forth in small, sensuous curves, loose from his shoulders down.

He hadn't been able to get into a buoy on his own. He and Ressk working together were unstoppable.

"Goes to prove . . ." Craig leaned back and caught one of Torin's hands in his, holding it against his cheek, stubble prickling her skin. ". . . di'Taykan don't do well alone."

"You reading my mind again?"

He turned his head and kissed her palm. "Wouldn't think of it."

"Gunny." Frustration bled into Binti's voice. "The container's on board. We're closing now."

Werst hadn't had to suit up after all. "Seems the Trun have spatial skills."

"*Attention,* Commitment, *this is Drone Control. We will sound an all clear when drone 77A has exited your departure area.*"

"Ressk?"

He shook his head, nostril ridges definitely fluttering now. "We need more time."

Torin reached over Craig and thumbed the communications board live with her free hand. "Attention, Drone Control, this is *Commitment.* We need to examine the contents of container twelve dash eight for damage before we can allow you to leave the area."

"*Attention,* Commitment, *this is Drone Control. We are not responsible if the contents of container 77A shifted during delivery. Drone Control out.*"

"Atten . . ." She frowned at the readings. "They've blocked us. They really want us out of here."

"Yeah, well, really can't, not yet," Ressk muttered.

Hair moving in choppy arcs, Alamber pushed in between the two chairs, thumb tapping a one-two, one-two-three rhythm on his slate. He pinched up a small section of the board, dragged a line of code free, and tossed it to the left where it expanded into four fast moving screens.

"What . . ."

"Wait." The screens disappeared, half a dozen sections of the board in front of Craig lit up, and Alamber returned most of his attention to his slate. "I sent a surge into the docking clamp and froze it. Reads like an overload, sort of thing that happens when someone's a little too anxious to blow and it's set so anyone leaning on the controls'll think it was them. Best part, the clamp'll have to be manually released."

"One of Big Bill's?" Craig asked, releasing Torin's hand.

"One of mine for Big Bill. He liked people to leave on his schedule, not theirs."

"And you had it preloaded in my ship?"

Craig's growl flattened Alamber's hair. "Look, I'm kind of busy . . ."

Torin tugged Craig back down into his chair and nudged him

toward the board. "Discuss it later. Right now, you need to call the station master and let zir know how you feel about being held hostage by poor maintenance. They won't see coordinates until their incompetence allows us to leave. Go big."

He frowned. "Won't that get the clamp fixed faster?"

"Not if you're obnoxiously clear that's what you want. They already think we're violent and inferior; they won't want to do us any favors."

"No one said inferior, Torin."

"Not out loud."

Three coffees later with Werst and Binti back in the control room and the station master refusing further contact from anyone on the *Commitment*—Torin counted that a win—Ressk stiffened and said, "Alamber."

"Unclench. I can stay out front of security. Get the data."

"If they . . ."

"I know. Just snatch and grab, I'm right behind you."

"*Commitment, you are clear to go.*"

"Just snatch and grab?" Ressk snapped his teeth together. "They haven't cleared their fukking caches for years."

"*We require that you upload your destination coordinates . . .*"

"Got it!"

"*. . . immediately.*"

"Fukking hell." Craig lurched for the board as the ship jerked away from the docking arm, all clamps releasing at once. "I've been asked to leave a few places, once or twice, but I've never had an entire ship thrown off a station before."

"We are terrible ambassadors for the Younger Races," Binti snickered.

Torin could think of worse.

"I'm out clean." Alamber slid his slate into a pocket and rolled his shoulders. "Ow."

"Come on." Binti stood and moved up behind him. "I'll rub the stiffness out."

He sighed and sagged against her. "Can we just pretend I made the expected response?"

"Sure."

"Good work, Alamber."

He paused at the hatch, Binti's arm around his waist and flashed a wide smile at Torin. "Short and bristly couldn't have done it without me."

"We know."

We needed you. You were useful. Your place here is secure.

He made a small, pleased noise and let Binti lead him away.

"Kid's got more issues than the *Marine Corps News*," Ressk said softly.

"How long have you been waiting to use that line?" Werst demanded, helping him out of the chair.

"A while," Ressk admitted. "Doesn't make it wrong." He stretched. "I'm for food and sleep in that order, unless someone objects. Fuk it, I just solved the mystery, owned a traffic buoy, saved the day for the good guys, I don't care if anyone objects." His nostril ridges suddenly snapped halfway closed. "You, uh, you don't object, do you, Gunny?"

"No reason I should," Torin told him as Werst rolled his eyes and hustled the other Krai toward the hatch. "Good work, Ressk."

"You know it, Gunny."

"Do you have any idea how impressive that was?" Craig asked when they were alone in the control room, watching the proximity pings as the docking computer maneuvered them through traffic out to what passed for open space in the Core.

"Absolutely." She settled in the other chair, the seat still warmed by Ressk's body heat. "On a theoretical basis anyway. It was boring as fuk to watch, but no one got killed, and I'm all in favor of no one getting killed on my watch a . . ."

"Torin?"

She frowned at the board where the last of the proximity pings were fading.

"*Commitment, you are cleared for independent control in three, two, one.*"

"Return acknowledged. Have to admire how much that sounded like don't let the door hit you on the ass on the way out," Craig muttered as he checked that they were locked on the buoy.

Torin made a noncommittal noise and tried to identify the pattern she'd seen in the pings.

Not troops on the ground.

Not ships in space.
Not defensive.
Not offensive.
But familiar . . .

FIVE

"**N**ow that's something you don't see every day."
Torin turned and frowned at the side of Craig's face—
he continued to stare out the front port. "It's the same type of net
as at the end of our last jump," she said. "Mictok constructed,
absorbs the Susumi energy wave, stores it until . . ."

He reached out, laid two fingers against her jaw with an aim
Binti would've envied, given that he still wasn't looking at her,
and pushed her head until she faced forward again. "Not the
net. The line of red giants, port side."

Even in the brilliance of the core, even through the polarized
port, the red giants stood out, although only the smallest star of
those Torin could see looked red. The rest were yellow-orange
to orangey-red at best.

"Do you think it's one of those?"

Gaze locked on the stars, she could hear the shrug in Craig's
voice. "We're looking *for* a red giant and we're looking *at* eight.
Odds of success are better than they were at Abalae."

They'd followed the jump Ressk and Alamber had pulled
off the buoy to a trinary system; two hydrogen/helium stars
designated Nuvivic Ah and Nuvivic Se as well as a more distant
and fainter red star, Bru Nuvivic. The system had eleven planets,
two inhabited by a mix of the Elder Races, five by mining
colonies and science stations—mostly Mictok—and the other
four long stripped of anything useful. It wasn't the system they

were searching for. They'd have to follow her again.

First they'd have to find out where she went.

"The exit buoy is two days away. We couldn't get there much faster than that even if we hadn't dumped momentum, there's a couple of big ass ore carriers out in front of us. Good news is, the buoy'll won't ping us for coordinates until we're eight . . ."

"Are we there yet?"

Torin turned away from the red giants in time to see Alamber sweep into the control room on a wave of wine-dark ribbons and pheromones. "Masker."

"It's at seven."

"Turn it to nine. And no, we have to jump again. You and Ressk have forty hours to crack the next buoy." She expected a protest, a declaration of how, having done it once already, he'd need only a small fraction of that even if he were working on his own.

To her surprise, he nodded, one hand rising to his masker. "Forty's good. Before we start, we want to check and make sure we didn't leave any litter strewn about behind us. Cracking code at that speed means there could possibly have been a few ones and zeros left lying around," he explained when Torin raised a brow. "If the wrong people find them, it'd be like identifying burn marks on the smoking debris left behind after a boarding party."

"Thank you for clarifying." She couldn't help but return his grin, glad in this instance to have left the Corps behind so she didn't have to. Standing, she beckoned Craig up from the pilot's chair. "Come on, let's get something to eat."

"Binti's cooking." Alamber slid gracefully past Craig and into the chair the instant it was vacated, fingers spread and already on the board.

"What's she made?" Craig asked, joining Torin at the hatch.

Alamber's hair flicked back. "Does it matter?"

"It only matters that it's not Werst," Torin answered, stepping over the lip. Werst in the galley resulted in unique food combinations at best, fond memories of field rations at worst.

Craig crowded through behind her, close enough she could feel his warmth against her back, his breath against her ear as he murmured too low to be overheard, "What was all over Alamber?"

She leaned back far enough to enjoy a moment's contact. "Confidence."

"Fuk, Ryder, you're like a Taykan with your need for heat."

"Flattering." Craig grinned, stirring the hot sauce into his chili. "But even I can't wrestle down pure Taykan tucker." He tossed the pouch to Torin, who caught it one-handed, added about half as much, tasted and added a bit more—Binti's spice baseline kicking less than her mother's curry. "And the things they say about Taykan food are true," he continued. "You think it burns going in? It'll take the hair off your ass going out."

Binti snickered. "Got a classy guy there, Gunny."

"Don't I know it." Torin crumbled a piece of hardtack into her bowl, ankle hooked around Craig's under the table. Most of their food came in preprocessed packs, but every now and then one of them would make something from scratch. It was usually a nice change.

"Remember Alyx, Gunny?" Binti asked, spoon scraping the bottom of her bowl. "He carried a dozen kinds of spice packets in his gear. I had to take Myrin to the ground to get a couple after he died."

"I don't remember that." She remembered pink hair and eyes and repeated orders for him to keep his damned helmet on. She remembered the weight of his cylinder tucked into her vest.

"Why would you? You were busy single-handedly bringing the Silsviss into the Confederation." Pushing her empty bowl away, she added, "Alyx used to wonder if field rations had been designed to make everyone equally miserable. You know anything about that?"

"Above your pay grade, Corporal."

"Not getting paid by the Corps anymore, Gunny."

Torin saluted her with a spoonful of chili. The Corps' field rations had been designed to be equally palatable to all three species. They defined lowest common denominator, and bland was the polite description.

"I don't get people who sound off about the food in the

Corps," Werst grumbled, dipping a slab of hardtack into his bowl and watching the line of sauce rise, absorbed into the pressed carbs. "*I* liked it."

"You ate a piece of a sentient, plastic, hive mind disguised as a big, yellow spaceship," Torin reminded him.

"Your point?"

Her mouth full, Craig answered for her. "You're not exactly discriminating, mate."

Werst shrugged his acceptance, Binti laughed, and Craig grinned, pointing his spoon at Torin as if to say, *you go ahead and eat, I'm on this.*

So she did. Because he was. She ate her food and noticed that over the last year, forms of address aside, most of the military had been rubbed off the team's interlocking relationships. They were comrades, friends, lovers. They hadn't been assigned to this duty and were making the best of things; they were all there because they wanted to be.

For the length of the bowl of chili, she switched off the paranoia that came with the need to keep everyone safe. Switched off the feeling of vulnerability fueled by the missing weight of a KC-7. Switched off the heightened awareness that maintained a background threat assessment and decided to be aware instead of the taste of her food and the way Craig's eyes crinkled at the corners when he smiled and the warmth of Binti's elbow brushing against hers and the sudden huff of air and flap of nostril ridges that meant Werst was trying not to laugh.

Because if she didn't switch it off occasionally, one day she wouldn't be able to.

"We backtracked our buddy Jamers on the traffic buoys and according to the entrance codes, she's jumped in from all four of the locations Intell knew she'd used." Ressk drummed his toes against the edge of the board, clearly annoyed by what they'd found. "The buoys have her jumping out to those same locations."

"Only those locations," Alamber added. "As far as this system's traffic is concerned, anyway. She's jumping into this system, but she's not jumping out."

"Only explanation we can come up with..." Ressk took over. "...is that she's making unregistered jumps. Probably going out simultaneously with ore carriers or freighters so they mask the energy wave of her Susumi engines coming on. When she jumps back in, she probably skims one of the mined-out planets. There's little chance of slamming into other ships and the emergent wave slaps against rock."

"She'd have to come in dangerously close for that to work." Craig waved Ressk up out of the pilot's chair. One hand resting on the upper curve, ready to take her place behind it, Torin answered Ressk's silent request for intervention with a raised brow. The ship had few rules—they were all adults and expected to behave as such—but when Craig was in the control room, the pilot's seat was his.

Nostril ridges opening and closing in a put-upon sigh, Ressk stood, muttering, "A life of crime is not without risk."

From the mix of expressions around the room, Torin wasn't the only one who'd needed a moment to realize he'd been replying to Craig's comment, not the seating change. He dropped down into the chair beside Werst who asked, "If we find the point she's jumped out from, can we work out where she's going?"

"No," Craig said simply before either Ressk or Alamber could respond.

Torin shot Alamber a look that snapped his mouth shut. Craig had been making solo jumps for about as long as the young di'Taykan had been alive.

"Even if we had a magic way to track a ship through Susumi, we can't find the point she jumps from because we're in the Core." Ressk slouched low, arms crossed, toes curled in close to his soles. "There's layers of energy trails out there, frequent enough that each new one burns through the old ones before they dissipate."

"Big corporate freighter came through a while ago, heading in-system." Alamber nodded toward the screen. "Days out in front, but still burning bright enough that's all we can track along that vector."

"And if a tracker exists that can sift through multiple layers and rapidly dissipating energy signatures," Ressk added, "Justice hasn't given one to us."

"All right." Torin swept her gaze around the room. "Options?"

Alamber spread his hands, the chair complaining about being tipped back as far as it would go. "We can track her if she comes through on a supply run while we're sitting here. Maximum wait, three tendays, likely a day or two less."

"Why so often?" Binti asked.

"Water. Eighty percent of what she picked up from the Trun was water."

Promise had a converter; they snagged ice when they needed it. On a dead planet, a converter's constant and specific energy signature would be like sending up a flare, pinpointing its location to any ships in orbit. But Humans needed two to three liters of water per day. Di'Taykan a little more. Krai a little less. A small ship, trail obliterated by the traffic in the Core, would definitely be a low impact way to deal with that.

"So, there's no water on this planet?" Binti shook her head. "Gotta say, when the H'san bang a planet, they do a thorough job."

"Red giant, no water . . . Look at us narrowing it down." Alamber slid down until his tailbone was barely balanced on the edge of his seat.

They were looking for a single planet with no real idea of where the hell it was and no apparent way to find it short of capturing some H'san and forcing them to talk. Torin missed clear orders to follow so badly that, at this point in time, she'd welcome a shiny new second lieutenant just to have a point of reference she could work against. *Stop a war*, Colonel Hurrs told her. *Well, thank you very fukking much.* There was always the chance the bastard had been setting them up to fail.

"I've eyeballed plenty of jumps." Craig swept the screen clear and began scrolling new data. "I can do it again. We need a red giant and there's eight front and center if you want to give them a burl."

"Eleven," Alamber corrected. "We ran the numbers. Angle's bad for the other three."

"Eleven. Eight." Torin ripped a thread from a fraying edge of the duct tape holding the front of the chair to the frame.

"We haven't time to search . . ."

The first four bars of a Krai pop song that Ressk had been warbling for the last three months rang out, the volume loud enough to echo off the back wall. Loud enough to yank Ressk up onto his feet as a line of red light bisected the board.

"Ryder! Don't touch!"

Craig jerked both hands away, the same motion curling them into fists.

"We've maintained a ghost link to the traffic buoy," Ressk explained, glared Alamber out of the second's seat, and brought up a new screen before his ass had fully settled. "There's a ship coming in."

"Not the first since we arrived," Werst snarled, straightened out of a crouch and slid his knife back into the sheath strapped to his thigh.

Ressk moved a foot to the board as Alamber answered, "Yeah, but this one, this one's using coordinates identical to ours."

"They're jumping out at the same buoy," Torin began.

He cut her off. "They're jumping *from* the same buoy, Gunny. Out from Abalae, using the first open slot after ours."

And Torin remembered the pattern she'd seen.

Not defensive.

Not offensive.

Familiar.

"There's someone following us."

"The facilitators?" Werst shifted his weight from foot to foot, ready for a fight, the line of tension across his back showing his frustration with an opponent who wouldn't close.

Torin understood that frustration. Could feel the same line of tension. "No, the facilitators are dirtbound and the Trun wanted us gone."

"Yeah, well the facilitators might be dirtbound, but the Wardens aren't, and if the facilitators called in the Wardens . . ." Binti paused and met Torin's gaze. ". . . we've got some serious bullshitting to do."

"If it's the Wardens, we're screwed," Alamber amended, his attention still focused over Ressk's shoulder on the board. "And not in a good way."

"We didn't do shit that would justify calling in the Wardens." Still shifting from side to side, Werst ran both hands back over his head, the bristles making a soft shuff shuff under his palms. "Oh, wait. I forgot, the Trun don't actually need us to *do* anything; we're dangerous, murdering animals. *Revenk* fukkers."

"It's not a Justice ship." Ressk had another screen open, registration numbers scrolling past. When the scroll stopped, Torin had only a quick glimpse of a line glowing orange before Ressk opened it, exposing the data. "It's a Katrien ship."

"The *Seelinkjer?*"

Alamber shook his head, hair moving in counterpoint. "Not possible. Jamers wasn't on Abalae."

"Entirely possible," Binti contradicted. "It's a big planet, and we saw one small part of it."

"Granted. But once we had the ship, we searched the other stations' docking records. She wasn't there."

"She isn't here either," Ressk added. "Incoming ship isn't the *Seelinkjer*, it's the *Tinartin Hur Tain* registered to the family Valinstrisy."

"Valinstrisy? Are you sure? We're running under a false reg," Torin explained as Craig twisted around and frowned up at her, his reaction no surprise, as he was probably the only other person on board who recognized the name. "Jamers is a smuggler, a false reg would make sense."

"Could be," Ressk agreed, "Isn't. We checked specs not just names and numbers on Abalae. And yeah, she doesn't need to have been docked at Abalae to use that buoy—space is big, right? But if she's got a fake registration, it's better than anything the Corps can provide. I know where the edges are in *our* code, and this ship is smooth. Evidence suggests our buddy Jamers isn't smart enough to load in anything that clean. The incoming ship is the *Tinartin* and it's everything it says it is, I'd bet my breakfast on it. Current course and speed'll bring her right to us. I'll contact . . ."

"No." Torin had to breathe deeply before she felt she could control her voice and maintain anything resembling a neutral tone. "Call me when it catches up."

She had one foot out of the hatch before Craig asked, "Where are you going?"

"To hit something."

Weight pushing the soles of her bare feet against the deck, far enough away to keep the entire bag in her field of vision, Torin slammed in a combination that would have landed mid-torso on an opponent her size. They'd be head shots on a species significantly shorter. She shuffled back, shuffled in, arms relaxed, throwing quick, snapping punches. Then again. Then faster. Normal combinations. One two. One two. One two three. A few less orthodox. One three two. Three one two three three. Lips pulled back, she sucked air through her teeth. Fights seldom came with convenient breaks to breathe.

"You're dropping your hands."

"I'm aiming low."

One two. One three two.

"Torin . . ." Craig moved behind the bag and braced it.

"I'm getting it out of my system before she arrives."

One one three two.

He grunted, feet slipping back a couple of centimeters. "Presit is not your enemy. She's been there when we've needed her, more than once, and yeah, a good part of why she was there was vested self-interest, but she's not the arrogant self-absorbed show pony we thought she was."

"Yeah, and she's hot for you."

"She's a different species."

"I *know*." Torin stepped back, took a deep breath, and rubbed the sweat off her face with the bottom of her shirt. "Presit a Tur durValinstrisy is a reporter and she's followed us in the past knowing we'll lead her to a story. But this, this is a story she can't have, so what do we do with her? And not just her, she'll have a crew."

"A pilot at least," Craig agreed. One hand on the bag, he stepped around it. "You can't . . ."

There were a lot of things she couldn't do. There were a few things she might have to and she could hear all of them in the pause after Craig's voice trailed off. "Then what can we do? It's Presit versus a war we're supposed to stop. We can't let her tell this story and we've never been able to shut her up. If we tell her we're in the Core on a Justice Department op we can't talk about, Presit will go to the Justice Department and demand transparency."

His brows were drawn in so deeply they nearly met over his nose, but he didn't argue. He knew Presit. "She's compromised in the past. Waited to go public. Underplayed certain aspects of the situation."

"A compromise isn't good enough." Torin tapped the release tab and began unwrapping her left hand. "We're doing this job because the Corps can't and the Corps can't because the press not only demands full disclosure, but makes damned sure they get it." She dropped her first wrap into the recycler and released the tab on the second. Her hands ached in spite of their protection. "Now we've got our own member of the press—who knows what kind of work we do—following us, planning to bolster her reputation by exposing details that could start a civil war."

"To be fair, Torin, she doesn't know that." He kept his voice light, even, but Torin could see the dawning realization of just how badly they were screwed on his face. "We could blow. Leave her hanging."

"We don't know where we're going yet. And leaving won't stop her from following us."

Craig nodded, a silent acknowledgment to Presit's commitment to the chase. "What are we going to do?"

"Do what you must to stop the grave robbers. To stop a war. We've all seen too much war. That, Gunnery Sergeant Kerr, is the mission should you choose to accept it."

The second wrap followed the first. Torin reached for a water pouch, took a long drink, and said, "What I have to."

If he noticed the pronoun change, Craig let it go.

Eventually, the two ships sat motionless, less than a kilometer apart.

"Anything?" The upper curve of the pilot's chair creaked under Torin's grip. With Ressk sitting second, she stood behind Craig, able to see and be seen—the moment there was something to see or see her.

Ressk frowned at the board. "Nothing yet." He smacked Alamber's hand away without looking.

Tall as he was, and he had five centimeters on Craig, Alamber wasn't quite tall enough to reach the board from his position behind Ressk's chair, but that hadn't stopped him from making a regular attempt. Torin had no idea if he'd maintained that position the entire time she'd been gone or taken it up again when Craig reclaimed his place. As Ressk hadn't told the di'Taykan to fuk off, she allowed him to remain.

Werst had been sitting reading, one foot working a bright red spring grip, when Torin and Craig returned to the control room. He'd acknowledged them, switched the grip to his other foot, and returned his attention to his slate. Binti had returned a few moments later, ignored the three empty seats, and leaned against the rear bulkhead, arms crossed, eyes narrowed. Fully aware she was the source of Binti's suspicions—the other woman hadn't spent enough time with Presit to have reached that level of suspicion on her own, not to mention that Presit had saved their collective asses during their run from Vrijheid—Torin appreciated having another set of eyes on the target.

"There's something happening," Ressk muttered. "I'm only reading it because I've got a broad . . ."

::You are being where you are not needing to be!::

Training kept Torin from reacting to the voice booming out of her jaw. "Why are you following me, Presit?" As heads turned, she mouthed, *implant.*

Ressk snorted and danced his fingers through a pattern of blue and yellow lights.

::I are not following you! It are . . .

". . . not always being about you."

Torin nodded her thanks. The Katrien were loud and high-pitched regardless of what language they spoke, and switching the implant feed to the ship's speakers would keep her skull from vibrating off the top of her spine. "There's no story here, Presit. Go home."

"I are not going anywhere. You go home!"

It always sounded strange when Katrien syntax matched up to that used by the rest of the Confederation. Since they spoke perfectly understandable Federate, Torin had always assumed the syntax was an affectation.

"If I are ever having done anything for you, Torin . . ."

Presit usually addressed her by her rank, her tone anywhere from fondly mocking to full-out derision. Torin frowned. This was serious, then. And personal. "Presit, you're on speaker. My whole team can hear you. Do you need me to switch you back to implant?"

"Your whole team are listening?"

"You followed us from Abalae. We all wanted to know why."

"Why I are following you?" Her voice sharpened to a familiar edge. "We are chasing the same shadow, that are being why. And you are knowing that if you are spending half a moment to actually be using your brain. Still perhaps I are better off appealing to consensus than your better nature, Gunnery Sergeant Kerr . . ." There was the derision. ". . . but if I are discussing this with the whole lot of you, then I are looking you in the eyes while I are doing it."

"She's off implant, Gunny. Switched to ship to ship." Hand just over the board, Ressk glanced up at her. "Do I put her up?"

The ability to throw visuals onto the glass of the front port was new as of the post-Vrijheid refit. *Promise*'s visuals, when Craig had bothered to snag more than the audio signal, had been confined to the board. Fine for one or two people, completely useless for six.

"Do it," Torin sighed. "Before she puts on a suit and tries to kick in the air lock. Give her visual on the whole cabin, we don't want her to think we're hiding things from her. That never ends well."

"But we are hiding things from her, right, Boss?" Alamber raised both hands when Torin turned toward him. "Hey, I don't want to say the wrong thing."

"Don't mention the mission."

"Well, duh."

A running red light delineated a meter-by-meter section of the glass, the internal area filled with the head and shoulders of Presit a Tur durValinstrisy, the stars still faintly visible behind her image. She combed the claws on her left hand through the fur on her cheeks, the pale, green metallic polish gleaming against her thick, silver-tipped dark fur, and sighed. "Well, the whole gang are being there, aren't they? Fine. At least I are being comforted by knowing I are not going to be misquoted during the retelling of my story."

Craig leaned in and Torin fought the urge to put a possessive hand on his shoulder. Full awareness of how ridiculous she was being wasn't enough to stop it.

"You look exhausted, Presit." She could hear the concern in his voice. "Is everything all right?" He'd spent a lot more time alone with her than Torin had. She couldn't see tired.

"No . . ." Her tone added a clear *idiot*. ". . . everything are not being all right. If everything are being all right, would I be here?"

Of course not. If everything was all right, there'd be no story.

"So, what brings you into the light of glory?"

She wrinkled her muzzle, sharp white teeth gleaming against the black gums. As it was Craig asking, they might actually get an answer. "If the light of glory are being your unnecessary Human dialect way of asking what are bringing me here into the Core, then I are here for the other side of the reason you are being here."

Or not.

"Details," Torin prodded.

"You are going first."

"You followed us."

"And again, I are *not* following you."

"All right, then. We were here first."

"Are we being kits now? You are going with that?" When she sighed, her fur ruffling, Torin could see the exhaustion Craig had noticed earlier, the effort it took to hold her head high. "Fine. I are searching for a dependent of my house, and I are not finding her. She are having fought with the *strectasin* some years ago when she are young and are having left, announcing as the young are doing that she are better off on her own. The clan are all expecting her to come back having proven her point, but time are passing and she are not home. She are sending messages . . ." A flick of her fingers dismissed the messages. ". . . to her *armenai*, but then, even that are stopping. More time are passing and no one are hearing from her for years. Finally, her *armenai*, who are having grown very old and are near dying, are having gone to the *strectasin* and are saying, I are wanting to be seeing her again before I die. We are a dependent of your house, and you are failing us. The *strectasin*, who are not being happy about the accusation, sends for me. She are totally ignoring that I are being in the process of putting together a story that are blowing the corruption in the office of the Ministry of Commerce wide open and she are sending me out as her representative. Granted, I are obviously being the best choice, and not only because I are direct blood line descent from the *strectasin*, but it are not like I are having nothing else to be doing with my time. She are, of course, not being willing to listen."

Strectasin ruled the matriarchal Katrien clans. Too many years of interacting with Presit, the reporter, made it difficult for Torin to see Presit, the put-upon family member.

"I are finding a contact who are putting her on Abalae recently, but the Trun are not telling me anything of use. They are recognizing me, of course, and . . ."

"They don't want to spill to the press," Craig said. "Because the people you were speaking to weren't exactly on the up and up."

Presit nodded. "If I are understanding your up and up, yes. They are most definitely not wanting to talk to the press, and I are too well known." She turned her attention back to Torin. "That are being thanks to you. Then I are seeing you speaking with Bufush . . ."

"That was you arguing with zir in the backroom," Torin realized.

"Zi are an idiot," Presit sniffed. "I are not being concerned with zir or the not entirely legal aspects of zir business and, although I are making that very clear, zi are being stupidly suspicious of my motives and are accusing me of attempting to be blackmailing zir. Like I are new at gaining information. All blackmail are ever going to be accomplishing are sealing zir mouth and that are being the opposite of what I are wanting. You are imaging my surprise, when I are seeing you . . ." She nodded at Craig. ". . . and Gunnery Sergeant Kerr, on zir security system. So I are following you . . ."

"How?" Ressk demanded.

"You are maybe not noticing you are the only ones of your

respective species on Abalae?"

"On the entire planet?"

She waved the specifics off. "People are talking and if you are forgetting what I do for a living, don't. I are seeing you speaking with the facilitators and that are deciding me it are not a good idea to be having this discussion on Abalae where the facilitators will be doing what they can to be overhearing. How convenient it are being, you are being asked to leave. It are ridiculously easy to be finding where you are docked . . ." She focused on Craig and frowned. "Why are you having changed the name of the ship?"

"We're working, Presit; why do you think?"

"If you are trying not to be noticed, that are not really working out for you."

"Micro notice is fine. Macro notice is not."

Her lip curled. "I are being sure you are thinking you are making sense. Point I are making, while I are traveling to the tether—and I are certainly not traveling freight, thanking you very much—I are finding you. You are taking so long to leave, I are half thinking you are knowing I are on my way and are giving me time to be reaching my ship . . . ?"

Craig shook his head. "Technical difficulties. Nothing to do with you."

"So you are saying. I are ready to leave as you are finally detaching and I are following you."

"How did you crack the buoy and find our jump coordinates?" Alamber demanded.

She turned an unimpressed gaze in his direction. "I are asking."

"You just *asked*?"

"The government is required by law to provide full transparency to the press and the buoys are government run," Torin reminded them.

Alamber's hair flipped out. "Yeah, but what if they ask you why you're here?"

Even given the full black of Katrien eyes, Presit put in enough effort to make the eyeroll obvious. "I are not hiding. I are searching for a family dependent. Although . . ." Her ears flicked, the Katrien equivalent of a shrug. ". . . everything I are doing are being press business in the end."

And water was wet. "You're searching for Jamers a Tur fenYenstrakin," Torin said before Alamber could continue the argument.

"Yes. Yes." She'd clearly expected Torin to know the name. "The fenYenstrakin are being a dependent of my family within the clan." Her gaze locked on Torin's. "Whatever Jamers are having done, whatever are bringing you in here after her, I are not having heard of it, not through any of my sources, and I are having the kind of sources the Wardens would be weeping to have. If I are not having heard of it, it are not being bad enough for you . . ." The rude gesture included them all. ". . . to be involved."

"You haven't heard half . . ." Alamber began.

Torin glared him silent, then exchanged a look with Presit where they both agreed to ignore the interruption.

"So . . ." Presit spread her hands. ". . . I are saying one more time, go home. If we are being friends at all, allow me to be finding Jamers and be bringing her back to our family. I are even saying please if it are helping, although I very much doubt it are."

"We . . ."

Hand clamped on his shoulder, fingers digging her need for his silence into his flesh, Torin cut Craig off. "We need to discuss this without an audience, but I'm sure, at the very least, that we have information, that we *both* have information on Jamers we can share. When the block goes down, get back in touch. Ressk."

The board went black.

"Block's in, Gunny. Full spread, implants as well."

"So, we're sharing information with the press, Gunny?" When Torin turned, Binti pushed herself up off the bulkhead. "What happened to no one knowing?" she asked, folding her arms. "What happened to if the news of the grave robbing gets out, it'll start a war even if the H'san weapons cache is never found?"

"I reminded Presit there's information we *can* share," Torin told her, voice falling into the familiar *I know what I'm doing* cadence designed for soothing second lieutenants and green recruits. "I didn't say we'd actually be sharing it."

Binti's frown deepened. "But she's going to think that's exactly what you said."

"No, she won't." Swiveling the chair away from the board, Craig reached up and wrapped his hand around Torin's—she loosened her grip on his shoulder enough he could tuck his fingers under hers. "Presit's dealt with Torin before. She'll have heard exactly what Torin said and she'll know negotiations for sharing information aren't yet on the table."

"How about this . . ." Werst snapped his slate onto his belt. ". . . we tell her that in exchange for what she knows about the H'san . . ." He broke off to close Alamber's mouth with a gesture significantly ruder than the one Presit had used. "Use your head, kid. She didn't mention the H'san by name, but she knows they're a part of this because she knows about the biscuit maker."

"Yeah, but . . ."

"If she didn't know about the biscuit maker, she wouldn't have been at Bufush's. If she tells us everything she knows, we, in exchange, will find Jamers for her and bring her home."

Ressk nodded. "We definitely need more information on the H'san."

Torin couldn't argue with that. "And how does Presit occupy herself while we ride to the rescue?"

"She goes back to work. Wins awards." Werst shrugged. "Why do we care what she does as long as she backs off?"

"She doesn't know how to back off. She'll follow us."

Alamber snorted. "Yeah, like we'll be handing over our Susumi equations."

"She doesn't need our equations," Torin reminded them. "She's followed ships through Susumi space at least twice before. Once into enemy territory. Considering what she's already done for her family, odds are she'll be willing to do it again."

"That shit needs a crazy pilot." Werst glanced over at Craig and his nostril ridges closed halfway in reaction.

Torin shifted far enough to see Craig's face had gone so completely expressionless, he had to be remembering the jump he'd made behind a Primacy ship, trusting Presit's equation, their survival owing as much to the little gray aliens as to either luck or skill. And if he wasn't remembering it, Torin sure as hell was.

Ressk broke the silence with a snort. "How many more pilots with Ryder's level of crazy can she find?"

"Skilled crazy pilots are rare." Torin leaned in until as much of her weight was against Craig's side as it was against the chair. "But Katrien clans are huge and as the *strectasin's* choice, Presit has access to everyone—and everything they have access to." The *strectasin* who'd pushed past her bodyguards to thank them after they'd taken down the furriers should have been wearing four stars. Torin had spent most of the meeting fighting the urge to salute. "I wouldn't bet against her having found exactly what she needs."

Binti drummed her fingers against the bulkhead. "What if we tell her that we know what Jamers is involved with . . ."

"Which we do," Ressk pointed out.

". . . but we make it clear that she doesn't want to know the details? That if they got out they'd damage the family— because that's what this is all about right, family? We make sure she's aware that Jamers isn't a victim, she's a participant, but if Presit leaves it to us, we'll pull her out when we shut the operation down."

"Yeah, but why would we do that?" Alamber demanded. "Why would we pull her out? What's in it for us?"

"What part about us needing information are you missing?" Werst growled. "We can't pull anyone out of shit until we know where that shit is."

"You're terrifyingly articulate, you know that right?"

Werst flipped him off, a Human gesture both Krai and di'Taykan had adopted by virtue of Humans being the first into the newly formed Confederation military and profanity being the first parts of language soldiers shared.

"Presit's a friend." Torin surprised herself a little with the declaration, but Craig's smile said it came as no surprise to him. "Also, Binti made an excellent point. If we don't give Presit the details of what Jamers is involved in, then she won't have to tell the *strectasin* and she can blame us. Knowing Presit, a chance to shift the blame will be a strong selling point."

"So we're lying?" Still leaning on the back of Ressk's chair,

Alamber fussed with his cuffs, his gaze on fabric and fingers. "Correct me if I'm wrong, but these grave robbers we were sent after, they aren't just rummaging about in boxes of bodies, they're searching for weapons. Weapons they'll either sell to a head case who figures they can profit from a few million more dead, or they'll try to collect that profit themselves. Either way, millions more dead."

"You're not wrong," Ressk muttered.

"And we're supposed to stop them without being spotted by the Elder Races because in retaliation they'd smack the Younger Races down and we won't stay down. War again. Millions dead. Rub. Repeat. Now the point of the recap . . ." Alamber held up a hand when Werst tried to jump in. "The point of the recap is that we're not shutting these guys down and calling in the Wardens; we're being paid to stop them. Where 'stop them' means no one who went on the treasure hunt for planet buster weapons in order to, you know, actually bust planets survives to spread the word and/or make a second attempt."

Judge. Jury. And executioner.

Torin tightened her grip on Craig's fingers.

Or millions more dead.

Alamber swept the room with eyes darker than the light levels called for. Dark enough, Torin suspected, that he'd opened the light receptors he thought he needed to catch nuance. It wasn't the answer that was important to him, it was the reason behind it. "So if we tell Presit we'll find Jamers and get her out, are we lying? Now me, I don't have a problem with lying, just so we're clear on that, but for the sake of consistency, I'd like to know up front."

"Or are we actually going to get her out?" Ressk asked.

"Against orders," Werst added.

Craig pulled his hand free and folded his arms. "We don't take orders from the Corps."

"We took money from the Corps," Alamber reminded him.

Torin listened to them argue for a moment, Craig against Alamber and Werst. Binti against Ressk. Ressk and Binti against Alamber, Werst, and Craig. Four to one. Two to three. Argument passing as democracy. Finally, she said, "Best guess says Jamers a Tur fenYenstrakin is an independent contractor. We've already agreed only the Younger Races would go after the weapons, so we are *not* . . ." The negative was a definitive negative. ". . . revisiting that argument. It's significantly less noticeable to have a Katrien flying in and out of this part of the Core than any of the Younger Races, and smart people would hire out rather than be that visible. Given that Jamers has been skimming artifacts off the top, she may have no idea of what the end goal is."

"Because only the Younger Races think weapons before they think cash," Binti said dryly.

"Weapons will get you more cash." Alamber pointed out.

"And that's made my point."

"If we say we're getting her out," Craig growled, "then we're getting her out."

"Gunny?" Werst was more of a realist.

"We don't lie, we're the good guys." Torin ignored Werst's snort of disbelief. "We don't disobey orders—even when those orders are phrased as requests by the people paying our bills. We'll stretch their parameters as far as it takes to get the job done, but that's it. And we don't tell Presit one thing and then do another."

"Although we're not responsible for her expectations."

Torin touched her nose. "Point to Binti. We'll do our best to get Jamers out, but we don't know how deep in the shit she's sunk and we can't make promises we might not be able to keep."

"And that'll be enough?" Werst looked dubious.

Craig didn't. "I think *Torin's best* will be enough."

Torin shook her head. "That's not . . ."

He cut her off. "She likes you a lot more than the two of you pretend. More importantly, she respects you. She's seen your best, Torin, a couple of times; she knows what it means."

"And, Gunny?" Ressk waved a hand to get her attention. "Not to continue chewing an empty *trysh*, but we need more information on the H'san or we're not going anywhere. She scratches our backs, we scratch hers."

"She grooms our backs, we groom hers," Craig amended.

"You've groomed her, have you?" The edges of Alamber's hair flicked out around his face. The di'Taykan equivalent of wagging eyebrows.

"Mate, I have groomed the hell out of her," Craig sighed. "And no one can dummy out a way to make cleaning forty kilos of undercoat from the vents sound sexy."

"What makes you think she knows more than we do?" Werst demanded before Alamber could accept the challenge.

"Presit makes it a point to know more than I do," Torin told him.

"What makes you think she's going to tell you what she knows?"

"We're following Jamers, she's following us. Odds are, she thinks we know where we're going."

"You know what you should do, Boss?" Alamber sketched possibilities in the air with both hands. "You should . . ."

"No." Torin didn't care how enthusiastic Alamber got. "Craig does the talking." She considered ordering the rest out, but she was staying and Presit had never minded an audience. "He has the best poker face, and she's annoyingly overt about how much she likes him."

"Jealous?"

"Shut up."

"Why would the best of Gunnery Sergeant Kerr not be being enough for me? Is she not being responsible for having ended the war?" Presit spread her arms in what might have been surrender but was more likely a benediction. The sarcasm had sounded unexpectedly sincere. "If you are wanting it, then I are giving my word I are not going to follow. I are well aware there are being many things a dependent of my family could be doing that I are not wanting to have to pass on to the *strectasin*. Nor are I wanting to be giving the H'san an opportunity to be linking my family's name to the desecration of their dead and the selling of their grave goods like so much *frincreesten*. So . . ." Her smile held relief and curiosity and small, white, pointed teeth about equally mixed. ". . . what are you needing to know in exchange?"

Craig leaned back and swung his feet up onto the edge of the panel, crossing them at the ankle, his lower heel on the worn edge that marked a thousand such positions. "You assumed you'd turn up Jamers on Abalae?"

"That are right, but then you are always having been smarter than you are looking." She fluffed her ruff, not quite selling the indifference. "If Jamers are finding a market on Abalae, then she are going to be returning to it when she are having new . . . items. Me, I are not following her into the H'san home system, abandoned though it are being, if I are not having to."

Where the fuk did you find the coordinates for the H'san home system? Torin closed her teeth on her response. Heard the sharp click of enamel against enamel that said either Ressk or Werst had been less metaphorical about it.

Craig ignored the equivalent of four of a kind hitting the table. "You sure that's where she was heading, then—the H'san home system?"

"Where else are she going to be going? She are not going to abandon an easy money maker once she are having found one, and the abandoned planet where they are having been ridiculous about their dead are the only place it are possible that she are finding the pottery. Who else are wanting to be buried with a H'san biscuit warmer? Well, maybe you." Presit shifted her focus off Craig just far enough to shoot Alamber a narrow-eyed glare. "Your collar are being ridiculous."

His collar was half a dozen rows of silver-tipped, black ruffles held in place by his masker. "What do you know about fashion, fuzzball?"

"Clearly, I are knowing more than you."

Eyes lightening, he smiled. "Get mange."

Torin took advantage of Presit's lengthy response in her native language to hold a silent conversation with Craig—who cut off the stream of irate Katrien with a raised hand. Proving once again, Presit really *did* like him. "The Justice Department tends to be sanctimoniously vague where we're concerned, so as a favor, can I put eyeballs on your coordinates? And if you could toss out a little more good oil on the H'san, it'd be helpful in finding your . . . Jamers."

Her fur ruffled again. "She are not my Jamers. I are never having even met her. She are a dependent of my house, no more. But the sooner you are finding her, the sooner I are getting my life back, so . . ." She turned slightly away from the camera, shouted a Katrien command, turned back and said, ". . . I having sent over everything we have." Head cocked, she wrinkled her muzzle until the sharp points of her front teeth showed. "You are knowing that changing the name of the ship are not being exactly covert if I are still able to contact you the same way I always are."

"We aren't hiding from you, luv."

"*You* aren't." She flashed more teeth in Torin's general direction. Torin flashed teeth back and they held their positions until the board pinged and Presit shifted her attention back to Craig. "My files on the H'san are not being in Federate, so I are having sent them through a translation program—I are not guaranteeing they are not having been scrambled." Her eyes narrowed. "*Are* Justice been talking out of their collective *byz*?"

"Talking out of their collective *byz* is business as usual for Justice. But comparing these . . ." He dropped his feet down to the floor and leaned in over the board. Torin wasn't sure if he was trying for innocent or curious, but trusted him not to overplay his hand. "These coordinates are . . . Where did you get them?"

"How are I knowing?" Her fur rippled over the shrug. "It's not like they are being a secret. How long are you thinking this are going to be taking?"

"As long as it takes."

Her lip curled and a little energy returned to her voice. "Craig Ryder, I are hearing Gunnery Sergeant Kerr using your mouth. I are not waiting here indefinitely, never knowing if you are having been destroyed by H'san planetary defenses or murdered by the criminals Jamers are working with."

"Because you care."

"Because I are not wanting to be waiting here indefinitely."

"Two tendays," Torin said. Now they knew where . . .

"One. And then I are coming in after you."

. . . they were back to simple. Stop a war. Hell, she'd done that once already. "Deal."

Presit took a deep breath and Torin heard a faint clicking sound, identified it as her claws tapping together out of range of the camera. "Jamers are not a bad person. She are not being young now and she are having been away for a long, long time so no one are knowing what she are like, but . . ." The clicking stopped. "I are hearing that she are having been lazy, and are having been not very smart, and are having been always looking for the easy way, but she are being a part of my family so I are asking you are remembering that when you are finding her."

"I'll treat her like I'd treat you in the same circumstances," Torin said blandly.

Presit looked surprised, her ears up, then she laughed. Her image disappeared off the screen.

"Ressk?"

"Got it covered, Gunny. I killed both bugs she sent with the coordinates."

"Both?" Craig asked, glaring at the board as though he could see them slinking through the code.

"The obvious and the not so obvious."

Presit, Torin acknowledged, was fairly obvious herself. "Check for a physical tracker either on or heading for the hull."

CSOs depended on the strength and complexity of their scanners, sweeping a debris field for the remnants of working tech or a DNA smear that would bring closure to the family of a sailor or a Marine. At heart, in spite of the additions and the temporary name change, *Promise* remained a CSO's ship. She could find a recording device the size of a thumbnail attached to the upper surface of the shuttle's wing.

"Son of a . . ."

"She'll go, but she won't go quietly," Craig said, sounding fond. "Of course, she doesn't do anything quietly."

Torin hummed a noncommital response and stared out at the distant red giants. The control room grew as quiet as possible for a small area holding six adults. The chairs creaked as Craig and Ressk shifted their weight. Fabric rustled as Alamber twitched at his sleeves. Binti leaned against the rear bulkhead, arms folded, sniper patient. Werst cracked his knuckles. Torin contemplated tossing him out the air lock. No one made the obvious observation.

They were waiting for her to make it.

"So . . ." She shifted around enough to catch reactions. ". . . the coordinates for the H'san home system aren't a secret."

Binti drew in a deep breath and let it out slowly. "Either Presit . . ."

"And her pilot," Werst pointed out.

". . . lied . . ."

"Don't think so."

". . . or Colonel Hurrs lied."

The colonel was Intell. If it got the job done, he'd declare blue was orange. That's why officers had noncoms, to keep them from getting lost in the big picture, and Torin had been very good at her job. "He wasn't lying."

They took her word for it.

"It seems the more important point . . ." Alamber dropped into an empty chair. ". . . is that the coordinates to the H'san home system aren't a secret to everyone else. Just to the Younger Races." He frowned. "Or maybe just the military."

"No." Torin was sure. "Colonel Hurrs thought stopping this was important enough to run an unsupported black op. He'd have pulled information off civilian channels if the military channels were blocked."

Ressk nodded, nostril ridges opening and closing. "He said searching for the coordinates had started attracting attention, but he didn't say from who."

"We didn't ask," Werst snorted. "That was stupid."

Werst wasn't wrong. Torin trusted officers to tell her what she needed to know to get the job done. Without the power of the Corps behind her, she needed to stop doing that.

"Well, given that the Younger Races are still at the kids' table, it's a good thing Presit was on Abalae," Binti said.

"And it's a good thing Presit's cousin was flying the supply ship," Werst growled, his emphasis on "good thing" nearly burying the words in irony.

They all considered coincidence.

"Good thing it was Presit, because we have history." Alamber stretched out a long leg and pushed at Craig's boot with his. "You have a shitload of history. Given the given, she wouldn't hesitate to confront us."

"In fairness, she wouldn't hesitate to confront anyone, but, yeah." Craig met Torin's gaze. "Tidy."

"Very tidy," she agreed.

"Too tidy. And when things are too tidy . . ."

Duct tape cracked under Torin's grip. "Plastic aliens."

"Stop breaking the ship." His hands were warm as they pried her hands off the chair. She accepted the excuse to be held. "It could be a coincidence."

She searched for an apparent causal connection. In the Corps, gunnery sergeants were considered all but omnipotent, but just because she couldn't find a connection, that didn't necessarily mean there wasn't one. "It could be."

Coincidences happened.

Unfortunately, she'd stopped believing in coincidence when she found she'd been fighting a war the hyper-intelligent, shape-shifting, hive-mind plastic fukkers had engineered. That was one of the things she resented most about them, that she'd lost her ability to believe some things just happened.

"So what do we do, Boss?"

"Our job. And if given the chance to fuk over the little plastic aliens, then that'll be all pleasure."

On the first night in Susumi space, heading for the right red giant if they could trust Presit's coordinates, Torin sat in the pilot's chair, the scarf she'd bought on Abalae across her lap, the recorded sound of wind in trees blending with the hum of the Susumi engines. She stared down into the shimmer of translucent browns and oranges and thought of her dead. Of Marines she'd carried out. Sergeant Glicksohn. Private Haysole. Private First Class Guimond. Of Marines she'd had to leave behind. Captain Rose. Lieutenant Jarret. Technical Sergeant Gucciard. Thought of them being called *Visitor* by shopkeepers and facilitators, by people who'd never lived through an orbital bombardment or had any idea of how many had died to keep them safely ignorant.

Calluses caught on fine fabric as the scarf spilled over her fingers.

And she thought of the Elder Races still keeping secrets. Of professing peace and denigrating war even as they'd sent the Younger Races out to die.

SIX

"It's water, Major." Nostril ridges slowly opening and closing, Verr frowned at the readout on the canteen she'd just dipped into the pool. "No salts. No minerals. No fish shit. No organics of any kind."

Marine canteens contained the best purifier available, which was why Sujuno had acquired them. Although this underground pool was the first water they'd seen—orbital scans had shown no surface water at all—she didn't regret the cost. She had no idea where the *sanLi* the Katrien had brought their supplies in from, but it seemed *distilled* had multiple meanings and every drop of the water brought in on the supply runs had gone into the canteens before it had gone into her team. Fortunately, the enclosed tech was among the minimal tech that continued to work. "Is it safe to drink without purifying?"

"It'd be safe to use in a regeneration tank. It's pure water. Pure," Verr emphasized as though worried she wouldn't be believed. "One hundred percent H_2O."

Sujuno stepped forward and indicated the kneeling Krai should turn the canteen until she could see the readout. "Trust the H'san to set up a filtration system for an open body of water thorough enough to result in improbable purity and then abandon it. Get all available containers filled as quickly as possible."

"All of them, Major? I only ask," Verr continued when Sujuno frowned, "because we've accumulated a lot of empties."

"Do you have somewhere else to be, Lieutenant?"

"No, but . . ."

"If you trust that water is going to remain pure or isn't going to drain away, then you haven't learned the lesson the H'san are teaching in these catacombs."

Verr's nostril ridges closed. "Life sucks and death is no reason to stop expecting the unexpected?"

"Close enough." Sujuno nodded toward the pool and repeated, "As quickly as possible."

Dion was certain they'd nearly reached the weapons cache. While she had no faith in either his intelligence or scholarship, she'd seen for herself that there was only one stanza left after they found the mark that would lead them out of the inverted bowl. The author's style—by way of Dion's translation—leaned toward overwritten, poetic declaration and from the beginning the clues had come one per stanza. More importantly, she could feel it. Instincts honed through eighteen years fighting the Confederation's useless war told her they were close.

Experience gained during those same eighteen years told her close only counted in intercourse and WMDs and those who didn't take advantage of fresh water got no sympathy when they died of thirst.

As Verr barked out orders, Keo picked up the case of collapsed containers and followed Wen and Broadbent toward the water.

If the cavern maintained the planetary schedule the rest of the necropolis had been locked to, they had three hours of light remaining.

So far, they'd activated none of the cavern's defenses. She sincerely hoped no one was stupid enough to believe there *were* no defenses.

Circling the pond, searching for the mark, Dion had barely covered a third of the distance around the cavern, Toporov a meter behind to ensure there'd be no independent action from their investor's eyes and ears. From where she stood, Dion appeared to not only be examining the exterior wall of the cavern but each plinth as he passed it, bending low. She couldn't fault him for his thoroughness even as she wanted to scream about the time he was taking. There'd been a mark on a sarcophagus already, so stairs within a plinth weren't out of line.

He ignored the bodies posed on top of the stones.

Sujuno had seen and ignored a lot of bodies over the years she'd fought in the Confederation's useless war, but these, displayed like trophies, kept drawing her gaze.

The Mictok and the Ciptran exoskeletons sounded hollow when she tapped them with the hilt of her knife. The mammals, however, were plush fur over desiccated flesh over rigid bone. Both Krai had taken a single sniff of the Trun's haunch where she'd cut a triangular opening, simultaneously slammed their nostril ridges closed, and declared them *revenk*. Inedible. Possibly a first for an organic substance. Not even the H'san corpses had gotten that response.

As the sound of Nadayki's boots descended the stairs, quick, staccato jumps from step to step ringing out his annoyance, Sujuno leaned on the bench by the Mictok's plinth. Leaned, because given the H'san physiognomy, few other species could sit on the benches comfortably. Sprawl, perhaps, but she didn't sprawl. Up above, the Mictok's eight eyes gleamed, but at least they didn't look *moist*.

"I've searched everywhere, the walls, the ceiling, the door, every fukking step of the whole fukking set of stairs—there's no control panel on this side." The young di'Taykan sagged against the far end of the bench as his hair sagged down against his head. "We can't go back."

The only visible entrance or exit from the cavern was the one they'd come through.

To find death a thousand times, travel only forward.

The first stanza. It was one of the more specific instructions Dion had been able to translate. The others had gone back when the Katrien had landed with water and Toporov had gone back to dispose of the Katrien, but she had only gone forward, remaining at their farthest point of egress as Dion searched.

To find death a thousand times, travel only forward.

It could easily be a metaphor. It could just as easily not be. She wasn't going to risk it.

"We don't want to go back."

"Yeah, but before we always could. There's a big difference

between can't and don't want to."

She disliked Nadayki's tendency to whine, but not enough tell him to stop and have to then deal with his mistaken belief that she paid any attention to his opinion at all.

Luck had put the remaining eight of her team on the right side of the door. The stone carving they'd assumed large enough to prevent the door from closing completely had barely slowed it, splitting cleanly in half as though there'd been a fracture designed into it for that very purpose. She wasn't yet ruling a deliberate fracture out. Modern H'san were all about the sanctimonious sweetness and light. Ancient H'san, however . . . Their thought processes were . . .

She glanced up at the Mictok on its plinth.

. . . peculiar. On the bright side, the crack of the stone splitting and then the extended percussion as half of it bounced down the stairs hadn't evoked a response from volume sensitive security in the cavern. They continued to speak softly, but at this point, after so long in the catacombs, it was habit rather than necessity. Fortunately, all of the team's essential, as well as most of their optional, gear had been moved down into the cavern and piled back on the sled before the door slammed shut.

As she had no intention of leaving without the weapons they'd been hired to retrieve, she considered the closed door unimportant. They'd continue moving only forward.

"You know we're trapped in here, right?" Nadayki switched from Federate to the most common of the five Taykan languages. Given his low birth, it was the only one he knew. "I mean, I'm pretty sure Dion is making up half the shit he's been spewing about the H'san, so our odds of him finding a way out are not high. We're probably going to die in this cave. Sure, not of thirst . . ." He waved at the pool. ". . . but eventually even the Krai will run out of things to eat. We're going to die surrounded by what may or may not be dead bodies on display and then be eaten by short and hairless times two and you and I are the only di'Taykan around who understand about touch." His undertones added a request for comfort, properly pitched from lower class to upper, although he didn't move closer to her. The manipulative little shit had learned that much at least.

"I don't care." She answered in Federate. Taykan had seventeen different words for touch. The most basic, the one Nadayki used, meant *touch that calms*. "If you have needs, there are three Humans and two Krai in here and, in my experience, Humans are always willing to play."

"Yeah, but they're not . . ."

Turning only her head, she met his gaze. The green faded from his eyes as more light receptors opened. His hair flattened. He was young enough, he wore his need on his face as well as in his scent, and any other Taykan would have responded to it. Any other di'Taykan would have responded enthusiastically. Sojuno drew in a deep, defiant breath. She wasn't *any other* Taykan, di or otherwise, and her responses were her own. She would not break her vow to her dead. It wasn't enough that Nadayki had also lost his family and could be open to joining a new line. Nor that he was male—which meant nothing now, but would when he changed to qui. He'd bragged of the reason he'd run from his home, the deaths he been responsible for considered collateral damage in proving his cleverness, and he'd crowed about surviving the ruin of Vrijheid Station when his *thytrins* had died. She'd needed certain skills, certain outside-the-box skills for this job, and he was certainly able, but the moment they were paid, he would be as nothing to her for the sake of his dead *thytrins*.

For the sake of her dead *thytrins*.

She dug her fingers into her thigh, feeling the nails bite through the fabric.

For the sake of her dead.

"Dion better find that fukking exit," Nadayki muttered, when the silence extended. He stood and headed toward the water, his hair flipping back and forth in short, jerky arcs.

Sojuno agreed with the sentiment if not the petulance of the delivery. She felt her hair brush her cheek and willed it still.

"This, all this . . ." Dion waved an arm, the gesture general enough he could have been been indicating the entire cavern or any of its contents. ". . . the H'san considered an honor. The bodies displayed on the plinths? Fortunately for us all, I know more about the ancient H'san languages than any other member of the Younger Races. One line on every plinth translates as *your dead are our dead* and then the others, the other lines, they name each race and give a short description. A short, poetic description. Well, not on the plinth under the H'san, of course."

He looked so smug Sujuno almost broke her vows and slapped him. If it came to it, she decided, rubbing her temples, she'd order Verr to do it. Verr would enjoy it.

"On the H'san plinth," he continued, "it says only *we stand with you until we are needed.*"

Broadbent frowned, folding parallel lines into the pale expanse of his forehead. "So when they are needed, they won't stand with you?"

Dion rolled his eyes. "Don't be stupid."

"Don't call me stupid." Broadbent shifted his weight, his hands curled into fists. Slightly under average height for a Human, he hadn't a gram of fat on his body, only lean muscle. While not the brightest star in the cluster, he'd done his job competently enough, content to follow orders without question, reminding his superiors of the old joke: *What do you call someone who finished basic at the bottom of the group? A Marine.* A lifer, a career corporal, he'd been lost after he'd put in his twenty and available to be taken advantage of by anyone who could give him a job he understood.

She'd needed strong bodies who'd do as they were told, who wouldn't be missed if they disappeared. Broadbent had fit her hiring criteria perfectly and she enjoyed his uncomplicated obedience.

Ignorant of how close he was to a broken nose, at the very least, Dion waved off Broadbent's protest. "Then don't ask stupid questions."

"Told you, don't call me stupid!"

"Private! Stand down!"

He rocked back on his heels, Toporov's big hand splayed out, holding him in place with a touch. She could almost feel the warmth spreading over Broadbent's chest and she wrapped her right hand around her left wrist, skin to skin.

"Professor." Sujuno smiled when Dion turned toward her

and saw, from the corner of her eye, both Krai cover their teeth. He demanded the title when directly addressed. She doubted the validity of his claim. "Answer Private Broadbent's question. What do the words on the H'san plinth mean?"

"I don't think he . . . Well, yes, I suppose he was, wasn't he, although . . ." His gaze locked on her smile for a moment. Then he shook his head and looked away. "I believe that *we stand with you until we are needed* means that once they're needed, they stop standing."

"They stop standing? And then what?" Keo asked, stroking the heavy band the exoskeleton laid across her collarbone. "They sit?"

"I assume they fight."

Even Nadayki laughed at that, and he'd never worn the uniform.

"I'm obviously not speaking of modern H'san," Dion huffed. "Were the ancient H'san not fighters, I wouldn't be here leading the hunt for their weapons. And what's more," he continued, "given minute differences in the carvings, I am undoubtedly the only living scholar who can tell you that the H'san maintained this cavern for centuries after forming the Confederation."

"Yeah, well, good thing they stopped before we showed up," Verr muttered. Both Krai had climbed to the top of the bench and were curled together in one of the larger hollows, Verr sprawled across Wen's lap. "Waste of fukking food."

Wen snickered and slapped a foot against his bonded's hand.

Dion ignored them, rubbing at a rough spot on his chin where the depilatory had visibly worn off. "I can roughly date this cavern by the absence of the Katrien and the Niln, but with only a little more time, I can precisely . . ."

Broadbent had relaxed into glazed boredom, so Sujuno cut Dion off. "I don't care. Will knowing the date of the cavern's creation help get us out of it?"

He stared at her for a long moment, then he blinked, twice, as though erasing the picture from his eyes. "I feel that history . . ."

"Is irrelevant," she snapped, "unless it leads us to an exit which, in turn, leads us to the weapons cache." Arms folded, she kept her hair flat. "No one pays for history. While you were circling and searching, did you find the next mark?"

"I would have mentioned it, Major, had I found . . ."

She turned away before he could finish. "Sergeant?"

Toporov shook his head. "No, sir. I looked for the new marker he showed us, but I didn't see it either. And no sign of either a control panel or a closed door on the cavern walls."

"Because that would be too easy," Keo sighed. She'd tried to open the door into the cavern before Sujuno had turned it over to Nadayki, but pushing hadn't budged it and pulling had been impossible with nothing to grab.

"Easy is irrelevant." Sujuno swept a gaze around the remaining members of the team. None of this had been *easy*. The first marker within the catacombs had been right out in the open, but finding it had cost Timin his life. "The instructions tell us to go forward . . ."

"Unless *the professor* fukked up the translation," Nadayki drawled.

Dion's florid face flushed darker. "I know more about ancient H'san languages than anyone alive!"

"Talk. Talk. Talk." Nadayki waved a hand. "We're still trapped."

"We're not trapped," Wenn snorted. "I have demo charges in my pack." He grunted as Verr drove an elbow into his thigh and added, "Which I will not use until you give the order, Major. There will not be independent explosions."

Wenn liked demo charges. Five, no, six tendays ago, back while they were on their way through Susumi, Verr had informed her that a fondness for demo charges had contributed to Wenn leaving the Corps. Sujuno also had demo charges in her pack although, in her case, they had nothing to with her leaving the Corps. She hadn't wanted Wenn, but she'd needed a pilot and Verr wouldn't leave her bonded behind. Given that Dion hadn't translated a way out, Wenn's fondness for property damage could come in useful if they had to retrace their steps.

"I brought us here," Dion began, "to this cavern . . ." He tipped his head back and waved both hands at the ceiling. ". . . to this the H'san's inverted bowl, so . . ."

"So . . ." Sujuno cut him off before he could start in on yet another of his interchangeable, patronizing lectures on the H'san. ". . . there has to be a way out."

"Or the marks have been leading us on a wild H'san chase." Keo shrugged, the bands of the exoskeleton catching the light as it smoothly followed the rise and fall of her shoulders. "I mean, when we get right down to shit and giggles, Major, we only have Dion's word about the translation. None of us can read ancient . . ."

"Or modern," Verr added.

". . . or modern H'san, so we'd be totally lost if he got it wrong."

"Because we wouldn't know if he got it wrong."

Keo snickered. "He wouldn't know if he got it wrong."

"I don't get things wrong," Dion snapped.

Sujuno glanced at Toporov. Although quick enough to damp Broadbent's temper, the sergeant occasionally let the verbal sparring waste time for longer than she'd prefer.

"Enough," he growled.

"But, Sarge . . ."

He pinned her with a glare. "You forgot what enough means, Keo?"

"No, Sarge."

Keo was wrong; they had more than only Dion's word for the translation. They had the money their backer had been willing to put up. Money for a ship. Money for black market weapons and tech. Money to hire a crew that might stand a chance of succeeding. More money, *a lot* more money promised if they succeed.

Enough money.

Enough money when they delivered the weapons she'd be able to pay the price for progenitor. Dion had to be telling the truth.

That much money didn't lie.

"If the mark isn't on the walls . . ."

"I said it wasn't," Dion muttered petulantly.

Sujuno ignored him. ". . . then we search the floor, every inch of the plinths, the benches, and the trophies."

"I don't believe they're trophies as you understand trophies," Dion began.

"You want us to search the bodies, Major?" Verr ignored him, her nostril ridges so tightly shut, the pitch of her voice had changed.

"Yes, I do. We can't trust the H'san not to have trimmed the mark into the Trun's fur or carved it into the Ciptran's ass. If you see anything even remotely similar to what we're looking for, you call the professor for confirmation. You do not press, push, twist, poke . . ." A preparatory inhale from the right. She pointed at Nadayki without turning. "*You* do not comment." A beat of silence before she continued. "Search. Do not touch. Am I understood?"

"Yes, Major." A familiar chorus from the ex-Marines.

The silence from Nadayki and Dion was sullen and supercilious in turn. Sujuno ignored them as well.

She paired herself with Broadbent. Next to the sergeant—who continued shadowing Dion—he was the least likely to try and carry on a conversation during the search.

The ancient H'san had not left their mark on the body of the Mictok. Or on the plinth under it. Or on the floor around it. Or on the bench beside it.

"Hey, Major!" Keo stood with one hand on the Dornagain's plinth while Nadayki rubbed his hands and a few other body parts over the nearest bench. "Do we look inside, too?"

"The benches?" They sounded solid and their supports were definitely too narrow to hide an access to the next level. Although, she allowed, they could hold the tech that opened an access.

"No, not the benches. The bodies."

In the sudden silence, everyone waited for her response.

Extremities came off the insect species easily enough. Without the flexibility of life, a hard twist would crack the joints. For the mammals, the ex-Marines carried knives and both Krai had small axes on their belts—although she was fairly certain they had a religious more than a practical purpose. If it came to it, Keo's exoskeleton would probably augment her strength enough for her to rip the bodies apart.

Sujuno had seen a lot of bodies while she fought a senseless war, but she'd never given an order to dismember the dead.

With any luck, it wouldn't come to it now.

"Leave the bodies for now. If we don't find the mark anywhere else, we'll take them apart."

"I don't mind, Major."

They were standing close enough together she could see the heavy gunner's smile. According to the records Sujuno had managed to access, there was strong suspicion although no proof that Keo hadn't minded in the past. "Leave them."

"Yes, sir."

She was examining the side of the bench closest to the Trun when the lights went out, plunging the entire cavern into darkness and evoking a surge of whispered profanity. Turning her head away from the sudden, acrid scent of Broadbent's fear, she kept one hand on the bench—contact with the slightly off-putting textures the H'san preferred was preferable to being unanchored in the darkness—and tapped her shoulder light with the other. "Sergeant." The second light on, a third of the way around the pool, turned in her direction. "Set up camp by the stairs."

"You heard the major, everyone back to the stairs." Toporov had set off the decibel alarm three times in the first two days. It had taken Sujuno's promise to gag him to finally lower his volume. Here, without the constraints he'd been under in the rest of the necropolis, he put his sergeant voice back on. "Stay back from the water. If you fall in, I will let you drown."

They didn't eat communally, that would have implied community. They'd each claimed a fraction of the supplies, and it wasn't only the Krai who guarded the pouches on the sled they considered theirs from companions they merely tolerated. Sujuno maintained a strict control of the water supply only because the mission would fail without it and she would not have the mission fail.

Having pulled her pack off the sled, she leaned against it, pulled the tab on a pouch of field rations, topped the pouch up with the last of the water from off-site, and activated the heating unit. It smelled like *tomagoras*. Hardly surprising, as most Taykan field rations smelled like *tomagoras*. And tasted like *rinchas* until extra spices were added. No one knew why. It was a mystery that long predated her people's entry into the Confederation. Spices were off the table thanks to the ancient H'san's inane security protocols, so she flicked off her light—

it was enough that scent and taste disagreed, why add a third differing sense—and settled to eat. Field rations had the comfort of familiarity if nothing else.

As the temperature began its nightly four-to-five–degree drop, she allowed the ends of her hair to lift as she relaxed a little of her control. It helped she was far enough away from the others that they were shadow puppets in pools of light, barely more than voices in the dark.

"I hate this," Wenn whined. "Every night it's fukking freezing!"

"I know ways to warm you up," Nadayki offered.

She heard skin on skin as Verr snarled, "He's bonded."

"I know ways to warm you both up."

"That's different."

"Verr, Wenn, you're on first watch."

"But, Sarge . . ."

"Broadbent and Keo take second. I take third."

"Why don't Nadayki and the professor ever stand watch, Sarge?"

"Would you trust a Marine's life to their piss uselessness?"

"Hey!"

Dion made no protest.

Rank and privilege and the complete absence of any threat they could actually fight kept Sujuno from standing watch. If it came to it, she'd stand before the civilians did. If it didn't, she'd lose no sleep over whining from those unwilling to perform their contracted jobs.

Tucking the empty bag under a strap where she could find it later, she tugged her bedroll free, unrolled it, and, after checking that both her maskers were at their highest possible settings, lay down, closed her eyes, and got as comfortable as circumstances allowed. It would be light again in just under six hours; nights were short at this latitude at this time of the year.

The rhythmic sound of flesh to flesh overlaid with quiet panting meant Nadayki had found a willing partner. The scent told her it was Broadbent. Better than Dion.

She slid a hand under her clothes and touched the cylinder of ash hanging on a leather braid between her breasts. She had no guarantee it held any of her family's remains, but she'd taken it from the ruins of their compound, from as close as she could get to the center, and she'd claimed it as family when security had tried to take it from her, so family it was. All the family she had.

Sooner or later, they'd find the next mark the H'san had left to guide them. They'd empty the weapons' cache. She'd receive her payment. She'd file the registration of progenitor and her name would live again. Until that time, she'd do the job she had to do, but nothing more.

They finished searching the plinths, the benches, and the floor two hours before the lights were due to go out on the second day.

They'd discovered that a third of the benches were hollow, but that was all.

"Why a third of the benches?" Verr asked.

"I've discovered that the H'san have an intrinsic attachment to the number three," Dion told her. "An almost religious attachment to it."

Sujuno exchanged a glance with the sergeant. This was the first time they'd seen any evidence of such an attachment. Toporov's expression openly called Dion a liar. She doubted hers was any subtler.

"Do I take the benches apart, Major?" Keo asked. She smacked a fist-sized piece of broken stone against the underside of the nearest bench, punctuating the question with an echoing boom.

"I find it hard to believe you're even asking that," Dion sneered. "Had only one bench been anomalous, than we could assume the ancient H'san were indicating that we should investigate it. However, given the number of hollow benches, we can draw no such conclusions."

Keo shifted enough to fix Dion with a flat, unfriendly stare. "What the fuk does anomalous mean?"

His lip curled. "That basic education isn't a requirement for violence."

"I could kill you with this rock."

"And you've just made my point."

She tossed the piece of broken stone into the air and caught it.

"I could throw it with enough force it'd crush your skull. Throw it fast enough that you wouldn't have time to point at it."

Dion snorted disdainfully.

Sujuno found herself actually considering it for a moment; then she sighed. "Sergeant."

Toporov plucked the rock from Keo's hand.

"Once we've been paid for the weapons, you may kill each other with my blessing." Suddenly realizing she'd twisted a handful of fabric so tightly her pants had begun to dig into the back of her leg, Sujuno forced her fingers open. "Until such time, play nice. And, no, we will not be taking the benches apart. Not until we've exhausted all other possibilities."

"Like after we dismember the dead guys?"

"That would be one of the remaining possibilities, yes."

"I feel I should mention that the plinths, which none of you can read, makes it clear, although not overtly, that the bodies are important to the H'san."

"Cheese is important to the H'san," Wenn pointed out to laughter.

"I repeat, none of you know . . ."

"And neither do you." She was very close to ordering Toporov to give Keo back the rock, but it was less than two hours until lights out and they had no time for drama. "Everyone take fifteen, then we begin."

Verr tapped a finger against her slate. "If the fukking scanners worked, we'd have been out of here yesterday."

"Yeah, well, they don't." Wenn flicked a finger against her forehead. "Got to use your big, sexy brain, *churick*."

"Yeah, that'd be all adorable and shit if you didn't just call her delicious," Nadayki muttered, leaning against Keo, fingers of one hand rubbing the contact point between her exoskeleton and her hip. "And if you didn't mean it literally."

"Not that finding the other stuff was a breeze or anything, but it was hard mostly because of the area we had to search. We're all enclosed here; why would the H'san make finding this mark so difficult?" Keo smacked Nadayki's hand away and crossed her arms.

"Because they were seriously creepy. I mean, I'm not the

only one who thinks this whole dead bodies on display thing is seriously creepy, am I?" Wenn reached up and tugged on the Mictok's lowest leg. It came off in his hand. He stared at it for a moment—they all stared at it for a moment—then his nostril ridges slammed shut, his lips pulled back off his teeth, he made a high-pitched noise, and threw it into the water.

"Well, Major, you were right about the water not staying pure," Verr sighed. She smacked her bonded on the back of the head as she passed.

Sujuno caught up with her at the edge of the pool and they stood together, staring at the leg floating about a meter out.

"Should we grab it?" Verr wondered.

The three slender digits on the narrow end waved as the leg sank.

"Or not."

Opening more light receptors in order to track the leg all the way to the bottom, Sujuno frowned. "There's a pattern on the stone." Dropping to one knee, she braced a hand and leaned out over the water, trying to ignore the way the light flickered as ripples from the impact returned from the other side of the pool. The stone on the bottom of the pool was darker than the stone that made up the rest of the cavern, but she could see lines that were darker still radiating out from the center. Or radiating *into* the center.

"I don't see anything," Keo complained, behind her.

"Of course you don't." Human eyes were useless. "We examine this before we start tearing things apart." She ignored Keo's huff of disappointment.

Broadbent turned out to be the best swimmer. "Choice at school growing up was swimming or cross country," he explained. "I hate running."

"And that's why you went with boots on the ground," Wenn mocked.

After a moment's consideration, Broadbent shrugged. "I never did much running in the Corps." Stripped down, he ignored Keo's whoop at the purpling bite mark on his right shoulder, and paused at the edge of the water. "Uh, Major? We still drinking this?"

Keo snorted. "I'd rather lap up your manly musk than the essence of giant embalmed spider leg already dissolving in it."

"You get promoted to major, Keo?" Toporov asked.

"No, Sarge."

"Ignoring her personal preferences, Keo has a point." Sujuno snapped her fingers to get Broadbent's attention and indicated the closest part of the pattern. "See that line? Follow it. Find out what's at the other end of it."

"Yes, sir." Broadbent waded in, clutching one of the extra lights. The Corps designed their gear to be Marine resistant; a little water would have no effect. Three steps in and the water lapped mid-thigh, the skin between his shoulder blades glistened with sweat.

Nadayki hummed thoughtfully. "I remember him being bigger." When Broadbent made no protest, he sighed. "Still, it's probably cold in there. Who could leave a line like that dangling?" he asked when Verr snickered.

"Can you leave anything alone if it's dangling?"

"Why would I?"

"Quiet!" Sujuno felt her nails dig into her palms and ignored the pain. This was it. She knew it.

Three steps more and the water reached Broadbent's armpits. The ancient H'san had clearly angled the bottom steeply toward the center. One more step and he'd be swimming.

"Wait." He froze at her command. "Can you feel the pattern?"

The water was clear enough and he was still close enough she could see his feet move. "Yes, sir."

Her turn to wait. After a moment she growled, "And?"

"It's raised." Balanced on his left leg, he bent his knee and stretched his right leg out in front of him. "I think it gets more raised farther in."

"Are you saying," Dion demanded, "that the pattern is dominant in the spatial relationship it maintains with the bottom of the bottom of the pool and that it grows more dominant the closer you move toward the center?"

Wenn's teeth snapped together. "Oh, come on, seriously? Major, let me . . ."

"No." Dion either didn't know or didn't care about the threat inherent in the sound. She'd seen Krai teeth crush Human bone. "Not until we've been paid. Keep moving, Broadbent."

He swam with short, awkward looking strokes, neither hands nor feet breaking the surface. When he reached the center, she heard him take a deep breath then he flipped forward and floated for a moment, facedown. Sujuno had to assume that, in spite of the depth, the water remained clear enough he could see the bottom. After longer than she was comfortable with, his legs dropped and his head came up. He spent a moment breathing, then said, "Lines come together around a squiggle, Major."

Dion stepped closer to the edge. "I hesitate to ask, given your description, but does your squiggle happen to resemble the mark I've spent the last two days searching for?"

Broadbent bobbed up and down, the curves of his shoulders breaking the surface. He spat out a mouthful of water and stared at Dion for a long moment, his position inhibiting a physical response. "We've been searching for," he said at last.

"Is the mark raised like the pattern you followed to the center of the pool?" Sujuno asked before Dion could spit out another string of stupid.

"Looks like, sir. Hard to tell how high from here, though."

"At that depth, light's probably too diffused for shadows," Vree murmured.

"Does it appear to be the mark we've been searching for?"

"Um . . ." He glanced down. "Yes, sir."

"I expect, and this is an educated guess, that he needs to depress it." Dion took another step, glanced down as water lapped against his boot, and stepped back again. "You need to depress it," he repeated.

"Tell it it'll never amount to shit," Wenn snickered.

"Tell it it's weak," Keo laughed, flexing her exoskeleton.

"Tell it it's all alone," Nadayki said, voice and hair flat. "It'll always be all alone."

"The law is very clear; there is no line if the sole survivor is di'Taykan. We are sorry for your loss, Sujuno di'Kail, but there are many families who would be happy to have you join their name."

"But when I am qui, the law will allow me to declare progenitor and restore the line."

"The law will allow this, yes, but it is very expensive to register a new progenitor and you will not be qui for many years. The Taykan are not intended to remain alone as you will be until you change."

"Major?"

Only Toporov noticed. He was better at his job than she'd given him credit for.

"The professor's right." Her tone added how much she disliked admitting it. Vree laughed. Dion heard only the words and preened. "Broadbent, if you can reach the bottom, you should de . . . you should press the mark." The mark they'd found after days of moving rock and dirt had also been raised stone, protruding out of the wall beside a metal door. Simple. Uncomplicated. Obvious. It had sunk into the wall when Dion had pushed against it and the door to the catacomb had opened. "If you can't reach bottom, come back and we'll find something light enough for you to swim with that'll extend your reach."

Side by side along the curved edge of the pool, they all watched the light as Broadbent dove, pale flashes of arms and legs and torso following behind. His first dive took him nowhere near the bottom—refracted light had made the pool seem shallower than it apparently was. He surfaced, gulped in air, and dove again.

Closer.

When he surfaced the second time, he sucked in a desperate breath before his nose and mouth were entirely clear.

"Report," she snapped when he finally stopped coughing.

"I can do it, sir."

And then he did nothing at all but breathe for a ridiculously long time. She realized what he was doing just as she felt Toporov readying himself to bellow and said, "He's hyperventilating. Leave him be."

The sergeant grunted agreement.

On his other side, Nadayki murmured, "I feel like I should say something about heavy breathing, but who the fuk cares."

Broadbent dove again.

She felt the click through the soles of her boots.

"Was that . . ." Dion began and was drowned out by the crash of stone panels opening. By the roar of thousands of liters of water draining away. By ancient machinery pushing the nose of a small ship up through the absence of floor where the pool had been.

Her back slammed up against the Mictok's plinth and she realized they'd all stumbled back. They hadn't needed to, the floor had remained rock solid, but fight or flight had kicked in during the sound and fury and there'd been nothing to fight. Breathing heavily, she clenched her teeth and pushed herself up onto her feet to keep from reaching out and touching Nadayki. Pressure on new bruises provided potent distraction.

"Broadbent!" Toporov knelt at the curved line where the floor ended, leaning as far forward as the side of the ship allowed, peering down into the lower level. "Broadbent!"

"He's dead."

"We don't know that, Major."

"Look up, Sergeant. Two, two and half meters, forty degrees left of your zero." The ship looked nothing like modern H'san ships, but function put a certain form on anything intended for space that started at the bottom of a gravity well. The translucent smear she'd directed the sergeant's attention to was red and brown, topped with pinkish-gray froth. Water had feathered the lower edges, but impact had obviously occurred after most of it had drained away.

Toporov shook his head. "He could be injured."

"Those are brains," Keo said from behind her.

They'd all seen brains before. When she was a mere second lieutenant, Sujuno had found a bit of her captain's brains in a pocket of her combats while walking to the extraction point two days after her first battle had ended. Back at base, she'd thrown them in the incinerator and silently accepted the abuse the supply sergeant had thrown at her when she went in for a new set. By the time she got out, newly a major, she'd long since learned that a familiar set of combats, with dependable tech, meant more that random bits of brain.

Wen's arm rose, and a small stone rang against the side of the ship. "We should've tied a rope around him."

"I'm telling you, you'd have still lost him. Given the mass of the water and the speed with which it drained, the force on his body would have been enough to have dragged anyone anchoring the end of the rope in after him. The only possible result would have been multiple brains smeared on a magnificent, ancient vessel." As Wenn lifted his arm again, Dion put himself between the Krai and the ship. "Stop it!"

"It goes into space," Wenn sneered. "I'm not going to dent it."

"Do you have any comprehension of how priceless this vessel is?"

"I've got a pretty good comprehension of how stupid this whole thing is," Nadayki called from the stairs. He sprawled gracefully four steps up, having removed himself as far from the edge of the pool as he could. Sujuno reluctantly admired his survival instincts. "Why the fuk would the H'san set up a kill switch? Go for a swim, press a symbol. Oh, look, it's a spaceship, and you're dead."

Dion's lip curled. "Do not assume you understand how the ancient H'san thought."

"I understand stupid." He tapped his chest, his hair a lime-green aurora around his head. "Genius." Arms wide, he indicated the whole cavern. "Stupid."

Sujuno nodded. "He's right."

"I don't believe he is." Dion waved his slate, screen still showing the latest symbol. "Most of the Younger Races are barely able to comprehend how modern H'san think. I am one of the few, the very few, who have any small understanding of the ancients. And even given my scholarship, we have no context for what just happened and therefore no way of knowing their reasoning. And I guarantee, they had reasons for this cavern, for the bodies, and for the ship."

"I don't care. Ignoring for the moment that we've just witnessed a spaceship rising through a pool into an *underground* cavern . . ."

"Stupid," Nadayki muttered.

". . . it would be pointless to go to the trouble of creating the kind of treasure hunt we've been involved in only to have set it up so that it kills the treasure hunters before they reach the end."

Dion folded his arms. "Sacrificial intent."

"Seriously?" Wen sighed.

"If we allow that the ancient H'san were not acting pointlessly . . ."

"Acting bugfuk crazy," Nadayki muttered.

". . . and as Broadbent is dead," Sujuno continued over the

enthusiastic agreement to Nadayki's amendment, "we can assume that the mark Broadbent found may have *resembled* the mark we've been searching for, but was not, in fact, the actual mark."

"You asked him if it appeared to be the mark." Wen rocked back and forth, hands opening and closing. "Not if it *was* the mark. *Serley chrika*, Major, you killed Broadbent!"

"Chill, Wen. You didn't even like him," Keo pointed out.

"Not the point!"

"I'll allow that Broadbent was stupid," Dion sneered.

Wen charged, the staccato slap of bare feet against stone the only warning.

"Sergeant!"

Toporov grabbed the Krai out of the air, pushed him into his bonded's arms, and backed off, hands well away from snapping teeth. Verr gripped Wen's shoulders, pressed their foreheads together, and reminded him they could divide Broadbent's share among the survivors.

"Broadbent died. No one killed him. And you," Sujuno snarled at Wen, "do not need to threaten Dion in his memory."

"It wasn't a threat," Wen growled.

"I wasn't threatened," Dion muttered at his slate.

"You don't seem to care that he died." Arms folded, Keo glared at Nadayki. "You were fukking him last night, he's dead today, and you're all critical about the H'san."

"There's a lot to be critical about." Nadayki leaned back on his elbows and sighed. "And why should I care more about him dying just because I fukked him last night? Humans are so weird about sex."

"Yeah, well, don't even pretend that being a shithead is the di'Taykan default because I've known plenty of di'Taykan."

He grinned. "How well?"

"Enough!" Sujuno swept her gaze over the entire team, pausing only long enough to stare Nadayki down. "The weapons are on the lowest level of these catacombs, we've known that from the beginning, and the bottom of that ship is a long way down. I will not leave here without those weapons, so there has to be a way. Find it."

Verr pulled far enough away from her bonded so that she could shake her head. "I don't know, Major, we've searched everywhere."

"Obviously, we haven't." She could hear the Krai breathing, Dion's fingers tapping against his slate, Keo shuffling around in a small circle as though she could see what they'd all missed from where she was standing.

"All in favor of finding a better way to spend our time, wave a body part."

She turned in time to see Nadayki shove a hand in under his waistband, reaching for the body part he intended to wave. She opened her mouth. Closed it. Took a step toward him. "The stairs."

"Major?" Toporov moved to stand behind her left shoulder.

"We didn't search the stairs." They'd walked down them. They'd been distracted by the dead on plinths and the benches and the water. They'd searched the walls all the way around the pool and they'd searched the floor, but they hadn't searched the stairs. The stairs had brought them down into the cavern and they needed stairs taking them down farther still. Unless Dion had been talking out of his ass from day one, it was the kind of symmetry the H'san appreciated.

"Uh . . ." Nadayki reluctantly waved a hand. "I searched the steps for a control panel."

"But only for a control panel."

"I guess . . ."

The mark had been carved shallowly into the riser of the lowest step.

She had to press it herself.

"Forget it, Major." Verr spoke for all of them. "We're not touching it. Not after what happened to Broadbent."

This was the way to the weapons. To her progenitor. The grooves felt cold under her fingertips as she traced them. When she applied pressure, the entire riser shifted two centimeters in and a three-by-five–meter slab of floor slid back to disappear under the cavern wall.

Arms flailing, Verr staggered and would have fallen into the opening had Keo not grabbed her and dragged her back.

"Stupid," Nadayki reiterated.

"I've definitely started leaning toward your bugfuk crazy theory," Verr growled, nostril ridges tightly closed. "That's a fukking safety violation at the very least."

"I assure you . . ." Dion began.

"Shut up."

"Packs on, people. We can't carry the sled down that."

Keo grinned. "We could slide the sled, Sarge. Let it bounce."

"Packs," he repeated.

Sujuno had kept hers ready to go. The others, even the sergeant, had gotten sloppy, and she ground her teeth at the delay.

The stairs, carved out of the same pinkish rock as the cavern, went straight down forty-three steps to a landing. A one hundred and eighty degree turn and straight down thirty-seven steps to a landing.

The risers on H'san stairs were variable heights and seldom level, the off angles running between two or three degrees to just under twenty. On a single short flight, it had been annoying. By the second landing Sujuno's calves were cramping with the effort of maintaining her balance at speed and they all kept one hand on the wall. They'd done little resembling hard labor since landing, but compensating for heights and angles seemed to be requiring enough effort from all involved she realized the planet's pull had wearied them more than she'd thought.

They'd rest as they cataloged the weapons, not before.

"What do the H'san have against elevators?" Nadayki skipped a shallow step, stumbled, and caught himself by grabbing a handful of Toporov's jacket.

"This place is millennia old; you couldn't pay me enough to get into an elevator. Besides . . ." Toporov tugged his jacket free. ". . . what would power it?"

"Geothermal running to secure generators. Solar fields we didn't spot from orbit. Magic. Same thing that's powering the lights and whatever they used to pop a fukking spaceship through the floor."

Forty-one steps. A turn. Fifty-three steps. A turn.

"What's with their hard-on for prime numbers?" Verr wondered.

Fifty-nine steps.

The lower corridor was the darker pink of the bottom of the pool. It was damp, but there was no standing water. The pool had drained through it, not into it. At the bottom of the stairs, the corridor to the left ran straight for approximately thirty meters and ended—although light and shadow suggested a ninety-degree turn and the corridor continuing. To the right, it did the same although it also curved around the end of three enormous cones, narrow ends anchored in the body of the ship, stone following the same arc as the pool on the level above .

"Engines," Wen said, after a visual examination. "Ship takes off, it'll slag this level."

"The ship is an antique," Sujuno reminded him. "Older than antique. What makes you think it'll work?"

Wen shrugged. "Everything else has."

She couldn't argue with that. They'd expected ruins and faced a fully operational security system. The H'san built to last. Some of what they'd built even made sense.

"Where's the machinery that lifted it through the pool?" Nadayki demanded, head turned three quarters of the way around as he stared up between the ship and the wall. "For that matter, where's the floor of the pool? And what's holding this in place besides bits of Broadbent?"

"The H'san move in mysterious ways," Dion told him, and Sujuno wanted to smack the smug, sanctimonious smile right off his face.

Nadayki straightened and smiled back at him. "Fuk you."

"We're wasting time, people! Let's get this area secured!"

Verr patted Toporov on the arm as she passed. "Thanks for checking that the decibel security is still off, Sergeant."

The straight walls of the corridor were bare, but the curve that circled the ship had been covered in multiple lines of inset stone.

"That's a lot of H'san. How do we find which one we need?"

"Don't touch it!" Dion grabbed Keo's arm and landed on his ass up against the far wall.

"Sorry, you startled me." She flexed her exoskeleton. "Don't know my own strength." She hadn't bothered to sound sincere, they were all aware she knew her own strength down to the micro-newton. "And I wasn't planning to . . . Why does it smell like shit down here?"

"Broadbent." Verr's voice boomed against the walls, the

sound wrapping around the engines, smacking against the straight wall of the corridor, and curving back around. "He's been crushed. Bowels blown out all over the place. There's barely five, maybe ten kilos of uncorrupted meat." Shaking her head, she appeared around the left side of the curve. "What a waste. Oh, and the H'san shit, as opposed to Broadbent's shit, goes all the way around, Major."

Dion ghosted his hand a centimeter above the wall. "Not shit. Letters. Words. Sentences."

"Thank you, Professor . . ." After nearly seven tendays of Dion, Sujuno figured she could handle anything the progenitor bureaucracy threw at her. "I understand how language works. What do the sentences say?"

"I don't know." His eyes were locked on the marks they'd been following, flicking by screen after screen on his slate. "There's a possibility I could find familiarity and extrapolate from position and context, but it could take years. Decades. This is a lifetime's work. This is the kind of find H'san scholars dream of."

"Illegal?" Nadayki snorted. "Or just boring?"

"Lieutenant, was there evidence of a door . . ." At this point their working definition of *door* had become somewhat variable. ". . . back there?"

"Didn't see one, Major."

"All right." She turned to Toporov. "We go out two groups; one left, one right. Fifteen minutes out, then back."

She went left with Keo and Nadayki and Verr. Toporov, Wen, and Dion went right. Dion had insisted he stay behind to work on translating the curved wall, but Sujuno played to his ego and convinced him the sergeant would need help should they run into new writings by the H'san.

"Don't trust him on his own?" Nadayki asked as they reached the corner.

"Nor you," she replied.

The light hadn't lied and they turned right into yet another corridor that appeared to have no end, walls joining at a distant vanishing point. The left wall was unbroken stone. Ten meters from the corner, they passed the first of three large metal doors on the right.

"What do you think is behind there, Major?"

"There were centuries' worth of dead H'san interred on this planet. I assume the doors lead to new catacombs."

"Or maybe the shipyard where they built that shuttle," Keo said, fingers trailing over the metal of the third door.

It wasn't that far-fetched a theory. She had no idea why she was so certain they weren't the doors to the weapons cache.

"Holy shit, they're . . ." Keo snatched her fingers back. ". . . vibrating?"

The distant slam of metal against stone caused Sujuno's hair to lift and while she forced it down, the three of them stared at the doors.

"That wasn't our door." Verr twitched, toes flexing against the floor. "But if there's another corridor like this to the left, then who's to say there aren't other doors?"

Sujuno started to run back the way they'd come, the others falling in behind her. Her boots slid against the slick stone as she cornered. She braced herself against the wall, grabbed Keo as she slipped, and together they raced for stairs and the ship. Almost there, they saw Toporov, Wen, and Dion running toward them, the sound of boots and bare feet echoing back from the hard surfaces of the surrounding stone.

Dion held his arm across his body, fingers dripping red, and it wasn't hard to see that only Toporov's grip on the back of his jacket kept him on his feet.

"We found the entrance to the weapons cache, Major."

Her heart pounded too violently for her to speak.

"What happened to him?" Nadayki demanded as Verr checked her bonded.

"He tripped the defenses." Wen pushed Verr's hands aside.

And Sujuno realized that the sounds of boots and feet had stopped, but the sound of marching, of claws, of buckles and leather, had not only continued but had grown louder.

"Sergeant?"

He shot a glance over his shoulder and his face wore an expression as close to panic as Sujuno had ever seen on an NCO. "Incoming H'san, Major."

Her hair pulled free of her control and clamped close. "All

H'san on this planet are dead, Sergeant."

He shook his head as though denying what he was about to say. "Yes, sir, they are."

She glanced at the stairs. From the top, they could hold the stairway. Hold it. Block it. Blow it up. But the sergeant said they'd found the entrance to the weapons cache—her mind skittered past what exactly he'd just agreed with—and the entrance was on this level. If they went up, would they ever get down again?

. . . travel only forward.

Thirty meters to the corner. An infinite corridor beyond that.

"We found the entrance to the weapons cache, Major."

. . . travel only forward.

"Run," she said.

SEVEN

"Exiting Susumi space in ten. Everyone, strap in."

"You expect to hit something, Ryder?" Werst asked over the sound of the entire team pulling webbing into place.

"No." Craig leaned right and dragged a run of scrolling equations closer to the center of the board. "But uncertainty'll cark you before expectations. We've only got Presit's word that her equations were for the H'san's system of origin—at this point, who's to say the H'san aren't keeping the Katrien away with false coordinates? Satisfy curiosity, assume they'll never be used. I have no idea what we'll exit into." The ancient chair complained when he shifted his weight. "And when I say *into*, I hope I don't mean that literally."

"Presit wouldn't kill you." Binti sounded sure.

"Not on purpose. I'll withhold my opinion on the H'san's intent until after I know we've survived the jump."

"Wow," Alamber muttered. "That's grim."

Sitting second, Ressk twisted far enough around to see Torin's face. "Gunny?"

"I'm withholding my opinion on his pessimism until after we've survived the jump."

Craig laughed, reached back, and squeezed her calf. "Sounds fair."

They emerged just outside the elliptical orbit of an icy dwarf planet about as far from the red giant as they could get and still be in the system. If there'd ever been enough traffic for a buoy and a web, there wasn't now. With nothing in their way, they rode their momentum in, engines off, scanners on and slaved to the maneuvering thrusters—at the speed they were going, flesh and blood didn't have a hope in hell of reacting to a potential collision before it became actual. And over.

Thumbing her webbing open, Torin stood, stretched, and folded her arms on the top of Craig's chair. "Well, what've we got?"

"There's another dwarf, almost at its far aphelion, a gas giant we're going to pass at an uncomfortable 3.7 million kilometers—probably far enough out to avoid the gravity well, but that is one fuk of a big planet."

"Thus the term gas giant," Alamber muttered, draping himself over the back of Ressk's chair. Ressk reached back and smacked his leg, indicating he knew the di'Taykan was there rather than with an intent to do damage.

"After the *gas giant* . . ."

Torin grinned at Craig's emphasis. Alamber's hair flipped him off.

". . . we'll cross the remains of an asteroid belt. Fortunately, the belt's close enough to big G, most of them were probably sucked in, minimizing the potential for impact. Finally, over there . . ." Craig pointed left. Torin didn't bother looking, she knew she wouldn't see anything she could understand. ". . . is a planet at the inside edge of what was the habitable zone before the star went red. Nine and a bit AU. Everything closer in, fried. Three habitable planets," he answered before Torin could ask.

"But if this is the right system, the H'san got everyone out, right?"

"That's what history says." Torin appreciated Binti's caution. As they hadn't been greeted by signs saying *welcome to the H'san's system of origin, proceed at own risk,* they were still relying on Presit's information, ignoring, for the moment, the accumulating evidence that suggested there was history the Elder Races hadn't shared. "Any sign of the defenses Presit mentioned?"

"Not this far out."

"If this is the right system and the coordinates are available . . ."

"To the right people," Alamber interrupted, making *right people* sound like an insult.

"Available to the right people," Ressk amended, repeating the emphasis, "then the H'san clearly don't give a shit about visitors this far out. Any defenses will be protecting the planet with the weapons cache, keeping non H'san from landing, and we're about twelve hours out from being able to pull any readings. Until we get something that says stay away from our ancient weapons or we'll kick your ass, we could be anywhere."

Staring out at a whole lot of nothing, Torin shook her head. "If she had to do this run every two tendays, Jamers must've been bored spitless."

"She wouldn't have done this run more than once." Torin stepped to the side as Craig leaned the chair back, then tucked back in against his shoulder as he swung his feet up on the edge of the panel, still talking. "Once she had a chance to look around, she'd adjust her Susumi equations to match the orbital path of her destination and slide in tight and tidy. It's what I'd do."

"Is it? Well, if working for Justice ever gets dull, we could always try smuggling."

He wrapped an arm around her waist. "Torin, love, you couldn't smuggle a ship's biscuit unless you were convinced it was for the greater good."

"Hey, I could . . ."

A piece of biscuit bounced off her elbow, and she turned in time to catch a second piece. Binti grinned and ate the rest. "Not a chance, Gunny. Listen to your pretty man, he's right."

The gas giant was beautiful up close. Swirling bands of purple and yellow and gray—darker at the poles, lighter at the equator.

Perched on the edge of the pilot's chair, Ressk leaned forward, toes digging into the padding. "Weird."

"What is?" Werst asked absently, distracted by the muscles flexing in his bonded's feet.

"When's the last time you saw a gas giant without a harvesting station or six?"

"Sixty satellites in orbit, powered up and scanning. I'm not reading weapons . . ."

Civilian salvage operators had specs for every Confederation and Primacy weapon. No one wanted a salvaged hunk of metal to blow up their ship. Torin suspected they had some of both allied and enemy specs *before* the Corps got them. Specs for H'san weapons, on the other hand, hadn't been included in Intell's IP. No one had been surprised.

" . . . I am reading a shitload of high energy crap I can't identify, so I'm going to step into our metaphorical vacuum and suggest that's what'll fry us."

"Agreed." They looked enough like weapons signatures to Torin; she had no trouble labeling them as such. There was plenty about astronavigation she still didn't understand, but weapons, weapons she knew. "Or if not fry, hold us until the H'san arrive."

"And then what?" Binti demanded.

The whole team was back in the control room.

"We disappear," Werst growled.

Ressk tapped the board and scowled down at the new line of numbers. "Or they wipe our minds."

"Or use us as slave labor in the cheese mines of Traxus." Alamber's hair was a pale nimbus around his head.

"I think that's covered in *we disappear*," Binti said thoughtfully after a moment.

Werst made a noise halfway between disbelief and insult. Binti bounced a wadded-up piece of rice paper off the back of his head. Alamber laughed. When Torin cleared her throat, Werst pointedly ate the paper and sat down.

They all needed to get off the ship and do something. Torin looked at the planet in the distance and shook her head. "And then nothing good happens," she said. "What about ships in orbit?"

"No ships. And no energy trails either."

"I found . . ." Ressk began.

Craig cut him off. "You didn't find a trail."

"I found mathematical evidence of multiple trails. One of them significantly larger than the rest. I think this is the right place, and I think both Jamers and her employers are using a brush."

Torin raised a hand before Craig could protest again. "A brush?"

Alamber answered before Ressk had a chance. "It's a burner that disperses your trail. They've been a rumor in the darker corners for years. If someone's actually managed to build one that works, that takes all the variables into consideration, then that someone is a decent engineer and a fukking brilliant coder. I'm in love."

"Good for you. Don't let it affect your aim."

He grinned. "Never has before."

Torin ignored the increasingly salacious suggestions of what he'd been aiming at and tipped Craig's chair back far enough for her to see his face. "So, a burner?"

"Possible," he admitted reluctantly. "Probable even, if Presit sent us to the right place."

"It raises the odds that she has." Torin let the chair drop level again. "Are we in danger?"

"From the satellites? Not yet. Ressk's right, they're set up to keep people from landing."

"Keep scanning, then. We need to know how to get past them."

"You think?"

"Gunny. We found their ship."

"On my way." She dropped off the back of the treadmill, grabbed a towel, and peered into the complex system of ropes and pulleys dangling in the corner. "Coming, Werst?"

"No." He grabbed a passing line with his left foot. "Not until I can hit something."

"How could the satellites miss that?" It wasn't a small ship. Even allowing for Craig pulling the front port to full zoom, it looked at least as large as *Promise*'s current configuration.

"We're not reading it either, Gunny." Toes gripping the edge of the panel, Ressk's fingers flew over the board. "It's eyeballs only. Invisible to nonorganics."

"Love the twisty and brilliant mind that came up with the code," Alamber murmured, hair sweeping slowly back and forth. "The blocker's essentially broadcasting *you don't see me* so sincerely that tech doesn't see it." He slid around in the pilot's chair, unable to turn it due to Craig's white-knuckled grip. "We need a third station, Boss. I can't work under these conditions."

He had a point, Torin acknowledged. Alamber and Ressk together had been able to beat every security system they'd come up against, but doing it on the move left Craig standing and required a dangerous game of musical chairs if they needed to maneuver—like during those instances when they were in range of multiple satellites armed with unknown weapons. And gods help them if a situation arose where Binti needed to shoot back. By law, nonmilitary craft were unarmed, but salvage ships carried cutting lasers and *Promise* had kept hers when she'd changed trades. No one who'd ever used a benny during a boarding party would argue against a cutting laser being a weapon. "I'll bring it up with Justice next time we're docked. If Justice is still speaking to us after this." She frowned and leaned in, uncomfortable behind Ressk's chair, but refusing to admit it. "Is that a second Susumi engine?"

"It's probably the Susumi off Jamers' ship. She unhooked so she could land, hooked it to the larger ship to take advantage of their block. There's a shuttle missing off the big ship as well."

So Jamers was dirtside with their grave robbers. "Looks like we're in the right place."

"Looks like you owe Presit an apology for doubting her."

"Not if she doesn't know about it. Besides, I didn't doubt her, I doubted the H'san. All right, while you work out how they got down without being shredded . . ."

"Odds are they put the same blocker on their shuttles."

". . . and duplicate it, let's cut off their escape route. Mashona, to the control room."

"On my way, Gunny."

"You figure we can fit the grave robbers and Jamers in here?" Craig asked in the silence that followed Binti's response.

Judge. Jury. And executioner.

If they worked out a way to get past the satellites and down to the planet, they'd be the only ones leaving.

"They'll fit in the gym." Werst wouldn't meet Torin's eyes when she turned. "We can slack off for a while."

She assumed Alamber would redirect the conversation. He didn't. Like Ressk, he kept his eyes on his screens, but they were both listening.

Craig folded his arms. "We don't know how many there are."

"So they'll be crammed in."

Or they might not.

Judge. Jury. And executioner.

Just before the silence stretched to the point where Torin would have to remind them of what their orders had been, Alamber sighed and said, "Won't a dead ship in orbit eventually get noticed by the H'san? I thought we weren't supposed to be noticed."

"We aren't," Torin began.

Craig cut her off. "Once we get her Susumi equation, I can tow her. I've towed bigger wrecks." The fingers of his left hand dug deep dimples into his thigh. "Salvage I can deal with."

Judge. Jury. And executioner.

What couldn't he deal with? Torin wondered.

Binti stared at the grave robbers' ship. "If I hit it right . . ." She pointed at something no else in the control room could see. ". . . there, I can disable it."

"And if you don't?"

"Then boom."

"Boom is bad." Craig reminded them, although none of them, singly or collectively, needed reminding. "If any debris heads dirtside, the satellites could backtrack the shot and decide we need to be dealt with."

"Not to mention the radiation wave from the Susumi engines," Ressk added dryly.

"And that." That uncontained Susumi radiation only affected organics at the cellular level wasn't particularly comforting. Torin had always been fond of her cellular levels. That said, she trusted Binti to make the shot. She'd trusted her to make harder shots. "Since sweet fuk all about this has been under our control, let's at least stop them from running. Do it."

Binti took over Ressk's chair. Rolled the tension out of her shoulders. Pulled up the cutting laser. Set it on pulse.

"Wait!" Eyes still locked on his screens, left hand dancing over numbers, Alamber waved his right, hair waving in time. "I've cracked the satellite system!"

"Hairline crack," Ressk snorted, ducking the di'Taykan's flailing arm and leaning in over his lap to check the scrolling code.

"Got further than you got, old man."

Ressk snapped his teeth together.

Alamber murmured, "Promises, promises." And then continued. "The block they used that's keeping instrumentation from spotting the ship? It's not just on the ship. It extends into the lower atmosphere—it's why they bothered setting up a geostationary orbit. If we stay inside that narrow corridor, it'll not only keep the satellites from spotting us but take us right to where they landed."

Binti lifted her hands away from the laser controls and glanced up at Torin.

"You're sure?" Torin wouldn't have asked any of the others— her ex-Marines, Craig—if they weren't sure, they wouldn't have spoken. Alamber's more flexible world view made his definitives surprisingly malleable.

He opened his mouth. Closed it. And finally said, "Eighty percent sure, Boss. I can't get any further into the satellites without being spotted."

"Ressk?"

Ressk backed away, shaking his head. "If he can't get in, I can't get in, Gunny."

Twenty percent chance of dying, then. "Everyone gear up. Shuttle in fifteen." She could live with twenty percent.

"I'll lock the board." Craig moved Alamber out of his seat. "How narrow a corridor?"

"Please," Alamber blew out a dismissive puff of air. "There's plenty of room. It's four meters, six centimeters wider than the shuttle."

Two meters, three centimeters on each side. For all Craig owned vacuum, he didn't have the hours in on VTA. Torin shifted the odds to a twenty-four, maybe twenty-five percent chance of dying. Still doable. "Marines, meet me at the galley in ten."

Halfway out the hatch, Binti glanced over at Werst before asking, "For snacks?"

"For weapons."

"*Chrick!* Not," Werst added hurriedly, "that I want to shoot someone, I'm just tired of feeling naked."

Torin thought of how she'd felt before the drop to Abalae. "I understand."

Alamber grinned. "I like feeling naked. I like feeling you na . . ."

"Gunny?"

"And that's why we keep the guns locked up."

It didn't look like secure weapons storage. It looked like a drawer for storing perishables. Enemies boarding the *Promise* would first have to find where the weapons were being kept, and then get it open without Torin's DNA.

"Look, if anyone gets as far as this drawer, they're already well armed and my DNA has been spread out over a few parsecs of space."

While acknowledging that the entire point of using Torin's team was that some people couldn't be stopped by the Justice Department's current methods, the Wardens still hadn't been happy about it.

Torin winced as the needles jabbed into the fingers wrapped around the drawer's handle. Prints weren't enough, the security system required living blood and, once disengaged, more paperwork than Torin had ever seen, and she'd filled in as Sho'quo Company's First Sergeant for a while before the drop to Silsvah. She assumed the paperwork was Justice's guarantee that she'd open the drawer only when absolutely necessary. They weren't wrong.

"What are we going to tell them?"

She turned to Ressk. He was already in the modified version

of combats Justice allowed them, minus the boots, and he didn't look happy.

"I can't scrub the lock report without scrubbing the ship's entire memory." He squatted beside her as the drawer opened, her identity confirmed. "Alamber thought he could corrupt the file, insert joke here, but after about thirty-six hours, he had to admit defeat." When Torin raised a brow, his nostril ridges closed slightly. "We heard Colonel Hurrs' orders the same time you did, Gunny, and we had time in Susumi to fill."

The first KC-7 was Werst's, but Ressk was there, he could help. Hers next. Then Binti's.

"Gunny?" His tone was a worried poke. "What are we going to tell the Justice Department when they ask why?"

"I . . ." Torin emphasized the pronoun as she reached up and set Binti's scope on the counter. ". . . don't know why, not yet. When I'm sure, that's what I'll tell them."

"Yeah but, that's . . ." He stared at her for a long moment, then nodded. "Okay."

She pulled out an ammo pack and wondered what he saw.

The shuttle cabin looked a lot like *Promise*'s control room—six chairs instead of five, three rows of two; pilot, second, four passengers. Behind, a small cargo hold. The biggest differences were the weapons stations to both port and starboard—the weapons removed before decommissioning. Every now and then over the last year, particularly when Justice could give them no definitive answer on the firepower they'd be facing, Torin considered using Alamber's contacts to pull a couple of missile launchers off the black market. It wasn't the law that stopped her—she wasn't sure how she felt about discovering that—it was that, in the end, with a fairly good idea of how those "contacts" would respond, she refused to add herself to the list of those who used Alamber.

Discolored patches in the gray paint and empty sections behind unlabeled panels indicated that the weapons weren't the only things missing. Torin figured if the Navy wanted to clean and shine before they designated the shuttle as surplus, she was all for it. Werst had pointed out that no one had wanted the Navy's porn stores anyway. Alamber had begged to differ. Which had led to a conversation about begging and differing Torin was still trying to forget.

"I'm not reading surface water." Torin, a fan of knowing what kind of shit they were likely to land in, had no problem giving up the second seat so Ressk could work the scanners. "Looks like we were right about what supplies Jamers was bringing in."

They'd loaded water enough for five days. Two and a half days in, Torin would have to make a decision about whether or not they continued the hunt. She could only hope that people who didn't give a shit about the death that would come with another war would give an equal lack of shit to covering their tracks.

"Didn't someone say this planet was inside the edge of the old habitable zone?" Binti asked, securing the knives in her boot sheaths. "Doesn't habitable require water?"

"Variable definitions of habitable?" Werst offered.

"Surface water probably burned off when the star went red. It's a good thing there wasn't more oxygen in the atmosphere or we'd have lost that also and would have to spend our entire time dirtside in HE suits." As it was, the Humans wouldn't be running any marathons, and the Krai were likely to get headachy and cranky. Crankier. Alamber would be happy about the air quality and unhappy about the heat, although the environmental tech in his clothes would deal with most of it. She made a mental note to prod Justice once again about getting them actual combats. Half the people they faced had managed to find sets, and it pissed her off that while her team had to wear biometric cuffs to synchronize their medical data, the bad guys got to take advantage of embedded tech significantly better than that provided by civilian wear.

The snicker slipped out before she could stop it.

"Gunny?"

"Just thinking about choices." She'd agreed to work behind Justice's back. To lie to every person in known space except two Intelligence officers and the five people on the shuttle with her. But she drew the line at buying black market combats. There was something very fukked up about . . .

The shuttle jerked. Torin slammed up against her webbing. She heard swearing, boots leaving the floor and banging back down. A hundred drops had her teeth clamped together and her tongue safely out from between them. It sounded like Alamber hadn't been so prepared.

"Craig?"

"Lightning." Strain tightened his voice.

"This high?" They were still in the upper atmosphere.

"Apparently."

The shuttle wobbled.

They'd shifted close to a meter with the first hit. Five centimeters with the second. They had two meters three centimeters clearance. Still plenty of room.

Then the left side of the shuttle tipped up and they slid hard to the right, Craig swearing like a sailor—a steady and unimaginative stream of *fuk fuk fuk fuk*.

This wasn't her first drop while taking fire. She knew the feel of an energy weapon impacting with the solid plates of a military shuttle. She knew the smell of ozone. The feel of free falling in a heavy, spinning can with no way to control her descent. The need to trust in the pilot's skills because she had no choice. That this time the pilot was a man she loved made no difference to how much she hated the lack of control.

The maneuvering thrusters shoved her hard into the left side of the webbing. Held her there for one heartbeat. Two. Three. The spinning stopped and technically she supposed they weren't free falling any longer no matter what it felt like.

"This part always takes too *serly chricka* long," Werst snarled behind her.

"Brace for impact!"

"About fukking time."

Torin set her pack down in the shade at the base of a huge, red slab of rock and looked back along the impact ditch to where the shuttle rested, half buried in sand. They'd been twice lucky. First, that the satellites had only been able to get off one shot and, second, that Craig had threaded the shuttle into a gully instead of flattening it against one of the many cliffs. "Nice landing."

"Tell us another," Craig snorted.

"We walked away and no one's shooting at us. I'm counting it a win."

"You have very low standards."

She turned to find him squinting up at her, deep creases at the corners of his eyes. There was a still a smear of blood on his upper lip. His nose had turned purple and had begun to swell. He never tightened his webbing—said it interfered with his flying—and when the ship had hit, he'd slammed his face into the board. Only experience had kept her from overreacting to the amount of blood as she'd worked to get him free.

Later, when she checked his cuff, his stats indicated no real damage and it appeared the greater damage was to the tech; all five cuffs had stopped transmitting to hers. Or hers had stopped receiving. She hated not having access to the physical status of her team. *I'm fine* could and had meant anything up to and including broken bones.

But, this time, they'd all walked away.

Nothing broken, not even Craig's nose, no one badly hurt.

She smiled. He smiled back at her, the red between his teeth familiar. "They work for me."

"What do?"

"Low standards."

He laughed, winced, and spat a mouthful of blood to one side. "Lucky me."

"Maybe later."

"We can't be too far off course." Standing just outside the hatch, Ressk held out his slate at shoulder height. "If I scan for the Younger Races, I should be able to get a read on the position of the grave robbers."

Werst glanced up from where he was piling salvaged supplies up against the side of the shuttle. "You think they're stupid enough to leave organic evidence?"

"I think they're stupid enough to . . ."

The impact threw Werst about four meters and slammed him

down on his ass in the sand. "Ressk!" Nostril ridges shut, he forced himself up onto his feet and staggered back through the puddle of melted sand by the half-buried hatch. "Ressk!" He dropped to his knees when the sand grew too hot underfoot, but even a meter away, smoke stinging his eyes, he could see no remains. Smell nothing but scorched glass and steel. When he reached out to dig, a hand closed around his wrist just as the skin on his fingertips began to blister and pulled him back.

He fought. Against the hands holding him. Against the arm locked around him. Against screaming. Howling. Wailing.

"Hey! Werst! *Churick*! I'm okay!"

A familiar palm against his cheek. He blinked. Focused. Took a deep breath as the hands and the arm released him and fell forward against Ressk's chest, gripping handfuls of his jacket. "How?"

"I saved him."

Werst lifted his head to see Alamber grinning down at them, brushing sand off his clothes.

"It occurred to me, thinking about the H'san, that the way they're built, they've got to be all about redundancies, right? So, they're going to have something in place in case intruders actually get through the whole death by satellite thing and make it to the surface. I was about to point out that locking onto a slate—or the antique H'san equivalent—would make an efficient targeting system for that redundancy when I saw Ressk put thumb to screen, so I grabbed his ankles and hauled his ass back in the shuttle as fire fell from above. Metaphorical fire. I think it was actually the same type of high energy pulse that hit the ship."

As terror and grief bled away, Werst could hear adrenaline burning off in Alamber's explanation, see it in the speed pale hair flipped around his head. He touched his forehead to Ressk's, opened his nostril ridges so their edges touched, and exhaled. Then he pushed himself away—although not entirely away, his fingers still crushed the thick fabric of Ressk's jacket—and looked up at the di'Taykan. "Thank you. *Agro se terker tesergerr ih*."

His hair stilled. "You're welcome?"

"There's a life between us," he translated. "A debt."

"He cracked my elbow on the edge of the hatch," Ressk muttered. "Hurts like fuk."

"You're not a puddle of melted glass," Werst reminded him, punctuating his observation with a shake. He heard a soft huff of breath and turned to see Gunny's lips—it had been her arm around his chest—pressed into a thin pale line, Ryder's hand on her shoulder, and he remembered how Sh'quo Company had died, melted into the planet's surface by a Primacy weapon.

"I think we can safely say . . ." Binti poked her head out of the hatch and jerked back at the heat still rising off the ground. ". . . that the ancient H'san are a bag of dicks."

Eyes over the edge, Torin could see no danger, so she lifted herself up onto the top of the cliff. The Krai were better climbers, but she needed to get the lay of the land. Stepping away from the drop, she brushed off her hands and shifted the strap of her KC so the weapon rested more comfortably across her shoulders. Craig's flying had been even better and, given their speed, luckier than she'd assumed. He'd hit the only surface in sight that gave them a chance of surviving the crash, sand being more forgiving than rock. The plateau she stood on stretched out unnaturally flat, kilometer after kilometer of red granite, the edges of black slabs rising up at irregular intervals. A long shadow hugging the ground in the distance might be another cliff, might be low clouds.

Off to her right, the huge, red sun hung low on the horizon. The light seemed—not artificial, she'd spent a good portion of her life under the artificial lights of ships and stations, but like it had presence. Substance. Like they'd feel it sliding past their skin as they moved through it. She didn't like it.

Not that it mattered.

The gravity was a little heavier than home and a noticeable amount heavier than ships and stations. It wasn't optimal for any of them, but hopefully they wouldn't be here long enough for it to become a problem. The smell of scorched metal covered any local scents although she had to admit there were valid reasons the Human sense of smell was generally considered to be piss useless. The air was completely still and the silence a little unnerving.

Returning to the edge, she braced a forearm against her thigh and leaned forward until she could see faces staring up at her. "The people we're looking for are about ten to twenty klicks back that way." She jerked a thumb over her shoulder. "We might as well climb out here, I don't see a faster route. We'll secure a line and send the packs up first. Ressk, to me."

"On my way, Gunny." Coil of rope over his shoulder, Ressk started up the rock face.

Torin moved back, out of the way. Arboreal, no Krai would need help making a climb a Human had managed. Eyes on the horizon, the comforting weight of a weapon in her hands, she made a note of how clearly voices carried in the silken air.

"We can't use our slates. How does she know where to go?" Alamber protested. "It's not like she was looking out the window and spotted them on the way down."

"She was Recon," Werst told him.

"And what? That gives her magic mapping powers? 'She was Recon' explains exactly nothing."

"It would if you were a Marine."

"It would if I was a Marine? Seriously? That's really not helpful. And technically, doesn't Ressk owe me a life?"

"Shut up."

The black slabs were giant symbols set into the red rock, large enough they could probably be seen from space. If the whole planet was a cemetery, then odds were high they were walking across the surface of a massive tombstone. The odds were high everyone on the team had figured that out, but as no one else mentioned it, neither did Torin.

About fifteen kilometers from the crash site, the low shadow became another red rock cliff.

Breathing heavily, cheeks flushed, Alamber sagged against the rock. "Look, all I'm saying is that with the slates off, you can't tell how far we've come."

"We were infantry," Werst reminded him. "We humped over a shitload of terrain. Plateau's flat, Gunny's moving us at about six kilometers an hour, took us two and a half hours to get here. Fifteen klicks."

"Do we go up, Gunny?" Binti asked.

Torin shook her head. "Look to the left, about three kilometers along the cliff face. What do you see?"

"Big pile of rubble. Section of the cliff probably collapsed."

"Or someone dug into it."

Someone had.

A small mechanical digger had been partially hidden behind the pile of rubble that reached nearly to the top of the cliff. On the other side of the digger was a door.

Craig folded his arms. "I can't dux out what H'san were overcompensating for, but they're the opposite of subtle."

Binti moved up beside him. "It's very shiny. You'd think it would have dulled down over the millennia."

"Protective layer of dirt."

"There's that."

The door stood four meters high, three meters across, the top arcing up another two meters. Constructed of a bronze-colored metal, it had been outlined in black stones inset into the red cliff. The metal might have actually been bronze, but as they planned to open it, not go through it, Torin didn't care about its composition. A metal pallet, just large enough to hold the digger, rested on a packed dirt base to the left of the door. Connected by cables to a mechanical pulley system that hung out over the top of the cliff, the pallet held fourteen empty six-liter water containers. She ran her palm over the closest and frowned at the layer of grime.

"I wonder if it's locked."

"Don't touch it," Torin snapped, and Alamber froze, one hand reaching for the door. She swept her gaze around the ex-Marines. They shrugged out of their packs and moved toward the rubble.

"Alamber, Craig, wait here while we secure the shuttles." Torin leaned her pack against Werst's. "Stay up against the cliff and get out of sight if the door opens. We won't be long."

"And if they left a guard up there?" Craig asked, pushing Alamber's hand down.

"We still won't be long."

"Good thing a hardware-to-hardware hack still works," Ressk muttered as the telltales on the air lock turned orange and the outer door opened. "Don't let it close again, Gunny. I'm not a hundred percent sure I can do that again."

"Noted. You and Werst, secure Jamers' ship. Mashona, you're with me." Dividing up along species lines was a poor use of resources, but ceilings in a Katrien ship were no more than a meter and a half high.

The Taykan shuttle was empty. Torin flipped the catches on the floor plate leading to the engine compartment as Binti examined the weapons locker in the stern bulkhead. "Nothing in here, Gunny. Space for eight KC-7s and a rack for a 9. They've got a heavy. We should get a heavy."

"Someone in mind?"

"No, but I hate being outgunned. "So . . ." Her pause was weighted. ". . . our grave robbers are mercs. At least now you've got something to tell Justice."

"Half of something," Torin amended.

"Fair enough. Why hire mercs to go after the H'san weapons? There's nothing down here for them to shoot."

"Best guess, person who put the team together is military and they're sticking with what they know." Belly down on the floor, Torin reached in, slid her hand between two panels, and snapped out the SIE27.

"So they're following a map?"

"Or they're following a person holding a map or holding a list of clues or a historian's best guess. Or they're supporting rogue archaeologists. Doesn't matter, we're following them." She wrapped the circuit in the protective sleeve Justice had them use for evidence and tucked it in her pocket. According to the specs Craig had taught her back when they were nothing more than recently coupled civilian salvage operators—whose ships were often cobbled together out of a variety of spare parts—Taykan ships didn't carry a spare for the two-seven, and without it the engine wouldn't fire.

"We didn't hear any shots."

"We didn't have to fire any."

"Remember what to pull?"

Alamber's hair flew out and he snickered.

Torin raised a brow and Craig shrugged. "Takes so little to make him happy."

"I wouldn't say yours was little. Door opens in the center," Alamber continued. "Hair's breadth crack between them, and not my hair, a skinny Human hair. It opens out and there's nothing to pull."

"It's a theme," Ressk sighed, as Torin pinned the di'Taykan with an unimpressed glare.

"You tried the door." Torin's blood pounded in her ears, as half a dozen worst case scenarios clamored for her attention. "What if the door had been trapped?"

Alamber waved her off. "I'd have died a hero. Isn't that a Marine thing?"

"Dead heroes are a Navy thing," Werst growled. "Marines prefer live heroes; none of that single use shit."

"We're not Marines," Craig told her quietly, jaw tight. "But we're not entirely incompetent."

"The grave robbers are mercs," Torin told him. "Or with mercs."

"The door's still closed," Craig pointed out.

She took a deep breath and reminded herself that after the last year neither Craig nor Alamber could be considered civilians, having acquired the same sorts of skill sets that had shifted the rest of them away from being Marines. Glancing over at the sun, she noted that it hung distinctly lower on the horizon. "Then let's figure out how to get it open."

"That was close," Alamber said to no one in particular. "I hate it when *sheshan* and *irsin* argue."

Torin ignored him. "Zero the door. Mashona, one to ninety. Werst, ninety to one eighty."

"It's a dead planet," Binti pointed out as she moved into position. "What are we watching for, Gunny?"

"Zombie H'san?" Werst suggested.

"Don't even joke."

The door had been opened at least once from the outside. Therefore it *could* be opened from the outside.

"Hidden control panel?"

"Really fukking well hidden," Ressk muttered, running his fingertips over one side of the surrounding black stone. "If I had a working scanner . . ."

"Why not wish for a key?" Alamber answered. "And I already searched there."

"Using Krai senses?"

"Only if I ask first. How tall are the H'san?"

Torin lifted a hand. "About here."

"And their reach?"

"That's a little trickier."

Fingers spread, Ressk froze in place. "This feels rough, but I don't see anything."

Hair spread, Alamber leaned over Ressk's head and breathed against the stone, condensation rising in two shades. "There's a pattern."

"Black on black," Ressk said. "Yeah. That's brought up the definition. Do it again."

Another breath and Alamber stepped back and swept his gaze around the door, his eyes as dark as the stone. "The pattern's everywhere."

Torin did the same and saw nothing. "Do you . . . ?"

Craig shook his head. "Not a thing."

"Face it, Boss, Human eyes are crap. It goes all the way around. Black on black. Very stylish. Not carved, raised . . . Relief. That's what you call it in stone, right? Not actually . . ." He took another step back. Stepped in again. "It's not a pattern, it's lots of different symbols."

"Written H'san?"

"Not like the samples Intell gave us, but why not? Things change. The relief's too flush to throw a shadow, but that could be more because the light sucks balls. Big red balls." Shifting his attention back to the first piece, he ran his fingers over the area Ressk had identified. "Even seeing it's there, I can't feel the edges." He rubbed Ressk's head and danced away from the answering swing. "Yay, teamwork."

"Can either of you get a scent off the symbols so we can figure out which ones have been handled?"

Alamber shook his head, slid a hand beneath layers of fabric and began to scratch. "Normally, I'd be all about the handling, but honestly, Boss, I'm hot and sweaty and I can only smell myself right now."

"And it wouldn't hurt if you hiked your masker." Craig shifted his weight from foot to foot.

"It's as high as it'll go. But I can take care of that for you."

"Let's concentrate on getting through the door, people."

"I'll try." Ressk moved forward, nostril ridges flaring open. "Jamers has to be about my height so there's no point in checking above my reach."

"Maybe she stood on a box." Alamber rose onto his toes, graceful in spite of heavy boots, and waved his hand above Ressk's head. "Then took the box inside with her. Or rang the bell for entry and they sent someone up to open the door."

"We'll leave that as a last resort."

"Why would a tomb have a bell?" Ressk asked absently as he tucked his face in close to the stone. First the left side, then the right. "Right here, there's a concentration of Katrien." His lip curled. "And not healthy Katrien either."

"Jamers?"

"I've never met her, Gunny, how the hell would I know?" He stepped back, nostril ridges fluttering, and used a finger to delineate the edges of the scent. "Here to here to here. Roughly."

"Mashona. Werst."

They turned and took up positions covering the door. Torin ordered the others back behind the rubble and rested her palm against the stone. She wanted to say it felt greasy. She wasn't positive it didn't. Alamber could see it, Ressk could feel it, she could take the risk. "On three. Two. One."

She felt the click as she pushed although, as far as she could tell, the stone under her hand didn't move.

The door swung silently open, exposing a long dark corridor.

"It's not just me right? That's creepy." Alamber peered over her shoulder, not quite touching but close enough she could feel the heat coming off his body, his pheromones making her skin feel too tight.

"It's an empty hall and an automatic door," Torin muttered, moving forward. "Now get clear and stay put." The grave robbers had left evidence of at least one piece of heavy equipment in the lines of scoring that cut across the threshold. The distance apart looked familiar and Torin added anti-gravity sleds to the list of things shut down by H'san tech. They'd have had to flip out the metal wheels and wheels, especially with the weight they seemed to have loaded, meant they'd be moving significantly slower than with a working AGS. Slower was good.

She saw nothing she recognized as a trap, realized that meant SFA, and stepped inside.

Lights came on, an illuminated line of glass ovals set into the rock. Level with her shoulders, they shed the same thick, red light as the natural light outside on the plateau. This part of the necropolis had been built after the sun had gone red. After the H'san had fled their planet of origin. After they'd given up war.

Another step. The ceiling was high, the corridor both long—the walls met at the infinity point—and wide. A balcony had been cut into the left wall about ten meters up, running the full length of the corridor, the stone balustrades carved into . . . *interesting* shapes. The stone, all the stone, was a slick pink. A closer look showed flecks of both red and gray but that wasn't enough to change her initial impression of climbing into the body of a living creature.

The air didn't smell the way imagination suggested a catacomb should. But then, the dead here had been dust for millennia; the air smelled of history, not rot. Analysis on both cuff and slate remained down, so Torin breathed in and, in her entirely unscientific opinion, the air in her lungs felt the same as the air outside. Had the grave robbers cracked a seal, allowing the air outside in? Or had the H'san built a ventilation system into a catacomb they then buried?

As long as her team could breathe, Torin didn't much care.

It felt five to ten degrees cooler than out on the plateau.

"Werst, on our six." She'd seen too many bodies to believe the dead required reverence, but she kept her voice low. Respectful. Less likely to be overheard by lurking mercs even if the response of the lights suggested none lurked in the immediate area. "Everyone else, inside. Stay close. Be quiet."

"Do we jam the doors open, Gunny?" Binti asked, matching Torin's volume.

"No. Let's not advertise our presence any more than we have to." They had a fifty/fifty shot the doors would stay open until they were deliberately closed or they'd close automatically the moment no one stood in the way. "Alamber, look around in here for the symbol that opened things up. The mercs didn't believe they were trapped, or they'd have tried to break free."

"We're calling them mercs now?" Craig asked, carrying her pack in.

"Evidence in the shuttle says armed ex-military. Mercs."

He nodded at her KC.

She shrugged. "We're the good guys."

"The mercs are working with more information," Alamber protested, peering up at the balcony, arms out from his sides so the cooler air could get in under his clothes.

"But our hearts are pure." A hand on his shoulder, Torin tugged him around to face the door. "It won't be up there; it's a door control."

"Yeah, but those freaky carved balustrades? They're like the symbols around the door. Letters, or whole words maybe."

"Still not going to be up there unless the last H'san out had a ladder." She pointed. "Pretend the H'san occasionally default to logic and search around the door."

It didn't take him long to find it. Pink on pink this time, not black on black.

"Probably a di'Taykan flying that Taykan shuttle, then," Craig said, squinting at the place Alamber insisted the symbol had been carved. "And the H'san either have good eyes or a sick sense of humor."

"Whole planet of dead people." Binti adjusted her grip on her weapon. "I vote sick sense of humor."

Torin agreed. "Werst, inside."

"We know the external control works, Gunny. Maybe, I should stay out here."

"We're not splitting up." The thought of one of her people on the other side of those doors, sat like a rock in her stomach. She beckoned him forward. "Clear the doors, people, let's see what happens."

The doors closed as silently as they'd opened. Torin nodded at Alamber.

The doors opened.

Thirty seconds later, they closed again.

"You know," Craig said thoughtfully, "I don't really care about them not telling us where their home system was—is—but I'm a little pissed about them hiding a way to keep machinery working perfectly after being left on its own for millennia."

Torin frowned at the wall. "Mark the spot so if Alamber's not with us, we can still get out."

"Why wouldn't I be with you?" Alamber demanded, hair expanding into a sudden, pale aurora around his head.

"Plenty of reasons," Werst told him.

Ressk smacked his bonded's shoulder and added, "Not all of them bad."

"Some of them bad."

"True."

"Mark the spot," Torin snapped.

The wall wouldn't take a mark. They couldn't chip it, carve it, or write on it.

Alamber's hair smoothed out as he purred, "I guess you'll have to take special care of me."

"Not in a crypt," Binti snorted.

"The dead don't care."

"You don't know that," Ressk said trying to scrape an arrow sign into the floor with the point of his knife. "Zombie voyeurs."

"Stop saying *zombie*." Torin frowned down the corridor, mostly to stop herself from smiling. Armed, taking a small team into enemy territory. Complete the mission. Bring her people out alive. This was the first time she'd felt settled in her skin since Colonel Hurrs had shown them a biscuit maker. "All right, they've moved on, but we're looking at approximately four klicks of corridor straight out with no way of knowing how much farther it goes or if they took a sudden turn at any point on the way. They left no sign out here . . ." The sled had marked the threshold but not the floor. "So we check the crypts—out of sight, out of mind, and anything they left behind is information we don't have."

The crypts, evenly spaced along the right wall, had no doors. Internal lights came on in the first when Torin stepped over the threshold.

"Yeah, that's not creepy at all," Ressk muttered, heading for crypt two.

The first crypt was a large, square room with a black stone sarcophagus, about a meter and a half high, taking up most of the floor space. The empty meter of space all around left barely enough room for an adult H'san. Black-on-pink symbols covered all the walls but the one with the door.

"Oh, sure," Craig muttered beside her. "These we can see."

Hands folded over her weapon, Torin studied words she couldn't read and thought about how the Confederation had been given form by the H'san, how the H'san had determined from the beginning what would and wouldn't be allowed. She thought about how they'd hidden their weapons when they gave up war rather than destroy them. She wondered what else they were hiding with their dead.

And so much for feeling settled.

"Torin." When she turned, Craig had a triangular piece of the sarcophagus lifted up out of place. "The corner's been broken off. You want to rob graves, you need to get the graves open."

He waited until she stood beside him before shining a light inside. It took a moment to separate substance from shadow.

"Six?" Craig asked.

"Maybe seven."

The sarcophagus clearly extended down below the floor line. Inside, multiple H'san lay curled in what might be a fetal position—with the H'san it was hard to tell. They were desiccated, not rotted. Flesh tight to bones, mouths and eyes sealed closed.

"Dehydrate before interment?"

"Probably."

He pointed. "Some arsehole's dug in."

The dead in the corner farthest from the break lay tidily interlocked, limbs around each other, wicker baskets tucked in curves and hollows. Under the break, the bodies had been tossed around, ends of broken bone gleaming, baskets empty.

"They're looking for something."

"The weapons?"

"Only if whatever map they're following stopped at the doors." She rubbed her thumb against the smooth stone. "Which it could have. They'd have to check every sarcophagus to make sure the weapons weren't in the baskets and/or hidden under the bodies."

"Because as unlikely as that is, that's what you'd do?"

"If I had incomplete information. A general location, but nothing specific."

"Lovely."

A moment later, it wasn't Alamber's yell that had her racing for the third tomb; it was the familiar sound of an energy weapon that followed.

Werst charged out of the second tomb as she passed, Ressk behind him.

"Mashona!" She caught the flicker from the corner of her eye and dropped to the floor, rolling over, weapon ready, nothing to shoot. On a hunch, she reached over and touched the place where she'd been standing. The stone was warm.

Werst's nostril ridges were shut, his weapon pointed at the far wall, his voice barely loud enough to hear. "It came out of the lights, Gunny, reacting to the noise. We take them out, if we *can* take them out, and we're in the dark."

"A security system protecting dead H'san," Ressk snarled softly.

Torin rolled up onto her feet. "Protecting a weapons cache that could plunge known space back into war."

"And that," Ressk allowed. "Guess we're in the right place."

"Plunge?" Craig asked as they ran toward the third tomb, boots making barely more noise than the Krai's bare feet.

"Too much?"

"Little bit."

The third crypt looked like the first. The symbols were in a different order—different words, sentences, obituaries—but, otherwise, an exact match, including the broken corner on the sarcophagus.

Just inside the door, Alamber leaned close to Binti's shoulder, hair jerking back and forth in short, quick arcs. His fingers weren't quite touching a strip of blistered skin that followed the curve of Binti's shoulder.

"She shoved me out of the way," Alamber whispered. "Took the shot meant for me."

"Second part of that was an accident." Binti nudged him with her hip, and he settled into the contact. "The security's sound activated," she explained when Torin came closer.

"Yeah, we got that; it took a shot at me in the corridor. You okay?"

"It's minor. Hurts like fuk, though." It looked minor, a finger-width burn, six centimeters long, and past it about a centimeter of her shoulder strap turned to ash. "I think," she continued as Torin checked the damage, "it's a warning to be respectful of the dead, and I stand by my observation that the ancient H'san were a bag of dicks."

"Not arguing," Torin told her. Craig shifted her out of the way, pulling the first aid kit from his pack. They'd needed a corpsman, he was as close to Navy as they had, and he wouldn't carry a weapon. She didn't . . . *no one* wanted him carrying a weapon. She took another step left until Alamber was close enough he could lean into her side. "What surprised you?"

"There's a body. Not H'san," he continued, before she could point out the obvious. Reluctantly breaking contact, he led the way around to the rear of the crypt.

A dead Katrien had been propped against the carved rock; her head flopped over onto her left shoulder, her fur dry and patchy, eyes glazed gray, lips pulled back off pointed yellow teeth. There were no visible wounds, except for the broken neck.

"You've seen bodies before." Torin dropped to one knee and tugged the worn shoulder pouch out from under a mangy elbow.

"Like you said, it took me by surprise."

"Jumped out at you?"

"Funny, Boss."

The Katrien's slate was an older model with nearly a full charge. It wasn't locked, so Torin flicked through to the first level. "The slate's registered to Jamers a Tur fenYenstrakin. I doubt she's lent it out."

"So they killed her. Because she was stealing from them?"

"Hard to say. It could have been an accident." Torin didn't bother trying to sound like she believed it.

Alamber hummed noncommittally, and held out a hand for the slate. "I'll see what she's got on it. Might be something useful. What do we tell Presit?"

"The truth. Jamers was dead when we found her. Wait here." She shrugged out of her pack, both shoulders at once, catching it easily before it hit the floor.

"Hey, Boss? Do you remember that vid Presit took when she and Craig found you guys on the prison planet?"

"I don't need to see the vid, I was there." He'd watched everything about her that Presit had shot, including rough footage that had never aired. Torin wasn't too happy about it, but she had no reason to stop him. Craig encouraged him. Sometimes, he watched with him.

"Right, well, the way Jamers' eyes are all glazed over and gray, it reminds me of the way Presit's eyes were when the gray aliens were leaving her brain."

Torin shot him a look of disbelief.

He shrugged. "What can I say, it's a creepy similarity."

"Keep it to yourself," Torin told him, shaking out a Corps body bag and laying it on the floor beside the corpse.

"I know Presit said she'd been gone for years, but I thought she'd be younger. Younger than Presit anyway. She looks old." He huffed out a breath. "And dead."

Jamers had been dead for a while; rigor had left the body and the flesh compacted under Torin's fingers. The moist interior had begun to rot. She wasn't wasting sympathy if there were gray aliens trapped in there.

Alamber watched her seal the bag, eyes dark, hair still.

"There's a hundred bits of the Corps you didn't pick up, but that you brought with?"

"I don't leave anyone behind."

"And you told Presit we'd bring Jamers out."

"And that." With the slates restricted, she had to set the charge by hand. The bag stiffened, pushed against her boot, then flattened. She flicked the ash to one end and poured it into the attached cylinder, having practiced the motion more often than she cared to remember. Her hand paused halfway to the vest she wasn't wearing and, grateful she had Alamber with her and not Werst who would have noticed the truncated move, she tucked Jamers into her pack instead. "Come on, let's tell the rest what you found."

The fifth crypt had pieces of torn paper on the floor, an empty coffee pouch behind the sarcophagus, and a crumpled filter. The eighth had a small pile of empty food packs, refilled with waste.

"I guess if you're willing to start a war . . ." Binti straightened and rubbed her palms against her thighs. ". . . you don't have a problem with littering."

"We carry ours out," Torin growled.

"If the H'san want to find out who broke in, they can build up a DNA profile by isolating epithelial cells excreted in urine." Alamber spread his hands when everyone turned to stare. "What? I picked up a lot of odd information working for Big Bill."

"We carry ours out," Torin repeated.

"Hey, I'm on your side, Boss."

The sarcophagus in crypt twelve was the first the mercs had broken into at the far corner. If it had taken them that long to notice their previous vandalism would be visible from the door, Torin could only conclude grave robbing didn't attract the sharpest knives in the armory. A half a dozen pieces of ceramic had been shoved in on top of the bodies, and she'd bet this was where the biscuit warmer had come from.

"Loot abandoned on orders."

Craig shot Torin a silent question as he slid the broken corner back into place.

She shrugged. "When you've risked your life chasing the

enemy out, picking up a few things for yourself doesn't seem unreasonable. The Corps frowns on it."

"Egregiously?"

"What do you think?"

"Gunny!"

Again, it wasn't Ressk's shout that started them running, but the weapons fire after it.

"Garn chreen ta dirin avirrk!"

That, and the profanity.

"Fukking inedible testes?" Craig asked as they ran.

"Close enough."

Ressk was sitting on the floor across from the twenty-first crypt, Werst checking a burn that ran diagonally across his scalp.

"I think the security system had a little trouble calibrating for the lack of height," Alamber murmured as Torin stopped beside him.

Torin thought about the burn on Binti's shoulder, painful but not debilitating, and doubted it.

"Again nothing serious," Craig said as he sealed it.

"Hurts like fuk," Ressk growled.

"If fukking hurts," Alamber began. He stopped when Torin shot him a warning glare. "Oh, come on, Boss. Classic straight line. More than I could resist."

"Try harder. Can I assume," she returned her attention to Ressk, "you weren't shouting about a body?"

"Uh . . ." Ressk flushed, the darker green mottling across his cheeks darkening further still. "It wasn't so much about the body, Gunny, but where it was. Is. I got uncomfortably close." He nodded across the hall at the polished stone wall under the balcony. "Beneath the loop with the double curved lines through it."

Torin checked the railing, and crossed carefully. She couldn't see . . .

And then she could.

The floor had been laid in such a way that the missing section remained hidden until she was almost on it. Pit trap. Basic, but effective. Head up, she sniffed, smelled the five of them, the omnipresent dust, and nothing else. The lower temperature in the catacombs had kept Jamers from smelling much different than the dead H'san, but a body introduced to the bottom of a pit trap would have had its physical integrity breached and even a Human nose should have been able to smell that.

She moved closer, sliding her boots across the floor, and looked down.

Polished stone walls enclosed a square meter of air. Three meters down, the pink turned gray. At six, darkness. Evidence suggested not even the H'san put lights in a pit trap.

Directly over the pit, she thought she could catch a faint whiff of the unforgettable mix of shit and blood that lingered over battlefields and wondered how far the poor s.o.b. had fallen before hitting bottom. Were they standing dead center on the trap when the floor collapsed beneath them? Or had they been moving quickly along the wall and not seen the trap until too late?

"Do we drop a flare, Gunny?" Binti asked beside her.

"No. Whoever they are, we can't get them out, so we leave them buried with the H'san."

"Bag of dicks," Binti muttered.

"Still not arguing."

Crypt twenty-one hadn't been tossed. Nor had twenty-two, or twenty-three through thirty, all left to the dead without the detritus of the living. They returned to the pit trap together.

"All right." Craig folded his arms. "Where did they go? And if they kept going straight ahead, why did they stop searching the tombs for the weapons?"

"They weren't searching for the weapons," Torin said slowly, staring at the infinity point as she put the pieces together. She turned and looked down at the pit. "They were searching for a sign of where to go next."

"That's an emphatic sign."

"Could be another corridor at the bottom of the pit," Ressk said thoughtfully, one finger tracing the edge of the burn on his scalp. "If my scanner was working . . ."

"It's not," Werst snarled. Ressk got hurt, Werst got crankier. They'd all learned to ignore it.

"All I see is dark." Binti leaned in. "What do we do if there's an opening halfway down?"

"If you can go halfway, you can go all the way and get your people out."

"*You* could," Craig pointed out as Torin squatted and cocked her head, changing the way the light hit the wall on the other side of the pit. "What?"

"There's a chip out of the stone. I thought it was a fleck of the gray but from down here I can see the shadow. Alamber?"

He crouched beside her. "Oh, yeah. There. I don't see any symbols or anything, Boss, but the stone's smudged in a line about half a meter over and a meter up from the chip."

"That's it." She straightened. "Craig's taller, but Alamber's lighter." Hand around the di'Taykan's arm, she tugged him up. "Stand here. Lean forward, open the door."

He pulled against her grip, not enough to get free, only enough so she knew he wasn't happy. "What door?"

"The one under the smudges. Werst. Mashona."

"On it, Gunny."

She waited until they were in position, back-to-back in the center of the corridor, then checked that the buckle was as much functional as decorative before taking a hold of Alamber's belt. At her nod, Craig took the other side.

"If I slip . . ."

"I weigh twice what you do, kid. We've got you."

Hair flat against his head, he leaned forward and pressed a palm against the wall. A one-by-two–meter section swung away from the pressure. And closed as he released it. And swung open again.

"Looks like the pit on its side. Only taller," Ressk added after a moment.

The biggest difference was that passage behind the door ended in a rectangle, not a square, of darkness and that a hunk of ceramic—probably not a biscuit maker, but Torin wasn't taking bets—had been left leaning against the wall about a meter and a half in, a prop to keep the door open while they moved their gear through. The chip had likely been caused when the mercs had lifted the sled up into the passage.

"We're moving into an area with no apparent access to outside air. Filters on."

"I hate filters."

Filters for the Krai covered everything below their eyes, loose enough within the seal to allow for movement of their nostril ridges.

"You hate being gassed more."

Ressk didn't seem convinced, scowling as he slapped the clear film over his face and secured the edges.

When they—in every possible combination of *they*—found no way to manipulate the door from the other side, they left it propped open behind them. Since they'd ultimately closed it, Torin assumed the mercs knew another way out.

"If this gets narrower . . ." Craig touched the walls with his elbows. ". . . I'm not going to be happy."

"At least if the floor goes out you can brace yourself."

"There's that."

"How did the H'san fit through here?"

"Less chatter, people." Although the question about the H'san was valid. There had to be a limit to how far a sentient species could compact.

"Lights on, Gunny?"

Lights would paint a target on them should anyone be waiting at the other end of the passage or heading back toward them. On the other hand, the H'san had put a pit trap in with their dead within sight of the main . . .

She glanced back, shifting until she could see the perfectly square hole in the floor, too small for a H'san. Unless the floor had been designed to collapse in variable ways depending on who triggered it and a H'san standing on the same spot would have opened up a hole twice the size. One of her brothers had a game biscuit with traps that used those parameters. She wondered it if had been designed by the H'san.

"Torin? What are you thinking about?"

"That Mashona's right and the H'san are a bag of dicks." Turning her back on the pit, she shifted her pack. "Ressk and Werst, lights on, aimed at the floor. Ressk up front with me, Werst on our six with Mashona. Craig and Alamber . . ."

"Tucked snug in the middle, Boss?"

"No talking. No noise. We smell, see, hear anything, lights out. Questions? Let's go."

The PIDs—Personal Illumination Devices—clipped to the straps of their packs beamed golden circles onto the floor. Barely enough light to maneuver safely. Possibly enough light to be dangerous.

Torin set the kind of pace intended to eat distance without tiring the team unnecessarily and soon the sounds of movement, the circles of light, the smell of three species in an enclosed environment, became background and she could extend her senses beyond their position. She knew Werst and Ressk had fully opened nostril ridges and that Alamber's eyes were dark and his hair flipped away from his ears.

If the mercs were waiting ahead of them in the passage, if they'd set perimeter beacons Torin's team had tripped, then she was leading them into a shooting gallery.

After three hours and twenty-seven minutes, Alamber whispered, "Light ahead."

They stood in sudden darkness as both PIDs turned off.

Twenty-four minutes later, Torin could make out a patch of gray.

The gray grew paler and became a two-by-three–meter opening. What little sound they were making began to dissipate into what had to be a larger room beyond the exit.

"Hold here." Beckoning Ressk forward with her, she added, "Remember what was under the welcome mat at the other end."

Behind the faint glimmer of the filter, Ressk's nostril's flared. "Smells like . . ."

"Impact boomers," Torin said, edging up to the doorway, her back against the stone.

As her elbow broke the line of the door, the lights came on.

EIGHT

Torin looked out into the middle of another wide corridor an indefinite distance long; vanishing points to both the right and left, the opposite wall approximately six meters away. She missed being able to ping it, but the difference between approximate and exact was immaterial without the need to target artillery. Which she didn't get to do anymore. Although, it looked like someone had.

"Looks like they emptied the magazine," Ressk said beside her.

The entire visible length of wall they faced had once been covered with floor-to-ceiling, glass-and-metal display cases. Directly across from where they stood, the cases and their contents had been destroyed, broken glass and twisted metal and unrecognizable debris extending some distance beyond the immediate impact zone.

The mercs had cleared a path for the sled through the debris field exposing a floor made of tiny colored tiles laid out in geometric patterns, and she could clearly see where one of the sled's metal wheels had crushed the tiles on both sides of a grout line. The tiles were surprisingly delicate given that they were on a floor and Torin appreciated the new ease of tracking. Following the path, she could see where they'd made camp to the far right of the debris field.

Off the path, debris kicked aside indicated exploration in

both directions, but, as the sled had only gone one way, they could ignore everything to the left of the door.

Torin stepped out onto the mosaic floor and followed the path for a couple of meters, then turned to face the door—and the mural around it. Painted in brilliant colors unfaded by time, the door included in the painting's narrative, it depicted H'san using the artifacts in the surviving cases. Occasionally in ways Torin hadn't expected. Or believed possible.

Large and small chunks of the wall had been chipped out by flying debris, exposing the stone behind the ancient H'san equivalent of plaster.

"Museum, Gunny?"

"Cache. Museum implies access by the public." She bit back the urge to tell Ressk to be careful as he followed her out onto the floor. The Krai knew better than she did how to keep from lacerating their feet.

"Holy shit." Craig braced his hands against the walls of the passageway, leaned forward, and looked around. "What happened?"

"Fun with explosives?" Alamber suggested, peering over Craig's arm. "Hey, Boss, can we come out?"

"Stay close." She moved to study the pitted wall where the impact boomers had hit and counted two twisted pieces of metal that had definitely been weapons as well as another four possibles, too damaged or too H'san for her to be sure. The question was: why would the H'san target this entrance? And not merely target, six weapons aimed at a two-by-three opening could only be called targeting with prejudice. Who had they expected to emerge?

Someone going after the weapons cache. Someone who knew the route well enough to find a hidden door, but who didn't have the codes to walk it safely.

Someone who got lucky.

"Werst, check the passageway. See if the defenses got a shot off."

"You think their heavy gunner reacted to an attack?" Craig reached out, but didn't touch the wall. Torin had been pleased to see that salvage paranoia, where any hunk of twisted metal floating in vacuum post battle could turn out to be deadly, had made a direct transition to feet-on-the-ground paranoia.

"No, I think it was instinct," she told him. "Unless the defenses fired a warning shot first, no one's reactions are that fast. But a gunner who's seen enough combat, well, a sound, a flash of light, a change of air pressure . . ."

"I've got something, Gunny!"

The two-finger deep gully Werst found hadn't been blasted out of the rock. Or burned.

"Disintegrated?" Alamber offered, running a finger along the smooth rock at the bottom.

Craig snorted. "Disintegrator rays show up on bad vids, not in the real world."

"Well, if it turns out we're in a bad vid, that's all the more reason to make sure their weapons don't leave this planet. Let's move." She beckoned Ressk back to her side and stepped out onto the path.

"What about the filters, Gunny?"

The air still smelled of impact boomers, but was clearly circulating through both crypts and corridor—or was it a tunnel?—and cache. She had no idea if it had begun circulating with the mercs' arrival, or if it had been circulating for centuries for whatever reason the H'san had thought was valid. Nor did she care. With no apparent exterior access, they were in an enclosed, potentially hostile environment. Granted, given the size of the place, the H'san would have to either use one hell of a lot of an airborne toxin, aim it specifically, or drop partitions to create a smaller airtight enclosure, but all three options were valid ways to keep the curious or opportunistic or bugfuk crazy away from the weapons.

"Filters stay on."

The H'san's decibel-based security kept complaints at a quiet rumble.

What she'd thought was a pile of coarse white sand along the boundary of the merc campsite turned out to be broken glass. The mercs had left bags of waste behind again.

The sled's trail continued to the right, tiles crushed in a double line.

"Why would the H'san save all this shit?" Craig asked after

they'd walked past about a kilometer of shelving. "I mean, grave goods are a stupid waste, but a guy can wrap his head around the reasoning. This? This makes no sense."

Torin glanced over at a completely featureless ceramic cube and shrugged. "They gave up violence, but kept all their weapons. That's a good indication they don't like to throw anything out."

They passed three sections of destroyed mural, the stone exposed, the plaster ground to dust underfoot. By the time they got close to the point the mercs had exited the corridor . . .

"Eight klicks from the door," Werst said, shifting his pack.

"*Senak*," Alamber snorted.

. . . they were no longer following the floor so much as aiming for the destruction. Huge chunks of the mural, a priceless and irreplaceable piece of ancient H'san art, had been tossed aside to uncover a metal wall. They'd cut the hole to the dimensions of the sled. Flesh compressed, gear didn't.

Body out of the line of fire, Torin unclipped her light from the strap, bent, and pointed it through the hole. If the H'san remained consistent, the dark meant the mercs had moved on.

"Gunny?"

"New catacomb like the first, crypts on the right, balcony on the left. If the corridor has an end, the light doesn't reach it."

Craig stepped forward as she straightened and ran his palm over the edge of the cut. "The metal's a composite. I'm not sure of what." He picked at a chunk of mural still stubbornly adhering to the wall. It didn't budge. "No evidence of solvent. It would've taken the better part of a day to pry the mural off the metal and days to cut through, even given the size of their torch."

"How can you tell the size of their anything?" Alamber asked, innuendo surprisingly absent.

"Heat of the burn," Craig explained. "The hotter it gets the smoother the cut. This, this cut is slick."

That helped to explain the weight of the sled. The torch could be used as a weapon, but as the mercs were also conventionally armed, Torin decided not to worry about it.

"It's not a door," Alamber muttered. "How did they know where to break through the mural?"

Binti spread her hands. "Sign on the section they trashed: this way to weapons, cut here."

"No, there's a door here." Ressk touched the seam where the metal joined the stone. "It's the only place they uncovered between here and the destruction where the wall isn't stone. They couldn't find the door, they got frustrated, so they took a shortcut. See, there?" He pointed to where the edge curved dimpled up into a half circle. "They burned through there first to check visuals."

"But how did they know? Scanners aren't working and they couldn't have been randomly digging through the mural for metal. There aren't enough holes, not over a distance of . . ." Alamber shot Werst a look. ". . . eight kilometers."

"I'm telling you, sign on the mural." Binti huffed out a breath. "Misinterpreted the first few times, got it right this time."

"What, you think the H'san left a trail of bread crumbs leading to the weapons?"

"They left a map," Torin said, drawing everyone's attention. "Notes. A recording of interpretive dance. The means don't matter. They left a way for future H'san to check that the cache remained secure. Someone found it." She considered the need for the impact boomers. "Or part of it."

"Yeah, but how did they know where to . . ."

"It doesn't matter," Torin repeated, cutting off Alamber's question. "We go where the mercs went only we move a lot faster." When she twisted to find the angle to get both her and her pack through the hole, Craig touched her hip, his hand warm in spite of multiple layers between his skin and hers.

"Torin, maybe we should bunk in here for the night. It's been a long day."

"Time isn't our . . ." she began. And then the lights in the corridor went out.

"*Garn chreen!*"

"Didn't mean to grab that, Werst. Swear to you, I was startled."

Not surprisingly, Werst's light was the first on.

"You know the other place the lights went out like this?" Binti said through clenched teeth, shadows of her fingers dancing over the display cases as she adjusted her light.

"Prison planet?" Ressk growled, sounding more like his bonded than himself.

"Yeah. That'd be the place."

They weren't wrong. Torin could feel the weight of the prison bearing down on her, the lives ruined, the lives she hadn't been able to save. The gray aliens admitting responsibility for millions of deaths over five centuries—a social experiment and they were the lab rats. She could hear that weight flattening Werst and Binti and Ressk's voices and wouldn't add the force of her feelings to it. Part of her job was to help carry them. If she was fine, they'd be fine. That was how it worked. She buried her reaction—the anger, the guilt, the betrayal—under the sound of mild irritation. "Looks like we're taking Craig's suggestion and bunking here for the night. Head back about ten meters, set up against the wall."

As Alamber stepped forward, Werst reached up and tugged the beam of his PID toward the floor. "Down and close to your body, like in the passage. You don't want them to see yours if they're coming back. And we want to see theirs."

"Did you want to see mine?"

Alamber hadn't been one of the POWs. Torin had edited her report to the Justice Department to keep him *out* of prison.

Craig's fingers on her wrist, skin to skin as though she were di'Taykan and needed the comfort of touch, made her think of the look on his face when he'd arrived on that prison planet and pushed back the helmet of the HE suit. That memory was strong enough to help carry the rest.

"Gunny?" Ressk pointed his light at his cheek and flicked the edge of the filter glistening over his lower face.

They could eat through the filters. Field rations had a nipple designed to pass through the membrane and reseal it on the way out. But it wasn't comfortable and field rations were only just palatable as it was. She pried a corner off the lower edge of her jaw and ripped the filter off. "Give me a twenty count."

"Why you . . . ?" Craig began.

Torin cut him off. "Because I'm fast enough to get another one on if I start to react."

"And if it sneaks up on you?"

"The cuff'll show any deviation from Human norm."

Alamber's hair flipped up. "Any deviation?"

"That's twenty. Gunny?"

She took a deep breath and checked her cuff. "No effect."

"Yes!"

A few minutes later, rubbing residue off the bridge of her nose, Torin looked at the bag of pale paste—the Corps cooks hadn't bothered to make field rations appear any more appetizing than they tasted—and considered asking for a splash of the spices Alamber pulled out of his pack.

"You can have some of mine." Craig brandished an identical spice pouch, her thought processes apparently so obvious he didn't need to see her face.

"Taste buds dead of boredom or taste buds fried." She shook her head. "Tough choice."

If it hadn't been so dark, she'd have missed the flicker as Craig opened the pouch. Grabbing a fistful of his jacket, she yanked him sideways across her legs. Light splashed against the wall where his torso had been. The mural cracked.

Alamber keened.

Torin didn't see the flash that answered the noise, but she saw Werst move, hand over Alamber's mouth as he took the di'Taykan to the floor.

They'd gotten used to keeping their voices low, not forgetting, but adapting to what happened when they raised them.

Alamber's cry of pain had been loud enough to set off the beams, but before that . . .

"The spices. It's the only thing they had in common. Are you . . ."

"I'm not hit." Craig's palm pressed warm against her cheek as they untangled their legs.

Alamber lay with his head in Werst's lap, eyes squeezed shut, rocking back and forth, noises muffled against Werst's palm.

"Second beam hit the inside of his arm. Ashed the fabric, fried the skin." Binti ran her hands under Alamber's clothes. "I can't find the first."

Torin caught hold of her arm, stilled her. "I see it." She

adjusted her light to illuminate a two-finger–wide band of hair burned away on the left side of Alamber's head. The centimeter-high stubble seeped clear fluid from every hair.

"Oh, fuk . . ."

"Craig." Torin reached a hand behind her. "Sealant with the highest level of pain killer." The tube dropped onto her palm. She thumbed off the lid and sprayed a thick layer over the burn. The sense organs that were Taykan hair could be bent, broken, or cut with manageable levels of pain. A burn was excruciating.

Alamber shuddered and hiccupped damply as Werst uncovered his mouth. "Boss, I didn't . . ."

"I know." Torin tossed the tube to Binti. "It was the spices. They took a shot at Craig, too."

"Fukking bag of dicks," Binti muttered, sealing the burn on Alamber's arm.

"Spices?" Ressk had moved to kneel behind his bonded, chest pressed up against Werst's back, a second layer of support. "That's the definition of arbitrary, Gunny."

"The composition of the spices could be similar to an ancient threat."

"I thought the beams were warnings?" Craig asked softly over her shoulder.

"They set it up a millennia before they made contact with the Taykan." Alamber's pulse was thready and the skin of his throat damp under her fingers. The biometric in his cuff told her nothing she hadn't observed. "They couldn't have known."

"You defending this, Gunny?" Werst nodded at Alamber panting against his thigh, teeth clenched so tightly a muscle jumped in his jaw.

"No, I'm still going to punch the next H'san I see. I'll add this to the list of reasons."

Craig pressed closer, copying Ressk's position. "Shouldn't the sealant have dealt with the pain?"

"Not yet." Torin cupped Alamber's cheek and he nuzzled into her palm. "It needs to be absorbed by the hair shafts."

"You've dealt with this before."

She thought of flamethrowers on the battlefield and heated metal in APCs hit with heavy ordnance, and electrical fires as they fought their way through stations captured by the Primacy. "Once or twice."

Craig's warmth moved away and she heard him digging through the medkit. "I brought *duwar*. Diluted, but it should put him out for about six hours."

"That's a Taykan drug."

"He's a di'Taykan. Seemed relevant to bring it."

"Clever." Torin's fingers lingered on Craig's as he passed over the vial. "Alamber." His eyes when he opened them were so uniformly pale blue, she doubted he could see her. "I want you to drink this." She dimpled his lower lip with her thumb. "Come on, open. There's no reason to be conscious for the next few hours."

His tongue swiped against her skin before he gasped, "If they come?"

Didn't matter who he thought *they* were. "I'll carry you. Or Craig will. Or Binti. Or Werst and Ressk together. You know we can."

"Yes." He opened his mouth, swallowed, sighed, and a moment later the rigid lines of his body relaxed.

Torin released a breath she didn't remember holding. "Someone touches him at all times."

"We've got him, Gunny." Supporting Alamber's head with both hands, Werst edged back far enough that Ressk could move in and wrap an arm around his body.

It took a moment to remember the reason they'd volunteered. He'd saved Ressk's life at the shuttle.

"You two, keep his head stationary. Mashona, get his legs. We'll lift him onto his bedroll, then I want Craig to take a look at Ressk's head and Binti's shoulder."

"The sealant's holding, Gunny."

"He'll check anyway. On three. Two . . ."

"Why aren't I standing watch?" Craig murmured, lips resting against the edge of Torin's ear. He hadn't said anything while watches were being set because he didn't challenge her authority in front of the others. Privately, however, with their bedrolls overlapping, he wasn't asking Gunnery Sergeant Kerr but Torin.

She tightened the arm wrapped around his waist. "You'll stand tomorrow night, if we don't catch up."

"If we do catch up, there's going to be fighting. You lot need your sleep."

"If you're going to fly an unfamiliar shuttle out of here, you need to be on top of your game."

"An unfamiliar . . . ?" He frowned and thought about turning on his light so he could see her face. "What are you talking about?" He could feel her thinking about how to answer him. "Torin?"

She went still against his side. "No matter what happens down here, we're not leaving in our shuttle."

Ah. "I keep telling you, luv, that wasn't a crash. I'll cop to a hard landing, but our shuttle's fine."

"Our shuttle's engines are full of sand and if you start them, they'll be full of glass."

"That's nothing to be all big note about." When she didn't fill the pause left for argument, he sighed, lifting her head as his chest expanded. They'd taken everything not bolted down, but since they hadn't been in the habit of keeping anything on the shuttle that they hadn't planned to use dirtside, that had been easy enough to ignore. But he'd known. He moved his nose to feel the ache, to take himself back to the pilot's chair as they fell through the lower atmosphere. "Ressk scrub her clean?"

"He did. We'd have blown her, but we didn't want to give our grave robbers a heads-up."

Craig rubbed his thumb in slow circles over the inside of Torin's wrist and reminded himself they'd all walked away. "Guess it's a good thing I didn't get too attached. So who's going to skite the loss to Justice?"

"Colonel Hurrs owes us. He can explain."

That sounded fair. "So, the Taykan shuttle?"

"Bigger than ours. Probably faster."

"Faster's good. It won't be as tough."

He felt the warmth as Torin huffed out a laugh. "You need to work on your landings."

On the last watch, assuming the lights came back on, Torin sat and listened to her people breathe, listened for her enemies' approach. She doubted the mercs would be back this way until they headed out with the weapons—odds were, part of the weight on the sled was a second, collapsed sled. It didn't matter how silently the mercs moved; the sleds would give their position away in plenty of time. She also doubted she'd ever reach a stage where she could trust her enemies to act as anticipated.

Alamber's breathing—shallower and faster than normal, even with the sedative—hitched and Torin rose up on her knees beside his boots. She flicked her light on at its lowest setting and slowly moved it up the length of his body, until the reflected light off his chest allowed her to see that his eyes were open. He licked his lips, swallowed, did it again. Swallowed almost frantically.

Torin gripped his ankle, fingers up under fabric against skin, and handed him a pouch of water. Hands shaking, he raised it and locked his lips around the nipple. A moment later, she pulled the half-empty pouch from lax fingers as he slid back into an undrugged sleep, the undamaged part of his head resting on Ressk's stomach. Ressk's left hand cupped the back of his neck. Werst's right spanned the line of pale skin below the rucked-up edge of his tunic.

She tugged his arm free of the tangle and turned it until she could see his cuff. Watched it until his pulse slowed and his respiration evened out.

Seven hours and twenty-three minutes and seventeen seconds after the lights went off, they came back on, red and almost translucent for a few moments until Torin's eyes adapted.

She let the team spend as much time as she thought they could spare fussing over Alamber while she redistributed the contents of his pack, halving the weight he carried.

He pushed them away before she could call an end to it. "I'm fine." The hair on the uninjured side of his head flicked forward and he sucked air through his teeth. "Okay, I'm not fine, but as long as the sealant holds, it's bearable. Let's go already, so we can get the job done and get out of here because I'm not only in pain, I'm also stuck eating the same tasteless muck you lot do."

Torin met his gaze, nodded once, and shrugged into her pack. "Ressk, you're on point."

"Gunny, he's . . ."

"What part of *on point* do you not understand?"

The lights came on in the catacombs on the other side of the hole when Ressk's boot touched the floor.

"That's a lot of wasted meat." He readjusted his pack and stepped away from the hole, weapon ready. "I'll never understand the way most species treat the dead."

"Most?" Binti twisted her upper body and pack through on the diagonal.

"Ciptran males fight to the death for the right to mate and the females lay eggs in the thorax of the loser."

"Didn't need to know that."

The sled left no marks on the stone slabs of the new floor, but the mercs were searching the crypts again.

"Let's assume we're doing a wash and repeat of corridor one. Find a crypt they haven't tossed."

"That's a lot of crypts, Gunny."

Torin looked toward yet another vanishing point and squared her shoulders. She could identify human-scale objects at just under three kilometers, given reasonably decent light and air quality, but the corridor stretched empty for so long, it seemed like an optical illusion. "We'll be done sooner if we don't stand around talking about it."

"Oh, for fuk's sake, Ressk, we don't need to baby him; Alamber's a part of the team, he's not a civilian. Would you'd be this annoying if it was me?"

Ressk glanced up at her. "Hell, no. Not if it was *you*."

Binti laughed, the sound ringing in the enclosed stone of the crypt.

They froze, Ressk's hand around her knee. The burn on her shoulder ached, the skin pulled under the straps of her pack and her weapon.

"Suddenly not so funny," she murmured after a long moment.

* * *

"So you saw Marines get burned?"

"Yeah." Werst kicked the empty coffee pouch back behind the sarcophagus. Bring it in, carry it out; what the fuk was so hard to understand about that?

"Will my hair grow back?"

He was about to snap that Alamber knew more about di'Taykan hair than he did, but then he saw the look on the kid's face, the barely hidden fear. Apparently Big Bill hadn't set any di'Taykan on fire during Alamber's tenure on Vrijheid Station. "Sure, eventually. After the injured hair dies and drops out."

"Will it hurt the whole time?"

He remembered his Recon squad working their way through the woods. Their corporal had been hit with the backwash from a Primacy terraformer they'd taken out, turning the back of her head into seeping stubs. Almost a tenday later, the muscles of her neck had cramped with the effort she'd put into not moving her head. Occasionally, she'd whimper as though she couldn't stop the sound. "You've got the extra- strength sealant and that drug Ryder brought, so probably not."

"Are you bullshitting me?"

Werst met the kid's pale gaze and opened his nostril ridges. "Absolutely."

"Thanks."

"War dead?"

Multiple H'san had been put into the sarcophagus in pieces. Torin could see shattered bone and torn tissue and an arc of teeth held together with gold wire. Desiccated organs had been tucked inside the cages of exposed ribs and laid within the cradles of gleaming pelvic bones. Her brain insisted on the faint smell of rot, refusing to acknowledge the cleansing of time.

"I hope so."

As they moved to check again, three crypts down, she could hear the faint murmur of quiet conversations from the other pairs as they passed the open doorways.

"All we're doing is tracking the bad guys, and I still feel like we're being tested." She stared down at another sarcophagus.

"Find your way through a labyrinth of the dead to prove you're worthy to wield our weapons. We're not dragging along an unconscious egomaniac and no one's shooting at us and the catacombs aren't likely to make a Susumi jump any time soon, but there's a faint whiff of Big Yellow about this setup." Torin could feel Craig's gaze. When the silence extended, she turned to face him. "What?"

"What?" he repeated, brows rising. "Big Yellow was a colony. A fukking enormous colony of the gray aliens."

"I know." The sentient, polynumerous molecular polyhydroxide alcoholydes could combine into any shape, creating a hive mind. Twice now, enough of them had combined to become their own ship.

"I know you know." Gaze never leaving her face, he dragged both hands back through his hair. "And now you think the gray aliens learned how to lay out a mind fuk from the H'san? From the route to the weapons cache?"

"You don't." Not a question. He'd made it clear he didn't.

"You said yourself that the mercs don't have the whole map. Or all the notes. Or access to the entire interpretive dance." When she raised a brow, he grinned and the stiff line of his shoulders relaxed. "The interpretive dance bit stuck. And then you said, given incomplete map, notes, and dance, this whole bullshit treasure hunt only looks like a test because the mercs don't know exactly where they're going or how to shut off the security system."

Not quite what she said, but close enough for government work. "True."

"Yet you don't sound convinced by your own argument."

Torin took a deep breath and let it out slowly, forcing her thoughts to march in straight lines. The gray aliens had been around for a long time, long enough to engineer the interstellar war the Elder Races had been too evolved to fight. The Elder Races had trusted the Younger Races to fight, to kill, to die, but not trusted them with the coordinates of the H'san home system where the H'san, the Eldest of the Elder Races, had hidden the weapons they'd used to nearly destroy their civilization. What other information had the Younger Races not been trusted with? Had the H'san nearly destroyed other civilizations? Sure, the gray aliens had said the war had been a social experiment, but if the H'san could withhold information, why not the gray aliens? She wiped a sleeve over the smudges Krai feet had left on the polished surface of the black stone sarcophagus. "There's no plastic here. Not in any of the crypts. Not in the eight kilometers of display cases we passed yesterday. Lots of stone. Various metals. Rubber. Ceramic. Glass. But nothing that even looks like plastic." She shook her head at his lack of reaction. "You saw that, too."

He shrugged. "It was a long walk and as much as I love your ass, after the first three or four kilometers, I took a look around. Hell, it could be they decided not to waste fossil fuels on shit that gets thrown out. We don't know." Craig's expression changed as the last piece fell into place. "And that's your point, right? That we don't know what the fuk is going on."

"Hard to run a successful mission with bad intell."

He reached out and touched her cheek with the backs of two fingers. "I have faith in you."

"How long do you figure they searched before they found the next exit?" Lounging against her pack, Binti gestured with a circle of dried apple. "I mean, we're moving pretty damned fast and yet . . ." She waved a hand toward the vanishing point of the corridor. ". . . we haven't covered a lot of territory, relatively speaking, and we're already past their base camp for this sector."

"Easy enough to work out the approximate time once we find the next exit." Ressk frowned down at his slate, refusing to take as absolute the loss of his scanner and his connection to the ship. As the satellites couldn't target him this far underground, Torin let him fuss. "Could have been a couple of tendays. But that's a couple here, a couple back by the mural, and at least one digging out the door. Six tendays and however long it took them to figure their way out of that first hall. Looks like the H'san don't check in very often."

"Why would they think they had to? Anyone who might want the weapons has been told over and over that the H'san home system has been lost in time." Binti folded her hands, widened her eyes, and sweetened her voice. "And the Elder Races don't do violence."

"Sixty or seventy days?" Alamber's protest rose over Werst's muted snort of laughter. "Oh, yeah, I'd love to spend sixty or seventy days in here talking in whispers, surrounded by a fuk of a lot of dead H'san, unable to use any sort of decent tech, eating flavorless sludge, and feeling like someone set my head on fire."

"Guess they figured the reward was worth it." Craig capped the tube of sealant and studied Alamber's damaged hair. It had stopped oozing, but that was the best Torin could say about it. "They must've been offered a bucket of lolly for the weapons."

"From who?" Werst demanded. "No one with that kind of money would be willing to whisper at dead H'san."

He wasn't wrong. The backer of this little junket would be waiting in comfort for the weapons to arrive, not be down here whispering in the dark.

"Not our problem." Torin shrugged back into her pack, the *not yet anyway* silent and understood. "Let's go."

Ten crypts further on, the mercs had begun to open only every fourth sarcophagus.

"They're broken into four teams," Torin said as her team gathered in the corridor. "They're still checking the crypts, but they've decided what they're looking for isn't in with the dead."

"And crypt number four, Gunny?"

"The heavy's still breaking the lid because they can."

Binti snorted. "The heavy's a bit of an ass."

"Good thing," Craig pointed out. "It's a more obvious marker than finger- and toeprints and the occasional bit of trash."

"Better thing, now we only have to check every fourth crypt . . ." Torin smiled. ". . . we can move faster."

They'd eaten again before they found three sets of four crypts, untouched.

"All right." Torin rolled her shoulders under her pack, the gravity beginning to wear. "We're looking for an exit somewhere between this crypt, which they stayed in long enough to urinate . . ."

"And my *jernine* didn't believe me when I told them about the prestige of working for the Justice Department," Ressk murmured.

". . . and that one." Torin pointed at the crypt four crypts away from the last broken sarcophagus.

"No pit traps giving hints this time." Perched on his pack, Werst stretched his toes. "Unless they missed the sweet spot. Doesn't mean we will."

"Yes, thank you, Werst. We're narrowing it down; let's . . ." Torin's slate chimed.

The lights went out.

"What if they left through the balcony?" Werst asked the next morning.

Everyone tilted their heads back. The balcony was four meters from the floor, the top of the railing—still made of H'san symbols—two meters from the vaulted ceiling. The angle made it impossible to get an accurate measurement on the width.

"So we waste some time searching for stairs?" Binti asked, tying her jacket across the top of her pack.

Werst secured his weapon strap. "Gunny."

"Not on my own, not in this gravity." She beckoned Craig over to the wall and bent, cupping her hands.

He stopped in front of her. "You're not going to boost me, right?"

"No." Torin nodded at Werst. "We're going to throw him."

The Krai weren't large, but their bones were dense.

"On three."

Craig glanced over at her, past Werst's hand resting lightly on the top of his head, and grinned. Torin rolled her eyes. Their first mission for Justice, after a short farcical interval involving wreckage, a lever, and a bucket of soft fruit, they'd settled the "on three" or "three and go" question. "One. Two. Three."

Werst grabbed the railing and swung up onto it, gripping the top rail with a hand and a foot. Instead of jumping down onto the balcony floor, he held his position. "It's not a balcony." His voice drifted down, barely audible at the base of the wall. "It's a pit."

"A pit?"

"Yeah, a big, long pit filled with polished bones; skulls along the back, bigger bones at the front, smaller ones filling in the middle. Top layer's H'san, don't know what's underneath.

It's . . ." He paused. "It's a fuk of a lot of bones, Gunny, and I'd just as soon not check that it's H'san all the way down."

The last H'san war had destroyed all life on this planet. Billions of H'san dead and it seemed as though all of them had been gathered up and interred as the H'san worked out their collective guilt. Torin touched the side of her pack over Jamers' ashes. She understood their motivation.

"Hope the exit's not in with them," Alamber sighed.

Torin ordered Werst down before responding to Alamber's comment. "It won't be. So far, they've been making it difficult to get to the weapons, not pointlessly messing with the people coming after them."

"So far," Alamber repeated, sucking air through his teeth as his hair jerked forward.

Craig stepped backed until he stood pressed against the opposite wall, squinting up at the balcony. "I wonder what the balustrades say?"

"Oops?" When everyone turned to look at Binti, she shrugged. "What? They repeat every seventeen symbols, so they're not saying much. I thought that was obvious," she added, as Ressk banged his head against the wall.

They found nothing under the symbol that had been above the first door. They activated no pit traps, so Torin acknowledged it could've been worse. They looked for the symbol in each of the three crypts they were searching. When they found it, it led nowhere and appeared to have attracted no more attention from the mercs than any of the other symbols.

Ressk sagged against the sarcophagus in the second crypt and sighed, nostril ridges fluttering. "They picked a great time to learn to clean up after themselves. No drag marks suddenly cut off, no food wrapper caught halfway through the door, and no grubby footprints leading into a wall."

"Still plenty of grubby prints." Torin rubbed a couple off the glossy black stone. She paused. Frowned. Bent her head, left ear nearly on the stone. The overlap of hand prints along the edge nearest the door created a dulled border.

She tucked her fingers in under the narrow lip and lifted. The lid was a slab of solid stone that should have weighed hundreds of kilos. Craig, who had enough upper body muscle that his legs looked disproportionately short, had struggled to lift the broken corners. With barely a fingertip grip, Torin shouldn't have been able to shift it.

The whole top swung up with minimal effort, exposing a flight of black stone stairs heading down into darkness.

The second step was chipped, as though someone had misjudged the weight of an unloaded sled.

"Well . . ." Alamber folded his arms, head angled to protect his injured hair. ". . . this is different."

Every other wall of the octagonal room held nine sarcophagi, in a three-by-three rectangle, the long sides of the sarcophagi facing the room. In the alternate walls were two upper rows of niches holding metal urns and, centered under them, a door. An eight-sided pillar stood in the center of the room ending two meters short of the vaulted ceiling. The sides of the pillar corresponding with the sarcophagi showed scenes of H'san life. The other four—the four facing the doors—held inset control panels.

Ressk slowly circled the pillar, nostrils flared. "They tried all four of them, I have no idea which is the right one."

"I do."

Torin crossed to where Craig crouched at the base of one of the doors. For a moment, she thought the line of red ground into the intersection of wall and floor was dried blood, but blood dried brown not red.

"It's been tracked around and scuffed up by boots and equipment, but . . ." He twisted and pointed back toward the center of the room. ". . . you can still see where the spray pattern extends all the way to the pillar. I'd start there."

She straightened. "Alamber, Ressk."

"We're on it, Gunny."

"A H'san panel . . ."

"Math is math, Gunny. Numbers are numbers. We just adjust for base seven and we're *chrick*."

"And that's why we brought them along," Craig said behind her, close enough he could rest a hand on her hip.

Torin grinned. "Yeah, but they're doing the conversions on their slates."

"And then applying them."

"Fair point. I guess we'll keep them."

Without looking up from his screen, Alamber flipped her off. The mathematical distraction eased the visible tightness in his bearing and smoothed some of the lines of pain from his face. The ends of his uninjured hair had begun to swing in small, careful, arcs.

"Gunny." Werst's voice rolled around the octagon, volume near the edge of what security would allow. "We've got rot."

"Bluebirds in the morning," Craig muttered, following her to where Binti and Werst stood beside one of the niches.

Even with her nose nearly touching the broken seal of the sarcophagus, Torin smelled nothing but the same stale air, combined with the body odors of three species who'd been restricted to basic hygiene for the last two days.

"Seal's broken all the way around, Gunny." Binti squeezed out from between the narrow end of the sarcophagus and the wall of the niche.

"Is it another set of stairs?" Craig asked.

"No." Binti shook her head. "Most of the mortar's been pushed out of diagonal corners . . ." She pointed. ". . . there and there. They didn't lift the lid, they twisted and slid."

This lid seemed to weigh the expected amount.

Torin drummed her fingers on the stone. "Time, Ressk."

"Ancient H'san, Gunny. Base seven."

"Okay, we have time." Torin shrugged out of her pack. "Binti, Werst, you're on the back corner. Craig and I will push from here."

If it hadn't been for the broken pieces of residual mortar reducing the friction, they'd have never budged it without a heavy. As it was, the four of them working together shifted it about eight centimeters before it ground to a halt.

Torin covered her mouth and nose as Craig scrambled backward. "Far enough."

Binti gasped out what could have been an affirmative, while Werst breathed shallowly through his mouth, nostril ridges shut.

"*Ablin gon savit*, Boss! That's foul!"

"Keep working, we'll close it in a minute." She pulled her light off her strap and aimed through the triangular space. "Full face filters, now!"

"Oh, come on, Boss. It's foul, but . . ."

"Now," she repeated, using the tone that negated argument. The three ex-Marines were already tearing open the outer pocket on their packs. Torin sealed the clear sheet, hairline to jawline, before she turned to help Craig. Again, salvage paranoia had worked in his favor. "Ressk!"

"I've got him, Gunny."

With minimal bristles on a mostly bare scalp, the Krai could slap on a 3F faster than either of the other two Marine species, and with Alamber's hair already injured, he'd be more tentative than usual.

"Sound off."

"Sealed."

"Sealed."

"Sealed."

"I fukking hate these things."

"He's sealed, Gunny."

"Good." The pain in Alamber's voice cut him the necessary slack. She leaned in again. "Human. Can't tell male or female at this point." The green-and-gray mottling was disturbingly Krai-like. "There's red dust plugging nose, mouth, and eyes; fluids and gases had to have been released anally." Shaking her head, she straightened again. "It's cool and dry enough in here, I wouldn't even try for a TOD. Anyone?" She thought about the body bags she carried. Thought about how the mercs were probably ex-Marines. She glanced at Werst and realized he knew exactly what she was thinking. The familiar crinkle of the filter punctuated a deep breath in and out again and she opened another pocket on her pack.

"DNA sample," Binti said as Torin reached into the sarcophagus with the probe. "That's good," she added as Torin slid the probe back into the slender tube and sealed it. Whether she meant *good* they were taking a sample out or *good* they weren't scooping the entire body up off a bed of dead H'san,

Torin had no idea. Not that it mattered.

"You do realize that while you discovered that the gray aliens had been manipulating both the Confederation and the Primacy for centuries, you're not responsible for the deaths they caused."

"I know." Torin met Dr. Ito's gaze and held it. *"But someone is."*

"All right, then . . ." She moved to the other end of the sarcophagus. ". . . let's close it up."

A cloud of red dust billowed out with some force when they opened the door. Not explosive enough to reach the previous coverage, but the pressure had recently been released and hadn't had another millennium to build up again.

"Same codes to open it from this side?" Torin nodded toward the control panel, protected from the dust by a sheet of glass.

"Can't tell until we try, Gunny."

"Leave it until we want out, then."

"And if they don't work?"

"We'll try something else."

"Why, Gunnery Sergeant Kerr, do you have demo charges in your pack?"

She shot Ressk a lifted brow. "Not counting broken lids, that's two irretrievable bodies and a hole cut through a metal wall. The ship for subtle has left the . . ."

The floor quivered. Torin felt it through her boots and all the way up her legs until it set her stomach vibrating. Teeth clenched, she fought the urge to vomit. Binti had her hand over her mouth. A muscle jumped in Craig's jaw, and she could see his throat work. The two Krai lifted their feet into the air; one, then the other, then again. Alamber whined, fingers fluttering over the silk shirt he'd wrapped around his head to protect his injured hair.

Puking in a filter was unpleasant. Torin swallowed and watched the dust swirl until it felt safe to speak. "Anyone hurt?"

"I'd forgotten field rations taste as bad going up as they do going down," Binti muttered, attaching a nipple to her canteen and pushing it through her filter.

"So had we all."

A hand on Ressk's shoulder for balance, Werst stared at the bottom of his foot, flexing his toes. "What the hell was that, Gunny?"

"Let's go find out."

The dust tinted the air red, fine enough to be ignored as it covered everything it touched. The long corridor with the vaulted ceiling looked familiar, but the stone was gray, the ceiling was a good two meters lower, and there were crypts on both sides. Rather than the clean lines of the catacombs on the levels above, drifts of red settled on the loops and curls of decorative stonework. None of them knew H'san history well enough to tell if any of it was representational. They ignored the crypts, following the faint tracks on the floor.

The tracks became more visible the farther they moved from the door. Torin kicked the pace up.

"But I'm injured, Boss."

"You got shot in the hair, not the leg."

Two hours later, they followed scorch marks on the walls and ceiling to a slagged control panel. The thin slab of gray stone leaning against the wall beside it suggested the panel had been hidden in the wall. Given the H'san's skill at near invisible joining, Torin wondered how it had been found.

"Just a guess," Ressk said, squinting into the melted interior, "this wasn't the control panel they were looking for."

The closest sarcophagi were still sealed. No one had died in the blast.

"Gunny." Binti pointed at deep red marks above the doorways of two crypts. "They hung something to keep out the dust. Must've stuck around here for a while."

"Fortunately, we don't need to. Let's go."

They found two more crypts with residue over the entrances and then a second control panel left open beside the obvious outline of a stone door at the end of the corridor.

"That's new," Werst grunted. "This is the first time one of these fukking corridors has ended."

Pushed, the door remained closed, and there was nothing to grip in order to pull. About a meter away was a broken piece of decorative stone.

Torin rocked the stone under her boot. "They didn't want the door to close so they blocked it. Like the door by the pit."

"Yeah . . ." Craig shrugged out of his pack and rolled his shoulders. ". . . except that rough edge says the door closed with enough force to break the block."

"There's a couple of jackets, a half empty pouch of *sah*, five pieces of rigid tubing about two centimeters in diameter, an articulated hose, and three lights in that crypt, Gunny. One of the jackets is Human, but the other . . ." Binti tapped her nose, the filter crinkling. ". . . is di'Taykan and no more military than ours."

"So not just mercs, then." Craig looked thoughtful.

"I wouldn't have sent mercs in without some kind of expert on the H'san." Torin would have preferred an expert in her pocket as well. "Search the jackets for identification. Alamber, Ressk—control panel?"

"Okay, this is really complicated. We could crack it. Someone else did and I'm very hot for them right now because of their brains, but it'll take time." The rhythms of Alamber's voice were choppy, and he was breathing through clenched teeth. "Couple of days, maybe. Probably. And we'd have to suck all this dust clear first."

"We'd also have to build some kind of filter to keep the dust out while we're working," Ressk added, catching Alamber's swinging arm by the wrist and holding it still.

Alamber needed another dose of *duwar*.

They needed to get through that door.

"How long is the tubing?"

"About a meter five. Clip them together, and you could build a frame," Binti continued, answering the question Torin had actually asked. "We know they were hanging sheets of something to keep the dust out. They could build a shelter around the panel. Hose hooks to an external filter."

"We're a bit short of equipment," Craig pointed out.

Torin laid her palm flat against the door. "We blow it."

Werst's eyes gleamed. Although that could have been the filter.

With stealth abandoned, they all agreed better a bigger bang than a loud noise and an intact door.

"Definitely a big enough bang," Craig noted when they emerged from the nearest crypt to find a door-shaped hole in the wall and no rubble larger than a Human fist.

"The decibel security targeted the door as it blew. Might've helped break things up." Beyond the opening, Torin could see pink stone rising into a massive dome and what looked almost like the nose of a ship. Underground. She checked the dome again. It seemed solid.

At the threshold, using the wall for cover, she stood at the top of a long flight of stairs leading down to the floor of a circular cavern—given the dome, not entirely a surprise. The ship rising up through the center of the floor looked like a vacuum-to-air shuttle, much like the one they'd landed in allowing for species and millennial differences. A ring of alternating statues and benches surrounded the ship. Not far from the bottom of the stairs, a rectangular hole in the floor led to a lower level.

If the mercs had been in the cavern, they couldn't have missed the door blowing. In their position, Torin would wait silently, using the pedestals and angle of the stairs for cover until the new arrivals were exposed descending the stairs. Then she'd order her people to open fire.

"I'll go," Werst growled from the other side of the door, as able to read the room as Torin. "I'm a smaller target."

"Mashona, covering fire."

"On it, Gunny." Binti dropped prone in the doorway.

Torin went to one knee beside her. "Werst, go."

No one fired.

He darted right at the bottom, around into the blind spot. Came back into sight a moment later, investigated the second set of stairs, the nearer pedestals, and finally gave the all clear.

"Alamber, Ressk, Craig. One at a time. Move."

The cavern secured, Torin had Werst cover Binti's descent while she investigated the abandoned sled. Sleds. She'd been right about them taking along a second. It lay almost diagonally across the first, wheels still folded flat. Cases holding the cutter, the filter, tools, power packs, more tubing, a large roll of clear plastic—unresponsive plastic—and food were stacked messily on top, clearly having been carried down the stairs piece by piece. Four six-liter containers and eight four-liter containers of water had been lined up to one side. There were no empties.

The mercs had found water somewhere in the catacombs.

Water with zero impurities according to her canteen.

"Craig." She nodded at the containers. "Let's get started topping everyone up."

Two packs had been stripped and left; one rigged for Humans, one for Taykan. The body rotting with the H'san had been Human, so the body in the pit trap was di'Taykan. Unless they'd lost someone else, and there was a pack at the bottom of the pit.

"What a lot of crap." Ressk flicked the catch on the cutter's container.

"They had no idea of what they'd face."

"They had Jamers making runs."

"They wouldn't want to wait for her." Torin didn't blame them, not for that. And that was fine; there was plenty of blame to go around. "Given how she ended up, I doubt they'd have trusted her to buy most of this. She'd have attracted too much attention."

Ressk picked up the cutting laser. The power connector dropped off. Metal crashed against stone.

Binti dove off the stairs and flattened against the floor.

"Security's off," Craig said after a long moment of nothing happening.

"Decibel security." Binti rolled up onto her feet and shrugged her pack back into a more comfortable position. "H'san are too fukking crazy not to have something going on down here."

"Spread out. Quick recon." Torin sent Mashona and Ressk right, Werst and Alamber left. "We're not heading down those stairs until we know what we've left behind us."

"They think they're close, don't they? That why this stuff's here." Craig twisted the top back on a canteen. "They've already carried the sleds down two flights of stairs, but this time they only took what they could carry."

"Those aren't statues, Gunny," Ressk called before Torin could answer. "They're bodies, but they're *revenk*. The H'san did something."

"The H'san did a lot of things." Meat that wasn't meat was

not her concern, although she wasted a moment wondering why they'd left a pedestal empty. She walked to the edge of the floor. "Craig, what can you tell me about that ship?"

"No guarantees until I see the rest of it, but, yeah, it's a VTA. Design's similar to what the H'san used about ten years ago. Knew a guy at the station . . ." *The* station was always Salvage Station 24. Home, even if Craig could never return to it. ". . . who boosted a control panel out of an old H'san shuttle in a junkyard on Borin. Installed it in his wreck of a Drop Beetle and actually got the damned thing working. Until this trip, that conversation was as close to the Core as I've ever gotten. She looks like she's in good shape."

Torin glanced up. The dome still looked solid.

"Yeah." Craig followed her line of sight. "No idea. One thing the last couple of days have taught me, the H'san might've able to start up a galactic democracy, but they never got around to inventing the doorknob."

"Boss?" Alamber trotted across from a bench, and thrust a pile of discarded filters toward her, his own still a shimmer in front of his face. "There's no dust down here."

The dust swirled up to but not over the threshold at the top of the stairs—air currents or H'san tech, Torin wasn't sure, but there was no dust in the air in the cavern, although they'd all brought in a patina of red. Habit had her glance at her slate. Externals remained shut down. "How many discards?"

"Five or six. They're in a disgusting clump, I don't want to count them." He looked miserable and had started to sound sulky.

The mercs had been in the dust catacomb for days and while they'd have needed to change their filters, Torin could think of no reason they'd have dumped the used ones so far from their gear unless they'd been standing by the bench when they took them off. "Give me thirty seconds. If I don't collapse, you can remove yours." She pulled the release tab and ran her thumbs in under the seal to break it.

Alamber threw the discards back toward the bench. "It was twenty last time. Why thirty?"

"Larger space." She scratched at the residue around her hairline. He locked his eyes on his cuff and at thirty made a noise very like a whimper as he peeled his filter off and dropped it. When he unwrapped the shirt around his head, his uninjured hair had curled in over the wound. The injured hair had begun to die.

"Filters are optional, people."

"Filters are gone." Ressk's was off before he finished speaking.

"So the cavern's secure—for Navy definitions of the word secure." Filter off, nostril ridges opening and closing, Werst nodded toward the rectangular hole in the floor. "We go down?"

"We go down." Torin crossed to the narrow edge and leaned forward, forearm braced on her thigh. The stairs ended in a landing so there was more than one flight. The lights were on. She glanced up the stairs, past the rubble, at darkness. So far, following the light had worked for them. As the others gathered around, she laid her finger across her lips, then tapped her ear. One by one, they shook their heads. If the mercs were close, they weren't making the kind of noise three different species could hear.

"They could be waiting quietly at the bottom of the stairs," Binti murmured. "Waiting to pick us off, one by one."

"If they shoot the person in front of you and you continue forward, you deserve to be shot." She settled her pack, checked her weapon, and stepped down. "Let's go."

"Hey, Ryder. You think there's a hatch into that ship from a lower level?" Ressk asked, one step behind her.

"I'm not ruling out the possibility that the H'san built that ship around themselves," Craig told him, the timbre of his voice changing as his head moved into the stairwell, below the level of the floor, "and didn't bother installing hatches."

"You think it'll work?"

"Everything else has."

The five flights of stairs were as annoyingly variable as the short flight under the sarcophagus had been. Significantly more of Torin's attention went to not falling rather than to an analysis of what they might be walking into. The arboreal Krai were having the least amount of trouble, but even they stumbled over sudden angle changes. Werst had begun to swear softly under his breath.

Given the pink walls and the restricted real estate, Torin

found herself remembering a rebirthing process the psychologist before Dr. Ito had suggested they try. They hadn't.

On the fourth landing, Alamber said, "Prime numbers. Each flight of stairs is a different prime number."

"Why?" Torin asked. If they were walking into another H'san trap . . .

"The H'san are dicks," Binti said from the rear of the descent.

"Good a reason as any, Boss."

The lower corridor was empty and the stone the darkest pink yet. The air held battlefield odors of blood and shit. Both to the left and right, the corridor ran thirty meters straight to a corner. Torin held her position and sent Ressk around the curve that circled the bottom of three engine cones, mirroring the arc of open stone on the cavern level.

"Body parts," he said as he returned, nostril ridges half closed. "Human. Residue suggests they got caught between the ship and the stone."

The vibration they'd felt earlier could have been the ship moving. Torin pushed questions of both how and why aside.

"Looks like the blood and viscera got washed to the next level down," he added. "There's a constant thirty-five-to-forty–centimeter gap all the way around between the engines and the stone. Oh, and the writing . . ." Ressk nodded toward the black on pink. ". . . also goes all the way around. Seems like they had something to say. Almost a shame we'll never know what it is."

"Almost," Torin agreed. Foot on the bottom step, she leaned up the stairs and said, "Down and to the right, tuck back out of sight by the engines. We've got corners in both directions, and we don't want to set up a shooting gallery. I'll cover your six."

By the time she joined them, Ressk had quietly explained about the body.

"So they're down three," Craig began.

Werst cut him off. "That we know of. And they could be down three archaeologists, so we'll be facing as many guns."

"You sound like Torin, mate."

"Except I don't want to . . . Gunny!"

"I heard it." The ex-Marines moved into defensive positions

as she tried to determine which direction the shots had come from, the echoes from all the hard surfaces . . .

A single shot. Shooter wasn't as close as she'd first assumed. No ricochet. That round had hit a soft target.

"To the left. Marines, with me. Leave your packs with Craig and Alamber." The last year had forced her to change a number of the ways she did things, but she did not take civilians into a potential firefight. "You two, stay here. Anyone heads this way who isn't us, get out of sight around the curve."

"With the body?" Alamber demanded, the ends of his hair lifting.

Werst rolled his eyes. "You could probably take it in a fight."

"You could probably . . ."

"We'll try and get into the ship." Craig cut him off, a hand around his wrist. "Be careful."

Torin didn't look his way as she slipped out of her pack, checked her weapon, and motioned the others into movement. "You, too."

They ran to the left. Paused at the corner. Turned right into yet another vanishing point corridor.

"Gunny."

"I see it."

Blood. Dried brown. Iron-based blood. Not specifically helpful.

On the right, they passed three metal doors, scaled-down versions of the one that led into the catacombs from the plateau.

Ten meters past the last door, a side corridor joined the main from the right. Torin brought them to a stop just before they reached it and took a look. It ended in a broken door at roughly the same distance the ship's engines had been from the first corner. Signs of destruction equaled signs of life. She'd long since grown immune to the irony.

Dangling from its top hinge, the broken metal door had been built to a basic rectangle proportionate to the H'san. Dim lights were on in the big room it opened into. If the lights were on, someone was home.

Shelves and broken shelves, scattered and broken content, provided a hundred hiding places.

Torin sent Mashona and Werst to the left; she went right with Ressk.

The lights in the corridor went out the moment they stepped over the threshold. Looking back, the dark appeared to be a solid sheet of black, as though the light in the room were somehow contained. Which was a bullshit optical illusion created by the contrast, but it wasn't hard to see why so many sentient species feared the dark. Imaginations were often a pain in the ass.

The shelves still standing held supplies. Food, bedding, soaps—she didn't need to be able to read the labels. Assuming certain species' similarities, they were making their way through the storeroom for a bunker.

When they reached the back wall unopposed, they found a door flat on the floor of a dark hall, darker rectangles at intervals on the left. The door was wood, the hall barely two meters wide—it looked like the low rent crypt district. Torin signaled for Ressk to keep watch and stepped into the hall. The lights stayed off, but there was enough spillover from the storeroom for her to see into the first of the darker rectangles. Not a crypt. A barracks. Her light picked out two rows of beds, ten per row, unmistakably shaped for the H'san. Someday she'd love to know what the spiral thing between the beds was for. Not today.

Light off, she returned to the storeroom.

"Mashona says they have an opening, no door, on their side. What now, Gunny?"

"We join them." She waved to catch Binti's eye and signaled that she and Ressk were on their way.

They dropped back into the shelves rather than remain exposed at the rear wall, and ran. Even still carrying a fighting load, her knees appreciated the absence of the full pack. The four of them met up between two shelves of sealed, octagonal tubes.

"From now on we maintain eyelines." Torin glanced into a hall identical to the one on the right except that it had never had a door. "With no way to communicate, that was as much separation as I'm willing to risk."

The lights stayed on in the storeroom when Werst, on their six, stepped into the hall. The lights in the hall stayed off.

She left Werst in the dark, at the door of what looked like a multi-H'san office complete with species-specific workstations and tech that might once have been computer interface systems. Or it could have been an extremely angular, multiple-client, sexual-relief unit for the barracks.

"Sure, save the bureaucracy." Binti approached a tall glass cabinet with deep drawers and found herself unable to grip the pulls with Human fingers. "Permission to break something, Gunny?"

"Denied."

Inside the cabinet, rectangles of glass had been racked on their sides and they gleamed with a rainbow of colors as Binti's light passed over them. "This is depressing. I always thought the H'san were above all that."

"All that?" Ressk asked, holding a small metal spiral up to his light.

"You know, forms and memos and business shit."

"If that's what that is."

"That's what it looks like. So much for the idea that they ran their empire on song and ca . . ."

"Incoming!"

Three lights went out simultaneously, and Torin dropped behind a solid piece of meter-high glass and metal. She could hear Mashona and Ressk to her right and, as she hadn't heard Werst move, assumed he'd slipped into the room and taken a position by the door.

A familiar beam of light illuminated the doorway, the person wearing it safely back behind the protection of the wall.

"Who are you?" The voice was female and di'Taykan and it sounded as though she was one wrong answer away from either screaming or emptying a magazine into a room full of glass.

Torin could work with the first, but she doubt any of them would survive the second. She shifted into a crouch. "Gunnery Sergeant Torin Kerr."

"Lead big," Ressk muttered.

If the di'Taykan was ex-Corps, Gunnery Sergeant Kerr's reputation would get them a conversation or get them killed. Odds were about fifty / fifty.

"Of course you are." The incipient panic had disappeared like it had been switched off, the tone now so neutral it could have been machine generated. "Come out where I can see you."

"Into the hall? No. You step into the room."

"By all means, let's make it convenient for you." It wasn't sarcasm. It was . . . nothing. The light dropped to the floor, and a moment later, the PID was kicked over the threshold. It rolled forward about half a meter and ended up shining a cone of light toward the ceiling.

The spill was enough that Torin could make out shapes and shadows.

Taykan could see clearly even in lower levels, but she didn't know Werst was by the door and when she reacted, she aimed high.

Glass shattered.

Torin picked up the PID and pointed it at the di'Taykan on the floor, Werst's blade at her throat, her turquoise hair surprisingly sleek.

Her lip curled. "I should've known they'd send *you* after us."

Assuming *they* meant the Justice Department, Torin didn't correct her. The emphasis on the pronoun only reinforced how exposing the gray aliens had made Gunnery Sergeant Kerr enemies in the Corps. Some people didn't deal well with discovering everything they'd been fighting for was a lie.

"You don't remember me, do you?" Knife still at her throat, she didn't seem upset by her position. "Major Sujuno di'Kail. Ex-major, I suppose, but then why should I ex out if you haven't? I was at your lecture on Ventris after the Silsviss incident. You followed us, didn't you? Didn't need to work anything out, didn't need to spend days finding the way. We did that for you." Wrist held in Werst's foot, she waved her fingers, Taykan graceful. "You just followed. Except, you followed a little too far and now you're as trapped as we are. Surprise. There's no difficulty getting into the bunker system, but you can't get out."

"Automated defenses." Ressk fell in on Torin's right, his KC pointed at the major.

Major Sujuno had her voice under control, but her laugh teetered on the edge of hysteria. "Did I say that?"

NINE

Torin looked down at the strangely familiar body on the floor of the third and final barracks. "That's a dead H'san."

Major Sujuno folded her arms, hair tight to her head. "It was dead before we killed it."

That explained the feeling of familiarity. Torin had never met a live H'san, but she'd spent the last two days looking at dead ones. The flesh appeared to have been dehydrated. The joints protruded. The biggest difference between this dead H'san and the occupants of the sarcophagi was that the eyes and mouth of this H'san hadn't been sealed shut. Or the biggest difference might have been the three holes in the front of the head and the two center chest, all seeping clear fluid. Given the lack of exit wounds, the head shots had ricocheted around inside the skull, dicing the upper brain, and the chest wound seemed to be lined up with the superior heart. She assumed either clumping would have killed a living H'san, which this wasn't. "So, zombie H'san?"

Werst made a sound that might have been a choked-off laugh.

The major spun around to face him. "You think this is funny? They killed two of my people!"

Torin glanced over at the two Krai who'd been in the room when the major had led them in. They stood with their backs to the wall, nearly out of the circle of light around the body, their weapons ready. Clearly a bonded pair although she had no idea of their genders and just as clearly ex-Corps from the way they held the KC-7s. The major had lost a Human and a di'Taykan on the way to the cavern and the body around the curve had to have been one of hers, so the question became: how many more in her crew?

One of the questions.

"Major Sujuno." Torin had spent years being the support that allowed officers to give the orders that sent Marines out to die. Her tone turned the major back toward her, her expression shifting from rage to . . . nothing. A mask Torin was not permitted to see behind. "Where did the attackers come from?"

"From behind the metal doors you passed on the way to the bunker." The major's turquoise eyes were darker than the light level required. "You can call the rooms barracks, or storerooms, or crypts, but the doors leading into them were barred from the outside when we passed them the first time."

"If they were locked from the outside, how did the . . ." Werst flared his nostrils at her when Torin paused so she skipped the word zombie. ". . . H'san get out?"

"We didn't let them out, Gunnery Sergeant Kerr." The Krai on the right's nostrils were closed and the lip curled, showing teeth. "If that's what you're implying."

Officer. Lieutenant at best or there would have been confidence enough to let that first statement stand on its own. "Only a request for information." She kept her tone even.

"The H'san from the plinth released them." Major Sujuno's tone, on the other hand, said, *I know how ridiculous that sounds, and I'm entirely out of fuks to give.*

"From the cavern?"

"Unless you know where they've propped up another dead H'san on a plinth, Gunnery Sergeant, yes, from the cavern. Dion, Lieutenant Verr, and Sergeant Toporov found the other entrance to the bunker—the corridors loop the perimeter—when they emerged, the H'san attacked and wounded Dion . . ."

Verr was the Krai officer, still no idea of gender although both Werst and Ressk would know. Dion was species nonspecific.

". . . but it was unsteady on its feet, so Sergeant Toporov was able to break up the attack and get Dion and Verr moving back toward the rest of us. He wanted more intell . . ."

Understandably, Torin allowed.

". . . so he waited until he saw the plinth H'san unlocking the doors. Fired four shots center mass to no effect and ran. There's three rooms of guardians by each of the bunker entrances."

"We call them entrances because we can't fukking use them as exits," muttered the other Krai.

Major Sujuno squared her shoulders. "The sergeant died so the rest of us could get to safety. It didn't take long before we realized we were trapped. If we cross the threshold, on this side or the other, the H'san roil out through those doors like *seratts*. We've examined their armor, and a standard round will go through certain points . . ."

At which point Torin realized that the pile of junk the pair of Krai stood beside was metal plate and leather straps and entirely the wrong level of tech for the H'san who'd buried the bunker under their interred dead.

". . . because the armor is designed to protect against the energy weapons they're carrying, not a tungsten carbide core designed for maximum penetration."

"The energy weapons?"

"They're biometric, keyed to the H'san. Every weapon in here is keyed to the H'san. I've got someone working on cracking it, and if we can get one of the big guns operating, it may turn the tide, but—bottom line—Gunnery Sergeant Kerr, there's too many of them. We're trapped."

"If there's that many of them, why didn't we see them in the corridors?"

"You wouldn't. If no one crosses the threshold for . . . What is it, Lieutenant?"

"Forty-nine minutes, Major."

"If no one crosses the threshold for forty-nine minutes, most of them regroup, taking the dead with them behind the doors. We can't get an accurate count of the number left on patrol, but if we stay by the threshold for more than seven minutes, one of them will charge the door. The first time it happened, the outer door went down. We lost the middle door the second time. So far, we've stopped them before they reach the inner doors. I'm not certain they're intentionally sacrificing themselves to drive us back, but that's the end result." She turned, shining her light toward the rear wall of the barracks where five or six H'san were piled between the ends of the final two platforms, looking even more familiarly dead than the single body at Torin's feet. "There's another pile like this on the other side. Just after we dropped the third H'san, Corporal Keo thought she could use the flamethrower in her nine to simultaneously seal all three doors before another patrol showed up."

The doors were approximately seven meters apart. Torin tried to work out the angle. "That's not possible."

"How unfortunate you weren't here, Gunnery Sergeant."

Too flat to be disdain, Torin couldn't work out what the major's voice was hiding. She decided not to ask if anyone had tried to stop the heavy gunner from making a suicide run. Odds were, the answer would make her angry and, if the major was telling the truth, they had to work together to get free of the guardians. At the moment, she saw no reason to believe the major was lying. Her reaction to Ressk's suggestion of automatic defenses had been entirely honest.

"They ripped Keo's exo off after they killed her," the lieutenant said, teeth yellow in the light of the PIDs. "They don't like technology."

"What happens if you leave all your tech behind?" Ressk asked.

The major laughed, all shards and edges. "They don't like *us* either."

The silence stretched. Torin contemplated having common ground with a dead H'san, then Ressk crouched beside the body. "Is this blood?"

"What else would it be?" the major snapped, half a centimeter of hair curling dismissively.

"Don't know yet. Have you done a dissection? Checked to see if you can affect their operating system?"

"They're dead H'san. Walking around," snarled the second of the major's Krai.

"Using weapons," the lieutenant added.

"Okay." Ressk poked at the liquid and sniffed his finger.

"*Revenk*!" He scrubbed his finger against the floor. "Point is, there's no such thing as zombies. This isn't blood; rough guess it's a vector to keep the current running through desiccated tissue. And just because we wouldn't turn our dead into an automated security system, doesn't mean the ancient H'san haven't."

Since Torin was clearly not intended to hear Binti's response describing the ancient H'san, she let it go. "How long have you been trapped, Major?"

The mask stiffened. "Not quite two days."

Torin glanced back at the pile of dead H'san. In less than two days, the major's team had made a dozen or more attempts to break free. She couldn't decide if she admired their tenacity or was appalled by the way they kept repeating the same action, expecting a different result.

"What happened to her body?" Werst asked suddenly, locking a flat unfriendly stare on the major. "Your heavy gunner's body? And the sergeant's? You can't go out for them and we didn't see them. Are they both around on the other side?"

"She told you." The second Krai stepped away from the wall, hands curled into fists, nostril ridges half closed. "They take the dead in with them."

Werst glanced over at Torin and when she nodded, curious about where he was going with this, asked, "Has anything other than dead H'san come back out?"

"This is Dion, our expert on the ancient H'san." Sujuno prodded Dion in the hip with her boot. "He's the next thing to useless, but he's all we've got."

Even in the big common room with its jellied chairs and feeding rounds over by the food prep area, non-H'san were more comfortable on the floor, so they'd laid out Dion's bedroll near the counter where he could sit up, leaning back against the glass. Right arm curled against his body, Dion had spread the rolled sheets of acetate they'd found in the offices out around him and had used a multitude of colors to isolate symbols and symbol sets. The word *wet* had been written in blue next to a series of symbols circled in blue, then crossed out and replaced with a red word Sujuno couldn't read. *Maybe staff?* had been scrawled in black over the red.

He ignored both her boot and her comments.

"That wound's infected."

Sujuno glanced over to see Kerr studying Dion's bare right arm, too swollen now to fit comfortably in a sleeve. Purple/red lines snaked out from under the dressing, climbing both up toward his shoulder and down into his hand. According to the Krai, his fingers looked like uncooked sausages. When Dion had recoiled, they'd snapped their teeth in unison and laughed.

"Really? Infected? Thank the gods you're here, Gunnery Sergeant or we might never have noticed that." When Kerr did nothing but raise a questioning brow in her direction, she drove her fingernails into her palms and kept her voice level. "We sealed it, but modern antibiotics are barely slowing the progress of what's in the wound."

"Dead H'san."

"Probably."

"I don't know her," Dion muttered, glancing up from his notes and back down again, as though the sudden appearance of strangers at the bottom of a necropolis wasn't worth his time. His eyelids were pink and puffy. "Is this a rescue? If it isn't, and it certainly doesn't seem to be, I'd prefer another scholar or an actual physician rather than one more example of how an appalling number of theoretically civilized people prefer violence to thought."

Sujuno considered proving his point by prodding him again with some force behind her boot. "Gunnery Sergeant Kerr works for the Justice Department. She's here to arrest us."

"Is that so? So scholarship is a crime now?" he demanded, smearing the sweat on his forehead with the back of his left hand.

Kerr's lip curled. "No, but trespass, theft, desecration of multiple grave sites, and murder are."

They were to be blamed for more than trespass, theft, desecration, and murder; she could read it in the stiffness of the gunnery sergeant's posture, although her expression gave nothing away. Out of the Corps she might be, but Torin Kerr was still the definitive career NCO. Sujuno hated how comforting she found that on a deep level, and she promised herself she'd take the time to gouge the feelings out once they were free of the H'san. "Dion, have you found any reference to the guardians creating more guardians out of the dead?"

"Are you telling me they're created from other than dead H'san, Major?"

"Corporal Werst makes a credible argument that there's no reason for the H'san to regroup behind closed doors unless they're performing repairs and there's no reason to take the bodies of our dead with them unless they're repairing them as well."

"Who the fuk is Corporal Werst?"

"He is." Kerr nodded at the Krai watching suspiciously over by the door to the weapons cache, just out of eavesdropping range.

"Dion!" Sujuno snapped her fingers to attract his wandering attention. "*New* guardians from the newly dead—have you found a reference?"

His lips moved as he repeated her words silently, then he flipped through the sheets until he found one nearly covered in alternating green and red. "I believe," he said, tapping a messy green square, "that this says *guardian*."

She still couldn't tell if the square enclosed six symbols or seven. "So you said earlier. And?"

"And what? This is entirely new text in ancient H'san, Major. It took me five years to translate the guide to the weapons; you can't expect an instruction manual for the guardians in less than two days. We're just lucky these pages are also in what we in preConfederate languages call storytelling mode, which was dialectically stable for centuries or the vocabulary I have stored would be entirely worthless. And," he glared up at the gunnery sergeant, "no one was murdered. While you can certainly argue that they didn't perform them to a high standard, the dead members of the expedition died performing the duties they were hired to perform."

Going out in front so you don't have to. Sujuno could see the words cross Kerr's face and dug her nails in deeper to keep from saying them aloud. To keep from marching in step with the gunnery sergeant. But all Kerr said was, "Jamers a Tur fenYenstrakin."

"The smelly Katrien? You had her killed, Major?" Dion pointed a red stylus up at her, the tip wobbling.

Sujuno sighed. "The grave goods the Katrien sold alerted the Justice Department to our presence here. I realized that was a possibility from the moment I discovered she'd taken them. Given the progress we were making, I assumed we'd be out of here before the wheels of justice made one of their *oh, so slow* revolutions."

"Yet, in spite of that assumption," Kerr said, "she's still dead."

"To prevent her from doing further damage. And, in the end . . ." She waved a hand toward the doors out of the common room. Five downed H'san beyond one. Six beyond the other. Through the storerooms and over the threshold, countless dead H'san. "In the end," she repeated, "we're all dead, Gunnery Sergeant."

"Not yet."

Sujuno watched Kerr turn away and cross to join Werst. The Krai, in turn watched her until Kerr was close enough to speak quietly with him.

"If they're here to arrest us, why are you welcoming them?"

"Why am I . . . ?" She shook her head. "You weren't lying about ignoring popular media. Gunnery Sergeant Kerr, by her own admission, does one thing well. She gets her people out alive."

"You want us to become her people? Fine. But I can't see what she can do in this situation. Even with the four of them—and, yes, they're Marines, oh my, I'm so excited . . ." Sweat rolled down the side of Dion's face. ". . . we're vastly outnumbered and surrounded by an enemy that's not easy to kill."

"That hasn't stopped her in the past."

"Why does the major hate you?" Werst asked, eyes locked on the di'Taykan who continued talking to the infected Human. "When you're not looking at her, she looks ready to crack your bones for marrow."

Torin gave it a moment's thought. If Werst had noticed, the major wasn't trying to hide it from anyone but her. "If it's not about exposing the gray aliens, I have no idea why she'd hate me."

"It's not about the aliens. It's personal."

"I personally exposed them."

"It's not that. There's something off about her."

"Besides wanting to crack my bones for marrow?"

The corners of his mouth curled up. "Not everyone has to love you, Gunny." And curled back down again. "We're not here to make friends. It would've been easier if they'd been loading the weapons on their shuttle when we arrived."

Judge. Jury. And executioner.

"It's not supposed to be easy."

"The more time we spend with them, the harder it'll get. We work together to get out of this trap and . . ."

"Thank you, Master Corporal Obvious."

They watched the major shift through Dion's notes. "She says she saw my brief on the Silsviss. We've never met."

"It's not all about you. I've been around di'Taykans every day since I joined and almost every day after we got out, and she . . ." Werst shook his head. "You ever see a di'Taykan with hair that still?"

While not entirely motionless, Sujuno's hair moved significantly less than most di'Taykan, and Torin had seen her force it down at least once. More noticeably, she hadn't touched any of her people—not the two Krai as she passed them and not Dion, even though Dion's head was at hand height. He was clearly suffering, and among the Taykan, a touch for comfort only required the need for comfort. "I'd wish Alamber was here to figure it out, but there's enough of us chin-deep in shit already."

"You worried about them?"

"Alamber's a survivor, and Craig's almost as paranoid as I am." Of course she was worried about them. With the comms useless, she'd already given half a thought to testing the acoustics of the tunnels. Hard surfaces, straight lines, di'Taykan hearing—if sergeants and above wanted to be heard, they were heard. "Besides," she said, weight back on her heels, hands crossed over her KC, "it's Craig's turn to rescue me."

"I admire the equality in your relationship."

"Thank you. And speaking of relationships . . ."

Gripping a double handful of blanket, Ressk backed into the big common room dragging the H'san body into the light. Binti,

Lieutenant Verr, and Wen, Verr's bonded, had the other three corners, Binti towering over the three Krai. Even desiccated, the H'san probably outweighed all four of them, but the blanket slid easily over the ubiquitous polished stone.

". . . how did you get out of helping with that?"

"If you were going in here with the major, someone had to stay with you, given the potential bone cracking and marrow eating. The Human have anything to say?"

"He's positive that one of those sheets says *guardian* on it."

"*Guardian* like dead H'san being called guardian or what?"

"No idea. Also, the infection in his arm is killing him and he's in so much denial about that, he's pretty stress free about the bigger problem."

Werst made a noncommittal noise.

"What does that mean?"

"Our orders are to execute these people."

"To stop a war, I know." Four lives against millions.

"Just saying. Denial."

"Delay. Until we deal with the . . . zombie H'san keeping us in this bunker." She squared her shoulders and watched the major talk to Dion. "I'll complete the mission, Werst."

"You're not alone, Gunny."

They'd talked about that, the two of them in Susumi space, sharing a watch while the others slept.

"All right." Ressk straightened and headed over to join them, Binti right behind him. "If there's no saws down here, I need a heavy knife with a serrated edge."

"We didn't see any saws, but there's a shitload of blades," Wen said as he and Vree caught up. "There's got to be something that'll work."

"Heavy ax?" Verr touched the small ax on her belt. Torin had seen new recruits wearing them. Visible religious icons were against regulation, so she'd never had the opportunity to see how useful they were as a weapon.

"I haven't done any ax work in years," Ressk said thoughtfully.

"A *ser tyrin plee kerstirin* like you with an ax?" Wen scoffed.

Werst growled and showed teeth. "What did you call him?"

"Enough." Torin's voice cracked out and four sets of nostril ridges snapped closed, lips quickly covering teeth. "Insults in Federate only. If there's going to be blood spilled, it is not going to be over a misunderstanding."

Verr remembered her rank in time to not answer, *Yes, Gunnery Sergeant*, with the rest.

Binti leaned in close. "Admit it, Gunny, two days of keeping it quiet—you missed the yelling."

"Corporal, if I'd wanted to yell, I'd have reflected those security beams back off my shining personality."

Grinning, Binti stared across the room at the food prep area. As her grin slipped, Torin realized she was actually staring back toward the stairs and the ship and the two people they'd left behind. "We've got to get out of here."

"I know." If Craig came after her, they'd be trapped together and she wouldn't be distracted by worry about a patrol stumbling over him. On the other hand, if he didn't come into the bunker, they'd still have a potential front outside the perimeter. On yet another hand, Alamber and Ressk's complementary skills hadn't yet hit code they couldn't crack. If Ressk was right about the H'san, he could use Alamber beside him.

"Situation means a truce until we get out?"

"It does." Given the numbers, she suspected that having the major's people on their side meant sweet fuk all, but it was a legitimate reason to delay the inevitable.

"And after?" Binti's expression said, *I trust you to do the right thing.*

Torin would've preferred her expression to say, *I trust in our orders.* But, in the end, that was Torin's job. "Let's get out of here first."

The weapon cache was huge. Torin had expected an oversized Marine armory and not crowded shelves and vaults following a spiral both up and down—like Bufush's junk shop made deadly and rearranged inside a giant snail shell. The architecture was entirely different from anything else they'd passed although, granted, taking the shortcuts through the catacombs on the weapon's trail meant they'd likely missed a few chambers. The structure looked to have been built of polished concrete and the same brassy metal as the guardians' doors.

The section nearest the entrance held blades. Curved, straight, short, long; apparently every culture went through a phase where they jabbed holes in each other. Torin doubted the H'san had been using them at the same time as the planet busters, but, for all she knew, they might have.

"I assume the blades weren't going with you, Major?" The mercs' ship had a decent-sized cargo hold as well as expandable pens—most of the weapons would be fine riding out the trip in vacuum. The shuttle, however, had significantly less space. Either they were after something specific, or the reward was great enough to risk multiple trips in spite of the satellite defenses.

"*Aren't* going with me," the major corrected. "I won't be paid for weapons a decent blacksmith can re-create."

"So you're working for someone. Not Dion, or you'd care that he was dying."

If the major had been Human, Torin might've been able to read the expressions chasing each other across her face, but the physiognomy was just different enough they moved too fast for her to translate. Anger. Pain. Maybe resentment? With only four letters in her family name, Sujuno di'Kail had definitely come out of the Taykan upper class. Had her family cut her off? If she was willing to dump the seeds of another war and millions more dead out into the Confederation, the bar had been set pretty damned low when Torin considered what else she might have been willing to do.

The clash of steel and Ressk's voice cut off her response. "It's big enough, but it's too flexible."

Torin half expected a comment from the major, but she only huffed out a disapproving breath. Fair enough. Alamber had been the only di'Taykan Torin had spent time with lately and he'd never have let that go, but officers were taught to be more circumspect.

"Hey, Major!" Wen's voice bounced down from an upper level. "We might've found another whatchathing."

"Might have?"

"Not sure. It's got attachments."

Alamber wouldn't have let that go either. The major only headed up the spiral, long legs taking her quickly out of sight. The Taykan were, as a species, effortlessly graceful—it had to do with the way their joints were connected according to a bored tech during one of Torin's lengthier stays in Med-op—but the major moved as though she were holding pieces of herself in place. Torin made a mental note to ask about injuries when she reappeared.

If the three cases stacked by the door also contained *whatchathings*, ready to be carried out to the ship, Torin had to reluctantly admire their industriousness. Two piles of re-dead H'san and still time to find the weapons they'd been sent for. She also wondered why the H'san were so hot for pink. The cases were almost exactly the color of the darker stone at the bottom of the last flight of stairs.

About to join the search for a saw . . .

"In what universe do two serrations make a serrated edge? For fuksake, Mashona, do you even know what a saw looks like?"

. . . Torin heard a noise from lower down the spiral. The major, the lieutenant, and Wen were still up the spiral—she could hear them speaking, though she couldn't make out the actual words—so the banging had to have come from the last member of the major's crew. The one trying to get a larger energy weapon to work.

She saw the bright flash of lime-green hair first, then, a few steps lower, the di'Taykan whose head it covered. He was leaning over an open case twice the size of the three already gathered and swearing softly to himself in a dialect Torin didn't know—although he might have been praying. Torin had heard Marines do both and the rhythm and emphasis were almost identical. He straightened, turned, and dropped the tool he'd been using. It bounced almost to Torin's feet as the light receptors in his eyes snapped open and his hair flattened to his head.

"*Ablin gon savit!* Who the *sanLi* are you? And where the fuk did you come from? Hang on." His hair started to lift. "I've seen you before. You were with Big Bill on Vrijheid. You were fighting the Grrr brothers right before the station blew the fuk up."

She remembered him as well. Nadayki di'Berinango. He'd

been with Craig, attempting to crack the Marine armory the pirates had stolen. He'd been one of the pirates.

"The station didn't blow up, Nadayki."

Blood pounding in her ears, Torin hadn't heard the major descend to stand behind her. The trick was not reacting.

"Gunnery Sergeant Kerr blew it up. Blew up the station and the pirates who'd taken her *vantru*."

Nadayki's hair flattened again. "You blew up the *Heart of Stone*? You? My *thytrins* were on that ship and you killed them."

"I'm sorry for your loss." Craig had locked Nadayki out of the cargo bay, kept him from boarding the ship. That was the only reason he hadn't died with his *thytrins*.

"Keep your sorry," he spat. "You don't care that they're dead."

Torin considered it for a moment and not for the first time. Every now and then, she thought about the *Heart of Stone* exploding as it made ready to jump into Susumi space. The pirates had been escaping with a Marine armory after killing three CSOs and capturing and torturing Craig. She was self-aware enough to know that they'd died as much for what they'd done to Craig as what they could do with the contents of the armory. "No," she said. "I don't care." If she felt anything, it was satisfaction.

"I'm going to kill you!" His hands curled into fists, but he was smart enough not to attack. As he'd said, he'd seen her fight the Grrr Brothers. He shifted a dark-eyed gaze to the major. "Why is she even fukking here?"

"She's here to arrest us. For, what was it, Gunnery Sergeant?" Sujuno sounded as if she was asking about the price of drinks in the officer's mess. "Trespassing, theft, desecration, and murder?"

"Murder?" Nadayki folded his arms. "Nobody got murdered!"

"The Katrien . . ."

"She doesn't count!"

That opinion had begun to piss Torin off.

"So why is she *here*?" Nadayki's hair whipped back and forth so quickly it looked like a solid curve rather than individual strands. "If you know she's here to arrest us, why haven't you shot her?"

"We need her help to get out of the bunker."

Nadayki waved that off. "No, we don't. I'll get this thing working and we'll blow the walking dead away."

"It's not the walking, it's the attacking. And I've told you, the controls are biometric, but feel free to keep trying." The major sighed. "He might as well keep trying. He's useless in a fight, completely untrained."

"He's a civilian."

"That's what I said. A close facsimile of a saw has been found, Gunnery Sergeant. I assumed you'd want to see the dissection."

"Lead the way."

At no point had the two di'Taykan come close enough to touch.

Werst crouched down beside the corpse, his KC balanced across his back, his hands dangling between his knees. "I didn't know you were all up on xeno-anatomy."

"I'm not." Ressk set the blade above the uppermost hole in the skull and began to draw the saw back and forth. It caught on the desiccated flesh, bucked, then bit into bone.

"And yet . . ."

"I used to hunt with my *jerta*. We'd go out into the wildland, him and me, and shoot a *vertak* or a *sinsac* and butcher it before bringing it home. It was his way of getting his city-born son back to nature and Ner forbid we just climb a tree like everyone else." He sighed and met his bonded's gaze. "Look, none of us knows squat about doing a dissection—our happy group of grave robbers didn't even think of it—but if I can find what's controlling these things, then I might be able to shut them down. I don't have to do this right or scientifically, I just have to get into its head."

"Have you tried communicating with them?" Binti asked, staying far enough away from Ressk's butchering to miss the details.

Verr flapped her nostril ridges. "They're dead!"

"But they're also up and walking around and working together. That implies internal communications, at the very least."

"Well, unless you brought a singularly useful linguist with you, *at the very least*, no one here talks ancient H'san and even if this lot doesn't predate the Confederation, they certainly predate Federate."

"What about trying music? Art? Math?"

"Sure, because while a shitload of zombie H'san are trying to kill you, why not introduce them to the tunes they missed while they were dead?"

"Or we could take them all down with Viridian Interval's last upload."

Verr snorted out a reluctant laugh. "Pretty sure that counts as cruel and unusual."

Torin counted the ammunition spread out on the table and then again, just to be sure. Her people had come in with four sixty-round magazines as reloads. Sixty rounds in the KC made three hundred all together. Each. The major's people had no reloads. One magazine. Sixty rounds for each of the six Marines and they'd been able to recover only one weapon from their three dead.

"It's a cemetery planet," the major snapped. "We were expecting static defenses, not a firefight."

Five or six shots to kill each of the redead H'san. Torin expected they'd blown most of their ammo during the mass attacks. In spite of the major's defensiveness, she put the blame for shorting the supplies squarely on the late Sergeant Toporov. The KC-7 wasn't designed to be decorative. If it was a part of operational gear, it needed to be supported.

She glanced over at the entrance to the weapons cache. What was it Hollice used to say? Water, water everywhere and not a drop to drink.

"They've been gone too long," Craig growled, walking back to the curve around the ship's engines. They hadn't found a way into the ship, so they'd been going up to the cavern, one at a time, and sorting through the supplies left behind. Sure, potentially dangerous and hard on the knees, but it was that or follow Torin, and he knew how that would turn out.

"Too long?" Alamber folded his arms and leaned gracefully against the wall. "That's a little arbitrary, isn't it? We haven't heard any more gunfire, so I expect the boss is trying to convince them of the error of their ways."

"She doesn't usually spend much time on that." Torin was more *you have one chance to see reason before I take matters into my own hands.*

"Good point. You think they've run into trouble?"

He ran a hand back through his hair. "I think the odds are very high."

"So it's up to us to get them out of trouble."

Torin would kill him if he charged in assuming she needed rescue. "A little more information wouldn't hurt, let's . . ."

Alamber's sudden grip on his forearm cut him off. When he turned to look—he hadn't heard the young di'Taykan move—Alamber pressed the finger of his other hand to his lips, ears swiveled all the way forward, more visible than usual because his healthy hair still wrapped the injured hair. *Something coming*, he mouthed. *More than two feet.*

All the younger races were bipedal.

More than one? Craig mouthed back, when Alamber freed his mouth.

He half shrugged. *No scent.*

It might be nothing, but Craig'd bet the papers for *Promise* it was nothing good. He moved them back around the curve where they'd be hidden by the ship's engines and covered by the scent of decay. In close to the ship, out of the line of sight from the corridor, they synced their breathing and waited. Craig had been at this for enough time now that he knew they hadn't been waiting long, definitely not as long as it felt, when he heard it, too. Creaking and tapping and metal whispering against metal. Not trying to be stealthy.

Robots? That would explain the lack of scent.

The sudden increase in volume suggested it, or they, had arrived at the part of the corridor closest to the curve around the ship.

The sounds stopped.

Time passed.

Alamber shrugged and pointed at the damp pile of entrails. He couldn't smell anything over it. Had there been anything to smell.

Steadying himself on the dark metal curve of the engine, Craig peered around the corner.

He'd seen enough dead H'san lying curled in sarcophagi over the last two days to recognize one standing. It wore what looked like metal-and-leather armor. Even before he'd joined up with Torin, he'd known that *looked low tech* was often a dangerous lie. In one appendage, it held a short, fat cone by a handle that looped out of the narrow end. Looking directly into the wide end, he couldn't tell if the cone was solid or hollow. The H'san stood completely still, *completely* still, and looked more like the statues up in the cavern than a living creature. The eyes that were a little too large for the face, giving H'san an appearance of youth and innocence to every species in the Confederation who birthed live young, were open and staring right at him.

Shite.

He whipped back. Motioned Alamber to silence. Held his breath.

Heard movement.

The movement was deliberate rather than quick, but they couldn't outrun a H'san. He knew that because he'd heard a H'san could outrun a Ciptran and he'd seen a motivated Ciptran keep up to a skimmer.

"Down."

Alamber grabbed his arm. "What?"

"Down into the blast bay."

"That's insane!"

"Only if the engines fire." He grabbed his pack, slid it between the curve of the engine and the floor, and dropped it. "It's not that far. Move!"

Credit where due, Alamber moved.

His pack preceding him, he moved faster through the narrow space. His head, instead of Craig's head and shoulders, remained stuck up over the edge of the floor when the H'san came into view. Eyes suddenly dark, he disappeared so quickly Craig knew he'd let himself go, free sliding between polished metal and stone.

Craig cracked his chin on the edge when he followed. He moved a lot faster when he ran out of engine, hit a solid surface, rolled, slammed into a warm body, and froze.

Alamber's arms went around him and when he looked up, instinctively given that it was pitch-black in the blast bay, he felt the di'Taykan shake his head.

They waited. And then, as their eyes adjusted and a gray ring began to define the walls of the bay, they waited some more.

Finally, he felt Alamber relax. "It's gone. It circled the ship and kept going. I guess the dead are all 'out of sight out of mind'; programming stripped down to the basics."

"The H'san programmed their dead?"

"Someone did. Necro-neuro programming."

"You made that up." The bottom of his chin was sticky and hurt like fuk when he touched it.

"Well, yeah, but the dead don't get up and walk around on their own. And speaking of up . . ."

Craig caught himself as Alamber released him and stood. "What are you doing?"

"Seeing if I can reach the bottom of the engines so we can climb out." He was a line of darker gray against the wall. "No. But we didn't fall that far, so if I stood on your shoulders, I could reach. Probably be able to inch my way up. Of course, once I was up, how would you get out? I doubt I could brace myself securely enough to pull you up into the crevasse."

"There's rope in Werst's pack."

"And nothing to tie it to. Nothing personal, but you'd drag me back down. Maybe we could tie a couple of packs together and jam them tight." His voice had begun to circle the bay. "Wait, I just remembered the collapsible tubes in the cavern! I could tie two or three of them together for strength and, no, that wouldn't work. There's nothing to brace them against."

Craig put out a hand, searching for his pack, touched something that rocked, and reached for it. Felt eyes, a nose . . . the jaw was missing. It was wet and cold. He swallowed. Tasted bile. Swallowed again.

"What?"

He didn't remember making a noise, but he must have. "Head

that belongs with the pieces, I assume." It was dark enough in the center of the bay, he couldn't see it. Death, he could cope with. Violent death, not so much. Teeth clenched, he wiped his hand on his thigh and stood. "Can you see?"

"Not right into the middle, too much contrast. I'm getting a good look at the walls, though."

"As long as the light doesn't go out."

"That's it. Look at the bright side. The boss has definitely rubbed off on you."

"Yes, she has." Craig fitted the response with a di'Taykan emphasis. When Alamber laughed, the dark seemed less grim. "How's your head?"

"Managed to avoid smacking it into the rock. Still feels like I set it on fire." He pushed Craig's pack into his hands. "Not that I've ever set it on fire. Turns out *I'll try anything once* is more of a guideline."

Untangling the straps by touch, Craig realized he could now see the blacker oval of the broken skull and found he couldn't look away, waiting for his eyes to adjust enough to see a face.

"Oh, hey. I might have found us a way back up."

Grateful for the distraction, he shrugged into the pack. "How?"

And blinked at the sudden spill of light as a rectangle opened in the curved wall.

Alamber grinned. "I thought we'd take the stairs."

"It's moving." Werst straightened and took a step back, aiming between the H'san's eyes.

Ressk grabbed the H'san's shoulder with a foot and continued to work the saw. "No, it isn't."

"Yes, it is."

It twitched violently enough to dislodge Ressk's grip and he fell back, nostril ridges slamming shut. "Yes, it is."

The saw blade wobbled, abandoned between the two pieces of bone. The H'san wobbled with it.

Werst watched Ressk reach slowly out, grip the saw, steady it, and push the blade forward again.

The H'san twitched.

"The metal of the saw is closing a contact in the tech that's controlling the brain."

Werst stared at him in disbelief. "You can't know that."

"Yeah, I can. This is nothing more than creepy engineering."

"You're not an engineer."

"I am."

They turned together to glare at Wen. The H'san twitched. All three Krai twitched with it.

"You're an engineer?" Werst asked, adjusting his aim.

"Sure." Wen shrugged. He was better at it than most Krai. "I was air crew."

Ressk sat back on his heels, lips rising off his teeth. "Then why weren't you taking this apart yesterday? We'd know what we were facing."

"We're facing zombie H'san," Wen sneered. "And they don't fly. Or does infantry not know what *air crew* means?"

"Seems to mean useless," Ressk spat. "Help us turn the body."

Wen backed away, both hands raised. "Not likely. It's your stupid idea and I'm not your bonded."

Teeth showing, Werst crouched again, grabbing on where told and flopping the body over on its other side, nostril ridges closing at the smell rising out of the cut. If he had to shoot Wen himself to keep the desecration of an Elder Race from starting another war, well, right at the moment, he was good with that.

Binti had gone back into the weapons cache to "keep an eye on Nadayki." He was messing with H'san weapons, so she supposed Gunny's order made sense in spite of the repressed feelings she could hear seeping through the words. She just hoped he didn't snip the wrong wire and turn the whole place into a smoking hole with her a meter from ground zero.

He gave her a dismissive toss of his hair when she arrived, the kind that said *why should I care about you; you're not good for anything but violence*. Although after the Trun, she might have been reading more into it than was there, given he'd been a pirate and all. Still, it pissed her off so she watched him from the top of a pile of pink-and-cream crates, flipping one of her knives from hand to hand. Werst and Gunny could roll a blade sharp enough to cut air in and out of their fingers, but she preferred her fingers attached.

After a few minutes, she realized Nadayki had moved as close to her as he could get and continue to work on his chosen weapon.

She frowned and leaned back. She was a sniper, she saw better from a distance.

His arrogance was less defensive, more an actual belief in his superiority, but, that aside, he reminded her of Alamber when he'd first joined them on the *Promise*, needing touch and not sure how to ask a non-Taykan for anything that wasn't sexual. Although he'd had no trouble asking for sex.

Nadayki wasn't asking, but he certainly seemed to be craving touch.

Which was weird because there was another di'Taykan around. And sure, she was a major, but rank didn't erase a di'Taykan's need for contact.

Binti sprawled a little more, stretching out her legs, and Nadayki shifted a little closer.

Yeah. Weird.

The top of the H'san's skull dropped to the floor, ringing in a way that didn't sound like any bone Torin had ever heard.

"Gunny, what's that thing Humans say when they want to show off something triumphantly?"

"I have no idea what you're talking about."

"Tah dah?" offered Dion. He'd been delirious a few minutes ago, but it seemed he was back with them.

"That's it." Ressk bent over the skull cavity, punched the air, said, "Tah dah. Hair-thin metal strands woven through the tissue, looks like gold and platinum, and I bet they're following neural pathways all through the body—the signals from a living brain replaced by control codes."

"They don't die unless we also destroy their superior heart," the major pointed out, leaning against the long counter beside Torin.

"Power source." He sat back on his heels and knocked his knuckles against the broad expanse of bone.

Torin turned toward the weapons cache. "Mashona! Bring up that ax we found!"

"On it, Gunny!" She sounded as though she was down a well. "Ax?"

"Yes, Major, ax. Careful maneuvering around brain tissue might have been necessary . . ." Given it was dead tissue, Torin wasn't entirely convinced of that. ". . . but I'm not waiting for him to saw through ribs that have been cemented back into place. We need to get out of here."

"To warn the rest of your people about the patrols, of course. How long until they come after you?"

"They'll stay where I told them to stay, Major."

"And the patrols will go where the patrols go. If I gave you an order, Gunnery Sergeant Kerr, would you obey it?"

The non sequitur pulled Torin around to face her.

Her gaze remained on the dissection going on across the room. "You still use your rank. I still use mine. They say there's no such thing as an ex-Marine, and I admit I used that belief to maintain discipline during our expedition. So, if I gave you an order, would you obey it?"

"I don't obey bad orders, Major." Although it would be more accurate to say that ensuring bad orders weren't given had been a large part of her job.

"Who's to say it would be a bad order, Gunnery Sergeant."

"Have you given any thought to what will happen if you get these weapons out of here?"

Again, emotions flickered across the major's face too quickly for Torin to read, but all she said was, "Yes."

Torin found herself wondering exactly what question the major had been answering.

"Hey, Gunny?" Binti emerged from the cache with the ax—or reasonable facsimile—and headed over to where the Krai were gathered around the body. "I don't think that biscuit warmer they showed us is a biscuit warmer, not unless they went to war over cold baked goods. There's a couple dozen more of them in a case by Nadayki's science project."

"If you're referring to one of the items the Katrien removed," the major said, while Torin was still figuring out how to respond,

"I assure you it was taken from a sarcophagus."

"I know what I saw, Major. Nadayki saw it, too. They were either tucking weapons in with the dead or biscuit warmers in with the weapons."

"I very much dislike not knowing what's going on," Major Sujuno said softly.

"The H'san like cheese." When that finally turned the major around to face her, Torin shrugged, "It's one thing we know for sure."

Her hair flipped up, just once, as she laughed. Reluctantly. "It might be the *only* thing we know for sure."

Torin understood the reluctance. She didn't find bad intell particularly funny.

Lieutenant Verr turned out to have the most ax experience of the four Krai, clipping the ribs neatly off the body, then taking a final swing to detach the narrow curve of sternum.

Bone cracked.

Ressk's nostril ridges flared, then slammed shut as he threw himself backward.

"Everyone down!" Torin dropped, pulling Major Sujuno to the floor with her.

The H'san exploded.

"Power source," Ressk shouted, as he lifted his head.

As explosions in an enclosed space went, it could've been worse. Torin's ears were ringing, but she could still hear. She got to her feet and habit held out her hand to help the major up. "Everyone all right?"

"Gunny!" It was Ressk's cry, but Werst's arm with a piece of bone protruding through a bloodstained sleeve. Hand around his bonded's wrist, Ressk stared wide-eyed across the room at Dion.

The major sighed. "He's Human. They're . . ."

Torin raised a brow.

". . . weirdly delicate. You'll be fine."

She didn't know that. She couldn't know that. But Sujuno's offhand, superior dismissal of the possibility that infection would eat Werst away from the inside was oddly comforting. That Krai bone and teeth were among the toughest substances in known space made little difference to bacteria. Although bacteria that affected Human systems might not affect them. Werst didn't look convinced, but Ressk looked less like he wanted to tear Verr limb from limb.

"If he dies, I will devour you!"

Not a lot less, but less. "Let's stop any chance of him dying before it starts." Historically, the Krai had a simple solution to potential infection: they bit the wounded area out. Torin had acquired firsthand experience of how effective it was just after she made corporal, when her Recon unit had been sent to scout a Primacy base on an OutSector planet and had gotten pinned down. She'd kept the divot in her thigh until she was tanked after Crucible to regrow her jaw. Torin closed her fingers over Werst's shoulder. "Ressk, if you could do the honors."

"Happy to, Gunny."

"No." Werst pulled free of her touch as he pulled the shard from his arm. He tossed it aside and clamped his palm down on the wound as blood darkened his sleeve. "It's bone-deep, *churick*."

Ressk shook his head. Torin wasn't sure what he was denying.

"If you manage to get it all," Werst continued, red seeping between his fingers. "I won't be able to use the arm. If the major's right about the number of guardians, I'm going to need to use the arm."

He wasn't wrong.

Ressk grabbed his wrist. "We need to take the whole arm off, then." He jerked his head back and forth, back and forth, looking, Torin assumed, for the ax.

"Hey." Werst's voice pulled Ressk's attention. "Did you miss where I said I needed to use the arm? We don't know it's infected. The major's right; just because it can take down a Human doesn't mean anything now that it's trying for a Krai."

"If you die . . ."

"We're all going to die sooner or later."

"Later."

"All right." He tugged and Ressk closed the distance between them.

Torin gave them a moment, forehead to forehead, but only a moment. "Ressk, will examining a power source help us get the hell out of here?"

"If I can figure out how to shut the guardians off . . ."

"Let his arm bleed for a while," Torin told Binti, who'd snapped the aid kit off her belt. Werst's cuff acknowledged a foreign substance in his blood, but wasn't able to identify it. So far, no symptoms. "Clean it out with water, don't seal it."

"I know the drill," Werst growled.

Recon occasionally had to improvise out on their own.

"Fine, doctor yourself. The rest of you, let's go get another H'san."

"Good thing we have spares," the major said, falling into step beside her.

Torin closed her teeth on the automatic *yes, sir*. It was the first one she'd had to stop.

"It's a hatch. It has two functions: it opens, it closes. Opened. Closed. All you have to do is work with that."

"It's a locked hatch."

"And locks have a single function."

"It's a very old lock designed a very long time ago by a species we apparently know jackshit about."

"Single function," Craig repeated. "How hard can it be?"

"Fuk you."

"Maybe if you get the hatch unlocked." He laughed when Alamber flipped him off. He had no idea what they were going to do if they got into the ship, but the stairs from the blast bay had ended at the ten-meter–square landing outside the hatch. Given the size of the landing, they were both confident there was another entrance, but neither of them could find it. Rather than go back down to the bay and stand around with their thumbs up their asses discussing how they couldn't get out of the bay, they'd decided to try and break into the ship. Turned out that Alamber's criminal career, pre–Big Bill, had included a certain number of hacked hatches.

"It's harder on a station; you have to get through the station security as well. Not all stations, of course," he continued twisting the upper half of his body 45 degrees and peering in behind the dangling faceplate. "Smaller stations, rougher sectors, security's shit. The contents are usually shit, too. These things tend to balance out. You're lucky you're with me; Ressk's useless at hardware."

"And yet, the hatch is still closed."

"At least we know the dead H'san can't get in here."

"The dead H'san probably know where the door is."

"They don't know anything they haven't been programmed with."

"If it was me, I'd program in schematics. Full blueprints."

"Good point. Shit." Alamber's elbows jerked, but his hands remained buried in the guts of the hatch controls. "Grab that long skinny tool with the copper head and the insulated grip and poke this."

Craig picked the tool in question off the kit spread out on top of Alamber's pack. He leaned over Alamber's shoulder and peered into the mess. "Poke what?"

In turn, Alamber leaned some of his weight against Craig's hip. "You see that shiny blue oval? Just back of my thumb?"

There were a lot of shiny blue ovals. He moved the tool. "This?"

"No!" Craig felt Alamber flinch. "My other thumb!"

"This?"

"The oval next to it. While I wish I was saying this under other circumstances, give it a good hard poke."

The power discharge blew Craig's fingers off the grip. The tool clanged against the floor as he staggered back, eyes watering and the world reduced to a flickering pattern of bright blue dots. Hands cupped over his eyes, he blinked until his vision cleared. He'd done his own repairs on the *Promise* for years; that was not his first discharge. And he'd rephrase if he mentioned it to Alamber.

"You okay?"

He lowered his hands. Alamber's question had been muffled because he had his fingers in his mouth. "Burns?"

"Yeah, but my head hurts so much, I can't really feel it."

"Did I poke the wrong oval?"

Alamber grinned. "No, you did it exactly right." Fingers trailing a gossamer line of spit behind them, he reached out and popped the hatch. "It's easier when you don't have to worry about relocking it. Ever again."

The interior of the ship was . . .

"Pink." He wondered how the H'san saw it.

"It's more cheerful than gray."

"It's pinker than gray," Craig muttered climbing the ladder to the upper level. The climb took a little concentration, given that the access had been designed for the H'san, who bent in non-bipedal ways. There was a wide port across the front of the control room—because the H'san for all their other strangeness were a biocular species who responded to visual stimulus. There were obvious, if not familiar, control panels—because the H'san were among the founders of the Confederation and their designs remained popular. They also lasted for-fukking-ever, which might be why it looked like they hadn't changed much in millennia.

In front of the panel were angles and curves and protuberances that, given their positions, had to be chairs no bipedal species could possibly be comfortable sitting on.

One finger back in his mouth, Alamber studied them appraisingly.

"Don't even."

He shrugged and turned his attention to the main panel. "You think we could get this thing going?"

"We can't close the hatch."

"We can't *lock* the hatch," Alamber corrected. "We've already closed it. And I'm sure we could seal it if we needed to."

"Why would we need to?"

"Boss is in trouble; bringing an operational shuttle into the game will change the rules."

"We don't know the game."

"Or the rules. But that's why you wanted to break in here, isn't it?"

He ran both hands back through his hair. "Alien ship. Alien systems."

"You said you had a friend with a H'san control panel, I'm brilliant, and physics remains a constant."

The control panel in question had been scrubbed of all

software and the hardware retrofitted into a salvage ship. This was a H'san control panel running a H'san system. A millennium-old H'san system. But Torin was in trouble, and it *was* why he'd wanted to break in.

He leaned carefully against the front of one of the chairs. "Did I ever tell you about how a Primacy bug flew a completely alien shuttle up to the *Promise*, ferrying Presit and me down to the prison where we blew the lid off the whole polynumerous plastic gray alien plan?"

"Yeah." Alamber sat a little less carefully. "Every time we watch those recordings."

"Well, it's a good story." There were dials, actual dials, on the control board. "Of course, it turned out the ship was made of the little gray aliens, so maybe the bug didn't fly it so much as it had an agenda and flew itself."

"Any chance this ship is made of little gray aliens?"

"Fuk, I hope not. Torin needs to move on."

"What about you?"

"I need Torin to move on."

"She never talks about them."

"She discusses them with Dr. Ito." Craig needed to find a way to connect with the ship's sysop. If it had one. "I don't know how much discussion happens, but I know she hates them. The aliens, not the sessions with Dr. Ito."

"She hates those, too."

"She says she does." He grinned at Alamber's expression. Torin had admitted to him, in the dark, when they were touching everywhere they could be and he could feel her heartbeat strong and steady under his palm, that Dr. Ito might actually be helping to clarify a few things. *Might actually be* was Torin-speak for *yeah, surprised me, too.* The grin slipped as he remembered. "She believed in something. Not in war or territorialism or whatever the fuk the Confederation thought they were fighting for. She believed in getting the job done and getting her people home alive, and it turned out not so much that she believed in a lie, but that it was a job that never needed doing."

"She still gets her people out alive, though." Slender fingers touched the coiled mass of his hair. "Every time."

"So far."

Alamber frowned at the control panel. "Dials?"

This was a bad idea, but she couldn't help Ressk—Binti was covering him, if Wen and the lieutenant weren't assisting, they weren't hindering—and she had no reason to wander among the weapons. She didn't want to talk to Nadayki. She wanted to wring his skinny neck, so she stayed away. Dion was delirious during his increasingly rare moments of consciousness. Werst was napping, curled up on one of the jellied "chairs."

Torin couldn't sit quietly. Couldn't settle. She needed to do something, but other than conclude the mission they'd been given by Colonel Hurrs, the only thing left to do was talk to Major Sujuno.

It was already too late to pretend she was a stranger if and/or when Torin killed her. She might as well get some answers.

"Major." Torin stood on one side of the long counter that divided the food preparation area from the rest of the room, the major on the other. "Werst says you look at me like you want to crack my bones and eat the marrow."

The major met Torin's gaze, and, after a long moment, stopped pretending.

Torin had been disliked often enough over the years—she'd never denied she could be abrupt and insensitive, arrogant and hyper-vigilant, all words that had been spat at her—but she'd never been hated. She'd stared into the eyes of enemy combatants as they tried to kill each other and she hadn't seen hate. She saw it now. Werst was right; Major Sujuno hated her. "Why?"

"You're here to arrest us." The major shrugged, the motion tight and controlled and at odds to the passion in her expression. "I'm committing a crime, and you're the weapon wielded by the Justice Department. Why wouldn't I hate you?"

"No." It wasn't a general hate, a hate of what Torin represented. It was personal. Werst was right about that, too.

"No?"

"No. Have we met? Was a *thytrin* of yours in Sh'quo Company when they died and I survived? Did I leave a *thytrin* of yours behind in the prison?" If either of those were the reason, Torin wouldn't blame her. There were days she hated herself.

"Nothing so simple." The major crossed her arms, one hand cupping her masker. One of her maskers; Torin suddenly realized she wore two. She'd begun to think that was the end of the conversation when the major said, "You were named progenitor."

"I had nothing to do with that."

"Of course not." Her voice had become a low growl, the edges unraveling, and the last centimeter of her hair flicking back and forth. "It means nothing to you. You're not Taykan. You'll never begin a family line. You have nothing to do with those who've lost everything and can't afford to keep their name. *You* were named progenitor. You. You have nothing to do with the bureaucrats who mock your mourning, who only care about squeezing blood from your pain. You have nothing to do with your name dying and you unable to stop it. No one listening to you. Do you know what it costs to be named progenitor? Of course not. Why would you?" she spat, her eyes dark as she threw herself up and over the counter, sliding on the polished stone. "You have nothing to do with that!"

Torin blocked the first blow and the second. The third got through, rocking her head back as she tried to take Major Sujuno down without hurting her. And yes, she recognized the irony. The major was taller, with a longer reach, but she was reacting, not thinking, and she hadn't had Torin's specialist training.

When Torin finally pinned her arms, she collapsed for a moment, pushing into Torin's touch before pulling back and hissing, "Release me, Gunnery Sergeant."

Torin dropped her hold and stepped away, a gesture holding her people where they were. The major's people were watching but didn't seem to care about the aborted fight one way or the other and clearly had no intent to intervene.

The major took another deep breath and stilled her hair. She squared her shoulders, nodded toward the cache, and said, "That is the survival of my name." Then she pivoted on one heel and walked away.

Torin stayed where she was. Looked down as Werst moved to stand beside her, his injured arm in a sling.

"Valid reason at least."

"Millions dead," Torin said.

Craig stepped back from the control panel and banged the side of his head against the bulkhead until Alamber grabbed his shoulder, pulling him too far away for contact. Since it hadn't been helping, he allowed himself to be pulled.

"What?" Strong fingers dug into the knotted muscles at the base of Craig's neck. "You expected to be in orbit by now?"

"Not orbit . . . something." He sighed. "The lights are only on because the H'san have an automatic light fixation. We've managed jackshit since we broke in."

"Since *we* broke in?"

"Maybe we should stop being so careful." Shrugging off Alamber's touch, he returned to the panel, turned dials, shifted slides, rubbed his fingers across what might have been a touch screen, and kicked the lower edge of the console for good measure, the metal booming under his boot.

"Hey! A light's on!"

The boom caught everyone's attention. Even Dion blinked and fought to focus.

"Hey! A light's on!"

"Alamber?" Torin couldn't see the speakers. Given her urge to look up, they were somewhere high.

"What does it do?"

"It lights up. How the sanLi should I know what it does? You're the pilot. What did you do?"

"I turned that. I moved that. I touched that."

"And you gave it the boot, right? Kicked it right . . ."

The second boom cut off halfway through.

"Sounds like they're in the ship." Binti swept a narrow-edge gaze around the edges of the ceiling and pointed at a dimple Torin had missed entirely. "At least we know they're alive."

Torin had a long swallow of water and wished she was the type of person who could drink on the job.

* * *

"Shite. The light's off again."

"Does it matter? We don't know what it did."

Craig turned, moved, touched, kicked. Nothing. "And now we'll never know." He dropped onto the pilot's chair, swore, shifted, and glared at the control board. "We might be going at this the wrong way."

"I thought we'd established that." Alamber rolled a dial under each hand.

"That . . ." Craig pointed with his second finger. ". . . is an alien control panel, the access to an alien sysop. The alien sysop controls an alien ship."

"Yeah?"

"Too many variables, mate. Remember the door. It opens, it closes. It's locked, it's unlocked."

"So, it's not turning on because the hatch isn't sealed?"

"Possibly. But you're missing the point; we need to simplify this."

Alamber's eyes darkened and he hissed as his hair gave an involuntary flip. "We go directly to the engines."

Craig grinned. "Engines turn on. Engines turn off."

"The weapons aren't exactly biometric, they operate on the same system as the body, powered through this contact." Ressk lifted one of the H'san's upper appendages to show the narrow metal plate in the palm. He'd been working nonstop since the explosion and Werst's injury. Werst's best chance was the medical unit on *Promise* and in order to get there, they had to get out. "There's no corresponding contact in the grip of their weapon, so there's a good chance the guardians could use anything in the armory."

"Another reason for not letting them get this far," Lieutenant Verr pointed out. "Right up there with not wanting to die."

Major Sujuno ran her thumb over the contact. "If we could use this to control some of the larger weapons, we could destroy the guardians."

"Once we destroy the guardians," the lieutenant added, "there's nothing stopping us from leaving."

Torin decided to let that go for the moment. "Ressk?"

"It wouldn't work with the bodies we have. When you shoot out the unit that powers them . . ."

"We stop them," Wen growled.

". . . you fry the whole system. Not to mention, you destroy the power source. Although, H'san metal to H'san metal, it gets a lot more destroyed when you hit it with an ax."

"Axes aren't really practical, given the scale." They could continue to take the guardians out one at a time, piling them in the barracks away from any chance to be rebuilt—if that's what was happening behind the metal doors—but, if the major hadn't exaggerated the numbers, they'd be at it for a couple of tendays, even working with teams at each threshold. Food and water needs aside, Werst might not have that kind of time. She definitely didn't have that kind of time. Torin pointed the H'san's cone-like weapon at the wall and squeezed the grip. Nothing happened. The same way nothing had happened when she'd twisted it. "What about the head shots?"

Ressk dropped the appendage into the major's hand and picked up the net he'd pulled out of the skull. "Hitting any of these blue disks . . ." A bit of brain dropped off the crumpled metal and bounced. ". . . fries the—for lack of a better word—wiring. I expect the surge scrambles the programming as well, but that's entirely redundant because there's nothing left for the programming to run through. You could skip the head shot entirely and only hit the power source and still take them down."

"Why were you shooting them in the head?" Marines were taught to aim at the dead center of the target's mass. Regardless of species, there was less chance of a miss and a greater chance of hitting critical organs.

"You shoot zombies in the head," Wen snorted, the *duh* implied.

The major tossed the appendage over onto the body and wiped her hand on her thigh. "Once the head's hit, they flail. Eventually their armor gets knocked askew so you can get a chest shot."

"You can't shoot through the armor?"

Her lip curled. "Not through the chest plate. Not unless you can hit the exact same spot at least three times."

"If we want to use their weapons to cut down their numbers . . ." Ressk draped the net over the open skull. ". . . I need an intact power source and an appendage with a working contact."

"How are we supposed to get that?" Wen demanded.

Ressk sighed. "You don't shoot them in the fukking head."

"You don't need the head?" Torin clarified while the lieutenant moved to stand between her bonded and Ressk.

"No, just a power source and a contact point."

"The wires around the power source?" On the second corpse, Ressk had skipped the step with the ax and cut a dozen or so wires running from the box out into the body.

"Only the box." He held it up. "And an appendage."

"Why not all of them?" Werst asked.

"I can only reconnect one per power source."

"All right, then." Torin lifted the strap of her KC off her shoulder, hung it on Werst's, and pulled out her boot knife. "Mashona."

"Gunny?"

"I'm going to go stand by the threshold for seven minutes and attract a guardian. I'll need you to shoot out its knees."

"I didn't know they had knees," Binti said as she checked her weapon.

"Closest equivalent."

"Gunny . . ."

Torin looked down at Werst.

He shook his head. "Never mind."

As they headed down the dark hall leading past the three sets of barracks to the storerooms and finally the exit, Torin realized they weren't alone. "What?" she demanded, without turning. Someone had their light on and she needed her eyes to adapt to the lower levels in the storeroom.

After a moment's silence, Wen said, "We want to watch."

"I want to see you die. Why not honesty?" the major demanded at the ripple of reaction.

Why not?

"Werst."

"I'll watch her."

"Ressk, keep an eye on Nadayki. It's long odds, but if he gets something working, I don't want him behind me when my attention's needed elsewhere."

"I need the power unit intact, Gunny."

She grinned. "Yeah, yeah, I heard you the first twenty times. Mashona will set up at the farthest point where she has a clear shot. I'm not guaranteeing the guardian won't get a few shots off, so the rest of you can wait where you like."

No one followed her across the storeroom. During her seven-minute wait at the threshold, she cleared the area; an accidental skewering on a piece of broken shelving was not a part of her plan.

At seven minutes and twelve seconds, Torin heard the approach of a patrolling guardian, the syncopated rhythm unnaturally constant. The lights in the side corridor, lights that had come on for both Major Sujuno's people and hers, stayed off.

She held her ground until the last moment, then dove right as the guardian surged over the threshold and Binti's first shot rang out. Old bone was brittle bone and the joint, unprotected by armor, blew. A lower appendage collapsed and it spun to the left, its shot shattering an already damaged set of shelves. Binti's second shot spun it left again around a second destroyed joint. Its weapon gouged a line across the stone ceiling. With a third joint destroyed, it collapsed to the floor.

Three running steps and a boost off the angle of its hip, and Torin balanced on the center of its back. With one hand on the top of its head, she reached around with the other, and slid her blade in under the metal collar that protected its throat. Cut through soft tissue. Found the join between two vertebrae. Cut up, not straight across. The sarcophagi holding the pieces of H'san had been an education.

The cone-weapon fired again, angle close enough that Torin dropped to her knees. An upper appendage reached back, hooked black nails around her lower leg, and gouged bruises into her calf as it tried to drag her forward. She braced her other knee and twisted the knife. Felt one bundle of wires give. Then the other.

Separated from its programming, its head bouncing over a pile of debris, the body ran straight for a wall on the shattered stumps of its legs. The impact flung Torin off, fingers still gripping tufts of hair. She rolled as she hit the floor, got her feet under her as the headless H'san spun in place, grabbed the appendage with the weapon, drove the point of her blade into the exposed elbow joint, popped it, cut the wires, and detached it from the body.

Arm and weapon flew in different directions.

The body rolled. Torin rolled with it, clawing her way around until she sat on its chest, the chest plate providing a secure handhold. Unfortunately, she had to cut the chest plate off. Fortunately, the leather strapping was nothing more than it appeared to be. Four quick slashes cut the plate free as what was left of the guardian thrashed from side to side, the plate clipping her in the mouth as it flew free. She spat blood and adjusted her grip, tucking in. Up close, she could see where repairs had been made in the center of the chest. See where three rounds had gone through its shoulder—chipping the bone and shredding the flesh, but not, it seemed, doing enough damage to require repairs. She ducked a flailing limb that could have eviscerated her had it any control, slid her knife between two ribs, leaned her weight against the handle, and pried the ribs apart.

The dead H'san—the guardian—headless, appendages both flailing and failing, made no noise. The re-animator hadn't given it a voice. Torin was good with that.

She appreciated the minimal fluids as well. A beheading was usually a lot messier.

The power source glimmered through the space she'd opened. She slid the tip of her knife around it, cutting it free from the gleaming golden lines that anchored it in the dead H'san's chest.

The guardian collapsed, one piece at a time, like a puppet having its strings slowly cut.

When it finally stilled completely, Torin tested the security of her front teeth, wiped the blood off her upper lip onto her sleeve, and climbed off to retrieve the amputated appendage.

Another guardian charged through the door.

Three fast shots took it out—the first dented the armor, the second opened up the bottom of the dent, the third went through the hole and destroyed the power source.

It slid to a stop at Torin's feet, shoulder nudging her boot.

"You might want to quit lingering near the door, Gunny." Binti sounded amused. "Unless you're planning to have me take the lot of them down one at a time."

"You'd just get big headed," Torin told her, tucking the appendage and weapon under one arm, grabbing the remains of the first body, and dragging it between the shelves and pieces of shelves until she met the others near the back of the room.

"Wen, Verr . . ."

Torin couldn't see the major's face through the light clipped to her shoulder, but she sounded disappointed.

". . . get the other one and get it back here. *We* don't leave it close enough to the door that the others can retrieve it."

"Feel better?" Werst asked as Torin handed him the piece of H'san.

"Little bit, yeah."

TEN

"**W**hat stinks?" Eyes squinted nearly closed, Craig rubbed his nose against his sleeve and sucked air in through his teeth.

Hanging in over the edge of the engine well, Alamber dragged his tunic up over his mouth and nose. "We must've vented something."

"In a ship that's been empty for millennia?"

"Hey, could be the zombie H'san hanging out in here bitching about how boring it is being a guard."

"You think there's more than one of them?"

"So do you." When he looked up, Alamber shrugged. "If there was only one of them, the boss would've been back by now."

Craig glanced at the timer on his cuff. Torin and the others had been gone just over four hours and if he'd had to bet on why, he'd bet they'd been cornered by the undead patrol. Maybe they were with the mercs. Maybe they weren't. Maybe Torin had already dealt with the *and executioner,* but he doubted it. Torin would be dummying up a way to get everyone out alive—although without the comms, he had nothing to go on but his belief in Torin's ability to get the job done. If precedent held, she'd come back to him bleeding and angry, but she would come back to him.

"You think firing up the engine will draw the zombie H'san away from her?" Alamber asked. "I mean, from them."

He'd meant *from her.* Craig was all right with that. "I think live engines on a dead ship should catch their attention, yeah."

"Okay, try this." Shifting up onto one elbow, Alamber handed over a small, curved tool with a long handle that looked like a close cousin to the tool he'd used on the hatch. "I've never slipped it into an engine before—insert innuendo here—but nothing else is working."

"What is it?" It was heavier than it looked and small enough to get past the conduit.

"*Ad sitina hunn.* Closest Federate would be a . . ." His lips moved silently for a moment. ". . . a spintite socket wrench with a male adapter and an extended grip."

"How close?" It didn't look like a socket wrench.

"Does it matter? You're about to stick it into the controls of an alien engine."

"Valid point."

They were counting on form following function. A shuttle engine provided enough lift to break out of the gravity well and attain orbit. With no identifiable antigravity tech, the H'san shuttle needed to provide one hell of a lot of lift, which should have simplified things. It hadn't. Craig had no idea what all the conduit was for.

It wasn't until they'd pried the access cover off and he'd lowered himself into the generous amount of space required for an adult H'san that he'd truly realized what *ancient alien mechanical systems* meant. It meant neither of them had recognized a damned thing. Still, duxing out the impossible beat sitting around doing nothing, waiting for Torin to return.

Throwing his weight against the conduit, he opened up enough space to slide the tool through. Probing individual circuits had accomplished a big fat nothing, but the curved end on the not-wrench would allow him to give two at a time a turn. Elbow jammed in the gap, he twisted the tool until . . .

The engines roared.

The flash nearly blinded him. Power surged up the tool, locking his fingers to the grip. He threw himself back, breaking the connection, losing his balance, and sliding down the metal bars on other side of the access well.

The engines shut off.

"You okay?" Lying on the deck, most of his upper body unsupported, Alamber stretched a long arm toward him.

Craig raised a hand to keep the kid from attempting the last six centimeters and falling on his head. It took a couple of tries to get his voice working. "I'm fried but fine. How long?"

"The engines? Not very. Microburst at best."

"Seemed longer."

"Yeah, well, you were busy watching your life flash before your eyes."

The fingers that had been clamped to the grip felt scorched, and he was both sweating and chilled. "It wasn't that bad."

"Looked that bad from up here."

"Let's . . ." He started to get to his feet, felt as though the gravity cut out, blinked, and sat down again.

"You need some help? The boss would give me such crap if you got hurt handling my tool." Craig looked up and Alamber smirked.

It hurt when he laughed. "On the bright side, we can start the engines. We just need to figure out a way to do it that doesn't hurt so much." Stretching out a leg, he hooked his heel over Alamber's not-wrench and dragged it toward him. "Now we know how to turn this thing on, let's chuck back to the control room and take another crack at the board."

"Now?"

His legs felt more fluid than he was comfortable with. "In a minute."

"That's an arm–ish–like thing." Nadayki stayed well out from the counter, eyes light as he watched Ressk cut the dried flesh back to expose the wires running down to the contact. "It's disgusting."

"Not arguing," Ressk grunted, snapping off about eight centimeters of exposed bone. "I've never handled so much meat I don't want to eat."

Nadayki tossed his head, lime-green hair feathering out around him. "Really, because I've got . . ."

Major Sujuno cleared her throat and he froze, hair clamping

in tight to his head, arms wrapping around his torso. Torin hadn't noticed it in the cache—they'd both been distracted by their history—but she'd had never seen a di'Taykan in such touch distress. Nadayki was undeniably a murdering shit, but she had to fight to stop herself from crossing to him and tucking him in against her body. Ressk was distracted by his combination of engineering and surgery, but Binti and Werst seemed to be having much the same reaction. Torin shook her head when Binti caught her eye. With Wen and the lieutenant taking their cues from the major, Nadayki probably hadn't been touched since Dion's injury. For it to be this noticeable, she'd bet the major hadn't touched him for all the time they'd been together.

Which meant the major willingly suffered from an even higher level of touch distress. High odds Nadayki had been going skin to skin with the Humans at least, but Torin would bet the major hadn't. Had Sujuno been Torin's major, she'd have done something about it—a destabilized officer made bad decisions. As she wasn't, and as Nadayki *was*, in fact, a murdering shit, it wasn't her problem, as hard as it might be to ignore.

Her expression entirely neutral, Torin stepped between them. "Nadayki, we need a weapon that'll cause maximum destruction without bringing the roof down."

"Destroy lots of guardians, minimal property damage?" Hair swinging, he turned and sauntered back into the cache. "It's a good thing for you that I'm a fukking genius."

He hadn't checked with the major. The major didn't look happy about it. Torin reminded herself that she didn't care.

Alamber had gone for the med kit the moment they'd gotten back to the control room and Craig's hand hurt enough he'd sat on the floor, leaning back against a relatively flat bit of the pilot's chair, and let him spray sealant on the reddened skin. He sighed and slumped as the pain receded.

Then straightened again almost immediately.

"Did I do it wrong?"

"No, of course not." He reached out and touched the back of his fingers to Alamber's cheek as he kicked the bottom of the control console on the visible dent one of them had left behind. A section of panel dropped off to hit the floor with a surprisingly dull thud.

"Well, that's going to make things easier." Alamber leaned in, eyes dark. "If we can hook the hardware together, I might be able to force cooperation. Hang on."

"Not going anywhere," Craig said as Alamber dove back into his pack and came up with a small case.

"Universal connection." He grinned and waved a wire before pushing one end into his slate and heading back under the control panel with the other.

"No such thing."

"You'd think that, but Big Bill was all about me getting into places I wasn't supposed to be and it's not like there isn't H'san tech all over known space. I mean, if even you salvage guys grabbed some . . ."

"It can't be that easy."

"It's not. This is one use only and I may fry my slate—even with the kind of firewalls that'd stop actual fire."

"And if you do?"

He shot a grin back over his shoulder, and a piece of hair unwrapped from around the injured strands to wave. "If the cable still works, I'll take a shot at frying yours."

"Stand back." Ressk, hand wrapped in a piece of H'san textile that Nadayki had sworn would insulate, completed the connection between the power source and the cone weapon. The beam left a scorched line the length of the counter and blew a circular chunk about half a centimeter deep out of the bunker wall.

"It did more damage when the dead guy was using it," Wen scoffed, curling his lip when Werst growled.

"That's because it's an energy beam used as blunt force," Ressk explained setting the weapon back on the counter. "Pull the trigger, swing the beam, and it's like swinging a big invisible bat."

"Well, this is a bigger bat." Nadayki dropped a . . . Torin assumed it had to be a weapon as Nadayki had carried it out of the weapons cache, but it didn't look like any weapon she'd ever seen. It *was* big. Triple barrels, each barrel slightly cone-shaped and wrapped in what looked like braided fiberoptic cable. The base of the barrels twisted around a . . . She had no idea. For a BFG, it was lighter than it looked.

"There's no contact point on the grip!" Ressk's teeth showed. "We need a weapon that'll work with the power source!"

"Calm down and cut the covering away. Here." Nadayki tapped the textile wrapped around the grip with a slender finger. "To here. It's what's stopping the entire grip from being a contact point on your little bitty weapon as well."

Ressk's nostril ridges fluttered. "I should've seen that."

"Yeah, you should have."

"Fuk you."

Torin stepped between them. "Nadayki, you've been in the cache since we arrived. Go get something to eat. Ressk . . ."

"I can't take a break, Gunny. We have to get out of here."

Torin tracked his gaze to the nearer of the two doors leading to the other side of the bunker—officers' quarters and Med-op instead of barracks and admin. The Med-op had held a number of cubes that flattened under a minimal touch and nothing any of them had recognized, biology being significantly more variable than engineering. As they watched, Binti and Werst emerged, having gone to check that the guardians had made no unexpected inroads.

"We have to get out of here," Ressk repeated as Werst gave the all clear. "I have to get him out of here and to the Med-op on the ship. Let me work."

"On the condition you take a break if you need one." Where *need* meant, *I'm trusting you to tell me if you can't do what I need you to do*, and they both knew what she meant.

"I have to set this up so the appendage holds the grip and the shooter's grip on the appendage controls the weapon. We test it. We're out of here. The end is in sight. I can do this."

"I know."

The big weapon worked on the same principle as the smaller one, smashing the first target to pieces. The second test against one of the redead H'san proved their armor absorbed the energy of the small weapons, but the energy of the big one overwhelmed it, slamming the body against the wall and pinning it there.

"Except broken bones don't stop them." Ressk broke the contact, and they watched the body crumple.

"Removed bones don't stop them," Binti pointed out.

Nadayki jabbed at a wire-and-ceramic oval with the point of a knife. "Crush their head and you'll disrupt the programming."

"We'll use it to sweep them aside, smash them into the walls, hope we crush a few heads, and open a path through the middle while we take out as many as we can with conventional weapons. BFG makes the run first, the rest of us haul ass after. At the far end, BFG turns and either orders a drop and fires, or fires with regular ordnance in support." Torin gripped Nadayki's shoulder, ignoring his sudden intake of breath. "Do you have any idea what that oval thing is?"

"Uh . . ." He looked up at her, his eyes so dark they were almost free of lime-green. "No?"

"Then stop playing with it. If you blow your hands off, I'm not sure I like you well enough to keep you from bleeding out."

"Yeah, well, I'd bleed out before I let you save me." But his hair swept across the back of her hand as he set the oval on the counter.

"Shouldn't I be giving the orders, Gunnery Sergeant?"

Torin turned, met Major Sujuno's gaze and held it. The hate was a constant presence now; acknowledged, it could be ignored. "If you believed that, Major, you wouldn't have asked."

"Rhetorical question."

Torin's lip lifted off her teeth into a curve only another Human would have seen as a smile. "I don't think so."

"Then perhaps you should think of how we'll need to bring more than one of these weapons into play." The major stroked a finger down the upper barrel of the BFG. "Granted, we haven't food nor water enough to take down all the guardians one or two at a time, but we only require seven appendages more to arm each of us. With eight of these weapons, we can destroy all opposition."

"We don't need to destroy the opposition, we need to get past it." Torin had no intention of gifting either the major or her people with any more firepower than they already had. "And I've fought the only one-on-one I intend to." She could feel bruises rising and, from the swelling on the side of her face, there was a good chance her cheekbone was cracked. Again. "Once, for a weapon we could use to get out . . ." To get back to Craig. To get Werst to the Med-op. ". . . that was acceptable risk. Now we have a way out, it's a pointless risk."

The major's eyes had darkened. "Not to me."

"Nothing's stopping you from cutting the appendages off as many H'san as your heart desires." Werst shrugged at the major's glare. "If you think you're badass enough, go to it."

"Gunnery Sergeant . . ."

"He makes a valid point. What's more, you, none of you have to come with us." The grave robbers trapped inside the grave they'd tried to rob would be poetic justice of a sort.

"You wouldn't leave us here to starve." Major Sujuno sounded smugly certain of that.

"Neither would I take your choice to starve away."

"*I'm* leaving with you," Nadayki muttered, shifting closer, his arm pressing against her thigh.

Hands curled into fists, the major stared at Torin for a long moment. "It seems I *have* no choice. I leave with you, under your terms, or I don't leave at all. Or . . ." She shifted her weight, and her breath came noticeably quicker. ". . . I kill you, we kill you all, and take the weapon. We take all the weapons. And my name lives."

"Try."

The major blinked. "What?"

"Try to kill me." Making it personal would make her life so much easier. She'd survived years of people trying to kill her; not always, but often enough by killing them instead. A war between interstellar civilizations had spent a significant amount of time being about mud and blood, and she'd been covered in both a little too often. Torin had no idea how much of that showed on her face, but she wasn't trying to hide it.

Major Sujuno took a step back. "Lieutenant!"

"Nothing to do with me, Major." Lieutenant Verr stepped back farther and faster. "It's not even that Gunnery Sergeant Kerr took down a dead H'san in single combat, it's that she even thought of doing it in the first place."

"Armed dead H'san," Wen called from beside Dion's pallet.

"Exactly, an armed dead H'san. Ignoring, for the moment, that she won . . . the whole idea was fukking nuts. Plus, her people are ex-infantry, they're all carrying, and our KCs are where we left them after the ammo check. Now . . ." Verr folded her arms, the poster child for an immovable object. ". . . I want to get paid for this job as much as you do, and I don't want to find out what the Justice Department considers a suitable rehabilitation for trespass and desecration, whatever the rest of the charges were . . . although, not the murder; we had nothing to do with that. We thought the Katrien had left. How did she die?"

"Broken neck," Torin told her, a little confused by Verr's reaction to her taking down the H'san. It hadn't been that hard. Living targets, targets that could react, feel pain, that had lives to lose were much harder.

Hair completely motionless, the major flipped her gaze between them. "That's not . . ."

Verr ignored her. "Toporov, then. Broadbent was strong enough, but he was uncooked at the core—soft—and McKinnon was an engineer. I doubt she either could or would. But my point is that even more than not wanting to deal with Justice, I don't want me and mine to die right here and right now, and I don't want to starve to death trapped in the bottom of this fukking tomb. And trust me, Major, me and Wen, we'll starve to death last. So we're going to let Gunnery Sergeant Kerr get us out of here, because, surprise, the vids were right, that's what she's good at, and maybe we'll reassess after and try shooting them all in the back and maybe we won't, but we won't die—fast or slow—because you personally think it's a good idea."

"I am in command of this expedition, Lieutenant!"

"Expedition's over, Major. It was a good run, but it ended when we were trapped by zombie H'san." Verr nodded toward Torin. "She's been in charge since she got here."

Major Sujuno stood for a moment, pinned between them, then she wrapped herself in the neutral Marine officer personae she'd worn before allowing the hate to rise to the surface. Everyone's gaze on her, she walked to her weapon and pointedly picked it up, hanging the strap over her shoulder.

"We'll leave at your discretion, Gunnery Sergeant."

As though she expected Torin to believe it would be that easy.

"Shoot us all in the back?" Torin asked Verr.

Who shrugged. "Just a thought. I doubt it would work."

"Gunny!"

Torin tightened her hold on Nadayki's shoulder for a heartbeat, his pulse having finally steadied under her fingers, then, ignoring the major entirely, crossed to where Werst crouched by Dion's pallet. The scholar hadn't been conscious since Torin's fight. As the red lines of the infection had spread out onto his chest and up into his throat, it had become obvious he wouldn't make it back to Med-op in time.

Werst glanced up at her, nostril ridges wide. "He opened his eyes, said, I told you so, and died."

"His last words were I told you so?"

"He went the way he would've wanted to," Wen said from the other side of the body. "Smug and sanctimonious to the end." He sounded amused, but sincere.

"Do we take him out?" Werst asked, nodding at Torin's belt.

An NCO carried a minimum of three things into a firefight. A weapon. Ammunition. And a promise that if it was up to them, no one would be left behind.

Torin considered Dion. It would be hypocritical to say it wasn't her choice. They couldn't get to Private Timin di'Geirah, whose body rotted at the bottom of the pit trap, and they couldn't get to enough of Corporal Katherine McKinnon shoved into a sarcophagus with the H'san. Parts of the crushed and dismembered Corporal Broadbent waited for her to get a DNA sample and the guardians had taken the bodies of Sergeant Yasha Toporov and Corporal Srey Keo. But Jamers was in Torin's pack and they had Dion.

"We take him out."

To her surprise, Ressk took Wen's place, helping Werst lay Dion out flat. A glance at the counter showed Nadayki working on the BFG, the major watching, arms folded—a nontypical position for a di'Taykan. Mashona watched the major, hands crossed on top of her KC—an entirely typical position for Mashona.

Ressk's nostril ridges fluttered as he sealed the upper edge of the bag. "They should've taken the wound before the infection got into his blood."

Torin assumed "they" referred to Lieutenant Verr and Wen, who had curled up together on one of the H'san . . . chairs. She waited until she held Dion's cylinder in her hand, the curves cool against her palm, before saying, "Werst."

"Little late, Gunny." He slipped his arm out of the sling. Binti had cut his blood-soaked sleeve off above the elbow so she could clearly see the skin around the wound had turned a darker green and one dark line ran up to disappear under the edge of the cut. "It'd be more than a divot at this point."

His temperature had gone up a full degree. Pushing the fabric back, she noted the infection ended a centimeter past his elbow. "We've got an ax. We can take the arm off."

Ressk jerked as though he felt the blow.

Werst flexed his fingers, and Torin watched the skin ride over the muscles of his forearm. "I still need both hands to help get us out of here and, after that, it's less than three days back to the ship now we know where we're going. Less than two if we hustle. Plenty of time."

Torin drew a line on Werst's sleeve about four centimeters from his shoulder. "It gets to here, we reassess."

Werst nodded agreement. Ressk shook his head.

"All right, let's get this show on the road." As Torin led them back to the counter and the BFG, she heard Werst say, "Then Colonel Hurrs will just have to approve a tank so I can regrow the arm."

"Without giving this whole shit-storm away?" Ressk growled.

"Sure. He's head of Intell. That makes him a *cark* sucker by default."

Nadayki had been adjusting the sensitivity of the contact point. "We're squeezing a dead H'san to fire this, and, while I might normally make a comment about that, just—no. Since squeezing a dead H'san isn't exactly a quantitative measurement of force, and again, no comments, I figured it needed to be cranked up a bit, so I slaved my slate in and tweaked the code."

Torin sneezed. "What can I smell?"

"Besides, dead H'san?" He held up a twisted and blackened

piece of almost familiar tech. "That would be my slate. Bit of unexpected blowback, ancient alien tech and all." Patting the uppermost barrel, he dipped his head and smiled almost shyly at her. "It's more sensitive to pressure than it was."

"Good work."

His hair flipped up and he snorted. "Of course it is."

But Torin had seen both his surprise and his pleasure and wondered what the hell the universe was doing sending her another damaged di'Taykan.

"You can't not, can you, Gunny?" Binti asked softly.

"Excellent question. All right, people." She raised her voice to a non-ignorable volume. "We are leaving. Get your packs, let's go."

"Leave your packs." Major Sujuno confined her gaze to the pair of Krai on the chair. "We'll come back for them after we destroy the guardians, when we come back for the weapons."

Lieutenant Verr and Wen exchanged a look and Torin hid a reluctant smile at how clearly they were wondering if the major had been paying attention. Finally, Wen shrugged. "I don't actually want to fight in my pack."

"No one's making you," Torin told him. "But we're not coming back for it."

"Fuk that shit." Both Wen and his bonded went for their packs.

"So . . ." Werst nodded at the FBG. "Who gets to squeeze a dead H'san?"

"Sounds so attractive when you put it that way. What?" Binti demanded, suddenly aware Werst had switched his attention to her. "Oh, no." She thumped her chest. "Sniper. Distance and accuracy, that's what I'm about. You don't want to waste that on blunt force trauma. You carry it."

"I'm a little close to the ground for the H'san."

"Don't look at me." Nadayki patted the KC he'd hung around his neck. "I'm good to go."

Torin only barely stopped herself from snatching it away from him. "You gave a civilian a weapon, Major?"

"I plan on selling a civilian a whole lot of weapons, Gunnery Sergeant, but in this instance, Nadayki gave himself a weapon when Corporal McKinnon no longer needed hers. And let's stop playing around, your *alsLan*'s right, the Krai are too low to the ground to do anything but break legs and we both know you have no intention of permitting me an advantage."

"You're right. We don't have time for this." *Craig must be going insane.* Good news, he hadn't shown up yet, so he was sticking to the schedule they'd evolved over the last year. She swung her KC across her back and picked up the BFG. The piece of dead H'san felt like fuzzy jerky laced through with wire. She'd handled pieces of bodies that had felt a lot worse.

"Their heads are big and unarmored, and their eye sockets are disproportionately large," she said as they passed the barracks. "You have a good chance of getting through the skull and disrupting their programming. Mashona, on our six. Odds are high the patrol will approach from one eighty, not the zero. Don't let them get close." Werst would keep an eye on the major. Verr and Wen wanted out of the trap, which made them a problem she could deal with later. Wen's pack bulged suspiciously, and she made a mental note to search it when they reached the cavern and dropped a couple of demo charges down the stairs. Halfway across the storeroom, she knew she couldn't put it off any longer. "Nadayki, do you know how to use that?"

Even without eyes on him, the hair flip came through loud and clear. "The explosive force of a propellant is channeled down a barrel driving a projectile out of the barrel and toward a target. To cause this to happen, point and apply pressure to the dangly bit. Ignoring for the moment how good I am at dangly bits, it's not rocket science."

She should take the gun away from him. That seemed hypocritical when she about to fire an ancient alien weapon by way of a piece of ancient alien, the firing mechanism worked out by members of two different species with no engineering training between them, who'd worked together under the inaccurate observation *the enemy of my enemy is my friend*. Bottom line, she wanted as many weapons she understood in the fight as possible. "Keep the end with the hole pointed at the guardians and only at the guardians."

"I'm not stupid."

"You're untrained. Finger off the trigger until you're ready to shoot." She paused on the threshold long enough to think, *how is this my life?* Then she stepped out into the corridor.

Around the corner, the metal doors slammed open like she'd flipped a switch, the sound rolling through the underground like thunder.

"Well, they're not trying to take us by surprise," Binti muttered.

Was the noise a warning? *Get back inside while you still can?* Probably not. The odds were higher it was intended to inspire fear. It was definitely deliberate. H'san engineering had kept the catacombs lit and the air fresh; they wouldn't have miscalculated the weight of the doors and the give in the hinges.

"We need to get to the corner before they box us in. Move!" Running full out, Torin wondered how Keo had thought she could make it all the way to the doors before there were too many H'san to . . .

"Holy fuk."

"Well put."

The first of the guardians wasn't quite at the corner. So many guardians and except for the sound of their feet and the creak of their armor, so silent.

"They need to make some noise," Ressk muttered.

"The dead will be ever silent unless the living give them voice," Major Sujuno called out, close enough on her right that Torin was thankful for Werst's steady presence. "In retrospect, we should have paid more attention to the less directional parts of Dion's translation."

Torin lifted the BFG as the surrounding KCs opened fire. Remembered the shot the Human's First guard had fired in the mining tunnel. It had been a lucky accident that the ricochet had hit the idiot who'd pulled the trigger. Here, the odds were high any ricochet would hit a H'san because there was one fuk of a lot of them pouring out of all three doors.

With the closest guardian a little too close, she squeezed the desiccated flesh and closed the contact. The energy beam punched a hole down the middle of the swarm, slamming bodies up against the far corner a hundred meters away. Swinging the triple muzzle from side to side, she slapped guardians against the walls and swept a tangle of them back in through the open doors.

"Clear path! Let's go!"

Her boots beat out a rhythm to follow as she charged toward the corner at the far end of the corridor. The H'san piled up against the wall would complicate things, but, once they got by, they could hold that corner until everyone escaped up into the cavern. She expected to meet Craig and Alamber at the corner; they'd have heard the doors open.

The guardians she ran toward lay still, too crushed between the beam and the wall to rise. Those she ran past, while tangled around each other and tangled around their own broken bones, attempted to struggle upright and get on with the job. She appreciated the sentiment in the abstract.

Past the first door.

Past the second.

Almost to the third . . .

Torin jerked back, yanked almost off her feet by the strap of the KC across her chest. The BFG in one hand, she slipped free of the strap and spun around. Metal slammed into her face, hitting the cracked cheekbone, flinging her sideways into a pile of struggling H'san. Focusing was . . . wasn't . . .

A boot drove into her stomach and the BFG was ripped out of her hands.

Gunnery Sergeant Kerr, who had chosen to both leave the Corps behind and carry it with her, assumed everyone would follow because she was Gunnery Sergeant Kerr. Sujuno lifted her KC, aimed and fired and fired again and waited for her chance. She watched how the first shot of the H'san weapon slammed the guardians against the far wall, and she heard their bones shatter and knew what she had to do. She watched the guardians swept to the left and the right. She shot at their power packs when she saw their armor dislodged. She needed them destroyed. She was not leaving here without those weapons.

And Gunnery Sergeant Kerr, who had no right to be named progenitor, in her need to return to those she'd left behind, had shown her how to do it without having the *seerint* to do it herself.

She had to get out. That was why she'd remained silent. Why she'd waited.

She had to get out with the weapons.

To do that, she had to destroy both the guardians and Gunnery Sergeant Kerr. With Kerr gone, Kerr's people would follow her. Of course they would. They were Corps and she was a major.

When Kerr opened the way and they started to run, she quickly outdistanced the Krai. They were at a disadvantage on the flat, and as long as she stayed close to their precious gunny, Werst wouldn't fire. Of course she knew Werst watched her. She wasn't a fool. The others aimed at the H'san. Back where his short legs had left him, he'd be aiming at her.

To her surprise, as she yanked Kerr back, the gunnery sergeant's KC came free. Her own hanging from her shoulder, Sujuno changed her grip and slammed the butt into Kerr's face when she turned. A boot driven into soft tissue, a grab from lax fingers, and ridiculously simply, the H'san weapon was hers.

"Major!"

Verr had no claim on her attention now. Maybe later. She'd need help getting the weapons out after she destroyed the guardians at the source. After she whipped the beam around the inside of the three rooms and destroyed their contents as certainly as a bullet unable to leave a skull. She'd sweep the others back and away again as she moved to the next room. And the next. With the guardians on this corridor gone, she'd cross through the bunker and destroy the guardians on the other side. Eventually, they'd all be dead and she could take her time getting all the weapons out.

Having all the weapons paid for.

A bullet took a chip out of the wall far above the thrashing H'san.

"Major!"

Werst had missed his shot. Or been made to miss. Lieutenant Verr would stay by her. Lieutenant Verr also wanted to be paid.

With all light receptors open, she stepped up to the third room and could see long, narrow metal arms joined together at one point like a nightmare insect, reaching high and dipping low, flexing multiple joints. An arm lifted a piece of H'san from one of the surrounding bins and laid it on a broad table. Wire dangled from another. She could smell rot and solder as waves of dry heat pulsed out toward the cooler air.

She had one foot over the threshold, weapon raised, when Sergeant Toporov lurched out of the shadows.

New scars cut across his skin, new wounds sealed shut, sensors visible in empty sockets evidence of the fragility of Human eyes compared to H'san. He wore Keo's exoskeleton, pieces joined by twisted wire to make up the difference in their sizes. The contact points had been driven into pale and damaged flesh. Gold wires emerged through the skin of his palms and wrapped around his fingers. When he grabbed her, Sujuno felt the wires and not flesh and bone.

Dead flesh.

Dead bone.

Dead like her entire family, only they would never rise and walk again.

It had been so long since she'd been touched.

The flesh that fired the weapon had shifted when she snatched it up. The beam had barely strength enough to blast back a pair of approaching H'san.

Her feet left the floor.

Alive, Toporov had not been that strong.

He yanked the weapon from her hand and tossed it aside as though it meant nothing. As though it didn't mean everything.

H'san, not all completely rebuilt, surrounded them.

Pressed tightly against Toporov, she reached back into the crowd, searching, fingers sliding over dry fur and desiccated flesh until they closed around metal. The metal moved. Boots braced against the sergeant's thigh, she yanked the knife from its sheath. H'san made. Two serrations on the blade near the handle.

The incision over the power source gaped, damaged ribs pulled apart by her weight dangling off one of Toporov's arms.

She would not be stopped now. She would not fail her family again.

One hand lay flat against his chest, soft pressure of hair against her palm. The other drove the knife in through the incision. It slipped easily between the curving bone; room for a blade left when they'd pried the cage apart.

"Major!"

"You are not my progenitor!" She thrust the blade into the power source.

"DOWN!"

Ears ringing, Torin lifted her head in time to see a piece of meat fall from the ceiling and land wet and quivering on the floor. She shoved a twitching H'san away and stood, holding out a hand to pull Ressk to his feet. She heard shots, muffled, saw Binti back toward them kicking a boot away, the jagged bone that stuck out of the top scraping against the floor. Saw Verr and Werst pulling Wen out from under a pile of pieces. Barely stopped herself from taking Nadayki down when he grabbed her arm and waved his hand in front of her face.

Beyond the blast radius, the H'san were rising.

She shoved Nadayki and Ressk toward the corner.

Grabbed Verr's shoulder and turned all three Krai.

Binti glanced over her shoulder and nodded.

And they ran.

By the time Torin reached the corner, more H'san were standing than not. She dragged a shattered H'san from the pile against the wall and slid it with all her strength along the floor.

Short fur and metal plate moved surprisingly fast against polished stone and the H'san in the lead went down in another tangled pile.

When Binti came back for her, she pushed her forward. "Keep running!"

No one waited at the bottom of the ship although their packs were still there, leaning against the curve of the wall.

"Up the stairs!"

"The H'san came off the plinth, Gunny! They can climb . . ."

"Incoming!" Nadayki pointed opposite to the direction they all knew the H'san were coming from, ears flipped forward through his hair.

"There's doors in the other direction, Gunny." Verr's nostril ridges were closed so tightly her voice was affected.

Had the explosion been enough to open the doors even with no one in the area the guardians had been left to defend?

"Torin! Slide between the engine and the stone into the blast bay!"

"Craig?"

"We're in the ship. We have visual but no audio. Trust me."

"Go!"

Ressk slid through the space.

"Knew I should've left it behind," Wen groused, dropping his pack before him.

Down on one knee, Binti made every shot count, a pile of redead at each end of the corridor moving forward in fits and starts, the guardians behind shifting the redead forward as they advanced.

If they used their weapons, they'd hit each other.

"They've been programmed to recognize other H'san as . . ." Nadayki slid out of his pack. ". . . oh, I don't know, allies."

Verr. Werst. Torin dropped the packs from against the wall. They still had to get out of the catacombs.

"Gunny! We're out of time!"

"Go!"

Binti sprayed rounds in both directions, then ran for the gap. Two packs still to drop.

"Leave them!"

Good idea. The major's people had left supplies and extra packs in the cavern. They'd be . . .

One of the packs was hers.

Jamers. And Corporal McKinnon's DNA.

"Torin! For fuksake!" Binti stood by the engines and fired as the first guardians came around into the curve.

She grabbed a strap and ran for the gap.

They slid through side by side and rolled at the bottom. Torin's pack smacked the stone a centimeter from her head. Glancing up, she saw, not a guardian, but the wider end of a cone.

"Get away from the wall!"

Wen screamed, his right leg flattened against the floor as the H'san fired down from above. He screamed again as Verr dragged him back.

"Gunny!"

Torin caught the painkiller Werst threw her, jabbed one end against Wen's throat, and depressed the trigger.

Silence, except for the rustling of the H'san up above.

"I think I found part of Broadbent's head," Nadayki whispered.

Below mid thigh, Wen's leg wasn't a leg anymore. It was bone—Krai bone, one of the strongest substances in known space, surrounded by a mess of crushed flesh in a wet fabric bag seeping blood because the ends of most of the blood vessels had been crushed closed. Given Krai blood pressure, that wouldn't last.

"We can't save it."

"No." It would have to come off to save Wen. "But we can't cut through Krai bone either."

"You can't, Gunny."

Torin turned to look where Ressk pointed. Verr sat by Wen's hip, her lips pulled back off her teeth. No point in asking if Verr was sure; they had no other option. "Get on with it, then. Ressk, give me the sealant. You hold him."

Ressk moved in behind Wen and tucked him up against his body so his head lolled on Ressk's shoulder, holding him still with hands and feet.

Verr reached up to cup her fingers around her bonded's face, then she sat back, pulled her boot knife, and cut the fabric away. Most of the flesh dropped off when not contained. Nostril ridges open, Verr bent, one hand holding Wen's, the other holding his thigh. Her teeth crushed the bone. As she chewed and swallowed, Torin pulled the lower leg away and sprayed the entire canister of sealant over the ragged stump. Tossed the empty, held out her hand, and sprayed the second Werst threw to her.

"That'll hold until we find Craig and the kit."

"Yeah, Gunny, about Craig . . ."

"Hey! there's a door. Oh."

Torin turned to see Alamber at the foot of a flight of stairs, light spilling out into the blast bay. He rocked back onto his heels as Nadayki rushed forward and pressed against his side. "Hey, Boss." Alamber buried his nose in Nadayki's hair. Frowned. Began to rub his hand up and down the other di'Taykan's back. "Craig sent me to get you. There's a fukload of dead H'san gathering around the engines, so this isn't the best place to set up housekeeping. You okay?"

Her ears were still ringing from the major's explosion, but none of the blood soaked into her clothes was hers. "I'm fine." She'd be carrying the major out with her. "Ressk, Werst, stay with Verr." Height was a bigger factor in moving the injured than species although, in this case, species also. "I'll take Wen. Mashona, on our six. Alamber, grab Wen's pack."

Bone density made the Krai heavier than they looked so when Ressk, grumbling about his pack being the only gear left behind, shrugged into hers, Torin accepted the help. Halfway up the stairs, Wen slid from semi to full unconsciousness and Torin, knees aching, climbed faster.

Craig waited at the hatch. "Put him there on the big rubber pad. It's both soft and firm, and I don't know what the hell it is."

Torin laid Wen down and got out of the way as Verr slid to her knees beside him.

"Almost six hours, Torin."

After six, he got to put himself into danger he'd never trained for and mount a rescue. It was a compromise they'd reached after a lot of yelling and some particularly energetic sex. "It seemed longer."

"You said you were fine. What happened to your face?"

"Broken cheekbone. I'd forgotten about that."

"You forgot about a broken cheekbone?"

"Hordes of zombie H'san." She shrugged and found a few bruises. "I got distracted."

"Fair enough."

"What happened to your chin?"

"Cracked it sliding into the blast bay having been spotted by a patrolling zombie H'san."

"Well, all right, then." He was warm and solid and strong and understood. Torin tucked the uninjured side of her face into the curve of his neck and shoulder, and breathed him in for a minute.

Almost exactly a minute.

She straightened, her hands on his biceps. "What's vibrating?"

"The H'san are packed in around the ship, beating on the

engines." Alamber gestured at the screen. "Tah dah."

From the angle, the lenses had been set into the edge of the ceiling. Torin squinted at the screen, mostly because it brought her right eye into line with her left, now starting to swell shut. "They're not beating on them. They're trying to climb them."

"No way that could be part of their programming." Nadayki leaned in. "Except it seems to be." He looked up and grinned. "Hey, Ryder! How's the toe?"

Alamber dragged him out of the way before Torin could move, growling, "Have you got a death wish?"

She nodded her thanks, forcing muscles to unlock. Colonel Hurrs wanted Nadayki dead for the sake of peace and, for a moment, she'd have happily obliged him. The moment passed. Peace had nothing to do with her reaction, and the adrenaline spike eased back into the lesser though still heightened level she'd been riding for the last few hours. "Is the hatch secure?"

"Not exactly." When she glanced over at Alamber, he shrugged. "I had to fry the controls to get it open. But don't worry, the H'san are too big to slide down into the blast bay and the stairs we used; they're the only way up here."

"That we know of," Craig amended.

"That we know of," Alamber repeated, sighing. "And there's always the chance the dead have been programmed with full schematics of the necropolis."

"The H'san are too big, but they're not the only zombies down there. The heavy gunner," Werst pointed out when everyone turned to stare. "The major blew Toporov up, but we have no idea where the fuk Keo is."

One of Ressk's hands twitched around his slate, the other closed around Werst's wrist. "Does this ship have any usable weapons?"

Craig and Alamber exchanged a look and smiled.

"Not exactly weapons, mate."

He hadn't wanted to leave Torin in the control room, not after nearly six hours when he'd had no idea of what was going on, but he could see that the idea of Gunnery Sergeant Kerr was holding everyone together and the whole zombie H'san thing, well, that was an excuse to fall apart in his opinion. Gunnery Sergeant Kerr would hold it together until she had time to be Torin, and he'd be there then.

Alamber hadn't wanted him to go alone, but as much as Torin could be rock steady through an apocalypse if she had to, he'd wanted another nontraumatized person in the control room and had cut Alamber's argument short.

"We've got two wounded, two distracted bonded—and, yeah, Ressk is faking calm like a champ, but he's still faking it—and an enemy who's willing to shit disturb for the sake of shit disturbing, voice of experience speaking. If I'm going to do this, I need you to keep an eye on things." Not entirely fair since Alamber's need to be needed was a big red "manipulate me" button, but every word was the truth, so Craig gave himself a pass.

Dropping down into the engine access, he pulled Alamber's curved-headed tool—median age of the universe, twelve—out of his belt. They'd wrapped another layer of insulation around the grip although they hadn't had time to test its effectiveness.

"No time like the present."

How many dead H'san did it take to rock a shuttle? How many dead H'san were down here? How long would it take them to find another route?

He leaned against the conduit and slid the tool through the open space. One eye closed, he lined up the contacts and pressed the curve across them both.

The engines roared on.

Eyes shut, the flash threw the blood vessels on his eyelids into silhouette.

He could feel a new, cleaner vibration under his boots, the deck singing along with the engines. The tool vibrated at double time, but the extra insulation was doing its job. Until it wasn't. Warmth. Then heat. His arm began to shake. Locking his other hand around a length of conduit, he held himself in place. No point in not finishing the job.

Seemed Torin had become a part of him at the ethical level.

If his smile twisted into a grimace—either the insulation was sticky or blisters were rising and breaking—there was no one there to see it.

Just . . .

. . . a little . . .

. . . long . . .

His knees buckled as the deck rose and he slammed down, the tool torn out of his hand. The conduit held it in place for a few seconds longer, then it was tumbling over and over itself while the engines continued to roar.

The hell? Without the contact the engines wouldn't . . .

The deck bucked. His vision filled with a flash of red and white, a moment of black. Then he blinked to find Binti on one knee, leaning over him.

"Dumbass." Her fingers ghosted over the back of his head.

"What did I do?"

"Where should I start?" She looked down at her fingertips, shook her head, and wiped them on her thigh. "You didn't mention how dangerous this was likely to be. You didn't seem to notice that the lower caverns were collapsing. You took us about four meters up. And you knocked yourself out when the engines shut off and we fell back down."

"Yeah, yeah. You lot do dangerous shit all the time, this was my time. As for the rest of it . . ." He pushed himself up onto his elbows, right hand curled protectively. "I couldn't hear anything over the sound of the engines." The caverns collapsing explained the noise continuing after the engines had shut off. "Everyone all right?"

"Given the landing, it was probably a good thing Wen was already unconscious," Binti said as she stood, "but yeah. Few more bruises all around, and Ressk clipped his nose on a corner of a control chair. Bled all over. Werst was adorably concerned. Oh, and Werst's temperature has gone up another degree fighting the zombie H'san infection, so we have to haul ass." She held out her hand. "Come on."

"And the zombie H'san?"

"Eleven seconds at around 1400 degrees—they've been fried, crushed, possibly drowned, and no longer our problem."

"Drowned?"

"Engines came on, water poured out of the fuk knows where, whole lot of steam. It was all very exciting. Nadayki tells me there used to be a pool in the cavern."

The bulkhead of the engine access now appeared to be the deck. "So, I flew this thing for four meters?"

She laughed. "Eight if you count the trip back."

The ship had twisted as it came down, and the control room had twisted with it, remaining level, which was an impressive bit of engineering. Chucking back to the control room, however, had become a bit dodgy.

"Yeah, kind of has a height requirement now." Binti pulled herself up into the passage. "Can you make it with that hand?"

"Not a problem. I can lift myself that far with one hand." And an elbow once he was high enough.

They entered the control room by descending a spiral slide. He had no idea how the H'san would have managed with their physiognomy. Nor did he have any idea of where the slide had come from. He'd been in and out while waiting for Torin and had never seen it. As he landed, he saw that the exterior hatch now opened into the cavern over a three-meter drop to the floor. Torin waited for him by the . . .

"Rope ladder?"

"We had rope and we had Krai. This is baby stuff; it took them next to no time." Torin directed his attention across the room to where Werst and Ressk were sliding loops of rope under Wen's pallet. "They've worked out a way to carry him comfortably." She gently brushed her fingers over the rising bump on the back of his head and looked at the smear of blood for a moment much the way Binti had before meeting his eyes.

"Minor. And this . . ." He held up his hand. ". . . already coated in pain reducer." He'd had the tube they'd previously cracked on his belt. "I keep from using it, it'll be fine in a couple of days."

"Okay." The corners of her mouth twitched. "So that's two shuttles you've crashed on this planet."

"I'll cop to two hard landings, but it's not a crash if everyone walks away."

"We're tipped over on top of a pile of crushed rock with the hatch popped off."

He matched her smile. "Still walking away."

"Hey, Boss!"

He turned as Torin did and saw a familiar figure standing by the wall of the cavern.

"They're light on their feet," Torin explained, warm against his side. "I sent them out to check the stability of the stone."

"And?"

As though he'd heard the question, Alamber continued, "Good news and bad news. Good news is, the ceiling's cracked, but likely to hold for as long as we'll be under it. The bad news is that the Mictok is missing off its plinth."

"Zombie Mictok?" Binti moaned over by the control panel. "Gunny, I quit."

"Never mind!" Nadayki's voice came from slightly farther away. He appeared, holding the Mictok up by one leg. "I found it. Must be hollow, it's really . . ."

The body hit the floor and rolled toward the shuttle leaving Nadayki waving the leg.

In all the time they'd been together, Craig couldn't remember Torin ever laughing so hard.

Nadayki lifted field rations off the pile left behind in the cavern and dropped them into his pack. "There's plenty of food, if you can call this food, but we're short of water."

Torin glanced over at Craig filling the canteens from the containers they hadn't emptied on the way in. "We're good. It's two days to the exit, less if we hustle."

"Two? Are you shitting me? It took seven tendays to get down this far."

"Well, like the major said, all we had to do was follow . . ."

The lights went out.

Torin took a deep breath, listened to some creative profanity, and decided as she tapped her PID that yes, it had been a long day. "Werst, let's see your arm."

The line hadn't gone higher, but two, three-centimeter–long lines had joined it. His temperature remained at two point two degrees above Krai norm. She weighed the spread of the infection against rest and food. Against the worry tightening every one of Ressk's expressions.

"Make camp. We leave when the lights come back on."

"You blew the door." Wen murmured the next morning as they carried him over the rubble at the top of the cavern stairs. "I wanted to blow the door, all the doors, but the major wouldn't ever let me. I have demo charges in my pants."

"Drugs?" Torin asked as Verr smiled fondly down at him.

"Euphemism worth exploring?"

Verr looked up at Alamber and laughed. "No, he really has demo charges in his pants."

Torin traced a mental line over their route back to the exit. "A few extra demo charges may come in handy."

They came in handy at the door leading back into the chamber where Corporal McKinnon's remains rested.

Ressk shook his head as he stepped over the mess. "I could've cracked that, Gunny."

"We crashed a shuttle and broke their Mictok, there's no point in subtlety now."

Double-time would do Wen no favors. If it came to it, she'd send Ressk and Werst on ahead. As long as it wasn't necessary, she wanted them all together, all moving as fast as possible past the dead.

"She wasn't well, you know." Nadayki stood close enough to touch as they waited for Binti and Alamber to spell Ressk and Verr on the net. "Major Sujuno, I mean. She was all twisted up inside."

Torin brushed the back of her hand against his. Seven tendays of rejection wouldn't allow him to make even so simple a first move. "Making excuses for her?"

"As if."

But she thought he might be.

Torin stared at Werst's arm, illuminated by the beam of her light. The skin felt hot and tight.

"Fuk, Gunny, your fingers are freezing. Respect to Ryder's warm bits."

"Ryder's warm bits are no concern of yours. Two hours, people. Eat, nap if you can. Then we move on."

"In the dark, Gunny?" Verr demanded.

It was a flat, straight corridor, thirteen pairs of feet hadn't found a pit trap heading in so were unlikely to do so heading out; every one of them wore a light, and it hadn't been one of the three civilians complaining. "Yes, Lieutenant," Torin snarled, "in the dark."

Nadayki and Alamber napped draped over each other, touching at every possible point. Very di'Taykan except that it went no further than touch. Torin wasn't sure why; two hours in the dark was certainly long enough and neither had been with their own species for a while.

On the other hand, criminal activity aside, Nadayki was a combination of acerbic little shit and clingy, so odds were high it was as simple as Alamber not liking him.

In the hall of useless old junk, Torin cleaned souvenirs out of everyone's packs. Nadayki had brought along the ceramic oval and both Wen and Verr had a number of small weapons. Wen also had a few large weapons.

"That's mine!"

"That's contraband. It stays."

Nadayki's hair flattened into a lime-green skull cap. "Who died and put you in charge?"

"Seriously?" Alamber jerked him back as Torin's hand rose to touch the vest she wasn't wearing. "Do you have a death wish?"

Wen hovered in the gray area between lucid and drugged and let his weapons go with nothing more than a sulky protest.

Verr watched Torin stack everything beside the pile of debris, met Torin's gaze with an expression that said she knew how this adventure was going to end, and turned her attention back to her bonded.

"You're setting a dangerous precedent . . ."

* * *

"Whose blood on your pants?" Torin only knew it wasn't his.

Craig frowned. "Uh, there was a face in the blast bay. Most of a skull, part of a face."

"Broadbent. One of Major Sujuno's."

"Yeah, well, I touched, I wiped."

"Good."

"Good?"

"I didn't have time to get a sample. You're carrying him out." Most of the blood dried on her clothes was the major's. They'd left three behind, but it could have been worse.

"Can you fly it?" Torin asked as Craig settled into the pilot's chair of the major's shuttle.

"I've flown Taykan controls before, and with a lot less sleep."

She made a noncommittal noise and leaned over the back of the chair. "Out of a gravity well? Up that narrow protected zone? Without crashing it into the *Promise* when we arrive?"

"Hey, third time's the charm. At least we aren't leaving anything behind we'll miss on our shuttle. We hadn't had it long enough." He turned his head far enough to kiss her wrist. "Now, set a good example for the children and the prisoners, and buckle up."

ELEVEN

"**D**o we blow the ships, Gunny?" Binti waited by Promise's board, pack at her feet. Her shoulders sagged with exhaustion, but Torin knew she wouldn't miss. She didn't miss.

Did they erase the evidence? If the H'san came by on patrol, and Torin wasn't convinced they did, they'd assume any debris remaining in orbit had come off ships taken out by the security satellites. Would they analyze the debris? Would they land? Could they tell from orbit that the weapons cache had been disturbed?

She stared at the screen for a long moment, then shook her head. "Go get cleaned up. Craig?"

"It's a universal shuttle lock, and let's hear it for disappearing diversity in engineering. It should hold. If we don't say anything, Justice may never notice we've switched shuttles. The people we deal with at least aren't exactly ship-heads." He settled deeper in his chair. "Plenty of time to rest when we're in Susumi. Jump in ten. Don't start anything you can't finish."

With the hum of Susumi space settling around her, an unbreakable shield, Torin made her way into their small infirmary to have her cheek bonded. Craig had argued an entire separate packet for the infirmary was a waste of space right up until their first job. When they got back to the station, he packed in as many upgrades as Justice would pay for and arranged for one or two on his own. Torin had only barely managed to talk him out of a full regeneration tank.

Wen lay on one of the narrow beds, a portable regen tank ready to be slipped over his stump as soon as Verr finished sterilizing the sealant. The tank would dissolve the sealant and include any reusable organics in the rebuild of Wen's leg. Way back when she'd had a single chevron on her sleeve, a med-tech had told Torin parts of the breakdown had been based on Krai digestion. Torin suspected he'd been amusing himself at her expense, but she'd never done the research to be certain.

Werst sat on the bed, shirt off, arm extended so Ressk could run diagnostics and determine what antibiotics were needed.

The siren was a surprise.

"The hell!"

Ressk stared at his slate, then threw it down on the bed so he could work the screen with both hands.

She flattened against the wall as Alamber charged into the room, slate in hand.

"Block it from getting into the queue!" Ressk snapped without looking up.

Verr muttered under her breath about contaminants. Torin and Werst exchanged a look of joint incomprehension. Apparently Alamber knew what was expected of him as he worked at Ressk's side.

"Torin? There's a medical alert trying to redirect us after jump!"

"We're on it!" Ressk snapped before Torin could respond. "Deal with the noise!"

"On it."

Nine and a half minutes after the siren shut off, Ressk sighed, and relaxed. "That's got it. Good thing we were in Susumi or we wouldn't have been able to stop it."

"Stop what?" Torin demanded.

"A warning that we had a proscribed substance on board. That infection? Any sign of it and a message goes straight to the nearest CDC base and Med-op will take control of the ship."

"Confederation Disease Control? Why?" Binti asked, leaning against the wall beside Torin, breathing a little heavily, her hair damp.

"It's a weaponized variant."

"Can we kill it?" The longest line on Werst's arm had nearly reached his shoulder.

"We can." His gesture took in the four Krai. "According to Med-op, we can fight it off long enough for the drugs . . ." He reached into the bio-chamber and pulled out the assembled dose. ". . . to take it out. Everyone else . . ."

". . . not so much," Alamber finished, staring at his slate.

"Partition the information off and save it," Torin told him. "We might need it."

"Biological weapons." Werst winced as Ressk jabbed the end of the dose into swollen tissue. "We should've hauled a planet buster up into orbit and used it."

"I knew you weren't going to execute anyone." Craig handed her a coffee and sat down between her and Ressk. "You're going to give the story to Presit, aren't you? Blow the secrets and the whole thing wide open."

She'd considered it. "No."

Her mouth twitched as the entire team except for Werst voiced personal variations of disbelief.

The expression Werst shot her was unmistakable. He knew, had probably known for a while that she'd decided not to bring Presit in at the end. Odds were high he'd worked out why.

Torin took a long drink, then stared at her reflection in the dark liquid as she tried to get the words she needed to say into formation. "We left two dead Humans, two dead di'Taykan, two shuttles, two ships, and one hell of a mess behind. Colonel Hurrs sent us in with . . ."

"A biscuit warmer? Ow."

"Thank you, Binti. Yes, a biscuit warmer. He'd extrapolated what he knew into a terrifying situation, but, bottom line, he *knew* sweet fuk all. I don't know if the position of the Younger Races in Parliament, in the Confederation, is as tenuous as Colonel Hurrs believes. I don't pay attention to politics, but I do know there's no point in executing the survivors of Major Sujuno's expedition to keep the attempt secret when the person who sent them for the weapons, who was going to pay them for the weapons, is still out there. And only Dion and the major knew who he was. And I'm not one hundred percent certain about the major," she added after a moment.

Binti leaned back, her chair protesting the angle. "So you're going to take the three of them to the H'san?"

Torin thought about the H'san as she knew them, as the Younger Races knew them; wise and funny, sweet smelling and kind. They sang every morning at sunrise. They loved cheese.

"Well, we can't take them to Justice, can we?" Alamber's hair rose to cover the bald stripe where the dead hair had finally fallen out. "Not after running off on a secret mission for the military."

"Who lied to them about us," Craig added. "At least the H'san won't start another war over it."

Torin thought about a giant snail shell stuffed with potential death and destruction. "You sure about that? I'm not." She drained her pouch, set it down, and laid her hands flat on the table. "This is what I want us to do; I want us to do our jobs. If I have to, I'll explain the entire situation to a tribunal. I want to trust the system and I want to give these three over to the law. I'd like to do it on the down low, just in case some part of the colonel's fear has merit. But it's a big universe and I'm going to assume we're not the center of it. After all, it's been proven that it's easy enough to hide things—like the H'san system of origin—when no one knows they're being hidden."

She could almost hear them thinking about it.

"You want to prove that the Younger Races can act like adults rather than sneaking around hiding things from Mom and Dad." The chair protested again as Binti shifted her weight forward, leveling it out. "Because Mom and Dad always find out. If they want to send us back to our rooms, we need to be able to argue as adults, not children throwing a tantrum."

Ressk snapped open another pouch of *sah*. "We might want to talk to the H'san as well. I'd like to give them a chance to upgrade their security system before we have to drag another set of assholes off their planet."

"You think we'll catch shit for not getting the name of the backer from Major Sujuno?" Alamber drummed his fingers on the tabletop until Binti covered his hand with hers and stopped him.

"She was attacked by her sergeant who'd been turned into a zombie. He grabbed her weapon, operated by pressing the flesh of a long-dead H'san, and she blew them both up."

"That doesn't answer my question, Boss."

"I think we're good."

"I think we're all going to be sent to therapy," Binti muttered.

"And the war we were supposed to be preventing?" Werst asked quietly.

"I believe . . ." And if she was wrong, she'd be carrying millions more dead. ". . . that Colonel Hurrs has spent his whole life at war. War is his default response. We . . . I defaulted right along with him. But he's never been to the Core and he's never realized how many people barely gave a thought to the war while we were dying in it. I spent too much of my life at war and, while I'm willing to clean up the debris, I'm done with it. I refuse to believe war is the default."

"Because the gray plastic aliens made us fight?"

She took a deep breath and let it out slowly. "Because we're better than that. We have to be."

Craig wrapped an arm around her shoulders. Ressk finished his *sah*. Werst and Alamber built a tower out of pretzels.

Finally, Binti grinned. "Intell won't be too pleased with us."

Ressk matched it. "Neither will Justice."

"Yeah . . ." Alamber pulled the lowest stick and Werst swore as the tower fell. ". . . we're going to put the *rinchas* in the *armee* for sure."

"The ducks in the pudding?"

"It loses a little in the . . ." Alamber paused. Frowned. "Yeah, okay, ducks in the pudding is pretty close. So, Boss, how do we deal with the fallout?"

"We become Wardens."

She sat and listened to the hum of Susumi space.

Binti recovered first. "But we already work for the Justice Department."

"On contract," Torin agreed. "Brought in as they need us because we have a special skill set. I want us to be actual

Wardens. With the title, and support, and the responsibilities that entails. We still work as a team, we still do the job we've been doing, but we do it as a part of a greater whole. A fully integrated part of the Justice Department, not merely weapons wielded by them."

Across the table, Werst grinned. "That's a pretty unsubtle metaphor, Gunny."

She shrugged and rose to get another coffee. "I'm not a particularly subtle person."

They discussed the truth of that until she sat down again, then one by one they fell silent.

"If we all agree, we put a sitrep together and shoot it to Lanh Ng the moment we leave Susumi. Colonel Hurrs' arguments. Our arguments. Every detail we can remember and as much as the major's people . . ." Although they hadn't been the major's people, not in any way that mattered. ". . . are willing to tell us."

Craig's thumb drew warm lines against her neck. "And if Justice doesn't see it our way? And we find ourselves facing an extensive rehabilitation?"

"For what?" she asked. "Acting as concerned citizens . . ."

"With a special skill set," Werst muttered.

". . . and stopping a group of mercenaries from stealing and selling ancient H'san weapons?"

"Justice isn't usually about the end justifying the means," Binti pointed out.

"I think this time they will be. But . . ." She raised a hand and cut off further protests. ". . . if the Justice Department thinks stopping ancient H'san planet-busting weapons from reaching the black market and being used by the sort of people who make Big Bill look both civilized and restrained isn't enough of an end to justify us acting independently, if the word *rehabilitation* is even mentioned, we'll break away, guns blazing."

"We'll be rehabilitated in their eyes by becoming Wardens."

Torin grinned across the table at Werst. "There's that."

"So are we telling the H'san?" Alamber dropped his chin onto his fist. "I mean, letting the H'san know we stopped a group of mercenaries from airing their dirty armaments couldn't hurt."

Binti grabbed a handful of pretzels off the table. "They might wonder why we didn't go to them in the first place so they could deal with it themselves."

"H'san against trained mercenaries?" Craig leaned back and snagged another coffee. "Like that would end well. What would they go in armed with? A cheese plate?"

"Don't," Torin pointed at Alamber, who closed his mouth and looked innocent, "say it."

"Hey, Boss." Torin took her feet off the second chair so Alamber could sit, but he waved them back and leaned on the pilot's chair instead. He nodded toward the window. "Staring out at a mathematical construct?"

"Working on my sitrep for the tribunal." She'd left Craig in their quarters, sleeping, satiated, and snoring.

"You should've recorded yourself convincing us and played it for them."

"They weren't there, they're going to need more detail."

"I guess." She could feel his fingers in her hair. "So, Boss, when you said we were going to be Wardens, you meant all of us, right?"

"I did. Although if anyone doesn't want to . . ."

His fingers stilled. "It's not that."

"They take all of us or none of us, Alamber."

"And we stay together?"

"Our value to the Justice Department is as a team, not as individuals. Yes, we stay together, or we don't stay."

His sigh sounded a little shaky, but his fingers began moving again, fingernails scratching lightly at her scalp, the heightened sensuality distracting from any hinted weakness.

It felt good, so Torin didn't stop him.

"Boss, you know how you're always saying we could use another di'Taykan?"

"Yes." Not entirely an unexpected conversation given that they now had another di'Taykan.

"The whole pirate thing aside, we could use one who hasn't slaughtered six people and not given a crap."

"He told you?"

"He bragged about how he did it. If he's my only option, I'd rather be alone."

"He isn't and you're not."

"I know." A finger stroked the top of her ear. "So can we . . ."

"No."

"You are being close to having run out of time." Presit folded her arms and glared up at Torin.

When they exited Susumi space, her ship had been waiting . . . not where they left it, but five hundred kilometers back of the jump point, safely away from the energy wave.

My pilot are not being entirely stupid. He are knowing you are having the equations to be jumping back where you are leaving from if you are returning Jamers to me as you are having promised. I are not wishing to be changed on the molecular or any other level, so we are having moved.

Craig and Torin had taken the shuttle over and once hooked in, Presit had come to them.

Torin smiled at her reflection in Presit's mirrored glasses. "Close only counts in horseshoes and hand grenades."

"I are not having the faintest idea of what you are talking about."

"I'm not entirely certain myself."

Presit threw up her hands, metallic nails glittering, and stomped over to Craig, the silvered ends of her fur flicking up and down with the force of the movement exposing her darker undercoat. "Why are you putting up with her again?"

"Must be love." He met Torin's eyes over Presit's head and winked.

"It are certainly not being good sense," Presit muttered. She sighed, combed her claws back through her whiskers, and turned to face Torin. The social aspect of the meeting had clearly ended. "So, I are not seeing Jamers with you."

Torin opened her hand and shifted the metal cylinder until she held it between thumb and forefinger. "Jamers was dead before we landed. Alamber found her body."

"She are being in that?"

"She ar . . . is."

Toenail ticking faintly against the deck, Presit walked over and held out her hand. The cylinder was large enough, her hand small enough, she couldn't close her fingers around it. "Her death are being an accident?"

"No."

Presit growled low in her throat. "And you are not being able to tell me the details?"

"If you knew the details, you'd have to tell them to your *strectasin*," Torin reminded her.

"And she wouldn't be happy," Craig added.

"And when she are unhappy, she are being all about taking it out on the messenger. So I are giving up this story in order to be getting out with my pelt intact." Her sigh suggested she'd given the potential loss of her pelt some consideration. Then her grip tightened on the cylinder and her muzzle rose, white points of teeth showing. "You are having brought whoever are having caused her death to justice?"

Torin remembered her only sight of Sergeant Toporov, his body moving to ancient H'san programming. "He paid for it."

Presit tapped her nails against the cylinder. "That are not what I are asking, but I are allowing it to be your answer."

"Thank you."

"I are not needing your sarcastic *thank you*, Gunnery Sergeant Kerr." She tipped her head up, and although Torin couldn't see her eyes, she knew Presit was studying her face. After a long moment, the reporter nodded. "So. Now what are happening?"

"You'll take Jamers to your *strectasin*. We'll go back to work."

"*Vortzma!*"

Torin had no idea what the Katrien word meant, but the delivery hurt her ears. From Craig's reaction, she guessed it wasn't a nice word.

"That are not what I are asking, and you are knowing it."

"Change," Craig said softly. "Change is happening," he repeated when she turned to face him.

Presit nodded. "Well, that I are not doubting if you are insisting on remaining with her."

"She's stuck with me."

Presit nodded again. "Good."

Torin folded her arms and didn't ask what she meant.

Lanh Ng met them at intake when the *Promise*, her registration reset, arrived at Berbar, Justice's station in MidSector Seven.

"He doesn't look happy," Binti said behind Torin's left shoulder.

"He never looks happy."

"I don't look happy," Ng snapped, "because, as the only Human Warden, I'm stuck dealing with you lot. Who, I might add, are more trouble than the other three special operation teams combined. And don't . . ." He pointed at Alamber. ". . . tell me it's because you're that much better than the other three teams combined. It's true, but I don't want to hear it. Intake forms."

Torin touched her slate to his.

Ng studied the forms—perfectly filled out—and then studied the three prisoners—Alamber had wanted to list them as two and three quarters prisoners, but had lost the vote. "Process them," he said to the Warden on duty, then pointed at Torin. "My office. Now. The rest of you, when Meticulously Records Every Detail is done with you here, stay out of trouble and keep your mouths shut. You're in the air lock, the lot of you, don't give me a reason to open the outer hatch."

Torin followed him to the vertical. They rode up to the admin levels in silence. She nodded at his assistant and followed him into his office and stood at ease in front of his desk. Ng hadn't been military, he'd been a lawyer with Justice when he'd made his lateral career move, and he didn't require military bearing. She didn't exactly require it, couldn't decide if her posture was habit or comfort, but fell into it automatically.

He finally put down his slate and studied her face. She stared over his left shoulder.

"You broke your face again. You should stop doing that."

"Yes, sir."

"Why didn't you come to me with this in the beginning?"

She'd included her reason in the sitrep. "Because I believed Colonel Hurrs when he said that taking it to the Justice

Department, allowing the Elder Races to know what was going on, could lead to a civil war."

"Okay . . ."

"We also had no idea of the grave robbers' time frame, we only knew they were close. There was a chance that while the Justice Department deliberated over what should be done, they'd have weapons off world and begin another war."

"That wasn't in your report."

"It only just occurred to me." Meticulously Records Every Detail was not the only Dornagain in the Justice Department. The entire species seemed to be natural bureaucrats, and when they deliberated, they took enough time to analyze every possible option. Every potential option. The lunch order.

"You do not know better than the entire Justice Department. You can't go charging off on your own because you think the Confederation needs saving."

"Yes, sir."

"What does *yes, sir* mean?"

"I do better work within a structure."

"Like the Marine Corps."

"Yes, sir."

"Or the Justice Department."

"Yes, sir."

"And when you do better work, your team does better work."

"Yes, sir."

"Although your definition of *within a structure* seems to be interestingly nuanced."

"Sir?"

"Stop doing that, you know it pisses me off." He looked down at the report, now on his desk, and flicked through the pages. "You broke the law when your team cracked those buoys. You know that, right?"

"In the pursuit of lawbreakers when speed is of the essence, if there is no danger to any citizen of the Confederation, laws may be set temporarily aside as long as a full report is made of each instance."

Ng stared at her. "Are you quoting the manual at me?"

Torin stared back. "Yes, sir, I am."

"I'm amazed you even realized there was a manual."

"I make myself aware of anything that'll help me do my job and bring my people home."

"And cover your ass. Well, done." He sighed. "You confuse the rest of the department. You know that, right? From Meticulous right up to the minister in charge. As a result, they've kicked your report, and everything it means and implies and insists on, back to me. And I am giving you and your team three tendays to pass the first-level Warden's exams. You're right, you're not weapons." His mouth twisted. "*We're* not weapons, and if we reinforce the separation between the Younger and the Elder Races, that's how they'll continue to see us. Not all of them, but enough to cause significant problems." He tapped the screen and the report flipped through to the final page. It took a while; Torin had been thorough. "In the end, I can essentially guarantee that you and yours will be treated as requested because, however you accomplished it, by stopping the sale of those weapons, you saved millions of lives and very probably stopped, if not a war, any number of armed conflicts."

"Those were our orders, sir."

"Were they? I'll see that whoever has words with Colonel Hurrs mentions you followed them." His lips lifted off Human teeth in a very Krai expression. "And someone *will* have words with Colonel Hurrs." Head cocked, he leaned back. "As Wardens, you'll have an entirely different relationship with the military."

"I thought you'd be happy about that."

"Oh, *I* am. Now, here's the fun part." He leaned forward again, elbows on his desk. "While I talk the Justice Department through the mess you've dumped in my lap, using small words and probably pictures, someone gets to tell the H'san all about trespassing and destruction of monuments and adventure time with their dead. Guess who that's going to be, ex-Gunnery Sergeant Kerr?"

"You, sir?"

"I'm amused you think that." He frowned at the report. "We need to find out who hired Major Sujuno. We," he added pointedly. "Not you."

"I was only going to mention that her ship's still in orbit

around the H'san planet of origin. She could have left information on board."

Ng shook his head. "Thank you. We've never held an investigation before. Drop by the housing office, Wardens get quarters on station. Three tendays, level one. We'll let you know when the H'san are available and there may still be a tribunal in your future. Now get out. And tell your di'Taykan to stop trying to suck up to my assistant, or I'll do a more thorough background check on him."

With a jaunty wave to the Niln at the desk, Alamber fell into step beside her as they left the outer office. "So, how did not defaulting to war work out for us?"

"Surprisingly well."

"Good."

"So far."

Torin gave Dion's cylinder to the Justice Department, but she sent the DNA samples for the three Marines back to the Corps. She trusted them to do the right thing.

Wardens' quarters weren't large, but they were larger than the quarters on the ship and, because everyone got the exact same amount of space, Torin and Craig, like Ressk and Werst, had both a bedroom and a sitting room.

"Good thing. I don't want that staring at me while I sleep."

"Him," Torin corrected, adjusting the way the Silsviss skull hung on the wall.

"Doesn't make it better, luv."

"We don't have to . . ."

"No." Craig cut her off. "You agreed not to put him on the ship, I agreed he deserved better than a storage locker. I'll get used to it."

He wasn't just talking about the skull. "We'll be on the ship more than we're here."

"Torin . . ." He tugged her around to face him. ". . . we have rooms on a station. Rooms that are a damned sight nicer than rooms we'd be in on the salvage station. I never planned for the two of us to live on *Promise*." When she raised a brow, he smiled. "I know, but not full time. As long as you're here with me, I'm good."

A few minutes later, on their way to the bedroom, his hand warm against the skin of her hip, Craig leaned back far enough to see the skull and said, "Wipe that smile off your face."

Yeah. They were good.

All six of them had passed the first-level Warden's exams before the H'san made time to visit the station.

The meeting was to take place in the station's park. The H'san preferred to be surrounded by living things and apparently living Wardens, lawyers, and support staff didn't cut it. Torin arrived first, as ordered, stood on the mark Ng had shown her, and waited.

The H'san had been appraised of the situation. They, or at least *this* H'san had read her report and she therefore, in spite of Ng's threat, had no need to fill in any background details.

Eventually, the doors hissed open again and a single H'san walked through, pausing just over the threshold to inhale and exhale.

A living H'san looked a lot less like a zombie H'san than Torin had anticipated. She fought the urge to tug at her cuffs as they approached. She kept her thumbs interlocked, her shoulders squared, and her weight evenly distributed. She thought of Alamber's hair, still not grown all the way in, remembered his pain, and Binti's and Ressk's, and found her desire to punch the first H'san she saw—amended to first living H'san—hadn't waned.

Alamber had made her get new clothes for the meeting.

"You need an outfit that doesn't look like it's designed for ease of mayhem."

"That's got nothing to do with what she's wearing, mate."

The new clothes went with the scarf she'd bought on Abalae,

currently draped loosely around her neck and falling to both sides of her left shoulder. Werst had helped her test the tensile strength of the fabric and, if she had to, she could use it to restrain someone.

As the H'san settled in front of her so they were eye to their ridiculously large eyes, they folded their face into an expression of joy—Torin had spent the days before this meeting learning H'san expressions. "Please, relax."

She moved from parade rest to at ease, noting the warm and fuzzy feelings everyone in known space insisted they had around the H'san were absent. Fighting off a necropolis full of zombies seemed to be a game changer.

Their expression sobered. "You fear I am here to punish you? It is true the Justice Department suggested we, through my speaking, be the ones to deal with what occurred on . . ."

The planet's name buzzed in her ears, not recognizable as a word.

". . . and to an extent, that is why I've come. Your report was very enlightening. We wanted, through my speaking, to thank you. All of you, through your hearing. By preventing Major Sujuno and the mercenaries she employed from removing our ancient weapons, you've prevented their use in a great many deaths. There is, after all, no other reason for weapons, is there?" The expression looked anticipatory.

Torin stuck with the safe response. "No, there isn't."

"And you and yours would know that. Thank you for lifting that responsibility from us."

"You're welcome. *Zegazt* . . ." It was a title. Learning to pronounce it correctly without spitting had taken almost a full day. Ng wasn't sure what the title meant.

"The H'san liaison to Justice doesn't use it, that's all I know, Kerr."

". . . have you, through your species . . ." Close enough syntax for government work. ". . . ever considered destroying those weapons?"

They blinked at her, inner lid first, then the outer. "No."

"Why not?" She hadn't been told she couldn't ask questions, and she wondered what answers the Justice Department expected her to get.

Another blink. Inner. Outer. "It's our past. We maintain it, through our holding. It remains ours, through our holding."

And that reminded her of her purpose at the meeting. "I'd like to apologize for the disorder we left behind when we prevented the weapons you won't destroy from being removed and sold and used." The disorder had been all she'd been willing to apologize for. One Who Examines the Facts and Draws Conclusions had supported her wording during the protocol meetings. The Dornagain were realists. Insanely methodical, but realists.

The H'san's face wore confusion momentarily on the way back to joy. "You have nothing to apologize for. We've already begun to take care of the disorder, and we'll make certain that no one judges the entirety of the Younger Races based the actions of those few who tried to break our peace."

"It's sad you have to."

An appendage waved. "Have to?"

"It's sad that you have to make certain that no one judges the entirety of the Younger Races based on the actions of those few who tried to break your peace."

That was definitely the confused expression. Torin maintained "speaking to a senior officer" neutrality as the H'san worked their way through her repetition to, "Yes. Sad. And it was a shame . . ."

That expression wasn't shame. Or sorrow.

". . . the scholar died."

Torin shifted her expression just enough to meet the H'san's gaze and hold it. "It was a shame," she said, as the inner eyelid slid halfway across and stalled, "that they all died."

"Of course." Inner. Outer. No expression Torin had learned. "I only meant we'd have appreciated knowing one who put so much work into learning about our past."

Was she imagining undertones around *appreciate*? "*Zegazt*, if you could tell me, why hide the coordinates of your planet of origin only from the Younger Races?"

"Ah. So what has happened won't happen, of course."

"And now it has happened?"

"Better it not happen again. I'm afraid there is no time remaining; so many calling." They rose until Torin stood eye to sternum. Noting the point where the power source would go in, she didn't feel intimidated if that was their intent. "We've accepted your apology, however little reason we feel exists for it, as you've accepted our thanks. I think I have come to know the Younger Races a little better through this, through your living, student Warden."

Torin came to attention as they inclined their head. "*Zegazt.*"

She stayed in place, as ordered, until they were gone. They undulated a lot more when they were alive.

The entire team waited outside the park when she emerged. "Where's Ng?"

"He left with the H'san liaison and an assortment of assistants. According to a lingering assistant, you talked them into spending more time with the Younger Races. She ran off when we said we'd meet you." Craig fell into step on one side of her, Werst on the other.

"I didn't talk them into anything."

Craig bumped his shoulder into hers. "You can be unintentionally persuasive. How did the apology go?"

"They agreed I didn't need to make one."

"Really?"

She smiled. "Essentially."

"Did you ask why they refuse to destroy their weapons?"

The smile slipped. "It's their past, they want to hold it."

"So, they refuse to destroy their weapons because they don't want to destroy their weapons?"

"Pretty much."

"And the rest of it?"

"Honestly, I don't know. I suspect I was speaking to a politician."

Ressk leaned out around his bonded. "Were they male or female?"

"No idea."

Binti shook her head. "You got *anything* for us, Gunny?"

"They smell a lot better when they're alive, like puppies and pie." She thought about that for a moment. "Sequentially."

"So, Boss . . ." Alamber walked backward down the corridor, still relatively empty after the passage of the H'san, "Something occurred to me. The Younger Races don't know where the H'san planet of origin is, right? And they think it's lost, so they don't know to ask, right?"

"Right."

"Well, whoever Major Sujuno was fetching the weapons for, they knew."

"Don't be ridiculous, rehabilitation isn't enough. He needs to be permanently silenced." Pale fingers tapped against the plastic display stand under the piece of ceramic, then rose to trace the metallic pattern in the glaze. "I don't care how. Make it as visible as possible; it does no good if no one hears about it. Wield knowledge as power."

The interior of the bowl had begun to warm, the temperature rising with every repetition of the pattern. "If that idiot Dion and the major arrive with the weapons, fine, wonderful, that changes things, but we won't wait for them." Enough repetitions and a harmless looking piece of ceramic would grow hot enough to melt through stone. With no understanding of how long the power source would last, not a particularly useful item, but fascinating. It was the only piece of ceramic in his collection. He was more interested in plastic. What could be done with it. What it had done. He'd been looking for the perfect piece for years now. Eventually, he'd find it. Or he'd create a situation where it would come looking for him.

"Yes, that's exactly what I mean. Human's First will become more than a mockery of a movement when we make Richard Varga a martyr to the cause."

ABOUT THE AUTHOR

Tanya Sue Huff is a prolific Canadian fantasy author of over 25 novels, including *The Enchantment Emporium* series and the *Confederation* series, also published by Titan Books. Her stories have been published since the late 1980s, including five fantasy series and one science fiction series. One of these, the *Blood Books* series, featuring detective Vicki Nelson, was adapted for television under the title *Blood Ties*.

ALSO AVAILABLE FROM TITAN BOOKS

TANYA HUFF
CONFEDERATION SERIES

VALOUR'S CHOICE

In the distant future, humans and several alien races have been granted membership in the Confederation—at a price. They must serve and protect the far more civilized species who have long since turned away from war. When her transport ship is shot down, a routine diplomatic mission across the galaxy becomes anything but, and Staff Sergeant Torin Kerr must fight to keep her platoon alive.

THE BETTER PART OF VALOUR

When Staff Sergeant Torin Kerr makes the mistake of speaking her mind to a superior officer, she finds herself tagged for a special mission to act as protector to a scientific exploratory team assigned to investigate an enormous derelict spaceship. Along with her crew Kerr soon finds herself in the midst of danger and faced with a mystery that takes all her courage and ingenuity to solve.

THE HEART OF VALOUR

Gunnery Sergeant Torin Kerr is a Confederation Marine's marine. Sidelined since her last mission, she jumped at the chance to go to Crucible—the Marine Corps training planet. While the exercise is underway, the drones begin acting aggressively, without regard to fail-safes or their programming. Kerr finds herself caught in a desperate fight to keep a platoon of Marine recruits alive...

TITANBOOKS.COM

ALSO AVAILABLE FROM TITAN BOOKS

VALOUR'S TRIAL

Unexpectedly pulled from battle, Gunnery Sergeant Torin Kerr of the Confederation Marines finds herself in an underground POW camp, where her fellow marine prisoners have lost all will to escape. Now, Torin must fight her way not only out of the prison, but also past the growing compulsion to lie down and give up—not realizing that her escape could alter the entire course of the war.

THE TRUTH OF VALOUR

Having left the Marine Corps, former Gunnery Sergeant Torin Kerr is attempting to build a new life with salvage operator Craig Ryder. Turns out, civilian life is a lot rougher than she'd imagined. Torin is left for dead when pirates attack their spaceship and take Craig prisoner. Determined to rescue Craig, Torin calls in her Marines.

PRAISE FOR THE CONFEDERATION SERIES

"Rousing military adventure."—*Locus*

"The fast-paced third military SF novel in Huff's Confederation series… The intriguing and well-designed aliens and intricate plotting keep the reader guessing."—*Publishers Weekly*

"Expect more of this military sf saga, which is a vast improvement over Huff's earlier, mostly fantasy, fiction."—*Booklist*

"The notable Tanya Huff proves herself equally adept at military sf as contemporary fantasy in her riveting *Valour's Choice*… Don't miss this one."—*Romantic Times*

TITANBOOKS.COM

ALSO AVAILABLE FROM TITAN BOOKS

TANYA HUFF
THE ENCHANTMENT EMPORIUM

Alysha Gale is twenty-four, unemployed, and tired of her family meddling in her life—personally and magically. So when a letter arrives from her missing grandmother, bequeathing her a junk shop on the other side of Canada, Allie jumps at the chance to escape.

But she arrives at the Enchantment Emporium to find trouble brewing. With dragons circling the town and a sorcerer wreaking havoc, even calling in her family may not save the day…

"The Gales are an amazing family, the aunts will strike fear into your heart, and the characters Allie meets are both charming and terrifying." —#1 *New York Times* bestselling author Charlaine Harris

"Fresh urban fantasy… plenty of humor, thrills and original mythology, along with refreshingly three-dimensional women in a fully realized world."—*Publishers Weekly*

"Enchanting, suspenseful urban fantasy."—*Booklist* starred review

TITANBOOKS.COM

ALSO AVAILABLE FROM TITAN BOOKS

TANYA HUFF
THE WILD WAYS

AN ENCHANTMENT EMPORIUM NOVEL

Charlotte Gale is a Wild Power, but there's nothing wild about the life she is living. When her meddlesome aunts start interfering, Charlie ditches her cousin Allie and their grandmother's Enchantment Emporium and joins a Celtic rock band on the summer festival circuit.

All Charlie wants to do is play music and have a good time, but she soon becomes embroiled in a fight between an extended family of Selkies and an unscrupulous oil company willing to employ the most horrific means possible to get what they want, including one of the Gale aunts...

"Combining Celtic folklore, musical references, and a love of nature and magic, this will appeal to readers who like their urban fantasy with more depth."—*Library Journal*

"Zingy characterizations and a quick pace."—*Publishers Weekly*

TITANBOOKS.COM

ALSO AVAILABLE FROM TITAN BOOKS

TANYA HUFF
THE FUTURE FALLS

AN ENCHANTMENT EMPORIUM NOVEL

When Charlotte Gale's aunt warns their magical family of an approaching asteroid, they scramble to keep humanity from going the way of the dinosaurs. Although between Charlie's complicated relationship with sorcerer Jack, her cousin Allie's hormones, the Courts having way too much fun at the end of days, and Jack's sudden desire to sacrifice himself for the good of the many, Charlie's fairly certain that the asteroid is the least of her problems.

But together there isn't anything the Gales can't deal with—except possibly each other.

"Enchanting urban fantasy… Geeky in-jokes, dynamic leads, convincing romantic complications, and a threat that is both unusual and wonderfully convincing."—*Publishers Weekly* starred review

"There is plenty to like about the Gale family."
Library Journal

TITANBOOKS.COM

ALSO AVAILABLE FROM TITAN BOOKS

TANYA HUFF
THE SILVERED

The Empire has declared war on the were-ruled kingdom of
Aydori, capturing five women of the Mage-Pack, including the
wife of the Pack-leader. With the Pack off defending the border,
it falls to Mirian Maylin and Tomas Hagen—she a low-level
mage, he younger brother to the Pack-leader—to save them.
But with every step into enemy territory, the odds against their
survival grow steeper...

"Huff delves into an overwhelming yet improbably seamless
mix of steampunk, epic fantasy, and paranormal romance...
Huff fans who prefer her second-world fantasy tales (e.g., the
Quarters series) will be pleased by this return to the form."—
Publishers Weekly

"This is an exciting romantic quest fantasy... Fans will enjoy
the trek of the werewolf and the mage into the heart of the
enemy."—*Midwest Book Review*

TITANBOOKS.COM

**FOR MORE FANTASTIC FICTION, AUTHOR EVENTS, EXCLUSIVE
EXCERPTS, COMPETITIONS, LIMITED EDITIONS AND MORE**

VISIT OUR WEBSITE
titanbooks.com

LIKE US ON FACEBOOK
facebook.com/titanbooks

FOLLOW US ON TWITTER
@TitanBooks

EMAIL US
readerfeedback@titanemail.com